ASTRA MILITARUM

More tales of the Astra Militarum from Black Library

SHADOWSWORD
A novel by Guy Haley

BANEBLADE
A novel by Guy Haley

ASTRA MILITARUM
An anthology by various authors

YARRICK: THE PYRES OF ARMAGEDDON
A Commissar Yarrick novel by David Annandale

YARRICK: IMPERIAL CREED
A Commissar Yarrick novel by David Annandale

YARRICK: CHAINS OF GOLGOTHA
A Commissar Yarrick novella by David Annandale

HONOUR IMPERIALIS
An omnibus edition of the novels *Cadian Blood*
by Aaron Dembski-Bowden, *Redemption Corps* by Rob Sanders
and *Dead Men Walking* by Steve Lyons

STRAKEN
An 'Iron Hand' Straken novel by Toby Frost

• **THE MACHARIAN CRUSADE** •
By William King
Book 1: ANGEL OF FIRE
Book 2: FIST OF DEMETRIUS
Book 3: ANGEL OF FIRE

• **GAUNT'S GHOSTS** •
By Dan Abnett

Book 1: FIRST AND ONLY
Book 2: GHOSTMAKER
Book 3: NECROPOLIS
Book 4: HONOUR GUARD
Book 5: THE GUNS OF TANITH
Book 6: STRAIGHT SILVER
Book 7: SABBAT MARTYR
Book 8: TRAITOR GENERAL
Book 9: HIS LAST COMMAND
Book 10: THE ARMOUR OF CONTEMPT
Book 11: ONLY IN DEATH
Book 12: BLOOD PACT
Book 13: SALVATION'S REACH

WARHAMMER 40,000

LEGENDS OF THE DARK MILLENNIUM

ASTRA MILITARUM

DAVID ANNANDALE, TOBY FROST, BRADEN CAMPBELL & JUSTIN D HILL

BLACK LIBRARY

A BLACK LIBRARY PUBLICATION

Hardback edition first published in 2015.
This edition published in Great Britain in 2016 by
Black Library,
Games Workshop Ltd.,
Willow Road,
Nottingham, NG7 2WS, UK.

10 9 8 7 6 5 4 3 2 1

Produced by Games Workshop in Nottingham.
Cover illustration by Raymond Swanland.

A CIP record for this book is available from the British Library.

ISBN 13: 978 1 78496 288 3

See Black Library on the internet at

blacklibrary.com

Find out more about Games Workshop
and the world of Warhammer 40,000 at

games-workshop.com

Printed and bound by CPI Group (UK) Ltd, Croydon, CR0 4YY

It is the 41st millennium. For more than a hundred centuries the Emperor has sat immobile on the Golden Throne of Earth. He is the master of mankind by the will of the gods, and master of a million worlds by the might of his inexhaustible armies. He is a rotting carcass writhing invisibly with power from the Dark Age of Technology. He is the Carrion Lord of the Imperium for whom a thousand souls are sacrificed every day, so that he may never truly die.

Yet even in his deathless state, the Emperor continues his eternal vigilance. Mighty battlefleets cross the daemon-infested miasma of the warp, the only route between distant stars, their way lit by the Astronomican, the psychic manifestation of the Emperor's will. Vast armies give battle in His name on uncounted worlds. Greatest amongst his soldiers are the Adeptus Astartes, the Space Marines, bioengineered super-warriors. Their comrades in arms are legion: the Astra Militarum and countless planetary defence forces, the ever-vigilant Inquisition and the tech-priests of the Adeptus Mechanicus to name only a few. But for all their multitudes, they are barely enough to hold off the ever-present threat from aliens, heretics, mutants – and worse.

To be a man in such times is to be one amongst untold billions. It is to live in the cruellest and most bloody regime imaginable. These are the tales of those times. Forget the power of technology and science, for so much has been forgotten, never to be re-learned. Forget the promise of progress and understanding, for in the grim dark future there is only war. There is no peace amongst the stars, only an eternity of carnage and slaughter, and the laughter of thirsting gods.

CONTENTS

CHAINS OF GOLGOTHA

DAVID ANNANDALE

PROLOGUE

ASCENDING

The creature climbed the shaft of its prison. Every step of the ascent was hard-won, and the creature's breath rattled from its lungs in a feral snarl. The sound was swallowed by the splashes and struggles of the scavengers in the depths below. It became one more echo in an eternal, reverberating song of violence.

The journey was slow. The creature didn't care, for time had no meaning in the well. Here were only darkness, the clash of tooth and claw, and the choking embrace of water thick with the decaying remains of the fallen. The creature was one of the victors. It had beaten down its rivals, always risen to be the predator and not the prey, and now it had risen again, using the bodies of its enemies to make its way up the shaft.

It had prepared its climb with a patience that had nothing to do with enduring the passage of time.

There was no time. There were only teeth. Claws. Meat. Bone. War.

Patience was the embodiment of necessity, of survival. It fought, killed, and worked in the unending night until it was ready and, by feel alone, began its journey.

The creature's ascent was so painstaking, so gradual, that if it had been seen, it would not have been a threat. But it was not seen. It rose, metre by metre through Stygian black. It had climbed before. It had made too many attempts to count (and counting was meaningless), and on each occasion, it had reached a bit higher before it had had to return to the roiling depths. But this time was going to be different. This *time*, events would begin once again. The creature would reach the top, and it would bring with it the tearing and death from below.

Black became grey. Above, a circle of dim light grew wider and brighter. The creature's breathing grew harsher from the strain of effort and the eagerness of rage. It no longer moved solely by touch. It could see. In jerking, spasmodic movements, clumsy but inexorable, it reached the lip of the well. There it paused. It waited, quieting its breath, holding back its snarl even as its killing impulse became so powerful that its entire frame vibrated. It listened to the guards. It tracked the sound of their movements as they strolled back and forth, trading bored insults.

The moment came. Time began. The creature surged out of the well. It roared as it plunged claws into flesh, and feasted on the panic of the guards.

CHAPTER ONE

THE GRAND ILLUSION

1. Yarrick

I should have expected the Stompa would charge. There were so many things I should have expected. So much for which I will have to answer, on the day the Emperor finally releases me from my service and calls me to His Throne. Most of all, I will have to atone for the sin of underestimating the enemy. This is the very sin I condemned so freely in others, the sin that had almost doomed Armageddon. How could I have failed to heed my own warnings?

I deserve no mercy. But I won't be alone. There is very little mercy to be granted for the errors of that day.

The clouds were low over the Ishawar Mountains. The clouds were always low on Golgotha, but tonight they had an extra weight, and pressed down on the peaks like an upended sea of tar. They heaved and bulged with the sick promise of dreadful storms. They pulsed with a red glow, and their force was coming down to crush the army of Ghazghkull Mag Uruk Thraka from above, just as mine would on the ground.

I rode in the open turret of the command Chimera. The wind had dropped, the atmosphere holding its breath in advance of the coming storm, and my rebreather was able to keep the worst of Golgotha's crimson dust from my lungs. We were moving into the foothills of the mountain chain. We had been pursuing the orks for days, grinding at them, pushing them deeper into the Isha-war range, into ever narrower valleys and passes. Open terrain was where their numbers, still greater than ours, could be most effectively brought to bear against our armour. So we didn't give them a chance. We blasted through the plains and plateaux, a storm of fire and steel that never stopped, never let up. We had the greenskins in retreat. I was coming for Thraka. Years after he had profaned Armageddon, I finally had him cornered. Years of searching, years of being just a step behind him, hitting planet after planet just days after he had departed, world after world that had nothing left to devastate. But I had caught up to him. He was here, on Golgotha, leading the routed horde ahead. I knew he was.

He had to be. This was my last chance to stop him.

He. Him. Thraka had long since ceased to be an *it* in my mind. To reduce him would be to underestimate him, and underestimating him had one guaranteed result: doom. I had seen what he was capable of on Armageddon. I had seen what he had done since, as I followed his trail of devastation through the galaxy. It was an article of faith that the orks were unthinking brutes. It was one of the human race's sole consolations when faced with their numbers, their strength and their endurance: at least the orks were stupid. But not Thraka. The invasion of Armageddon had not been a simple-minded affair. Some of the strategies Thraka had employed had been brilliant. Inspired. And he had made moves since then that not only might as well have been signed, they had been aimed at *me*, personally.

I had a nemesis. We were facing each other over a regicide board the size of the galaxy.

To admit this was disgusting. To deny it would be criminally foolish. And utterly political.

For the political mind, the years of my search had been an eternity. Attention is difficult to sustain, and easy to lose to the next new and urgent conflict. Each new emergency obliterates the memory of all others. Every year that passed without a new attack on Armageddon meant the danger was that much more remote. There were so many other urgencies of war calling. Spending time, treasury and men in the pursuit of a spent force was nonsensical.

It was perfectly true that there was no shortage of dire threats to the Imperium. I would never be so foolish as to minimise them. But it was perfectly false that Thraka was a spent force. It was suicidal to think so. He was a threat that was unlike anything else in the galaxy, and the fact that we had driven him away from Armageddon changed nothing. He had almost hammered a spike through the heart of the Imperium. That should have been reason enough to devote all necessary resources to his elimination. But what was worse, if such a thing were possible, was that if there was ever to be an ork warboss who could unite the entire barbaric species, then Thraka was that ork. As much as it disgusted me even to articulate the thought, there was a monstrous truth that had to be faced: Thraka had the potential to become the ork emperor.

That possibility should have been obvious to the greenest trooper. It probably was. But for too many in the high places, whether lords or admirals or generals, it seemed to be a possibility too awful to contemplate. Better to pretend it did not exist. Easier to believe it was impossible that the orks would ever follow a single leader, and so destroy us all. So much nicer to bury your head in the sand, and avoid all the fuss and bother of actually doing something about Thraka.

I had to fight tooth and nail for every tank, every rifle, and every man of my army, every single day since the enthusiasm for the crusade had evaporated in its second year. Somehow, I found men of will, intelligence and vision. But they weren't enough. I also needed men of influence, and for the sake of a mission so important that no compromise should have been brooked, I had been forced to do just that. There were many – too many – colonels with me who held their ranks by the sole virtue of their noble birth. Our venture had been plagued by mistakes, accidents and idiotic judgement calls. But numbers, faith and weaponry had seen us through. Even Golgotha, which waged war against us with dust and storm as viciously as any greenskin horde, could not stop us.

Now the orks were running. Now Thraka was at bay.

Thunder, deep-throated as an earthquake, boomed in the distance ahead. The Baneblades were unleashing hell upon the orks. The flashes of their bombardment were bigger and brighter than the anger in the clouds. I wanted to be at the front with those magnificent tanks. When we had mustered on the Hadron Plateau, I had climbed on top of one of them to address the regiments. Vox-units relayed my words to the entire army, but the image I presented to all within viewing range was important, too. Thronc, but I knew the importance of image. I also knew its curse and its weight. Doing what had to be done, I chose the *Fortress of Arrogance* as my pulpit. Even among the glories of the Baneblades, it stood out. It was a weapon of peerless art, a masterpiece of war. In keeping with its name, it disdained camouflage. Instead, it was black as the void. It was the very idea of power, summoned into material being and given metal form. It even had a true pulpit on its turret. When I stood there, I felt the strength of the tank surging through my blood. When I spoke, it was with the fire of true inspiration. I descended from the *Fortress of Arrogance* with a regret that bordered on bereavement.

Now I gazed with longing in the direction of the choir of tanks. But the Chimera had been outfitted for mobile command, and it was not strong enough to be at the tip of the spear. Communications on Golgotha were difficult at best, and I had to remain within the limited vox-range of as much of the force as possible. So I had to content myself with seeing the flashes of our strikes, and hearing the booming drumbeat of our advance.

I was *not* content. But I was satisfied. Baneblades were a rare prize, and the mere fact that we had more than one was a significant victory in itself. They more than justified every deal, compromise, and soul-wearying bargain

I had made. They were turning Thraka's army into pulp and cinder. The orks had nothing that could stand up to them. Not here, anyway. Not within useful range.

More war thunder, like an answer to the Baneblades, both larger and more distant, and this time from behind. I looked back the way we had come. Kilometres beyond the marching troops and growling vehicles, beyond the line of hills we had crossed hours before, visible only as blurred silhouettes in the grit of the Golgothan atmosphere, gods clashed. Our Titans grappled with their debased ork counterparts. The official designation of the ork machines was *Gargant*. The word was ugly, dismissive, and deliberately so. The Officio Strategos did not seek to dignify the enemy, nor should it have. But there was nothing to dismiss in the danger that the Gargants represented. They were colossal totemic monsters. As the Warlord-class Titans were to men – the human form rendered sublime in size and destructive power – so the Gargants were to the orks. They were tributes to the savage gods of the greenskins, towering, lumbering, barrel-shaped mountains of steel and cannon. They could have reduced all of our regiments to ash. The Titans had engaged them, and the giants had been locked in hellish stalemate for two days now. We had moved through that battlefield like a trail of ants. I had felt insignificant, my actions a trivial grace note to the awful symphony of the giants. I had been privileged to witness, once more, the struggle of myths, and had been humbled. To see the Warlords stride over our columns was to feel an awe so great, it moved many troopers to tears.

We had pushed past them. We needed momentum above all. If we could take out Thraka, the ork resistance would collapse. So we had left the god-machines behind. The fury of their war followed us, light and sound rolling over us like the death-cries of suns. But theirs was not the vital heart of the war. Their battle, in the end, was a parenthesis. Thraka was not there.

With me, backing up the Baneblades, were three regiments. Immediately behind the superheavies came the 52nd armoured regiment of Aighe Mortis. Following them, scouring the planet of any remaining xenos trace, were the 117th Armageddon mechanised infantry and the 66th Mordian infantry. Hundreds of vehicles, thousands and thousands of men, the pride of the Imperium marching with purpose and discipline, exterminating savagery with faith. They were a sight that could move a stone to song. When I close my eye, I can still see them with a clarity as sharp as pain.

The waste sickens me.

There was a tap on my lower leg. I dropped into the Chimera's compartment. Space that would normally have held twelve troopers had been cut in half by vox-equipment and map tables. Even with the powerful units here, communications were hit-and-miss. Golgotha's dust eroded transmissions the same way it did lungs and engines. Anything farther than a few thousand metres, perhaps a bit more with exceptional line of sight, was hopelessly unreliable. It had been necessary to establish a relay system stretching all the way back to the landing site on the Hadron Plateau. It was a precarious line, ridiculously stretched and vulnerable, but there had been no time to come up with an alternative. It was working, though. Imperfectly, but with just enough reliability to make coordination of the entire expedition possible.

'It's Colonel Rogge, commissar,' vox-officer Lieutenant Beren Diethelm told me.

'Here we go,' Erwin Lanner, at the Chimera's steering levers, called out.

I made sure the vox-unit wasn't transmitting as I took it from Diethelm. 'Sergeant,' I told Lanner, 'you are displaying appalling disrespect for a superior officer.'

Over the vibrating rumble of the engine, I couldn't hear Lanner snort, but I knew he had. He was a short, squat man with arms whose strength and reach had been the doom of many an ork and unthinking sparring partner. His face was narrow, and his features had been sharp until accumulations of scar tissue had turned them into a gnarled fist. He had been with me since Armageddon, and his insubordination was matched only by his loyalty. I had never met anyone less intimidated by a commissar's uniform. He had no reason to be. If every Guardsman were equal to Lanner in bravery, skill and faith, we would have cleansed the galaxy of our enemies centuries ago. He should have risen far beyond sergeant, but he had refused to leave my side. The idea of someone else driving my conveyance, whatever it might be, was, for him, a personal affront. He had turned down one promotion after another, and when he was not given a choice, he indulged in such egregious misbehaviour that not only did he ensure that he remained as he was, only my intervention saved him from summary execution. For my pains, my reward was a barrage of outrages too studied to be real. They were theatre for my benefit, and it was a theatre that I needed, especially since Armageddon. It was one thing to be aware of one's own legend. Lanner made sure I didn't believe in it.

The sergeant had no faith in Colonel Kelner Rogge. I understood. Rogge commanded a fourth regiment, the rearguard of our principle advance. The Aumet 23rd Armoured had been acquired at a price, and being saddled with the inexperienced sixth son of High Lord Gheret Rogge of Aumet was that price. Colonel Rogge had been with us a year and he had, to my pleasant surprise, acquitted himself well. Lanner remained sceptical, but I knew he would never forgive Rogge the sin of his noble blood. What even Lanner could not take from Rogge was his commitment to our cause. I had assumed, during the negotiations with the father, that the Lord of Aumet's goal had been the prestigious placement of a son who was far enough down the line of inheritance that his loss could be risked, but whose path still had to bring honour to the family name. Within minutes of meeting the colonel, I realised that I had been wrong. He wanted to be part of my crusade as much as I needed Aumet's tanks. Kelner Rogge believed in what we were doing. He didn't have the experience, but he had the fire.

The rearguard mission might not have been the sort that would stoke that fire, but it minimised the risk that a novice colonel presented to the rest of the army. We had a large reserve of Leman Russ battle tanks to draw upon, and all I asked of Rogge was that he keep pace and protect our rear. Lanner, I knew, was expecting Rogge to snatch defeat from the jaws of victory at the earliest opportunity. He hadn't yet. But the sergeant's view of things was, on a number of fronts, so close to my own that I couldn't avoid a slight wave of apprehension as I spoke into the vox. 'Go ahead, colonel.'

'Commissar, I'm sorry, but we've run into bit of a delay.'

Those words will never leave my dreams. They announced the loss of an entire planet.

2. *Rogge*

'If you can't fix it, get it out of the way,' Rogge told Captain Yann Kerentz. 'Blow it up if you must.'

Kerentz blinked at the suggestion of wilfully destroying a Leman Russ. 'It's only the treads–' he began.

'Which we can hardly take the time to deal with at this moment, and certainly not in this place.' Did the man not understand the meaning of the word 'urgency'? The Aumet Armoured had a mission, and it was not going to be stymied by the stupid mechanical failure of a single tank. Its treads had disintegrated at the worst possible moment. It was the lead vehicle of the lead column, and the route led through a narrow canyon pass before opening up again. There was barely room for two vehicles abreast, and this one had not only stopped right in the bottleneck, it had swerved sideways. 'The wheels can't find any traction at all?'

Kerentz shook his head. 'No, sir. We might be able to push it with a dozer blade–'

'For the length of the pass?' Rogge poured on the scorn. The defile was two kilometres long. 'And then what? We'll have to abandon it anyway. No. Destroy it now. I want us on the move again in five minutes.'

From the turret of his Leman Russ Vanquisher, the *Condemning Voice*, Rogge watched Kerentz walk back towards the front of the line of vehicles. The captain's gait was stiff with displeasure. Rogge grimaced. It was his duty to make the hard decisions. He had made the correct one. Every second, the main body of Yarrick's force was widening the distance between them. The commissar had been clear: the advance would not stop, not pause, not even slow. The momentum was with the humans, victory loomed, but the orks would seize on the slightest hesitation. Rogge had his mission. It was his responsibility to complete it.

So he would.

Kerentz carried out the order. There was a distant *crump* of the tank's destruction. But it was ten minutes, not five, before the tanks were moving forward. Rogge cursed under his breath. He did not drop down into the turret basket. He stared into the night ahead, at the vehicle lights turned into dirty smears by the billowing dust, and tried to master his fraying temper. He didn't want his crew to see him off his stride. All he could think about was the lost time. They would have to step up the regiment's speed by a large measure to catch up. The thought that he would be found wanting tortured him.

There was also the terror of arriving to find the war finished. *Son,* his lord and father would ask, *what role did you play in the Golgotha crusade?* And he would answer, *Father, I had a nice drive in my tank.*

His face burned with the anticipation of shame. He willed the regiment forward. Forward to Yarrick, forward to triumph and the glory of Aumet and the Imperium. Forward to the proof of his worth.

The *Condemning Voice* emerged from the pass. Like all the regimental command vehicles, it was in the middle of the advance, so communication with the entire regiment was, if not assured, at least as solid as possible. There was still half the regiment back in the pass, and the leading units were slowing down again. Rogge pounded the roof of the turret with his fist, winced, then lowered himself into the basket. The interior of the tank was a din of engine roar and vibrating metal, but it was easier to listen to his ear-bead here than it was outside. He was about to bark for Kerentz to be put on the line when the captain addressed him first. 'Colonel,' Kerentz said, 'we have just encountered a branching path going deeper into the mountains.'

'How wide?'

'Good for three vehicles, maybe four.'

'Signs of activity?'

'None, sir. But the pass makes a sharp turn. We can't see very far down it.'

Rogge hesitated, torn between two necessities. He couldn't protect the army group's rear if he didn't catch up, but he wouldn't be doing his duty, either, if he ignored the pass. The delay in following that route, and for the Emperor knew how long... 'All engines stop,' he ordered. 'I want complete silence.'

The convoy of tanks halted, coughing fumes as the engines shut down. In less than a minute, the entire regiment was motionless, and the only sound was the ticking of cooling metal.

'Kerentz,' Rogge voxed. 'I want a full auspex scan, and I want you to *listen*. If there are greenskins up that way, we should be able to hear them.'

'Sir, with respect, the wind and atmospheric conditions–'

'Those are my orders, captain. Execute them.'

Rogge waited, picturing the war he was missing, willing the orks to be sensible and be off with the rest of their fellows. The more he thought about it, the more he realised he was wasting time. Even if there were a few of the beasts hiding in ambush, what could they hope to achieve? The vast bulk of their army was in pell-mell retreat.

Kerentz checked back in. 'No readings, no sounds, colonel. But–'

'Good.' No orks. And even if there were, they were showing half a brain and staying put. And even, *even* if they were stupid and attacked, they couldn't amount to a threat. It simply wasn't possible. The decision was easy. There was only one to make. 'Move on,' he said. 'Full speed.' Risky, at night, but the way was clear, the rocky valleys giving them a clear shot toward the rest of the war.

The eerie quiet of the stilled regiment erupted with the battle-hungry roar of a hundred tanks. The sound echoed off the surrounding cliff faces, turning into a massive, formless din. Aumet's sons surged forward. Rogge climbed back up through the hatch. He sat behind the turret's heavy stubber and watched the craggy landscape roll past. He saw the break on the right, in the north cliff. His gut churned, just a little, as he passed it. It was a passage into the empty, crimson night of Golgotha, and was swallowed by darkness after a few hundred metres. He stared into it with what he felt was righteous confidence. He had made the right and only choice.

Still, as the gap fell behind, he turned and watched until it dropped out of his sight. He continued to face back until he judged that the last of the regiment had passed the defile. Then he turned to look forward again, and wish that anticipation alone could accelerate the armoured march. He should contact Yarrick, he thought. Let him know that they were coming.

The vox exploded. Reports and curses came in at such a flood over his ear-bead that meaning broke apart, becoming fragments of panic. Rogge whirled around. At first, he could see nothing wrong. The line of tanks stretched out behind him into the night. But then he heard it. He heard the enormity of his mistake. Its sound was that of a mechanised avalanche, rising above wind and engine, clutching the entire regiment in its grasp. It filled Rogge's ears and his mind. It filled his soul. And as it hammered at his chest, drawing closer and closer, it became visible. He saw the avalanche of metal and brutes chew its way up the regiment.

As the horror drew closer, the din acquired meaning. The rampage of xenos and guns and machines sounded horribly like laughter.

CHAPTER TWO

TRAMPLED

1. Rogge

The force that stormed out of the pass and onto the Aumet regiment was no mere ambush party. It was a horde such as Rogge had never imagined. He had no idea of its full scale, but the war machines that led it would only be in the service of a full army. Brushing aside their smaller brethren, crushing any of their own infantry who didn't move fast enough, were superheavy tanks. Battle fortresses. They were as large as the Baneblades, but were twisted, vulgar monsters. Bristling with secondary guns, they were also festooned with pipes belching oily black smoke, as if a manufactorum had turned itself into a rolling harbinger of doom.

Lumbering behind the battle fortresses came worse monsters. Stompas. Rogge had heard the designation often enough, and laughed at it every time. He had seen hololiths of the machines, and laughed then, too, at the

27

crude design: the slapdash overlapping of the metal plates into a monstrous skirt, the redundant piling on of armament, the pitifully savage attempts at art that gave the things horned visages in the image of the greenskin gods.

He wasn't laughing now. Though the Stompas were smaller than the Gargants, he had only seen the truly titanic machines from a distance. The Stompas were close. They were here. And there were no Titans anywhere in sight.

As the green tide clanked and roared toward him, a psychic wave of ork presence rushed ahead of it. It was overwhelming. It shut Rogge down. His limbs tingled, then went numb from anaesthetising terror. He seemed to float out of his head. He observed his reactions with a stupefied detachment. His jaw sagged open. His eyes widened. His hands hung limply at his sides. His strings were cut, and he could do nothing but watch as the greenskin wave washed over his forces. The night shook with the deep, battering rhythm of obliteration.

There was another noise, much smaller, but somehow more irritating. Rogge realised it came from his ear-bead. The vox-network was screaming. Orders to retreat collided with orders to counter-attack. He heard his name over and over again, in transmissions that were first questions, then pleas, then curses. He blinked several times, reintegrating himself. He shook away the lethargy.

'All units,' he began. He found the steel and determination his voice needed. He did not find the decision he needed even more. 'All units,' he said again, with such force that a command must surely follow.

He saw three tanks attempt a coordinated response to

the nearest Stompa. They were the *Extirpation*, the *Final Toll* and the *Advent of Silence*. He knew the crews well. They were all far more experienced than he was. He had worried they resented his command. Now he blessed their initiative. They were still moving away from the ork forces, but had swivelled turrets to the rear. They fired in such close succession, it was as if the shells were a single blow against the greenskin machine. The Stompa rocked back a single step. Its front armour dimpled. Then it moved forward again, shaking the earth with its steps. Its left arm was a cannon, and it now spoke its fury. The shell punched through the top of the *Final Toll*. The interior explosion was followed by an even bigger blast as fuel and ammunition cooked off. The tank blew apart.

Even as it fired its cannon, the Stompa swung its right arm at the *Extirpation*. At the end of the arm was a chainfist larger than a Space Marine. It sliced into the flank of the Leman Russ. The shriek of metal cutting metal scraped the night raw and bleeding. Rogge gazed in horror, his reactions slowing to a crawl as the images of war overloaded his senses. The Stompa butchered the *Extirpation* as if it were a living thing. The tank shuddered and bucked as though in pain, and then the chainfist found the flesh inside. The screams of men joined the choir of tortured metal. Blood splashed out of the vehicle.

The Stompa didn't bother with the third Leman Russ. An onrushing battle fortress had rammed it with such force, it had knocked the *Advent of Silence* on its side. Ork infantry swarmed over the crippled tank, bashing futilely at its armour until one of them arrived with an armour-piercing rocket.

'All units,' Rogge said again. His throat was dry. He was

whispering. 'All units...' He trailed off. He had nothing to say.

It didn't matter. There *was* nothing to say. The horde rolled over the regiment, crushing, annihilating, as if the Ishawar Mountains themselves were delivering the blows. Rogge pulled the vox-bead out of his ear, blotting out the cries and demands. Resistance to the orks sprang up at the company level, but it lacked coherence. Those companies were stones against the tide. They could not stop the flood. They simply survived a bit longer.

The storm surge reached Rogge. He was distantly aware that his crew was firing the *Condemning Voice*'s gun. He didn't care. As a shambling monster twenty metres high loomed over him, he was granted a sliver of grace: he was too numb to feel shame.

2. *Yarrick*

Our advance slowed. For less than one minute, I had the luxury of believing that we had the greenskins boxed in, and that the end was on the horizon. Then vox-traffic from Rogge's regiment turned to chaos. And then we stopped.

The vox-unit convulsed with static and cacophony. The messages, each more urgent than the others, smeared into white noise. I let Diethelm do his job, a sick certainty growing in my chest. The word from the forward regiments was easy to sort out. The orks had stopped running. At the precise moment of the vox meltdown at Rogge's end, the orks had turned and hurled themselves back against us.

Colonel Sinburne, commanding the Mortisian 52nd, tried to sound hopeful. 'It's a final stand, commissar,' he voxed. 'They're desperate. They know this is the end.'

'Is it?' I asked. I wanted the truth, not a fantasy.

'They're hitting us hard,' he admitted, 'but–'

I cut him off. 'Listen to the foe, colonel. What do you hear?'

He came back after a few seconds with the answer I expected and dreaded. 'They're laughing,' he said.

The situation to our rear took longer to establish. 'Colonel Rogge is not answering, sir,' Diethelm reported.

That, in itself, told me that things had gone awry. But I needed to know *why* and I needed to know *how*. 'Then find me someone who is.'

Diethelm did. He performed well, and there were enough officers with the Aumet 23rd who knew their sacred duty. Many of them died letting us know what was happening. Their transmissions were fragments of tragedy.

'... we don't know if we're retreating or counter–'

'... multiple Stompas and battle fortresses, we can't–'

'Who is in command? Who is in command?'

'There's nothing left! Throne take that bastard! I'll feed him his–'

I stared at the map table as Diethelm called out the updates. Like a hololith gathering dimension and resolution, the picture formed in my mind's eye. I felt my lips pull back in a grimace as I realised how badly we had erred. The force that was tearing up the Aumet tanks was an army fully as large as the one we were chasing. Thraka had managed to keep this second deployment hidden in the mountains, secret from us. We had blundered into one of the greatest ambushes in the history of the Imperium. For all my preaching, for all that I *knew* better, I had underestimated Thraka. Once again, the ork had outplayed, had *out-thought*, we humans.

We were caught in a pincer manoeuvre. The valley in which the bulk of our forces now advanced was long and wide, but it was still a valley, with orks coming at us from both ends. Even the foothills of the Ishawar were high enough that we couldn't go over them. We were boxed in. Thraka had done to me precisely what I had thought I was doing to him.

We had a chance only if the frontline units could bring the war to an immediate end. I could read the signs, and knew the odds were the same as my growing a new right arm, but I spoke to Sinburne all the same. 'Colonel, do you have any expectation of being able to kill Ghazghkull Thraka in the next few minutes?'

'With the blessing of the Emperor, there is no telling what we might–'

'Do you even know where he is?'

'No,' Sinburne admitted.

I could hear how frustrated he was. He was grief-stricken at the idea of having to give up so close to the goal. But the reality was this: we had not been pursuing Thraka. He had been reeling us in. Unless Sinburne had the ork lined up within the sights of a dozen tanks, there would be no defeating him this day. 'Disengage, colonel,' I said.

'Commissar,' he began.

'We will need you here.'

There was no response. Static scraped at my ear, formless sound shaping a bad truth. I had Diethelm search channels until he found me a tank company captain. It was Captain Hantlyn, and he rode the Baneblade *Fearful Sublime*. 'Captain,' I said, 'you now have command of the armoured regiment.' And I gave him the last orders any soldier wanted to hear.

There was no choice. Going forward was suicide: the chain of valleys led only to a cul-de-sac, the end-point where we thought we had cornered the orks. We had to retreat, and we had to punch our way through the second army. There was no question of hope, only of necessity.

Gather our strength, then. By now, Diethelm had all the regimental commanders on the vox. 'This is no fighting retreat,' I told them. 'You are to return with all speed and prepare to re-engage at the rear.' With the Baneblades, we might stand a chance, not of victory, but of successful retreat.

Might.

We began the murderous process of reversing the direction of an entire army. Thousands and thousands and thousands of men and vehicles, a sea of war power that would stretch to the horizon on an open plain, now had to arrest all momentum and turn back the way they had come. The perfection of discipline kept the disorder to a minimum. Unforgiving reality meant there was still plenty to go around. The worst was the vehicles. Leman Russ and Manticore, Chimera and Basilisk, they all had turning circles and little room in which to make them. Even with the priority being granted the HQ Chimera, it took us a full minute to re-orientate. Where before the Imperium's might had flowed across Golgotha like a roaring cataract, now there was nothing but eddying molasses.

I knew that my commands had been death sentences for countless loyal Guardsmen as the greenskins pressed their advantage. I wished again to be at the front. Before, I had wanted to witness Thraka's end. Now, I would have shared the awful moment of retreat with men who had given everything to this cause. I owed them that much.

I owed the Imperium more, though. Every human alive did. And at this juncture, my sacrifice would serve no purpose. I would be failing in my duty to serve the Emperor. The romantic gesture, then, would be nothing less than treason.

We were disciplined but slow. The orks were beings of speed. Discipline was a barely grasped concept for them. There was nothing to slow their advance except the mire of human blood beneath their feet. And so it happened. The armoured regiment had not reached the new front line yet, the rest of the army had not even begun to march in its new direction, and the ork onslaught fell on us. I had climbed through the Chimera's hatch again, and though I was thousands of metres from the initial collision of the armies, I heard it. I felt it, too: the entire floor of the valley vibrated from the shock of the impact.

We began to move forward, and we were marching into the jaws of a meat grinder. But the choice now was to advance and die, or wait and die. We advanced, the only route of honour, and the route of our only hope.

A hope that took us through battle fortresses and Stompas. I had to stifle bitter laughter.

'If we find Colonel Rogge,' Lanner's voice crackled on my ear-bead, 'please grant me the privilege of killing him myself.'

'That honour will be mine,' I snapped. We needed armour to fight armour, and we had already lost the regiment that should have been, at the very least, holding back the orks long enough for the Baneblades to arrive. Mechanised infantry was nothing against what Thraka had unleashed.

And still we headed for the slaughter, picking up speed.

Within minutes, I could see the shapes of our destruction. The Stompas towered over our forces. A Titan would have blasted the monstrosities back to scrap metal, but our god-machines were still distant, still caught in unwavering stalemate. And here, the Stompas were the kings of the battlefield. They were horned beasts, with pipes jutting up from their shoulders, spewing smoke. At irregular intervals, taking turns, they would shake the valley with a deafening sound, part howl, part furnace roar, part raging horn. Every time a Stompa roared, the swarming foot soldiers took up the cry and hurled themselves at us with renewed war-fever.

My Chimera reached the fullness of the chaos. The green tide lapped at the vehicle's treads. I manned the turret's stubber. I was an awkward gunner, with only one arm, but with the harness holding me firmly to the gun, it turned where I did, and it was impossible to miss. I pulled the trigger and scythed down the rushing beasts. My body shook with each shell, the rapidly heating gun burned my hand, the acrid stink of fyceline fumes stabbed my nostrils, and it was all good pain, honest pain, the purging hurt of war that meant my enemies were dying. Out of the corner of my eye, I saw an ork boss flank the Chimera and launch himself towards the roof. A quick twitch to the right and I would have cut him in half. But suddenly that wasn't good enough. I was thrumming with hatred for Rogge, for myself, for the orks. The xenos filth were revelling in their triumph, and I would be damned if I did not make them suffer. So I let the boss land. I unhooked myself from the harness as he took a step towards the turret. Then I jumped up from the hatch and stood on the roof, too, making myself as visible as possible. I raised my right arm, brandishing the battle claw that had been mine since Hades Hive. '*You dare?*' I shouted. '*Do you know who I am?*' I was Yarrick, who had sent the orks fleeing from Hades. I was Yarrick, who killed with an evil eye. And so I did.

The ruby laser from my bale eye pierced upward through the ork's gaping maw and blew off the top of his head. The beast's jaw sagged with idiot surprise and the body twirled heavily before toppling from the Chimera. I turned my gaze on the orks below. They knew me, and they hesitated. Lanner drove through that hesitation, crushing greenskins to paste beneath our treads. I took the stubber again while the gunner, a trooper by the name of Koben, opened up with the cannon. We blasted our way clear. We created a path to our doom.

But I would not accept that conclusion. Nor would my crew. Nor would any of the men who marched with us. We were not Space Marines. Individually, we were nothing. Collectively, we were the will of the Emperor, and His will acknowledged no obstacle. We would smash through the orks.

That is, if will alone were enough.

We closed in on the full crush of the battle, and it spread to envelop us. I was surrounded not just by the green tide, but by the rising, turbulent flood of war itself. In that vortex, organisation broke down, giving way to the random, the chance, the improvised, the chaotic and yes, sometimes, the fated. But the vortex didn't mean the abandonment of strategy. I looked ahead, at the reality of the orks' giant war machines, and sought my strategy, because, by the Throne, I would find one.

I saw it. The exit from the valley, the route we had to

follow, lay to the east. A Stompa, striding off the pace from the others, blocked the path. Between it and the Chimera, there was a company of Basilisk mobile artillery platforms. Their earthshaker cannons might penetrate the Stompa's armour. But they weren't tanks. Their own armour wasn't designed for front-line combat, and they were open-topped. I could see that their crews were trying to manoeuvre them into firing positions, dropping the cannons for short-range destruction, and the orks were hitting them hard before they could become a threat. The air was thick with rockets. Several of the vehicles were already burning wrecks. The crews of many others were being cut to pieces.

'Make for the Basilisks,' I told Lanner. 'To all within reach,' I spoke on the regimental channels, 'protect the artillery crews. Give them the chance to save us all.'

Infantry and Chimeras converged on the Basilisks. Men ignored their own safety to gun down the orks clambering over the gun crews. But the orks were numberless, and a cannon-boasting battlewagon smashed into the fray. In the time it took our vehicle to arrive within range, the artillery company had been decimated. Vehicles, the battlewagon among them, were massive, twisted metal corpses. The shafts of the guns reached, useless and mute, for the blind heavens. Ahead of us, the men of one of the last Basilisks grappled with the orks, their doom a simple matter of seconds away.

Koben fired. The Chimera's main gun was as nothing beside a Leman Russ's battlecannon, but it still packed an explosive punch, and the shot was a colossal risk. He could have finished the orks' job for them. But he placed the shell with a precision that showed there had

never been a risk after all. There was a geyser of shredded greenskin bodies a few metres from the rear of the
Basilisk. The orks just beyond the explosion staggered,
stunned. The artillery crew pushed their besiegers back.
Stubber rounds and las-fire slashed in from all sides and
cut deeper into the ork assault. Then the Basilisk's gun
was trained on the Stompa.

The report was deafening. The recoil was a giant's
blow on the ground, and the Basilisk jerked back a few
metres. The shell was designed to shatter bunkers. Even
so, against this kind of a foe, we needed something very
close to a miracle. We received one. The Emperor's hand
guided that shell. It hit the Stompa, and I blinked as day
seared the night. There was a gigantic bloom of fire, as
if a volcano had erupted over the battlefield. The upper
half of the Stompa vanished. Chunks of metal, and some
of flesh, rained down. I called for a concerted rush at the
gap we had created. The order was hardly necessary. The
moment of victory called all eyes and hearts. A roar of
hope and faith louder than the orks' rabid howling came
from the men of Armageddon and Mordian and Aighe
Mortis. With the strength of desperation and renewed
purpose, we pushed the larger ork army back. We pushed
through the orks. The speartip of the infantry reached the
mouth of the valley.

And ran straight into a battle fortress.

The ork superheavy's arrival had all the grotesque flair
of that race. It charged in from the pass faster than any
tank should move. It was as if a voidship engine had been
mounted in the vehicle. Its front actually rose in the air
as it crested a low rise, and didn't descend before the
fortress had raced over another several dozen metres.

Men vanished beneath it and were smeared over the crude teeth of its front armour. I found myself staring straight at the mouth of its immense turret gun. The cannon dwarfed the Basilisk's weapon, and it gave us the ork answer to our blow.

Day again, much closer. I was in the heart of day, and the *boom* of the cannon was so huge it seemed to issue from inside my head. The blow felt like air that had turned to granite. I was flying. The world spun. I couldn't think. Everything was fire and wind and hammering. I hit the ground as if dropped from space.

CHAPTER THREE

ARROGANCE

1. Yarrick

Pain was a million jagged fragments. I took a breath, inhaling scorching heat and dust, and the fragments glowed red. *Get up*, I told myself. *This is nothing. You've known worse. You aren't going to let a minor irritant stand in the way of your duty. Now get up!*

I staggered to my feet, squinting at the maelstrom around me. The battle fortress's shot had blown away the central core of the Chimera and knocked the transport end over end. I had been thrown clear. The vehicle was on its back, its flanks gaping with fire, its front armour buckled and torn like tin. The Basilisk had vanished. Where it had been, there was now a field of warped and blackened sculpture. Flames guttered on all sides. Bodies of men and orks lay burned, smashed and torn. The air was still filled with the din of combat, but in this space, in the hundred or so metres in any direction, there was a pause. It was the peace of the murdered, the quiet of scorched earth. The battle fortress had come to a stop when it fired. Its turret swivelled, looking for new meat, but here and now, there were only tiny figures like me scurrying around. Nothing of interest. The engine rumbled as the gigantic tank's attention turned to fresh killing fields.

I scrambled through the blazing hell to the Chimera. There would be nothing to salvage there but lives, and likely none of those, but I had to try. My duty, in this moment, had shrunk to the few metres around me. They were all I could reach, along with, Throne have mercy, maybe some of the men who fought by my side. As I came up to the wreck, I saw Lanner fighting his way out of the hole in the front armour. I rushed to him and pulled him out. The right side of his face was burned, and he was bleeding from a dozen wounds, but nothing was broken. He took a few steps away from the Chimera. I turned back to it.

He stopped me. 'There's no one else, commissar,' he said.

I turned to face him. '*Down!*' I yelled. Lanner dropped flat. The charging ork swung a massive chainaxe, missed, and overshot, momentum carrying the filthy xenos to me. I hit him in the face with my power claw. I punched clean through his skull.

The corpse fell. Behind it, I saw the battle fortress. It had not left. It was heading for us, gun at the ready. I remember that I wondered, sourly, why we were worth killing. Perhaps the crew had recognised me, and I was the recipient of a grotesque honour.

The turret erupted. But not because it had fired. A

massive armour-piercing round had struck it. Flames shot out of the hatch, and the gun was suddenly askew. I whirled around. A shape burst through a wall of flame. It was as huge as the ork tank, its treads alone as high as a man. It was a shadow made of steel. It was death.

The *Fortress of Arrogance* fired again, catching the battle fortress in the flank, tearing open a gaping hole in the armour. The tank ground to a halt. Unbelievably, the turret rotated, the torqued gun aiming at the *Arrogance*. Even the orks weren't stupid enough to attempt a shot, I thought, even as I realised that they were easily stubborn enough to do so. I hit the ground beside Lanner.

Time and again, I have seen ork technology that functioned for no other reason than the sheer belief of the greenskins that it *would* work. But even their mad confidence couldn't overcome this basic a physical reality. I heard a muffled *fffwhump*, and the entire battle fortress shook with the force of the blast that was channelled back inside the tank. Then two more explosions, gigantic concussions as first ammunition, and then the engine, blew up. The pressure wave of the superheavy's destruction pressed us hard into the red dirt.

Then we were up, sputtering, before the ringing had faded from our ears, or the dazzle of the glare from our eyes. The *Fortress of Arrogance* had stopped. Its hatch opened for us as we climbed up. As we did, I noticed that the Baneblade bore some wounds of battle. Its armour was gouged and scorched, and had been penetrated in at least one spot. Inside, there were more wounds. An ork shell had pierced the *Arrogance*'s hide and, fortunately, gone right through the other side without detonating. But it had killed the driver, and the tank's commander,

Sergeant Hanussen, had taken the controls. He relinquished them to Lanner with visible relief. Lanner was a man in love as he settled into his seat.

I turned to Hanussen. 'How are our communications?'

'Spotty, commissar, but workable. I have already sent out word that you are alive.' When I nodded for him to continue, he said, 'There are at least three more Stompas and an equal number of battle fortresses against us. Some are already in the valley, and some are still coming up the pass.'

I grunted. 'We can't fight them there. Too confined. We'll have to wait for all of the primary threats to reach the valley, and try to break through. How are the other Baneblades faring?'

'The *Final Dawn* is still fighting. We've lost the others.'

I cursed. The *Fearful Sublime* was gone, too, along with Captain Hantlyn. The leadership of the regiments kept being decapitated. 'Who took command?' I asked.

'I did,' said Hanussen.

And he had made it this far. 'Good.'

'There's more, commissar. Colonel Helm has been trying to reach you. Something about orbital bombardment.'

I frowned. 'What are we targeting?'

'We aren't the ones doing it.'

I grabbed the vox. Seconds we didn't have were slipping away. But I put my trust in the men in the fray while I learned the broader situation. The curse of seeing the greater panorama of war is that one can never look away.

Static of one relay after another, the chain still blessedly functioning, and I was through to the Hadron Plateau and speaking to Helm. 'What is happening, colonel?'

'Commissar, the orks have a space hulk.'

It took an effort not to close my eye in despair. I kept my face rigid. A *space hulk?* When we had arrived in-system, the orks had had only a few transports at high anchor over Golgotha. We had summarily dispatched them. The orks had no forces except the surface ones, so no reinforcements, no resupply... Only they had. Thraka had a space hulk. It was one of those monstrous agglomerations of stolen and salvaged ships attached to an asteroid core that had been the primary source of troops and materiel for Thraka's invasion of Armageddon. We had destroyed it, and so dealt a crippling blow to his power.

We'd been naïve. It seemed that we were always so when it came to that ork.

He had another. It was a chilling testament to the extent of his power and influence that he could have *two* such bases. And that he had managed to conceal it until now, hitting us on yet another front at the worst possible moment, was an even more frightening sign of not just strength, but skill.

Helm was still speaking. 'The fleet is being hit hard, sir. We don't have the ships to fight something like that. It's also bombarding the surface, primarily the sites being contested by our Titan forces.'

'What is your evaluation?'

'Sir, we are losing.'

There was a charged quality to his silence as he waited for my answer. To speak so openly of defeat to a commissar was normally suicidal, and I have shot men for expressing sentiments much less definite than that. It took a brave man to be honest at such a high risk to himself. But I had asked him for the truth, and he had given it to me. Helm had proven himself an officer of integrity

on Armageddon, when he had risked his military career
and worse by standing against the treacherous idiocies
of Governor von Strab. I appreciated that he was just as
willing to tell me what I did not wish to, but absolutely
must, hear.

In this case, he told me what I had already deduced.
The facts were horrific in their simplicity. With a space
hulk, Thraka had more than the upper hand. The outcome of this war was decided. The only question that
remained was what, if anything, we could salvage. The
next words I spoke tasted like ash and deadened my soul.
They hurt all the more for the ultimate responsibility I
bore. This was my crusade. I still did not doubt its righteousness or its vital necessity. But I had led us here, to
Golgotha. It was under my command that disaster had
befallen us. Whatever the role individual officers had
played (and I did wonder about Rogge's total silence),
this was my war, and the hated words were mine to speak.
'I am issuing an order for immediate evacuation. Colonel, take the men and materiel you can and abandon the
Golgotha system. Do it now.'

There was a pause. In it was the weight of Helm's
despair. Then he said, 'Commissar, the men will refuse
to leave without you.'

I was simultaneously honoured, humbled and outraged
by the promise of disobedience. I knew better than to
bluster or threaten. The situation required a solution,
not a tantrum. 'Have any transports landed in the last
few minutes?'

'Three,' he answered.

'Then I was aboard one of them. I am directing the
evacuation. I am departing with our heroic troops.

Understood?' There was no answer except a disbelieving silence. '*Understood?*' I demanded.

'Yes, commissar.'

'Maintain the fiction as long as you can. I'm sorry, Teodor.' I was ordering an honest man to lie. And the poor bastard was going to be stuck with the responsibility of preserving my legend longer than I would be. 'The Emperor protects.'

'The Emperor–'

A huge burst of static that became an unending gale. There would be no further contact with Hadron Base. Outside the *Fortress of Arrogance*, I heard another kind of gale build to a frenzy.

2. Helm

Teodor Helm threw down the vox-unit and ran from the communications centre of the Hadron garrison. He didn't know if the static meant that Yarrick was dead. He had been unable to regain contact with any of the vox-relay posts. The entire network was down. Between Golgotha's electrical storms and its dust, vox-traffic was immediate area only. The Hadron Plateau was cut off from the rest of the army.

Helm mounted the steps of the fort's outer wall. He looked north, in the direction of the Ishawar Mountains. Even if it had been day, the chain wouldn't have been visible from this distance, but Helm could see more than enough evidence of the unfolding disaster. Before him, at the base of the plateau, the horde had gathered. These were not orks from the Ishawar. They had been gathering for hours. Transports arrived like black hail from the space hulk, dropping down just out of range over the

horizon to disgorge their war-fevered cargo. And so a
third ork force had entered the war, yet another obeying
the will of a single warlord. The unity was terrifying. And
here was the irony: the more everything went catastroph-
ically wrong, the more Yarrick was being proven right.

The perpetual cloud cover raged and flashed, but not all
the fury was natural. There was the glow and the rumble
of the transports as they cut through the overcast on their
final approach. And there were the fires: streaks of flame
that flashed above like wounds in the sky. The bombardment had spared the plateau so far, but the lethal rain was
falling heavily in the direction of where the Titans fought
their ork counterparts. The ground shook faintly from concussions hundreds of kilometres away. The orks sending
death from the heavens didn't care if their kin were vaporised. Nothing mattered but the destruction of the foe.

Then there were the traces of the other war, the one
in the heavens. Sometimes there was no more than the
light. Other times, the debris was large enough that it did
not burn, but hit the ground with cratering force. Helm
could follow this war only through the occasional, fragmented transmission. He hoped some of that wreckage
was from ork ships.

But even as he watched, there in the distance, so far
away that it was nothing more than a lonely, broken silhouette, and visible only because it was wreathed in the
fire of its death, fell a shape that stabbed at his heart.
Shattered though it was, he still recognised the lines of
the ship on which he had travelled so long that it was
home at least as much as Armageddon itself. No longer.
The Firestorm-class frigate *Harrower* was making planet-
fall unseen and unmourned by anyone but Helm. It

disappeared in the polluted night. The thunderclap of impact was muted, but it had the resonance of a single, massive beat on a funeral drum.

Helm looked back at the orks below. Hadron Base was built to withstand sieges, but no fortress could do so indefinitely, and there was no reason to make a stand. The commissar had ordered everyone here to depart. If they did not do so soon, they never would, and the defeat on Golgotha would be total.

With a curse, Helm turned away from the spectacle of loss. As he descended the staircase, he shouldered the mantle of the commander who would oversee one of the most humiliating retreats of the millennium.

3. Yarrick

There is something freeing about hopelessness. I knew that we would not live to see the dawn. So did the crew of the *Fortress of Arrogance*. Suddenly, there was no destination to reach, no goal to slip from our grasp. There was nothing left except the honourable death. As that certainty sank in, I saw smiles on the faces of the tank crew. I believe there was a real lightening of their spirits.

I have told myself this many times since then. It is important for my own soul that this be true.

I felt no lighter as I climbed out of the *Arrogance*'s hatch and took up position in its pulpit. The failure to stop Thraka would mean no peace for me as I fell to the night of the grave. Even so, I had new energy. Something very like exhilaration coursed through my blood. If death was upon me, I was going to meet it with all the fury my faith would grant me, and exult in every ork I killed between now and my last moment.

'Warriors of the Imperium!' I called. I was speaking over the vox, but as the energy flowed, it seemed to me that my voice itself carried over the battlefield. 'Tomorrow will be our day of days, for we shall have rejoined the Emperor in glory at the Golden Throne. Tonight is our night of nights, for it is now, in these very moments, that we earn the glory that will carry us to the Throne.' I paused as ork stubber fire ricocheted off my claw. In response, I stood higher. 'The greenskins outnumber us. They laugh that we have nowhere to go. They think they are triumphant.' A large blast to my left: a Leman Russ torn open by multiple rocket blasts. A Hellhound avenged it by incinerating its killers. 'Show them that they are wrong. Show them that they have nothing to celebrate. Show them that they are trapped on this planet with a foe who will never leave. Teach them what triumph really means! *Become the true wrath of Golgotha!*'

I could not hear the response any more than I could truly hear my own shouts. But as I could feel my exhortation in the rasp in my throat, as if it were a primordial beast's roar, so I could feel the spirit that rose to my call from the Emperor's legions. Locked in combat, dying and killing, they all heard my words, and they responded. For all that the valley floor was very quickly becoming a savage melee on a monumental scale, with regimental cohesion breaking down in the collision between two vast forces of war, we acted as one, striking with renewed fervour, our hearts filled with something that was at once a song of praise and a howl of undying rage.

As the *Fortress of Arrogance* leapt forward, I raised my claw in defiance of the ork machines that bulked in the night ahead. A Stompa and another battle fortress were barrelling forward to meet us. Their guns and ours flashed-burned the dark. At the same moment, there was a jerk as Lanner took the *Arrogance* through a sudden course correction. The movement was sluggish by any normal standard, but was preternaturally nimble for a Baneblade, and was just enough to spoil the orks' aim. Their machines turned, far more slowly. Distracted by the inviting target we presented, they ignored the other cannons aimed their way. A unified barrage crippled them.

I became aware of concerted, organised movement on all sides. With the *Arrogance* as focus, the regiments were reforming. Our casualties were horrific. The landscape was strewn with the corpses of men and vehicles, but was also alive with an army reforging itself into a mailed fist.

'Commissar!' a voice called to me.

I looked down. A Steel Legion trooper was running alongside the *Arrogance*, so close he was a single wrong step away from being dragged under by the treads. He didn't care, but not because he had succumbed to despair. There was a spring in his step. 'Yes, soldier,' I said.

'It's Hades Hive again, isn't it?'

'You were there?'

'Yes, I was. The greenskins are in for another surprise, aren't they? Going to rip Thraka's head off, commissar?'

I opened my claw. 'No,' I said. 'I think I'll crush it instead.'

The trooper laughed, saluted, and moved off.

Doesn't he realise? I wondered. *Of course he does.* This was our final assault, and we all knew it. Every man was charging for the salvation of his soul, for the bond of comradeship, and for the glory of the Emperor of Mankind. In the hellish strobes of the stubber, las and cannon fire, the gleaming elegance of Mordian uniforms mixed with the Armageddon trench coats and the industrial-grey Mortisian fatigues. And we were all moving toward the pass.

We plunged back into the sea of orks. We punched forward, always forward, though there was nowhere to advance except deeper into the enemy's midst. 'Stop for nothing,' I called down to Lanner. In answer, he drove the Baneblade even faster, crushing orks by the score. For a moment, the treads spun in the morass of corpses, and then the *Arrogance* roared on. I snapped my claw closed, as if tearing out the collective throat of the foe. I sent a mental challenge to Thraka. *Here we are*, I thought as I cut down greenskins with my bolt pistol and my eye. *Do you dare face us? Do you?*

The orks fell back before our fury. But only so far. They bunched up, then gathered courage as something colossal loomed out of the pass. It was a Gargant, fifty metres tall, come from the battles with our Titans.

Hanussen, who was manning the main gun, realised what its presence implied. 'What happened to the Legio?' he voxed.

'That is not our concern, captain,' I snapped. 'Our concern is what happens to that abomination. Destroy it.'

Hanussen lined the cannon up and fired.

If the Gargant had not been fresh from another battle, our gesture would have been pointless. But I could see that it had already sustained serious damage. There was smoke pouring out of its neck, and what looked like a fault line running down the length of its frontal armour. Our shell hit at the base of the head. Hanussen must have loaded an armour-piercing round. There was no explosion, and for a moment, it seemed as if we had wasted our blow.

The Gargant took one more step, then rocked forward. The head slipped from the shoulders and plummeted to the ground. The giant leaned deeper. Then gravity took over, and the slow bow became a sudden drop. The monster crashed to the ground, crushing hundreds of orks and spreading panic far beyond the immediate reach of its destruction. The superstitious dread spread before the *Fortress of Arrogance* too. The orks could see who rode the tank that had felled a Gargant with a single shot, and they could believe anything of me.

My bark of laughter lacerated my throat.

We surged towards the pass. We punished and slaughtered. The greater the number of orks, the greater the number of kills. The *Arrogance* shouted its voice of justice, and though a crew of brave and skilled men operated her, the tank felt like an extension of my will, as much a part of my body as the bale eye and power claw. The *Arrogance* and I were one, the iron spear-tip that was tearing open the belly of the orks.

'Here come more playmates,' Lanner drawled.

Emerging from the night ahead was another Stompa with a battle fortress. Was there no end to the orks' supply of these engines? I pushed the irrelevant question away. We were committed to the pass, so we had to destroy the ork superheavies. That was all.

'Take them!' I cried. I was speaking to the crew of the Baneblade, but I saw the infantry around us charge the monsters, too. I thought there might even have been some uncertainty in the orks. The psychic oppression that accompanied their presence seemed lesser to me. And why not? We had felled a Gargant with a single shot. We were unstoppable.

Then something changed. Something else had entered the field. I couldn't see what it was, but the atmosphere of the struggle gathered a new, crackling charge. The orks hurled themselves back against us. They hit with renewed will, and with something else. The panic had evaporated, replaced with orkish exuberance at its most insane. The monsters were laughing, just as I had been, but with a terrible delight. Their joy in battle and indiscriminate death had returned with a vengeance, and their laughter was undiminished whether they witnessed the bloody end of a human or an ork.

The Stompa charged. It actually *charged*. Fire and oily clouds pouring from its smokestacks, it pounded towards the *Arrogance*. The valley floor shook beneath its monstrous piston feet. It was not a creation that could move fast, nor did it now, but there was a massive build-up of momentum to its advance. 'Captain,' I voxed.

'I have it, commissar,' Hannussen replied. He fired, hitting the Stompa dead centre. But this time, the armour held, and the monster came on. It launched a rocket that struck the front of the Baneblade. Flames washed over the top, and I ducked down beneath the pulpit. Lanner didn't slow, and the *Fortress of Arrogance* rushed out of the flames to meet the challenge.

Another exchange of fire, cannon against cannon this time, and impossible to miss. The armour of the behemoths buckled, but did not give way. And then there was no more time or space. It seemed to me that the totemic face of the Stompa was roaring. I was, my face almost torn wide by the adrenaline-fuelled cry. The giants slammed into each other. The impact should have shattered the world. The *Arrogance*'s treads rode up the Stompa's plating. The walker brought its arms in as if to embrace the tank. The chainfist screeched against the left flank. The tip of the blade whirled teeth the size of my hand just over my head. A geyser of sparks streaked the night. On my right, the Stompa's cannon was aimed point-blank at the join between turret and hull. '*Burn!*' Hanussen screamed. The cannon boomed. The explosion engulfed the *Arrogance* and the Stompa's arm. I was shaken like a pebble in a tin, and lost my grip on the pulpit. I slid down the length of the hull and landed on the ground, an insect to be trampled by the giants.

I looked up as I staggered to the side. The blast had peeled back the *Arrogance*'s side armour and shredded the Stompa's arm. Metal flaps from both war engines were tangled together, and the giants were locked in their dance of death. The Baneblade's treads were still turning as if it were trying to force the Stompa to the ground, but the walker's centre of gravity was so low that it couldn't be toppled. The *Arrogance*'s turret was askew, the gun pointing to the clouds. The sponson-mounted lascannons and bolters had fallen silent.

Head ringing, still half-deafened from the report, I yelled Lanner's name into my vox-bead.

'Commissar,' his voice came back, hoarse and strained.

'Are all of you still alive?' I couldn't see how.

They weren't. 'Just me,' Lanner croaked. 'And a shot ready to go in this gun.'

The demolisher cannon protruded from the front of the hull, and could be fired by the driver. Its muzzle was only a few metres from the Stompa. The shot would be even more insane than the one the orks had taken, and Lanner's protection had been badly compromised. But

I did not tell him to stop. I did not tell him to abandon the tank. I would not deprive him of his honour. And I would not deprive the Imperium of one more victory, however pyrrhic.

'Glory to the Emperor,' I said.

'Glory to the Emperor,' he returned, and fired the gun.

The Stompa's chainfist broke through to the *Arrogance*'s munitions at the same moment.

The shockwave lifted me off my feet and hurled me end over end. I slammed into a wall of oncoming metal. I was boneless, a broken toy. As I slumped, something grabbed the bottom of my coat. I was yanked to the ground, dragged along the stony surface, and finally came to a stop in a painful, half-reclining position. I had been caught by the treads of the battle fortress. If the tank had not stopped, I would have been ground to mulch.

My vision began to grey, growing black around the edges. I blinked, keeping unconsciousness at bay. I could not move, but I could see. I saw everything. I saw that the Stompa was no more, but the majestic *Fortress of Arrogance* was mortally injured. It crashed back down and was silent. It was only inert metal, now.

I saw the end of our war. The soldiers fought heroically, but the end was preordained. The orks simply kept coming until they overwhelmed. Their triumphant energy turned them into an unstoppable wave. Then, finally, I saw what had changed. I saw what had entered the battlefield. It came charging through the swirling melee of combatants, knocking orks aside and splattering humans. The silhouette was so massive that for a hallucinatory moment I thought I was seeing a Dreadnought of the Adeptus Astartes. It wasn't a Dreadnought, nor was it one of the ridiculous weaponised cans that were the orks' debased versions of those living martyrs.

It was too big to be either.

It was an armoured shape, and it was rampage personified. It tore through the night faster than anything that big should move, leaping from cluster to cluster of struggle, annihilating Guardsmen with a massive stubber in its left hand, crushing them to nothing with an equally colossal power claw on its right. Every movement, every roar was an expression of rage, glee and messianic fervour. A terrible perfection of destruction had come among us.

Ghazghkull Mag Uruk Thraka was here.

He was smaller than the Stompas. But his presence was so immense that he appeared to tower over the mountains themselves. I was sick to the soul at the threat he represented to the Imperium and I struggled to tear myself free. I had no leverage. I was bound fast. But I still had one weapon. What I could see, I could target and kill. '*THRAKA!*' I howled with every ounce of strength I still possessed.

It should have been a futile gesture. He shouldn't have been able to hear me. Not in the cacophony of massacre. But he did. I understand now that destiny decreed that he should know I was there. It seems to me, in my darker moments, that the perfect agony of the galaxy is shaped to no small degree by the crossing of our paths. So he heard, and he came pounding toward me, running faster as he recognised me, his footsteps leaving a trail of small craters behind him. Like me, he only had one natural eye, and my bionic one focused on it. He came up so quickly, I had trouble acquiring the target. I had him as he reached me. I glared at him with the hatred of complete righteousness.

Before I could fire the laser, his claw swung into my face. The blow was no more than a slap. It was like being struck with a meteor.

My last sight before oblivion was of that obscene face contorted with delight.

CHAPTER FOUR

THE WELL

1. Rogge

They didn't kill him. They took him instead. They dragged him away, along with the other ragged survivors the orks chose to enslave rather than slaughter. He didn't struggle. There was no point. Quite a few of the captives did. Very few of them were killed. Instead, the orks jabbed them with shock poles and hauled them onward while they were still convulsing. So Rogge did nothing. He walked where he was led. He squeezed into the suffocatingly overcrowded hold of the slave transport. Second by second, step by step, he felt the last dregs of his honour drain away. The pain of his failure was so profound, he didn't even have the strength to howl.

When he stumbled out of the transport, into the greater hell of the space hulk, he felt that he had been reduced to a body surrounding a core of nothing. The numbness was a relief.

It didn't last.

2. *Yarrick*

I woke to agony and an immediate temptation to despair. I was suspended by chains that hung from a ceiling in darkness above me. They were wrapped around my upper arms, holding them out from my body, crucifying me. The pain, like clusters of daggers stabbing my flanks, shoulders and back, was so savage that at first, I wasn't aware of how I'd been mutilated. Then, as awareness sharpened, I felt the losses. My bale eye was gone. So was my claw.

My right arm.

I twisted in the chains, snarling, transmuting the pain into rage. I cast about with my remaining eye, taking in my surroundings as I sought what had been taken from me. I was in a large metal chamber. It was about a dozen metres on a side, and lit by flickering, dingy glow-globes along the walls. The only exit was sealed by a massive iron door. At the other end of the room was a large metal table. It was surrounded by instruments that erased the difference between surgery and torture. The light was dim, but not so dark that I couldn't see the overlapping bloodstains on the table. The floor around it was slick with obscene debris. The stench was slaughterhouse-thick.

Beneath my feet, there was no floor. I was being dangled high over a circular shaft. It was about two metres wide, and the gaping black of great depth. Sloshing, scrabbling noises echoed up from the darkness.

There were three orks standing guard. When they saw

that I was awake, one of them dragged the door open and left, sealing the chamber off again with a bang. The other two watched me closely, growling as if warning me not to try anything. Thinking clearly was difficult through the haze of pain, but I noted their wariness. I had worked hard to create a fearsome legend for myself among the orks. Here was evidence of my success. I wondered how I might use this fact.

After a few minutes, the door banged open as if a giant had kicked it. One had. Thraka strode into the chamber. He stopped at the edge of the pit. Our heads were almost level, and we exchanged a long stare. Thraka's face was the purest essence of his benighted race. It was the monstrousness of war at its most savage – pure beast made more hideous by a crosshatching of scars. It was a leathered palimpsest of wounds. Some I had given him, and they were insignificant. The only wound that mattered was the one that had almost stopped him, but instead, following the dictates of perverse destiny, had been his making. The top of his skull was adamantium. I couldn't imagine what had happened to the brain beneath to transform him into a prophet of orkish victory, but the claws that had operated on this ork's mind were stained with the blood of billions.

Thraka watched me closely. He watched me *quietly*. He was *studying* me. I was suddenly drenched in a sweat that had nothing to do with physical discomfort. The only thing worse than being face-to-face with a raging, howling ork is being face-to-face with a quiet one. So many human victories have depended on the orks' tactical simplicity. They charged until they died, and that was all. But an ork who watched and learned, planned and strategised, an ork who meditated, and kept his thoughts to himself – there could be nothing more dangerous.

Then the silence was broken, and to my eternal dishonour, it was I who broke it. 'Filth!' I yelled. 'The Emperor's wrath will blast you and all your accursed kind to the warp!' My hatred burst the bonds of language, and in the next second I was baying an inarticulate '*Rahhhhhh!*' at the beast. He continued to watch quietly.

The irony of that moment does not escape me.

After a few more shouts of incoherent, impotent rage, I calmed enough to speak again. 'I will kill you,' I hissed. 'I make you that promise.'

No reaction. Still that unnerving studying. I didn't know what he was looking for, or whether he saw what he wanted in my face, but he stepped back after an eternal moment. The guard who had fetched him took that gesture as permission to have at me. It laughed and gave my left arm a hard yank, almost pulling it from my shoulder. There was a blur of movement from Thraka, and he stood with the guard struggling in the grip of his claw. The ork whimpered. Its feet pedalled air. Thraka held the other ork over the pit. His eyes, one real, one a targeting bionic, never left my face. His mouth spread in a grin of predatory challenge. Then he dropped the guard.

The ork howled as it fell. The acoustics of the shaft turned its cry into a choir of hurt. The sound of impact was wet, and a long time in coming. The howl stopped.

Thraka reached above me and took the chains in his claw. He was no longer smiling. The gaze of that eye was penetrating, evaluating. There was also a complicity, which I rejected with all the hatred of my own look. He gave a slight nod. To me? I was imagining that, surely.

I prayed to the God-Emperor that I was mistaken. Then I heard the deep, final *chunk* of the claw slamming shut and the chains parting.

The terrible pull on my upper arms ended, and with freedom came vertigo. I fell into darkness, into my final seconds and into a strange peace. There was nothing I could do. Nothing to struggle against. For the first time in my living memory, I was absolved of all responsibility. Duty ends only in death, and I had been vouchsafed a few moments to experience the release from duty. I commended my soul to the care of the Emperor, and went limp. I plunged into terrible sounds. A thick wind screamed against me. I saw nothing but the dark, and after the first second, it seemed that I was flying, not falling.

I felt the pain of unfinished tasks. I hoped for forgiveness. I thought that there were worse deaths.

I had the luxury of several long seconds to think these things. And even now, there are moments of marrow-deep exhaustion when I look back on this tiny sliver of rest with something like nostalgia before shame corrects my thinking.

It was not shame that recalled me to duty on that day. It was the brutal but non-lethal impact of my landing. I did not hit metal. I hit liquid. It hurt like being slammed into brick, and then it took me down, smothering and choking. I had been limp. Now I thrashed in the foul blackness. I had no sense of up or down, no concept of anything at all except universal pain and, overriding even that, the divine command to resume my struggle.

My agonised chest demanded I draw a breath. Filth flowed into my lungs instead. I spasmed, and I broke the surface of the stagnant water. I choked up the sludge in my lungs and flailed forward. My feet struck bottom almost right away, sliding on a slick pile that might have been stones and might have been skulls. The pile sloped up. Within a few metres, I was out of the water and crouched against the curved, slimy wall of the shaft. Breath heaving in and out of my lungs like a handful of claws, I turned around to face the darkness.

I was almost overcome by a sense of total helplessness. I was not alone in this space. I could hear large bodies struggling and splashing nearby. But I could see nothing, I had no weapons, and I had only one arm. I braced myself and waited. After a minute, my eye adjusted, and I saw that there was faint illumination coming from phosphorescent fungi on the walls. The shaft had dropped me in one end of what seemed to be a large cave. It stretched out into the deep gloom before me, twisting out of sight. There were narrow banks along the walls. I felt the surface of the wall at my back. It was porous stone, not metal. I realised where I must be: in the lower reaches of the space hulk.

The fact that I could breathe was another hint of Thraka's enormous power. Space hulks were not uncommon among the orks. Once a Waaagh! reached a critical mass, the hulks were a favourite method of conveying war from one system to another. Many, but not all, used a planetoid as the core around which the patchwork collection of ships was assembled. This rocky core had an atmosphere in its interior. That necessitated a care and effort far beyond the norm for orks. I could feel Thraka's presence and strength of will even down here.

The struggle I was hearing came to an end. There was

a high-pitched chittering that somehow conveyed fatal agony. For a moment, there was silence. Then splashing started again, drawing nearer. A large bulk was approaching, leaving a wake behind it. I looked about me, desperate for a weapon or a means of escape. The wall was unbroken, and there were no handholds. But just to my right was the half-submerged body of the guard. The greenskin had landed on this spur of rock, and been impaled through the neck. I knelt and searched the corpse. The ork's gun had shattered, but the brute's blade was still in its sheath. The weapon was a crude, massive cleaver. It was an awkward weapon for a human to wield, especially one-handed. It was also a gift from the Emperor Himself.

And from no one else. No one.

I remained crouching, clutching the blade, listening to the approach of the predator. The splashing became shallow, and then there was an explosive scrabbling. I whirled, weapon extended. It met a shadow twice as thick and long as a man. The blade sank between chitinous plates. The weight of the beast knocked me against the wall. My feet lost their purchase and I slid down. The creature was propelled by dozens of tiny legs, and they clawed at me, shredding and tangling in what was left of my coat. Tusks like sickles snapped at my neck. The thing pushed its head down, trying to reach my throat, impaling itself more deeply on the cleaver. The mandibles brushed my skin. I pushed up with all my strength, my arm trembling with the effort. I cut through something important and was drenched in a flood of blood and other noxious fluids. The monster collapsed. I squirmed out from under the dead weight. I examined the creature as best I could in the dim light. It appeared to be a species of squig. It had the spines and wide jaws of those beasts, but its long, segmented body and exoskeleton owed more to the arthropod. Its tail ended in a straight stinger half the length of my leg. I could hear more of its kind not far away, and I was about to kick the corpse into the water when, on impulse, I hacked off the stinger. I turned the corpse over to its fellows and, stinger tucked under my arm, moved away from the eating frenzy.

I kept to the wall that extended up the shaft. I made sure that I wasn't about to be attacked, and then began pounding the stinger against the wall at about knee height. The stone was weak, the stinger strong. After a few hits, the tip gouged a hole a few centimetres deep. I held the stinger in place by squeezing it with the stump of my right arm. I hammered it into the wall with the flat of the blade. I kept at it until just over half of the stinger was wedged between rock. I stood up. Holding onto the wall with my left hand, I climbed onto the stinger. The footing was treacherous, but the stinger felt solid. I stood there for five full minutes, much longer than I should have to if I attempted what I was contemplating. The stinger held. My balance felt sure enough, if I leaned against the wall, to pound in another spike.

It could be done. I could build a ladder for a one-armed man to climb. All I needed was enough stingers.

I looked up towards the invisible mouth of the well. How far was there to go? A hundred metres? More? No way of knowing. I thought about how many stingers I might need. How many of those monsters I would have to kill. How endless my escape attempt would be.

How easily I could die in the process.

I thought about all of these things. Then I stepped back down to the ground, tightened my grip on the blade, and made my way toward the thrashing movements.

I don't know how long I was down there. In perpetual night and perpetual struggle, time was not even a concept. There were no cycles, only pauses of unpredictable length between convulsions of bloodletting. Survival necessitated absolute focus, and it wasn't long before I was a creature of instinct and mechanical habit. I could afford no thought that might distract me. There was no space for either hope or despair. I fought, I killed, I sliced off stingers, and I built my steps. When I grew hungry, I ate the bitter, fatty meat of the creatures. It could easily have killed me, but I had no other choice. I was lucky. It kept me alive, and as rational thought shut down before animal need, I shed the pointless luxury of disgust.

I scavenged a belt from the dead guard. It was so huge, I had to cut it in half. Then I had somewhere to sheathe the cleaver, and free up my hand.

I became the most dangerous predator in that world. The squig-things were larger and stronger than I was, but they were mindless and incapable of learning. I grew adept at catching them from behind, leaping onto their heads and sinking my blade between the skull and the first segment of the armour, killing them before they could bring their stinger to bear. I killed, and killed, and killed, was wounded again and again, but was always triumphant. I like to believe that it was my faith that gave me the edge in those moments when my life teetered on a knife edge. I could barely artic-ulate a prayer, but the knowledge of the Emperor's

protection was always there, as basic a fact of my existence as breathing.

Sleep was the risk, the enemy, and the terrifying necessity. I did what I could to protect myself. I sacrificed
precious stingers by planting them in an outward facing semicircle around the base of my ladder. I scattered
armour plates in loose piles beyond my rough palisade,
so I might be woken by the approach of an enemy. I slept
in light, broken snatches, jerking awake at the slightest
sound. Sometimes there was nothing there. Sometimes
there was. My body learned never to do more than doze.

More than hunger or pain, exhaustion became the rock
against which my strength was eroded. But duty only ends
in death. I was not dead. My duty was clear. I followed
the path. I built my path. Step by step by step, hammering in one stinger at a time, rising one half-metre, then
descending to kill for my construction material. The ladder rose, and it took me longer each time to climb up and
down. My task became more and more difficult, dangerous and tiring the closer it came to completion.

The effort to keep going required such extreme tunnel vision that I almost didn't notice when I was within
reach of the lip of the well.

I killed the first guard with a single horizontal slash of
the blade. It was no longer an awkward xenos weapon
in my hand. It was my tooth, stinger and claw. It tore the
ork's throat wide open. Its head flopped backward. The
ork gurgled and staggered forward, then back a step, its
blood jetting over me. The beast hadn't collapsed yet and
I was already attacking its fellow. The other ork was staring at me, its jaw hanging low with incomprehension and

panicked indecision. The greenskin started to respond, reaching for its own blade, but it was too late. I rammed the cleaver deep into that maw. With a crunch, the blade came out the back of its neck. The guard stumbled away, choking. It clutched at the blade, slicing its hands as it tried to pull the cleaver out of its head. The ork slumped to its knees, dark blood pouring down the length of the blade, slicking it. The guard managed to grasp the hilt and yanked with stupid strength. The ork pulled the blade out, killing itself.

I checked the guards for firearms. They had none. I picked up my blade and approached the door. I placed my ear against it, but could hear nothing on the other side. No way to know if the guards' death cries had alerted others.

Nothing for it, then. I sheathed the cleaver, grabbed the door handle and leaned back. The door opened with a screeching grind. There was a corridor on the other side. It ran about twenty metres, and then opened into a wider space. There the light was brighter, and I squinted in pain, half-blind after so long in the darkness. There was noise ahead, a lot of it. Ork snarls, clanging, human moans. The sound of a crowd.

There were no options. There was no plan. There was nowhere else to go. I had nothing except my will, my struggle, and my Emperor.

They would suffice.

Blade out, its weight a strain to hold one-handed, I walked down the corridor and into the light. Before me was a vast open area filled with cages. The slave pens. Waiting for me, as if I were late for an appointment, stood a squad of jailers, my new chains in their hands.

I launched myself at them, and I did manage to cut the hand off one of them before they subdued me.

As they dragged me off to a cage, there was a guttural laugh to my right. I knew whose laugh it was, and was sickened by the knowledge that by having survived the well, all I had done was entertain Thraka.

Will, I told myself, fighting despair. *Struggle. Emperor. They will suffice.*

CHAPTER FIVE

THE SHAPE OF REDEMPTION

1. Rogge

It took Rogge a minute to recognise the new prisoner. Like the rest of the male captives, his hair and beard were shaggy. They were an iron grey beneath the encrustation of filth, and that was unusual. Older slaves did not last long. Nor did the disabled, and this one was missing his right arm below the elbow. It was only when he saw that the man's left eye was also gone, and what blazed in his right, that realisation dawned.

The temptation was to withdraw deeper into the cage and the anonymity of mass misery. But that was only delaying the inevitable. And it was not the path he had sworn to himself he would follow, if given the chance. So he shuffled forward. 'Commissar?' he said.

Yarrick turned that gaze on him. It scanned Rogge, seeing everything. Rogge knew the ork superstition about the power of Yarrick's look. In this moment, he absolutely

71

shared their belief. 'Colonel,' Yarrick acknowledged. He
turned away from Rogge and moved to the bars of the
cage. Rogge saw that eye flicking over the space of the
slave pens. 'Tell me what I need to know,' he said.

Rogge swallowed. No judgement, no condemnation, no
demands for an explanation. Instead, a simple request for
information, spoken with the confidence of a man who
had no conception of surrender. Rogge stood straighter
even as he felt the temptation to weep with gratitude.
He had his second chance. Redemption would be his.
'There is no pattern to the shifts,' he told the commissar.
'We never know how long we will be held here. When
we are taken out, we work until we drop.'

Yarrick nodded. Rogge watched him touch the bars of
the cage, testing their strength. The soldering was sloppy,
the construction of the cage crude, but the enclosure
would have been strong enough to hold orks, let alone
humans. There would be no breaking out from the cage
itself.

Yarrick grunted and looked beyond the bars at the huge
space of the holding pen.

'A former cargo hold, I think,' Rogge said. For all the
encrustations of ork scaffolding, totemic sculptures
and savage graffiti, the human construction of the walls
and floor was still evident. They were inside a captured
freighter, of that much Rogge was sure. Continual modifi-
cations by the orks had blurred the boundaries between
this ship and the adjoining ones, fusing them into an
indistinguishable hell of metal and refuse.

The slave cages had likely once been freight containers,
and they were stacked in ziggurat formations on all sides
of the hold. Ramps granted access to the upper levels. A

large mustering space occupied the centre of the floor. There, slaves were gathered, organised, sorted, abused, tortured, killed. The orks didn't allow the other slaves to clear away the dead until the bodies had piled up to the point that they were a nuisance. Rogge had seen many shifts pass with a dozen or more bodies left to be trampled into pulp. The cage he and Yarrick shared was on the floor level, and blood sometimes seeped in through the bars.

There were some yells and scuffling behind them. They turned around. A few of the prisoners were staring upward, spitting and cursing at the cage's ceiling. Rogge pointed. 'Cal Behriman,' he said with all the contempt he could muster. Sitting on top of the centre of the cage was a second, smaller one. It held only one prisoner. It contained no luxuries except space. The man inside ignored the taunts. He sat, impassive, eating something rank from a metal bowl.

Yarrick was frowning. 'Why is he isolated?' he asked.

'He's our overseer,' Rogge explained. He pointed back outside the cage, at the other small boxes scattered around the hold, all of them sitting on top of other, larger containers. 'There's one for every dozen or so enclosures, as far as I can tell. These orks like seeing us whipped and prodded by one of our own. The traitor is given a bit more food and space, but has to sit and hear what we think of him.'

Yarrick was shaking his head. 'Too elaborate,' he said.

'Sir?'

'By ork standards, that's a very sophisticated bit of cruelty.'

'I don't understand.'

'Just another example of the strength of our enemy, colonel.'

Rogge curled a lip. 'He's a little tyrant,' he said. 'A ship's cook with dreams above his station.' He shrugged. 'Well, I hope he enjoys his reign while it lasts.'

Yarrick said nothing in reply. He watched Behriman for a moment more before turning his attention to their fellows in the cage. 'All the prisoners are human?' he asked.

'Everyone I've seen,' Rogge confirmed.

'Good.' The commissar took a breath, and seemed to grow before Rogge's eyes. When he spoke again, he was taller than the cage. 'Fellow children of the Emperor,' he began, 'you should feel no despair. Prepare yourselves for struggle and sacrifice, but also for victory. The orks have brought us deep within the heart of their power. We should thank them for the opportunity. Let us thank them by showing them what a terrible mistake they have made.'

Rogge stared at him, dumbstruck. They had been speaking quietly, but now Yarrick was orating for the benefit of the entire hold. His voice echoed off the walls.

Orks came running.

2. *Yarrick*

The beating was a small price to pay. I had new bruises in the shape of boot soles on my torso, and my face was a swollen, bleeding mess. Trivial matters. Less trivial was the question of why the orks had held back. By their standards, I hadn't been beaten – I'd been gently admonished to behave myself. Why I was not broken or dead was a disturbing question. But I could not be distracted by it. What mattered was that I had spoken, and I had been heard. I didn't know how I was going to strike against Thraka, but strike I would. To that end, it was necessary that the slaves think of themselves not as prisoners, but as combatants. I wanted them predisposed to struggle. They should be thinking about strategy and retaliation instead of their own despair. I had no illusions. Whatever happened, it was very unlikely that any of us would be leaving the space hulk. But we could still achieve victory. The goals on Golgotha and here were the same: the end of Thraka. It didn't matter who the prisoners were. That ork was a threat to every human life, so it was the duty of every human to fight him to the death.

I didn't expect a mass uprising, which would be useless and suicidal. What I wanted was to see who would respond most concretely to my exhortation.

In the cage, as the hours passed, and we waited, too packed in to crouch or sit, they spoke to me, and made themselves known. They had all been part of the Golgotha Crusade, but in a variety of capacities. Lieutenant Benjamin Vale had been the pilot of the lighter *Inflexible*. The vessel had been captured as it left Golgotha and tried to rejoin the departing fleet. Two troopers from the Armageddon 117th, Hans Bekket and Hadrian Trower, had also survived that last flight and been taken alongside Vale. These men were soldiers. I salute their courage in stepping forward, but I would have expected nothing less.

There were two others who approached me during my first hours in the cage. I would have their valour noted. Aranaya Castel was a medicae who had been caught when Hadron Base itself was overrun. She had combat training, but had never served on the front lines. Now the orks were amusing themselves by forcing her to work in their grotesque surgeries. These were not places of heal-ing. They were houses of pain. The orks who ruled them delighted in experimenting with scalpel and syringe, and Castel's shifts were spent in hauling away the bloody detritus of those experiments.

Then there was Ernst Polis. He, too, had been on the base, and was a Munitorum logistician. He had no training at all, and had simply been planetside to assist the coordination of our supply lines when the disaster had struck. He was one of the most cursed men I had ever met. He had an eidetic memory, and had never experienced combat until Golgotha. Every atrocity and monstrosity he witnessed, he retained with perfect clar-ity. I don't know what this balding little man had been like before his capture. I imagine a rather tiresome obses-sive consumed by minutiae. Now his eidetic memory had become a curse. He was barely sane. Trauma had produced a deep autism that was the only thing keep-ing him alive. He held awful reality at bay by erecting a screen of itemisation. He catalogued and numbered everything he saw. It was possible to converse with him, but only just.

When, muttering and counting, he squeezed his way past the larger prisoners to tell me, eyes on the ground, that he wanted to help, I said, 'Tell me how you can.'

'What do you want to know? There are between twelve and fifteen orks guarding the hold at any one time, approximately a hundred prisoners to a cage, but twice as many prisoners in total than are in the hold right now because there are two shifts, and both shifts are never present at the same time, and when it is our shift we will be taken to work salvage in one of four ships in the immediate vicinity, away from this Carnack-class trans-port, but all salvage returns to this hub–'

He went on without taking a breath. I broke in a few times to ask about the other ships he had seen. His mem-ory did appear to be perfect. As fractured as he was, his ability to remember anything he saw was a useful one. He had also managed to scavenge, from a captured trader's ship, a scrap of vellum and a stylus. The orks didn't care that he had these objects. I did. We began work on a map.

As for Rogge, I wasn't sure. I did not know what had happened when that second ork army attacked our rear-guard. Perhaps no commander would have been able to stop, or even slow, that strike. But from the look of hungry guilt that gnawed his face, I judged that he had failed his men and the rest of the crusade. He was hop-ing, I thought, to wipe away that guilt through redeeming action. If so, then his guilt might be useful.

I didn't know yet if the man would be.

Three people died at Behriman's hands during my first shift. Five the next one. Come the third, I gave serious thought to killing him. But there was no opportunity. I was always too far from him, and fell under the whip of an ork or one of the other human overseers. Those traitors, too, deserved my special hatred, but Behriman, perched above my cage, was the perpetual presence. He was also the most savage. The others did not spare the lash, but they did not kill. They left that to the orks.

Before I had a chance to close with Behriman, I no longer knew how many shifts I had worked. As in the well, time had smeared, become senseless. Our duties were salvage. It was killing work: disassembling what

was indicated, hauling machines and scrap and whatever eccentric piece of material was desired in crude
carts that were hard enough to push when they were
empty. Whenever we left the cage, we moved through a
cyclopean collage of metal fused with stone. For the most
part, what I saw was a labyrinth of corridors and holds.
Ragged tears in bulkheads and hulls created links where
none should be. Waste, grime and orkish scrawls were the
universal constant, erasing the differences between the
ships. I passed through one set of corridors a half-dozen
times before I noticed that the construction beneath the
ork improvements was not human.

Sometimes, I would haul my load past a viewing block,
and see the exterior of the space hulk. It looked like a
city in an earthquake. Ships of every make and size were
crammed together, their sterns sunk into the planetoid.
They slanted crazily this way and that. The longer they
had been part of the hulk, the more they had melded
into each other, losing their identities as voidships. Some
structures no longer resembled vessels at all, if they ever
had been. Towering over the rest of the fractured skyline
was a massive shape, a broad-shouldered monstrosity
that must have absorbed a dozen freighters as it thrust its
way into being. The peak was in the shape of a gigantic
ork skull. It gazed down upon the rest of the world with
snarling satisfaction. Lights blazed perpetually inside its
eyes. It was a temple to savagery.

We dragged the salvage to an enormous pit to be sorted
according to whatever madness moved ork technology at
any given moment. The path to the depot passed through
what had once been a launch bay. Upended, all of its
equipment and shuttlecraft had wound up as treacherous

hills of debris on the new floor. It was here, in the space between the mounds of broken angles, that I had my opportunity.

I was about three cart-lengths away from Behriman. He was whipping an older man. The slave was younger than I was, I think, but his hair had turned the white of dirty snow. I had seen him a few times, noticed the way his shoulders sagged under invisible lead, and known that he would not last much longer. His eyes had the lifelessness of clay. Perhaps his end would be a mercy. Even so, when he stumbled, and Behriman laid into him, I let go of my cart. There were no other overseers nearby. The path took sharp corners around the heaps a half-dozen metres ahead and behind. I guessed that I had time to come up behind Behriman while he was busy and kill him before an ork saw what I was doing. In my load of salvage, I had been careful to add a large shard from a mirror that had been in the stateroom of a one-time civilian luxury yacht. I grabbed the shard and started forward.

The old man collapsed. The other slaves looked on as I closed in on Behriman. They kept dragging their carts. I was less than ten paces away. Behriman dropped the whip and crouched over the slave. He wrapped his arms around the man's head and neck. I raised the glass. Then I heard Behriman whisper. I couldn't hear what he said, but I heard the old captive's response: 'Yes.' He spoke with relief. And gratitude.

And I think, perhaps, joy.

Behriman snapped his neck.

He straightened and turned to face me. He said nothing. He didn't raise his whip. He waited.

I lowered my hand and returned to my cart. I began

hauling it again. Behriman was already bawling invective at a slave whose pace had slackened. Behind us, an ork driver appeared, laughing as Behriman dished out encouraging blows.

At the end of a shift, exhaustion was so total that we would fall asleep as soon as we were packed back into the cage. Since we couldn't lie down, we slept standing up, leaning against each other. This time, though, I forced myself to stay awake a little longer. I made sure I was standing directly beneath Behriman's cage. When the rest of the prisoners were unconscious, I said, 'What did you ask the old man?'

He didn't answer at first. He was sprawled on his back on the mesh floor of the enclosure, and I wondered if he was asleep. He spoke after a minute. 'I asked him if he desired the Emperor's peace.'

'You presume much.'

A tiny movement of his shoulders, as if he'd shrugged. 'The man had served to the limit of his body's strength. He was as loyal a servant of the Emperor as any decorated officer. He deserved mercy, and a moment's dignity to compose his soul.'

'And who are you to grant such gifts?'

'I'm the one who is there.'

I nodded to myself. I was impressed. The man was unafraid to be completely despised in order that he might do what was necessary. He had what he saw as a sacred duty, and he was being true to it.

Here was a rare find.

'What do you know of this sector's layout?' I asked. I had only seen the same narrow routes again and again.

'Quite a bit. Why?'

'Because I think we have bided our time long enough.'
It was time to strike.

CHAPTER SIX

DESPERATE GLORY

1. Behriman

He lay on the floor of his cage for another hour, listening to the clangs and snarls and wails that filled the air of the space hulk. He thought about the conversation he had just had with Sebastian Yarrick. He thought about how he had brutalised the bodies of others and his own spirit in the service of a greater mercy. He had carried the burden of this duty so long that he could barely remember his life before his capture. Now that weight was at last about to be lifted from his shoulders. He allowed himself a single, body-shaking sob.

2. Rogge

The commissar spoke. The prisoners listened. Rogge listened. His soul burned with purpose.

Yarrick didn't orate as he had when he first arrived in their midst. He didn't draw the orks' attention. He spoke quietly, to one small group at a time, and what he said spread in whispers during the shifts until, Rogge was sure, every human in the hold knew, word for word, what the commissar had said. Yarrick spoke of war. What Rogge heard, what he was sure all heard, were words of hope. They were going to be leaving this hell. The break-out was imminent.

3. *Yarrick*

'Where do we go?' Rogge asked, his eyes bright with fervour.

'The *Inflexible*,' I answered. I gestured to Polis.

The little man nodded, and continued to nod while he spoke. 'I have been past the *Inflexible* three times during the last eight shifts, during which time I walked 20,235 steps, including the return trip, which ended the shift...' He caught himself, closing his eyes tightly with the effort. 'The *Inflexible* does not appear to be significantly damaged or fused beyond basic docking apparatus to this construct.' He clamped his mouth shut so tightly his teeth clicked, and he stopped talking. Purpose was mending him.

'And we have our pilot,' I said. Vale nodded.

'What if he's killed?' someone asked from the deeper shadows of the cage.

'I can fly it,' Rogge answered.

That surprised me. He was a tanker, not Navy. 'Since when?' I asked.

He gave an embarrassed shrug. 'Since home. My father's private yacht.'

'Hardly the same thing,' Vale protested, offended.

'No,' Rogge began, 'but the basic principles–'

'Are sufficiently similar,' I broke in, ending the argument. 'A pilot is a pilot, and a ship is a ship.' If Rogge's privileged background proved useful, then we were the better for it. 'At the start of the next shift,' I said. 'That's when we hit them.'

There was no cycle of night and day in the hulk, just perpetual grimy twilight lit by torches, flickering glow-globes and filthy biolumes. We didn't have the luxuries of such concepts as 'morning.' People just rested as well as they could until it was time to work again. And no one could be said to be alone when one could barely move for the crowding. All the same, I was given a form of privacy as everyone in the cage fell into uneasy dozing. Everyone but Castel, who was still jumpy after her latest stint amidst the horrors of the ork surgeries.

'None of us will leave this place alive,' she said.

'More than likely,' I agreed.

'Then why give us false hope?'

'I haven't. I never said we would succeed in escaping. Even if we can launch the lighter, it will be recaptured or destroyed before we get far.'

'Then why even try for it?'

'*If* it becomes possible to escape, that will be the most likely means. More importantly, an operational ship could do a fair bit of damage, especially if we choose the target wisely.'

'You have a target in mind,' she realised.

'The temple.' So much work had gone into constructing that massive ork head. The structure was a symbol of power. That was where I would find Thraka.

Castel was silent for a moment. She was thinking. Finally, she said, 'Commissar, despite what you said, you must realise that most of the people here are thinking of escape, not war.'

'I do.' That was regrettable, but unavoidable. What mattered was that they were stirred to action. Even if people died fighting for a selfish reason, their struggle would still be serving the greater cause. They would die with more honour than they had now. 'What will you be thinking of?' I asked.

'These creatures have profaned every aspect of my calling,' she spat. 'I will be going to war.'

'Then I will be honoured to fight alongside you,' I told her. Though she had been unafraid to ask me hard questions a moment before, I felt the pride radiate from her now.

She had been praised not by a fellow prisoner, or simply a fellow human being. She had been praised by an idea, a myth called Commissar Sebastian Yarrick. Ever since the battle for Hades Hive, his legend had shadowed my every act and utterance. I was very conscious of this man's existence, but I wasn't sure that he and I were truly one and the same. The legend was a useful tool. He inspired men and he was feared by orks, and rightly so. But his continued existence depended on my being worthy of him.

I would do that the only way I knew how: by acting for the good of the Imperium. And I would accept the responsibility for however many deaths such action would entail.

Our shift began. We shuffled out of the cage as the returning slaves staggered in. We moved towards the main exit from the pen. It was directly across from the one by which

I had first arrived. One group of prisoners edged towards the left-hand wall. There was another, smaller doorway just beyond the last of the terraced rows of cages, near the corner with the far wall. Ork guards came and went though that passage. There was also a pipe that emerged from its ceiling and ran as far as was visible down the corridor. It was an ork modification of the original structure, and like all such ork construction projects, it was sloppy, clumsy, and arrogant in its invitation to catastrophe. Promethium dripped from numerous joints and splits. Combustible pools spread on the floor.

Behriman snarled at the wayward group and whipped them. His bluff worked because his blows were real. The guards paid him no attention. He was part of the routine. They didn't notice that he was herding his charges closer to the pipe. Leaning against the wall to the right of the doorway was a bored guard. He had his prod tucked loosely under an arm.

The prod was electrical.

I slowed my steps, braced for action.

Behriman snapped his whip around the guard's neck. The ork choked on his surprise. He grabbed at the coil around his throat. He dropped his prod. A slave grasped it. The man's name was Averon, and I celebrate his memory. He lunged for the doorway and stabbed up with the prod, jabbing into one of the weak joints of the pipe. There was a flash and sizzle, and a shower of sparks.

As the fuel ignited, the pipe bent and arched like a tormented serpent. For a long second, it contained the fire within itself, but there were too many little fissures though which air and combustible met. A fountain of liquid fire burst out into the corridor. It gathered strength and momentum. It became a blinding storm that raged out of the doorway. Orks and humans scattered. Behriman sprinted to one side. The grasping flames missed him, but the rest of his group was bathed in incandescent death. They greeted their reward for their heroism with screams to haunt a guilty conscience. Most fell, writhing, but some ran. They actually *sprinted* as each breath sucked flame into their lungs. As I saw these martyrs rush with open arms to fall unerringly on orks, spreading the contagion of their doom to their captors, I knew that I had done the right thing. If I had in any way inspired that woman, who had become a howling, whirling torch with flames leaping three metres in height, to incinerate not one but *two* greenskins before she perished, then I was following the true path of my duty.

Not far down the corridor, around the first bend it must have been, the inferno found something even more nourishing than the orkish promethium. It was, as we were about to discover, an ammunition cache. It must have been large. There was a boom deep enough to shatter breastbones. The floor heaved, knocking us off our feet. The left-hand wall bulged for a moment before it peeled back, the blossoming of a steel flower. The fireball roiled out and filled the upper half of the slave pen, a sudden sun baking our flesh. Below the deep thunder of the explosions came the high-pitched shrieks of ricochets as small arms ammunition cooked off. Then came the smoke. It was oily, thick, strangling, smothering. It was a cloud of black wrapping itself around eyes dazzled by the fire. A few moments later, I heard the groaning roar of tons of metal collapsing, sealing the hole again to everything but smoke.

The slave pen was a maelstrom. There was no order, only panic mixed with rage. Humans and orks ran and fled and clashed and died. Coughing, eyes streaming, I couldn't see more than a few bleary metres around me in the erupting, cacophonous murk. I rose to my feet. Hand over mouth, I took as deep a breath as I dared, and then, before the hack in my chest silenced me, shouted, '*With me!*' I sensed the presence of followers as I stumbled towards the smouldering corridor. The flames were little more than fading glows in the smoky night there now. The floor was hot under the tattered soles of my boots, and I stepped on things that crunched and cracked like burnt wood, but I knew them to be something far grimmer.

I was coughing all the time now. My chest was being scraped by burning nails, and great, wracking heaves were trying to toss my lungs up my throat. My head was being squeezed by a mailed fist. But I pushed deeper into the billowing smoke, crouching as low to the ground as possible. This was the one direction I could be reasonably certain the orks would not be going.

The corridor hit an intersection, and the left-hand passage was a ragged funnel into the devastation of the munitions depot. The fires were still fierce there. They filled the space with a pulsing, wavering red glow. The whines and reports of detonating rounds were still frequent, but I led the way in all the same. The warped floor was covered by burned things that had once been orks, but were now little more than organic shrapnel. The hold was a big one, and while to the left there was only the impassable collapse, the explosions had also blown out the decks above, so the air was a little clearer. It was like breathing inside an oven, but at least I was breathing. And I could see who had followed me.

Rogge, Castel, Bekket, Trower, Polis, Vale and Behriman. A small group, and I saw no others coming up in the corridor. Perhaps there were slaves even now storming down the other corridors. Perhaps indeed, but only in dreams. More likely, the orks were already regaining control. No matter. We who were free to act were what mattered, and I would make sure we mattered to Thraka in the most lethal ways possible.

'Find weapons,' I told the others. 'There must be some that are still usable. Do it quickly.'

They did. As I scavenged for myself, I saw the group act with a directness and efficiency of purpose that would have done credit to a well-drilled infantry squad. There was something rather like joy in their determination. I have seen the phenomenon many times before. When people have been deprived of ability to act, they will respond to leadership with gratitude and vigour. To have direction becomes a form of salvation in its own right. Harness this human characteristic, and there is very little that you cannot accomplish.

The ork weapons were massive, clumsy, untrustworthy horrors. But there were stolen Imperial arms here, too. I found a laspistol and a sabre. The pistol was no storm bolter. It was here, though, so it would do. My companions also armed themselves with blades and guns. Most of them had found lasrifles, but Castel held an eviscerator. In her choice of the two-handed chainsword, I saw the final repudiation of her previous calling. The orks had turned her into a butcher. Well, I would let that be added to the greenskins' debts. We were now a war party. My troops awaited my orders.

I thought for a moment. To venture into the corridors would be pointless. We needed another way to move through the space hulk and reach the *Inflexible*. I led the way through the heaps of guttering wreckage to the wall opposite the collapse. It seemed stable, though it, too, had been damaged. The metal had been punched open, but not all the way through. I looked into the wall, saw a tangle of struts and, further up, accessible though a bit of a climb, a duct. I pointed. 'We go there,' I said. 'We will destroy the greenskin filth from within.'

Grand words.

And I meant them. Absolutely.

CHAPTER SEVEN

INFLEXIBLE

1. Yarrick

We became worms, tunnelling our way through the darkness of the shafts, ducts, and access hatches that linked the component ships of the space hulk. We were blind, and for the first while, we did not even have a sense of the direction of our movements. We went down blind alleys, where ventilation shafts ended against exterior hulls, and had to retrace our steps and try other routes at random until we found one that took us to a connecting breech in the vessel skins. We could hear orks on the other side of the walls wherever we went. The sounds of the pursuing greenskins chased us down the byways of our journey. Sometimes the sounds of clattering boots and shouted, alien threats were distant echoes. At other times, capture seemed imminent. But the apparent distances were all tricks of the pipes, the random vagaries of acoustic perversity. Some metal arteries down which we travelled were large enough to walk in. Most were no more than crawl spaces. After about an hour, when I judged that we had left the slave pen safely behind, and were beyond the reach of any likely pursuit, I let us travel toward a light source. We had to take stock of where we were.

The light came from a split in an elbow of the shaft down which we crawled. I put my ear to the crack. There was no sound of nearby orks. I twisted until I was lying on my back and kicked out at the split. The noise of my banging sounded huge to me, and I stopped after every half-dozen kicks to listen again. No greenskin came to investigate. Another minute of blows and the shaft parted enough for me to poke my head through. I was look-ing down from the ceiling of a nondescript corridor. In the direction I was facing, the passageway ended about six metres further on at a bulkhead. In the corridor's right-hand wall I could see a viewing block.

I withdrew, kicked the opening wider, and dropped down. I asked Polis to come with me. We made our way to the viewing block. The temple dominated the scene. I watched Polis take in the angle of our perspective on that structure. His lips moved in silent calculations. His eyes glazed. After a minute, they cleared and he looked at me.

'Do you know where we have to go?' I asked.

He nodded. He looked faintly ridiculous, clad in his Munitorum rags and clutching his lasrifle. He was a little man playing at war, and desperately afraid of the game. But he continued to function, and when I said, 'You'll have to lead us,' he nodded again. That agreement made him perhaps the bravest member of our group.

We returned to the gap in the shaft. Behriman and

Bekket hauled us up. Polis took point. The nature of our journey changed. Though Polis had to pause often to get his trembling under control, he changed our wandering into an advance. We were no longer worms. We were spiders, the shafts and connections between ships the strands our web. We were tracing the links that would, I vowed, bring an end to Thraka. Three hours after Polis's single look at the world outside our scrabbling, crawling, climbing darkness, we reached light again, and another tear in a hull. Polis squeezed to one side so I could see what waited for us.

I choked back a bark of bitter laughter. Before me, across a few hundred metres of open space, stood the *Inflexible*. Polis had been right: very little attached it to the other ships. It was resting on its landing gear. Rough scaffolding rose from the floor, going as high as the canopy. There didn't seem to be anything affixed to the lighter that would stop it from taking off.

Except for one thing: the *Inflexible* wasn't tied to other ships because it was *inside* one now. I should not have been surprised. The lighter was too small to be used as anything other than what it was. The orks were modifying the craft, making it into their own creature, and had surrounded it with slapped-together scaffolding. The space before us was another cargo hold, a vast one, kilometres high. The ceiling was invisible, and I didn't wonder that Polis, in his state, had mistaken the darkness above for the black of the void itself. The obstacle might not be a fatal one, I thought. If the *Inflexible* were still armed, it might be possible to blast an escape through the hull of this freighter.

I could see a half-dozen orks at work on the *Inflexible*.

The rest of the floor, the decking which had been a bulk-head before the ship was upended, was a scrapyard of miscellaneous construction projects in various stages of assembly and disintegration. Glow-globes, fuel drum fires and flaring welding torches illuminated another ten or twenty ships, all about the size of the lighter. Towards the far end of the hold, I could see the mangled outline of a Thunderhawk, and I shuddered at the tragedy that its presence implied. New, roughly assembled catwalks lined the walls starting about thirty metres up. They went past entrances leading elsewhere in the giant ship's hull, but I saw no stairs down. Either the catwalks were no more than observation platforms, or they were part of a larger construction project that was abandoned out of boredom.

I pulled back inside the shaft to speak to the others. We didn't have to worry about being overheard. We were given cover by the noise of endless perverse construction. I outlined the vessel's situation. 'We're almost there,' I then said. 'But to reach the *Inflexible*, we will be exposed.' We could minimise the risk by hugging the wall some of the way, but at the last we would have to cross open ground to the ship.

Polis trembled, but was the first to nod. The gesture might have been a nervous tick, but it made sure the others followed with alacrity. I motioned Vale forward with me. We paused at the exit from the shaft so he could get a good luck at his ship. 'A shame we're at the wrong end,' he said. The engines faced us, not the cockpit.

'Will it take off?' I asked.

He shrugged. 'Its flight-worthiness doesn't look like it's been attacked. I can't know until I try to leave.' He looked around. 'Commissar, are you sure we can get out of here at all?'

'No. But I am sure that the attempt is necessary.'

'I see,' he said quietly.

I believe that he truly did see. I believe that he already knew the path that lay ahead of him.

He turned to me. 'Commissar,' he said, 'with your permission, I would like to lead the way.'

'That is your right,' I told him. 'You are our pilot. Yours will be the honour to take us from this place.'

We both knew that we were talking about a different sort of honour entirely. The set of his jaw was grim. His eyes were hard, sharp, edged iron that had been tempered to the strength that would sustain him in the coming minutes.

We watched the area near our refuge. The shadows were deep here, and there were no construction materials of particular interest. After several minutes, no orks had passed through. I slid out, feet-first. The drop was less than two metres, and it would be harder to climb down with one arm than simply to let myself fall. The others followed, and Vale headed off, glancing back to make sure we were staying close.

Rogge was eyeing the *Inflexible* with a sick intensity.

'Something wrong, colonel?' I asked. There was no concern in my tone.

'No.' He shook his head. 'No,' he said again, as if he hadn't believed himself the first time.

Trower snorted. I turned my eye on him, and he cleared his throat. 'I'm sorry, commissar,' he said.

I held his gaze a few moments more before releasing him. I would not have dissent and disrespect in our numbers. We were still soldiers of the Imperium. We would conduct ourselves as such. I expected the men under my watch to maintain the same discipline even as they arrived at the Golden Throne.

We moved in single file, hugging the wall, draped in shadow. We weren't spotted. After a few hundred metres, Vale stopped and crouched behind a pile of scrap metal. He was staring fixedly at the *Inflexible*. His lips were curled in pained anger. When I saw what he was looking at, I felt an answering pang of fury. The forward half of the starboard engine, which had been hidden from our view until now, had been partially dismantled. Its casing was open, and even my untrained eye could see there were important elements missing. There was too much empty space there. But the engine had not been removed altogether. I did not want to imagine what would happen if someone attempted a take-off. I did not want to, but forced myself to do so.

And then there was a cry. It did not come from any of us, but was on our side of the hold. I looked up in time to see a figure plummeting from the catwalk above us. The ork hit the ground with a heavy, sick crunch. I heard a few braying laughs, but no other reaction from the creature's fellows. It lay still. A weapon had fallen with it: a rifle with a long barrel. I had never heard of ork snipers – it wasn't in their nature to fight at such uninteresting distances – but that was a weapon that could have hit targets at a considerable range.

At least as far as the catwalk to the ground.

The back of my neck tensed. I felt the phantom kiss of a round that had never been fired. We scrambled back against the wall, seeking cover in the deeper shadows. I craned my head back, peering into the flickering gloom. Through the slats of the platform, I had a vague impression of a gigantic shape moving away. Metal creaked under heavy footsteps. Then nothing more. I looked back down at the corpse of the ork. How had it fallen? I couldn't see how even a greenskin could be that clumsy. It hadn't been under fire. There wasn't anything going on up there.

Somehow, the ork must have slipped. That was what I told myself, and I sensed that there was a vital imperative that I believe it. There was no other possible explanation. None that fell within any sane conception of the universe.

We waited, weapons at ready. Our position was bad. The only cover was the scrap piles, and the ones nearby were no more than chest-high. If an attack was coming, we had no time to move to better ground. Across the breadth of the giant hold, the distinctly orkish work that erased the difference between construction and demolition continued uninterrupted. We had not been spotted.

Vale had turned his attention back to the *Inflexible* once more. He said, 'There are only three greenskins working on this side. Do you think you can give me cover while I board?'

'Yes,' I said. I did not try to talk him out of what he was planning to do. His action would, at the very least, have a strategic benefit.

Beside me, I heard Rogge gasp.

2. Rogge

Vale was mad, and Yarrick was worse. The revelation was painful, terrifying, and unavoidable.

When the state of the *Inflexible* had become clear,

Rogge had felt the cancerous grasp of despair. The ship was supposed to have been his means of salvation. In co-piloting the craft, he would strike back at the orks, restore his honour, and leave this terrible place. But the lighter had been mutilated by the enemy. There was no hope here, and so there was no hope anywhere. What could Yarrick's little band accomplish beyond distinctly messy suicide? Rogge had thought the renewal of honour needed the commissar's respect. But the high regard of a madman was worthless. Vale was about to march to his death, and Yarrick was going to help.

Rogge remembered his offer to co-pilot, and feared that he was about to receive his orders. Yarrick didn't glance his way. He and Vale spoke quietly, as if what was about to happen was a rational, strategic operation. Rogge looked back and forth between the two men and the wounded ship. He saw nothing but madness, and the worst of it was not what was going to happen when Vale went running off to meet the orks on his own, but *why* he was about to throw his life away. Vale was going to die because of Yarrick.

Rogge felt as if a blindfold had been torn from his eyes. He had been as dazzled by the commissar's reputation and force of personality as everyone else. But now he could see the man for what he was: a tyrant who played lethal games with the lives of others because he had the power to do so. On Golgotha, he had sacrificed a magnificent army to his obsessive pride. Now he was repeating the pattern. How many prisoners had died in that little uprising? And where would that one-armed, one-eyed monster of war take them now? How would he choose to feast on the deaths of his new followers?

He won't feast on mine. But on the heels of that thought came another: *What do I do now?* He had nowhere to go. He took in the faces of his other companions, and their unthinking commitment to Yarrick's leadership. There was no help or sense to be found there.

Yarrick spoke to the entire group. His voice was low, and would be inaudible only a few metres away, but it filled Rogge's consciousness as utterly as if blasted from banks of vox-casters. Yarrick's face was half-hidden by months' growth of hair and beard. Hunger had made it gaunter than ever. Bruises and wounds bit into its flesh, and the eyelid over the empty socket did not close all the way, revealing a slit of darkness. Yarrick's was a face of weathered crags, a map of decades of war in all its forms – glorious, brutal, desperate, triumphant, annihilating. It was, Rogge thought, a face that no longer knew anything *but* war. Rogge flashed on his memories of luxury and pleasure back on Aumet. Some were still quite recent, fresh enough to inspire the hope that they might not be the last of their kind.

But though Rogge stared at Yarrick and feared him, that voice and the fire that fed it were mesmerising. Yarrick said, 'We will strike here, and we will hurt the greenskins.' And Rogge felt a dangerous excitement in his chest. Yarrick said, 'While the orks struggle with this wound, we will take the battle to the heart of this abomination, and they will fear us before they die.' And Rogge felt a sense of mission flare.

Then he remembered how that mission must surely end, and regained his senses. There was no way off the space hulk. The only true mission was to stay alive from one moment to the next.

Yarrick turned to Polis. 'Can you guide us to the temple?' Polis nodded, rapid bobs like a rodent. His lips were moving in an unending, inaudible commentary, but his eyes were clear, shining with deadly fervour. To Vale, Yarrick said, 'How long once you're aboard before you can take off?' He spoke, Rogge thought, as if the lighter really would be able to fly.

'Not long,' Vale answered. 'How much time do *you* need to get clear?'

'Polis?' Yarrick asked.

The Munitorum gnome scanned the wall behind them. He pointed to an opening about a hundred metres on. Unlike the one from which they had emerged, this was not a tear in the skin of the vessel. It was an actual doorway, now tilted on its side. 'There,' Polis muttered. 'There.' He cleared his throat, his lips moving all the time. 'A good start, good start, find the vectors from there, yes yes, kill the temple, twenty metres to *Inflexible*, three visible enemy, disassembled engine cowling a product of Armageddon manufactorum Megiddo III...' His muttering faded back into mouthed silence.

He's getting worse, Rogge thought. The extended journey through the walls, with no greenskin encounters, had calmed him. But since that ork had fallen, his incessant cataloguing had started up again. He wasn't trembling, but his eyes had the shine of the Yarrick fever.

'Understood,' Vale said.

You understand nothing, Rogge thought. *Mad. Mad. All of you.*

And he had no choice but to follow for now.

Still crouching behind the pile of discarded metal, Vale faced Yarrick and made the sign of the aquila. Yarrick returned a one-handed version. That was all. There were no further words exchanged. Rogge felt the blood drain from his face at the matter-of-fact manner with which Vale accepted his imminent death, and the ease with which Yarrick sent him to it.

Vale leaped over the cover and sprinted toward the *Inflexible*. Yarrick trained his pistol on the orks. The others raised their firearms and took aim. 'Wait,' Yarrick said.

They held their fire.

3. *Vale*

He had been freed. He had been given the gift of knowing his destiny and final duty. His captivity was over. His mission was glory and flame. His heart leapt, so consumed with violent joy that his body could barely contain it. His limbs were infused with an energy that he hadn't felt since the forced landing. He wondered that his feet touched the floor of the hold at all. He was flying. Suddenly there was wind. There had to be. He could feel it whipping past his face as he bore down on the orks and the ship. The greenskins weren't aware of his approach. He almost laughed. The eye of the Emperor was upon him as he ran towards his apotheosis, and it rendered him unstoppable. He could tear the orks apart with his hands, but the Emperor's fire was coming for them.

One of the orks spotted him and shouted. The others turned and reached for their weapons. Now Vale did laugh.

At his back, his allies opened fire. One ork dropped, his throat torn out by a well-placed round. The other two shot back, yelling as they did so. Vale saw another ork round the nose of the *Inflexible* at a run. He crashed to the ground, head blown apart.

Something brutally hard, round and burning cold slammed into Vale's left thigh. He glared in outrage at the ork who had shot him. His leg lost its strength. His sprint broke down into a hopping limp. Fractal pain shook his frame, radiating out from the wound. The final metres to the lighter stretched. He clenched his teeth and hauled the dead leg forward. When he put weight on it, the world flared white. He bit his tongue, and blood poured down his chin.

Three more steps. The other two orks died. There were many more coming. The hold was in uproar. Orks were firing at the *Inflexible*, at Yarrick's position, at Vale. The shots were still scattered. There were still precious seconds before the orks made their numbers felt.

He reached the *Inflexible*. The canopy was open. He hauled himself up the ladder left by the orks and kicked it away as he dropped himself into the cockpit. A few seconds more, and the canopy lowered as he powered up. He killed the fuel line to the starboard engine. *Not yet*, he thought. The port engine whined with pent-up rage. He checked the weapons. Still present, still active.

The pain in his leg had numbed. Something worse than pain spread from the wound: a lethargic, creeping darkness. 'Not yet,' Vale muttered, tongue thick, breath hissing. He looked to port. The others had left their cover and were running for the opening in the wall.

The darkness spread down his arms to his hands and fingers, leeching strength and dexterity. His vision dulled to a grainy, grey tunnel. No more time. *Now*, he thought. His hands did nothing. Night was falling behind his eyes. He found a last cry. '*Now!*' he howled, and hands responded.

The *Inflexible* lurched forwards. Vale changed the vector of the thrust. Now he let promethium flood into the starboard engine.

No more darkness. Only light and heat and pain, and seconds of the most awful, sublime joy he had ever known.

CHAPTER EIGHT

THE RUN

1. Yarrick

A phoenix rose behind us. It shrieked justice at the heavens as it filled the hold with the hell of its birth.

We had barely reached the opening when the *Inflexible* began its final strike. I paused as the others ran down the narrow, upended corridor. I looked back to bear witness to Vale's sacrifice. The lighter lifted off the ground, climbing vertically. It kept climbing even as it burst into flame. At the same moment, its lascannon fired and its Hellfury missiles launched. The air of the hold was redolent with spent fuel and carelessly spilled flammable materials. The missiles slammed into other ships. The *Inflexible* spun wildly in the air, still firing the lascannon as it transformed into a fireball. It hung in the air another few seconds before it smashed into the deck. It crushed. It incinerated. Fire rushed through the space of the hold with the roar of a hurricane. It drowned out the screams of the burning orks. It grew into a towering wave of fire, and now I ran.

There was a wind in the corridor as air was sucked into the inferno. I had almost left it too late. Heat followed at my heels, carrying the promise of burning death. The passageway ended at a T intersection. I broke left. Behind me, there was a roaring, as if one of the *Inflexible*'s engines had entered the corridor. Just ahead, the others waited for me on the other side of a bulkhead. I leapt through. Trower and Bekket slid a steel door shut. With the ship's new orientation, they had to lift it up rather than pull to the side, but they managed to close and latch the heavy steel before the flames reached it. The barrier became warm to the touch within seconds, and we moved on quickly.

Polis led the way again. I was relying heavily on the little man, and he was rewarding my trust. He was a prodigy. Given time, luck and room for error, we would eventually have found our way to the temple without his help. It was so huge, it was the one destination on the space hulk that could always be found. But we would not have made such good time, and in such relative safety. His fear was a boon. At the slightest noise, some of which only he could hear, he would change route. Whether all of the threats we avoided were real or not, he was keeping us out of unnecessary engagements, saving our striking power for when we reached our goal. His sense of direction was uncanny. Wherever possible, he took us out of the corridors and into the networks of ventilation shafts, crawl spaces, access hatchways, and all the myriad byways of a voidship's circulatory system. No matter how many times the path twisted, no matter how many branches we took, he always knew where we were. We made good progress. Whenever we passed a viewing block, I saw that we were drawing closer.

We were very close, and crawling through the abandoned guts of a freighter. We were slick with grease, feeling our way through the dark over coiled pipes, fragmented gears that could slice off a finger if touched too suddenly, and funnels like cathedral bells. 'We need to reach the top,' I whispered to Polis. 'Can you get us there?'

'No,' he said, then repeated himself, becoming his own stuttering echo: 'Nuh-nuh-nuh-nuh-no. No connecting structures, commissar. It's isolated.' His muttering moved off-subject and rasped against the blind metal shapes.

'Then how do the orks have access?'

'Below.' Echo: 'B'low-b'low-b'low.'

I realised that we had been crawling along a downward slope. After another few minutes, the iron beneath my hand gave way to cold stone. For the space of a twitch, I was back in the well. But there was no water, and gradually the slope levelled off. Then we could stand, and the way ahead of us was showing grey. There was a light source not too far away.

We were in a tunnel beneath the surface of the planetoid. Once more, I was astounded by the discipline necessary to have orks take the trouble to create a stable, breathable atmosphere down here. I would have thought they lacked the patience to pull off such a feat of engineering. *You also never imagined being outmanoeuvred on the battlefield*, I thought.

The tunnel was part of a network of intersecting caves. We were moving through a high-ceilinged warren, one that would take orks quickly from one sector of the space hulk to another. Now it would deliver us into the heart of the construct. There were no more shafts or crawl spaces for us. We had to travel the same routes as the orks, and every second increased our risk of being discovered. So we ran. We ran to keep ahead of our luck, and we ran to fulfil our duty.

We were fast, but our luck still caught us. We flew across an intersection. Trower, who was bringing up the rear, shouted a warning at the same moment as the greenskins snarled and started firing. We ran harder, and Polis tried to shake the pursuit by taking what seemed like random choices at the next few junctions. It wasn't enough. I could hear the pounding of boots coming closer, the sound bouncing off the stone like hammer blows.

We went around a sharp bend to the left, and I paused. 'They must be stopped,' I said. 'Slowed, at the very least.' They would catch us in the next minute, otherwise, and if they didn't, their uproar would draw other patrols down on our heads.

Bekket turned back to the bend and crouched. Trower joined him. He remained standing. He would shoot over Bekket's head, and they could provide each other with some degree of covering fire. 'We thank you for the honour, commissar,' Bekket said.

'You will be remembered,' I promised them.

The rest of us ran on. Behind us, I heard gunfire. First the isolated reports of Bekket and Trower's guns, then the rain of counter-fire from the orks. The two men wouldn't last long, but every moment they gained us was precious. The echoes turned their shouts of defiance into the battle-cry of a regiment. Their screams, when they came a couple of minutes later, were even greater.

Polis had taken us through several more tunnel crossings by then. Trower and Bekket had played their part. So, by the Emperor's grace, would we all.

2. *Rogge*

He had abandoned them. Not a blink, not a pause, just a quick commending of their souls to the Emperor, and then off. Rogge fought the urge to vomit. His skin was prickling with fear and horror. He didn't know who held the greater terror for him now, between Yarrick and the orks. They were almost the same thing, just machines of senseless death. He ran with the rest of the party because he was caught in Yarrick's undertow, and there were no other options open to him.

No options yet. For the first time, the idea of surrender occurred to him. The orks had kept him alive once. They might do so again. They would be short a few slaves. The idea didn't horrify him the way it should have, the way it once *would* have, before he had seen the truth of Sebastian Yarrick. There was no honour in following a madman, or dishonour in turning his face from him.

There was no dishonour in staying alive.

But the madness still held him as they ran through the warren of stone. The walls were damp and cold. Some of the tunnels were natural formations, while many more bore signs of having been hewn by the slaves. Here and there were the bones of captives who had been left to rot where they fell, their remains gradually trodden to dust. Enough traces remained to show there had been men here, men who had been forced to give up their lives for glory of the ork warlord. More glory. More senselessness.

Thraka and Yarrick deserve each other, Rogge thought.

The tunnel they took now ran straight and up. They had left the sounds of the greenskin patrol behind, but there were other noises ahead. Polis slowed, and whispered something to Yarrick. The commissar nodded. While Polis huddled close to Castel, Yarrick and Behriman took the lead. None of them glanced his way, and Rogge felt warring impulses of relief and resentment. He fought them both down and moved up to learn the worst.

The tunnel sloped up sharply for the last few metres, ending in a jumble of boulders at the entrance to a large, echoing cave. Rogge had to crawl his way forward. Polis was curled up a length back from the opening, keeping within the comfort of full shadow. His eyes glittered with terror, but he still clutched his gun, and he was still looking ahead, waiting to be given his orders of martyrdom. Yarrick, Behriman and Castel were crouched behind the last line of boulders. As Rogge joined them, Castel gave him a look. Her contempt was clear and cold and precise. *How does she know?* he thought. And then: *Know what? There's nothing to know.* He looked away, suddenly finding it quite easy to stare straight ahead, and learn his fate.

The cavern was a natural one. It extended about a hundred metres to the left, right and forward of the entrance. The ceiling was invisible in the gloom, but Rogge guessed it must have been at least twenty metres up. Off to the right, a smaller tunnel dropped into darkness. There was a large squad of orks milling about, guarding the far wall. This one was not stone. It was metal. It was part of one of the hulls used in the construction of the temple. There was an entrance here, and it wasn't original to the ship, nor was it an improvised breach. It was an actual gate, festooned with crude ork faces, jaws agape in roars or laughter.

After a minute's observation, Yarrick and his two aco-
lytes pulled back to where Polis hid. Rogge followed,
dreading what was about to be decided.

'Can we fight them?' Castel whispered.

Yarrick shook his head. 'Too many.'

Behriman said, 'We need to draw some of them off.'

Yarrick nodded slowly. He almost seemed reluctant.
'You realise...' he began.

'Of course I do.'

Polis uncurled with a snap. He sat bolt upright, staring at Yarrick and Behriman. His lips moved, shaping the
cascade of silent words. He arrested them long enough
to speak. 'No,' he said. 'My mission is accomplished. I
am expendable.' And then he was up and scrambling
over the boulders.

Castel stood up a mere beat behind him. 'Commissar,'
she said, 'make them suffer dearly.'

'I swear it,' he answered.

She took off after Polis.

Drawn to the spectacle of mad self-sacrifice, Rogge
moved forward behind Yarrick and Behriman. They
paused at the entrance to the cavern. Rogge saw everything. He saw the insanity of blind faith. Polis ran through
the cavern, shouting its dimensions and numbering the
days of his captivity. He fired his gun, but hit nothing.
He did draw the orks' attention. They didn't react at first,
staring dumfounded at the lunatic human. Polis was halfway across the cavern toward the other tunnel before
one of them moved. While its kin laughed, the greenskin came up behind Polis. It had its cleaver drawn. It
hauled its arm back.

It didn't land the blow. Castel sprinted over the space

between them. With a rasping '*Hhhhaahhhh*' of hatred, her arms straining, she swung the snarling eviscerator into the back of the ork's neck. It was a good blow, one born of rage, a repayment for all the atrocities she had been forced to witness aboard the space hulk. The chainsword sank in almost to the width of the blade. The ork collapsed, its spine severed, blood spraying over Castel, slicking the floor of the cavern. The medic, triumphant in her butchery, jumped over the corpse and caught up with Polis.

The laughter stopped. The orks yelled, and all but a handful took off after the two humans. They were a mob of muscle and aggression, coming to rend their prey into shreds. Castel and Polis had a lead measured in seconds. They didn't pause, didn't fire again. Their last mission consisted in nothing more now than staying alive long enough to be a useful distraction. They disappeared down the tunnel. Polis's litany was multiplied by echoes, merging with the snarls of the orks. The sounds of the pursuit receded, plunging into darkness and silence. Rogge didn't hear a scream.

Yarrick and Behriman exchanged a look, then readied their weapons. There were only four orks left guarding the gate. Yarrick turned his gaze on Rogge.

The silence from the other tunnel wrapped a frozen grip around his soul. There had been no ending, no final agony, only the drop into the unknown. A terrible vision unfolded before him, a vision of an endless flight through the undermaze of the planetoid, with nothing to anticipate except the delayed, raging inevitable. The image was a nightmare whose waking was worse, and Rogge wanted no part of it.

He ran. He ran back down the way they had come. He ran towards the certainty of capture. He ran from the judgement of Yarrick.

He ran towards surrender.

CHAPTER NINE

CRUCIBLE

1. Yarrick

And then we were two. A mutilated old man and a cook. Behriman and I grinned at each other. I was as aware of our absurdity as he was, and he knew our strength like I did. I don't think either of us had expected Rogge to be true to his oath. I wasn't surprised when he ran, but I was still angered. Betrayal and cowardice should always be met with immediate, unalterable justice. Rogge had confirmed my worst suspicions about what had gone wrong on Golgotha. That we had been outmanoeuvred by Thraka was still my failing to expiate, but more might have been saved if not for Rogge, a link weak with the rust of selfishness. If there hadn't been the mission before me, I would have tracked the colonel down and put a bullet in the back of his head. I found satisfaction in the certain knowledge that he was running to a fate far less merciful than the worst I could do to him.

We were the stronger for his absence. We could have used the fire of Castel, Bekket and Trower, but we still had the synchrony of warriors focused on a single task. Our goal awaited, and there were only four orks standing in our way. I was still grinning as I took aim from behind the boulder. I was eager for what was coming. I heard Behriman snort, unable to hold back violent mirth.

I squeezed off three shots from the laspistol. My target jerked twice, hit in the neck and chest, and then a third time as the centre of his face imploded. I jumped out of cover and ran forward as Behriman fired behind me. He had a rifle. It had a lot more punch, and needed it. His target was the leader, a massive brute made bigger yet by the spiked plates of his armour. A fanged metal jaw protected his neck and lower face. Behriman's first shot glanced off the jaw as I closed with the nearest greenskin. He did better with the rest of his salvo. The second shot took out the ork's left eye. The monster roared agony and rage. The slug had to have penetrated his brain, but he wasn't dead. He struck without sight or thought, his gigantic axe decapitating the ork in front of him. I dropped to a crouch, and my opponent's blade swished the air just over my head. I fired up, draining the rest of the power pack. The greenskin's chin and nose exploded. Blood showered down on me as the ork rocked back and forth on his heels before toppling over on his back.

There was only the leader still moving. He was an automaton, whirling and slashing at nothing with every random step. I scrambled back, out of the way. It took Behriman another seven well-placed shots to drop him.

The battle had taken seconds. No alarm had been

raised. Shots being fired were too mundane an occur-
rence in ork life to draw attention. The rest of the squad
hadn't returned from chasing Castel and Polis. I muttered
a prayer under my breath for the medic and the clerk. I
stopped to loot the nearest ork corpse of ammunition.
Behriman joined me and did the same. We found a few
power packs that fit our weapons. We found long-handled
grenades. Then we turned to the gate. Its mechanism was
basic. It was an effective barrier only if it had guards to
back it up. Otherwise, it might as well have been nothing more than a morbid bit of sculpture.

We opened the gate. We entered the temple.

Here I am, Thraka, I thought. *Are you still enjoying this?*

We walked down a long, straight, low-ceilinged corridor. Behriman and I both had to hunch down to avoid
banging our heads. It must have been an infuriating passageway for orks. After about fifty metres, it opened up
onto the central shaft of the temple. The space was circular, about fifty metres in diameter, and many times that in
height. A central column ran an iron elevator car up and
down. Spiralling up the walls was a rough metal staircase.
It had no railing. It was no more than an endless series
of metal planks welded to the wall. There were no exits
off the shaft. Stairs and elevators went from the ground
to the distant ceiling with no interruptions.

The elevators were in use, but there were no orks on
the stairs.

'Well?' Behriman asked.

'To the top,' I said. 'If he's here, he'll be there.'

We ran to the wall. We began to climb the stairs that
would take us to the heart of power.

* * *

2. *Rogge*

He didn't run long. He fled for about a minute, taking tunnels at random. He was not being tracked by their earlier pursuers. He knew that much. He didn't hear anything in front of him. So when he ran into the patrol, he was more surprised than they were. He had intended to present his rifle to the first ork he encountered, and so signal his submission to slavery. Instead, dumb instinct betrayed him, and he raised the gun, finger on its awkwardly placed trigger.

The lead ork batted the rifle out of his hands, and backhanded him on the return swing. His left cheekbone and nose shattered. The pain filled his eyes with a sudden nova. He fell into darkness with something very like relief.

The greenskins denied him the refuge of oblivion. Rough shaking woke him. His head jerked back and forth so hard it felt like his spine was going to snap. He howled, and the shaking stopped. He fell to the ground. The jar of impact rattled the length of his frame. He looked around, blinking rapidly. He was still beneath the surface of the planetoid, still in the warren of tunnels. The space was an intersection of several passages. It wasn't as large as the cavern before the temple, but it was big enough to contain the monsters that towered over him. They were laughing at him. Tears of hopeless frustration sprang to his eyes. He couldn't even succeed at surrender. They were going to kill him now.

Only they didn't. The ork who had been holding him looked back over its shoulder. It grunted, the noise sounding to Rogge like a mixture of religious fear and religious joy. From behind his captors came booming, metal-on-stone footsteps. Something was coming that could crush worlds beneath its tread. The other orks parted, making a wide berth for the being that strode forward. Rogge whimpered as Thraka, bent forward to fit in the tunnels, loomed over him. The ork prophet leaned down. Thraka eyed him dismissively, then began to turn away.

He was going to leave. Suddenly, Rogge feared Thraka's departure more than his presence. If he was beneath Thraka's notice, he wouldn't be worth sparing. '*Wait!*' Rogge cried.

The ork couldn't have understood Gothic, Rogge thought. But he seemed to recognise desperation. Thraka turned around. Rogge was abruptly conscious of the *silence* of the orks. That such a thing was even possible terrified him. He found himself thinking in a new way about the warlord. The idea at the forefront of his mind was *propitiation*. He was face to face with a terrible god, and he was desperate to give the deity what he wanted.

What did Thraka want?

'Yarrick!' Rogge gasped. 'I can give you Yarrick! I know where he is!'

Thraka continued to regard him. The hideous face, that primitive savagery made more brutal by adamantium skull, didn't alter its expression. Thraka was waiting.

How do I make you understand? Rogge thought. He stood and pointed down the tunnel that his instinct chose to believe was the way back to the temple. 'Yarrick,' he kept saying. Did the orks even know the commissar's name? Rogge tucked his right arm in and flapped his elbow. Thraka let out a short bark of amusement. A mountain laughed. Rogge quailed. He fell to his knees. Thraka's troops followed the cue of their ruler and fell about with cruel guffaws. But Thraka only laughed the once. His single real eye looked in the direction Rogge was pointing. *Yes*, Rogge thought. *Yes, that's right. You know what I'm trying to tell you. I can take you to Yarrick. Let me show you the way.* He forgot, in his need, that he didn't know where he was.

Thraka's gaze returned to Rogge. The ork's jaw split into a smile, the kind of smile that accompanies the torching of solar systems. Rogge did his best to return it. Thraka delighted in his effort, and the ork's grin grew wider yet. The monster nodded, once, and then turned to speak to one of his underlings. Thraka's voice rumbled and sawed at Rogge's ears. The ork language could only have been produced by throats gargling glass, rage and broken bones. Rogge had no idea what was being said, but he heard a pattern of syllables repeat a few times. It sounded like 'Grotsnik.' Rogge hoped this was a good thing.

His answer wasn't long in coming. After a minute, a different ork battered his way to the front. Anyone who didn't move from his path quickly enough was sent flying by his grotesquely huge power claw. His presumption of superiority ended only when he drew abreast of Thraka. He abased himself before his lord, and growled something interrogative. It occurred to Rogge that the word he had heard was a name. His hopes frayed.

Thraka pointed at him. Rogge now saw the massive syringes that Grotsnik kept stored in bandoliers and in his flesh itself. He saw the scars and the sutures. He remembered Castel's stories of ork surgeries, and of the vanished line between experimentation and torture. He took a step backward.

Thraka reached out with his claw. He picked Rogge

up by his arms. The colonel whimpered as he felt his shoulders dislocate. Thraka tossed him into the arms of Grotsnik. The ork medic laughed. Rogge began to scream.

For all the terror he had experienced, it was a fact that Rogge had never screamed before. Now, he would never stop.

3. *Yarrick*

I don't know if I can say that we were lucky. I don't know if I can say that luck ever had any role in the Golgotha catastrophe. I can see too much destiny at work in the events of those days. There was also too much will. I will not blaspheme and pretend to know the Emperor's, but mine and Thraka's decided much, and destroyed more.

So I don't know if Behriman and I were lucky or cursed. But we were better than halfway up the height of the temple's central shaft before the klaxons started. We had done well to make it this far without incident. But we were both winded. My legs were heavy with pain. Even in the dimness of the shaft, I could see Behriman's face looking pale and shiny with exhaustion. But then the warning sounded – a brain-shredding, metallic roar that rattled in the chest. Seconds later, orks streamed in through the ground floor entrance. While most of them pounded up the stairs after us, a small group waited for the elevator. Within seconds, there were over a hundred greenskins in pursuit, and the Emperor knew how many in the upper levels of the temple, alerted now and waiting for the mad little humans to show themselves. We had no hope. None at all.

The feeling was oddly liberating. It gave free rein to our determination. Behriman's face hardened with a cold exhilaration. I know what he felt, because the same dark fire suffused my being. We ran. Adrenaline from some hidden reserve coursed through my veins. I pushed through pain, exhaustion, and the impossibility of what we were attempting. We had no chance of breaking through to kill Thraka even if he was somewhere above us. But we would try, and we would fight. I knew my duty to my Emperor and to my species. There was no price too high to be paid, by me or by anyone within my reach, in the execution of that duty. To know this, as I did, was to render irrelevant such concepts as hope and probability. The way forward was clear. That was enough.

Up, faster somehow, but the goal stubbornly refusing to come any closer. The orks shot at us, but they were running as they fired. The distance was still too great. The rounds whined against the metal wall and left us untouched. But now the elevator was rising. It would reach us in less than a minute. If it could be brought to a halt, the greenskins inside would be within a few metres of us. Their fire would rip us to pieces.

I shoved my pistol into my belt and grabbed a grenade. I kept climbing, taking every granted second to take another step up. Behriman followed my lead. He didn't wait for the elevator cage to arrive. He tossed his grenade behind us. The explosive flew in a fine, long arc. It exploded as it hit the stairs, blowing open a gap several metres across. 'The xenos filth are adaptable,' he wheezed between ragged breaths. 'Let's see them grow wings.'

I grunted approval, but didn't answer. He was younger, had more breath to spare. He was also more right than he knew. The orks *were* adaptable. They wouldn't learn to fly, but they would find some way over the gap.

But maybe not before it was too late.

My eyes flicked back and forth between the rising cage and the stairs before me. If I tripped, I would fall, and if I fell, it would be off the stairs and into the void. I had already experienced the death comfort of a great plunge. I had no need of its touch a second time. I maintained the careful rhythm of my climb. I defied the exhaustion of my ageing flesh. I moved up and up. I let the cage rise closer. I waited as it began to slow and the orks fired through the bars. I waited as Behriman cursed and we both crouched and ducked. The rounds were a hard danger now. But still I climbed. Still I waited.

The elevator cage stopped. Its door opened. The cluster of ork guns looked close enough to touch. I gave them the grenade. I threw it to the back of the cage.

The orks in the front had time to squeeze their triggers once before they realised what I had done. Behriman gave a liquid curse as a round tore through his cheek. It spun him round and he crashed against the wall. He stumbled, sagged, but did not collapse, and did not stop moving. The burn of a shell slashed at my scalp. I took pride in the pain. I kept moving.

Movement, too, in the cage. The movement of panic. Orks jumped, some trying to reach the staircase that was close, but not that close, some forgetting they were well over a hundred metres up and simply jumping from one death to another. Then the grenade went off. It blasted the cage away from its pillar. The metal crate shot forward, smashed into the staircase, and fell. It turned end over end, banging against the wall, smearing some orks and dragging others off their perches. The shaft echoed with the crash of the tumbling cage and the howls of the plunging orks. The elevator hit the ground floor with a satisfying impact.

The howls grew louder, now the rage of the frustrated horde. Gunfire sought us, an insect swarm of rounds blackening the air. Sheer volume overcame inaccuracy. If I still had a right arm, I would have lost it again. A shot exploded off a step as I brought my foot down. I stumbled, lost my footing. I threw my weight to the left, and slammed against the wall instead of hurtling into space. The instinct was to curl into a ball, to be the smaller target. The instinct was as cowardly as it was wrong. I dismissed it and started moving again. Neither Behriman nor I could run anymore. My legs were columns of lead. They felt as useless as the twisted wreck of the elevator column. I moved them by will alone. I was in the well again, rising endlessly through a nimbus of pain and exhaustion. It would have been easy to fall into a numbness, to keep going by detaching myself from my agonised flesh. But I had to remain alert, had to be ready to counter the next threat.

Below us, the orks raged, their anger louder than the report of their guns. Behriman used two more grenades, destroying more of the stairs behind us. The orks were hauling lengths of scrap metal from the destroyed elevator and were using that to cross the first of the gaps, but the process was eating up time. We were pulling ahead.

I looked up for the first time in a century. The stairs ended at a landing. We were there. A few more steps, and the climbing would end. Relief turned into a last shot of strength to my legs, and I started running again.

The rocket hit the wall just beneath the landing. It tore the world apart. I was flying, eyes filled with light, ears stuffed with sound, mind battered empty of anything except a furious denial. I would not surrender to such a perversity. I reached my arm into the heart of the dragon's breath that enveloped me. I closed my fist, expecting nothing but fire, air and defeat. I found metal. I gripped with the ferocity of rage. The blast washed over me, the jaws of the dragon clamping down hard on my bones. Then the dragon departed, leaving behind pain and, with the return of conscious thought, despair.

I was holding on to a strut sticking out from the damaged landing. The stairs beneath me had vanished. The explosion had pushed me out, and I was dangling off the projecting lip of the landing. There was nothing below but the long fall and final rest.

And Behriman had caught my leg.

He was heavy. But perhaps, despite the added strain, he would be the salvation of us both. 'Climb up,' I rasped through clenched teeth. If he could use me to reach the platform, then haul me up after him...

Behriman tried. But as soon as he moved, we started to swing, and my grip slipped. He stopped. His features seemed to relax. His gaze shone with gratitude. 'We've taught them a thing or two,' he said. 'Commissar, will you finish the lesson?'

'I swear I will.'

He nodded, satisfied. He let go, spreading his arms wide to embrace his flight. He smiled as he dropped into freedom.

I looked away from his fall. I focused all of my attention on my goal. I shut out the din of the orks, the whine of the stray rounds, the possibility of another rocket. I confronted the hopeless. I had only the fading strength of my one arm. There was no purchase for my legs. There was nothing for the stump of my right arm to lean on and give me purchase. I squeezed tighter on the strut, imagined my fist as welded to the metal. It could not let go, but by the grace of the Emperor. I did not just tell myself this. I *knew* this. And when I knew it, I began to lift.

One arm for the weight of a battered old man. The pain exploded from my shoulder and upper arm. I could not acknowledge it. I believed only in the simple fact that I could lift this one object. If I did so, I would not fail my Emperor. Desperation can grant miraculous strength, and I was well beyond desperation. I become nothing but will. My arm was folded now, and my head and upper chest were above the lip of the platform. I rocked forward before I could think of the risk. My chin smacked metal. My stump shoved against it, giving me that tiny bit more momentum. My fist turned around the strut, and my grip was suddenly something that could be broken. I pushed down, gasping agony. My strength fled, but not before I straightened my arm, propelling myself forward. I cried out as I let go. Gravity tugged at me. It failed. From the waist up, I was lying on the platform. I rested for a moment, then squirmed and scrabbled until I had pulled myself up the rest of the way.

My body cried out for sleep. I stood up, wavering. I staggered forward. The landing had been buckled by the explosion, and the door wrenched partly out of its frame. I could, I thought, just squeeze through the gap. I reached for my pistol. It was gone, lost in the rocket strike.

'The Emperor protects,' I whispered. 'The Emperor provides.' I had faith that He would. It was all that I had left, and it was enough. I leaned into the door, pushing the

space between it and the wall open a few more centimetres. I crawled through.

Thraka was not waiting for me on the other side. No orks
were. The room was large, but not as huge as the grandi-
ose exterior had suggested. I was at the very peak of the
temple. I had expected a shrine to the savage greenskin
gods, perhaps some mark of Thraka's command. Instead,
I found command of a much more practical kind. I was in
the control centre for the space hulk. I was surrounded by
the ork version of consoles. They were massive, and ris-
ibly simple by human standards. Each console featured
only a single button: huge, red, central. In the middle of
the floor, a block of stone served as a dais. It was wide
enough and massive enough to support the monstrosity of Thraka. He would stand there, I thought, and give
his orders, which would be carried out from these consoles. No one was here now because the space hulk was
not on the move. The tedium of remaining at an inac-
tive station would have been beyond comprehension to
the ork mind.

I was alone, but would not be for long. Between grenades and rocket, the way up to the nerve centre had
been destroyed. But the temple was a fusion of ships,
and thus a honeycomb of passageways. I could hear the
orks forging a new path. The wall to my right reverberated with the shrieking of tearing metal and the *crump*
of explosive charges. They would be here soon. What I
would do, I had to do now.

One side of the chamber was given over to enormous
windows. They were the eyes of the ork idol that glared
over the wreckage-scape of the space hulk. As I thought
about how the construct travelled, and what damage I

might do here, I noticed for the first time what nestled between the clusters of upended ships: engines. Huge ones. None from anything smaller than a cruiser. Some belonged to ships that had been grafted nose-first to the planetoid. Others had been dismounted from their original vessel. They were all lower than the surrounding structures. I looked at the scattered disposition of colossal motive power, put it together with the consoles, and understood how the space hulk navigated: one button per engine, each engine propelling the hulk in a different direction. Simple to the point of imbecilic, too crude for any precision, but the orks had no need for precision.

The wall shrieked. The orks were on the other side. I heard the sound of chainaxe teeth grinding into metal. Behriman, Castel, Polis, Bekket, Trower, Vale: their sacrifices had purchased a few seconds. I owed them the honour of using that time well. I ran from console to console, slamming my fist down on *all* the buttons. I would destroy Thraka with his own weapon.

One after another, the engines blazed to life. Immense forces strained against each other. As the first punctures appeared in the wall, the shaking began. It was as if the space hulk were being hit by an earthquake, one that would not stop, and just kept building in strength. Thraka's base became a perpetual collision between voidships. Stolen fusion reactors lit up the night of the void. Forces beyond the tectonic buckled and twisted the space hulk. Plumes of stolen promethium shot up from the multiplying breaches in the fuel lines.

The shaking grew stronger yet. It knocked me off my feet, and I crawled to the windows to look upon my work. The construct was starting to break up. Ship hulls wrenched free of their foundations. Some fell, crushing smaller structures, setting off more explosions, gouging open deeper wounds. Others were blasted away from the main body, re-launched into the void by a force more powerful than the construct's artificial gravity. Twisting, rattling, whiplashing, the world was tearing itself apart with thunder and flame, and it was glorious.

There was an eruption at the base of the temple. A tower of flame roared skyward, all-consuming, all-purifying. The world beyond the windows disappeared in a glare of incandescent red. The structure groaned, dying, and it lurched to one side, as though trying to walk. The floor heaved.

The wall came down all at once, and the orks stormed in. But they were too late. I saw Thraka pound forward, trampling his minions. Then the floor heaved again, split, and collapsed. I fell, slipping from Thraka's grasp as he lunged for me. I plunged into a chaos of flame and tumbling metal. In the last moment before I was battered into darkness, I saw Thraka, above, in the exploding ruin of his domain. He was roaring, arms raised high. He was raging, I thought.

But he looked exultant.

EPILOGUE

THE VALEDICTION

I woke, and I was complete. I knew, before I opened my eye, that what had been taken from me was mine again. My right arm felt heavy, lethal. I looked. My claw was there, as it should be. There was no power flowing to it, nor was there to my bale eye. Still, their presence was reassurance enough.

But how had I been rescued?

I sat up, taking in my surroundings. I was lying on an operating table filthy with blood and reeking with the stench of a thousand atrocities. I was in a medicae bay, but the tools that I saw would have horrified the most fanatical chirurgeon.

I had not been rescued. I was still on the space hulk. My claw and eye had been reattached. *Correctly.* The two realities were incompatible at so fundamental a level that their co-existence made my skin crawl.

I swung my legs over the edge of the table and stood.

My injuries had blended into a general wash of pain. Nothing was broken, though. I was intact. I could walk. I approached the door.

It opened. I stopped. Beyond it, orks lined both sides of the corridor. They had been watching for me. The moment I appeared, they roared their approval. They did not attack. They simply stood, clashed guns against blades, and hooted brute enthusiasm. I had been subjected to too many celebratory parades on Armageddon not to recognise one when it confronted me. I went numb from the unreality before me. I stepped forward, though. I had no choice.

I walked. It was the most obscene victory march of my life. I moved through corridor, hold and bay, and the massed ranks of the greenskins hailed my passage. I saw the evidence of the destruction I had caused around every bend. Scorch marks, patched ruptures, buckled flooring, collapsed ceilings. But it hadn't been enough. Not nearly enough. Only enough for this... this...

I was living an event that had no name.

At length, I arrived at a launch bay. There was a ship on the pad before the door. It was human, a small in-system shuttle. It was not built for long voyages. No matter, as long as its vox-system was still operative.

I knew that it would be.

Ghazghkull Mag Uruk Thraka awaited me beside the ship's access ramp. I did not let my confusion or the sense that I had slipped into an endless waking nightmare slow my stride. I did not hesitate as I strode towards the monster. I stopped before him. I met his gaze with all the cold hatred of my soul. He radiated delight. Then he leaned forward, a colossus of armour and bestial strength. Our faces were mere centimetres apart.

My soul bears many scars from the days and months of my defeat and captivity. But there is one memory that, above all others, haunts me. By day, it is a goad to action. By night, it murders sleep. It lives with me always, the proof that there could hardly be a more terrible threat to the Imperium than this ork.

Thraka spoke to me.

Not in orkish. Not even in Low Gothic.

In High Gothic.

'A great fight,' he said. He extended a huge, clawed finger and tapped me once on the chest. 'My best enemy.' He stepped aside and gestured to the ramp. 'Go to Armageddon,' he said. 'Make ready for the greatest fight.'

I entered the ship, my being marked by words whose full measure of horror lay not in their content, but in the fact of their existence. I stumbled to the cockpit, and discovered that I had a pilot.

It was Rogge. His mouth was parted in a scream, but there was no sound. He had no vocal cords any longer. There was very little of his body recognisable. He had been opened up, reorganised, fused with the ship's control and guidance systems. He had been transformed into a fully aware servitor. I promised myself he would be one forever.

'Take us out of here,' I ordered.

The rumble of the ship's engines powering up was drowned by the even greater roar of the orks. I knew that roar for what it was: the promise of war beyond description. In silence, I made the orks a promise of my own. They were letting me go because I had lived up to my legend. I would do more than that when they came again to Armageddon. Legend would clash with legend, and

I would bring them more than war. I would bring them more than apocalypse.

I would bring them extinction.

EVIL EYE

DAVID ANNANDALE

There was a jitter in Bekket's eye that I didn't like. We were trained at the Schola Progenium to watch for the early signs of political deviance or dereliction of duty. That meant being able to read all the nuances of body language. Hans Bekket was no traitor, and he was no coward. But the time of our imprisonment was eroding him, physically and spiritually, as surely as the sands of Golgotha had eaten away at the metal and flesh of our forces.

I had been watching him for several shifts now. How many days those were, I had no way of telling. The concept of time as a series of moments arriving from the endless potential of the future to become a distinct and defining past was a luxury denied to the slaves on Ghazghkull Mag Uruk Thraka's space hulk. We had only the grinding scream of an eternal present. Existence was labour, whips, agony, death. I had tried, early on, to gauge the length of the shifts, but the orks made even that effort futile. They simply worked us until the numbers collapsing from exhaustion became annoying. Then they bundled those of us who were still alive back into our cages. There we slept as best we could, waiting to be turned out to suffer again.

Bekket and I were hauling salvage. It was junk of every description scavenged from the ships that, along with a central asteroid, made up the hulk. We dragged heavy, clumsy carts full of the stuff to a massive depot, where the orks' grotesque versions of enginseers pawed through the material. We pulled the carts with chains, but we weren't chained ourselves. The orks didn't bother. Where could we go? And what fun would there be in beating stragglers to death, if there were no stragglers to be had?

Bekket's eyes flicked back and forth as if he were a malfunctioning gun servitor seeking targets. He was unconsciously looking for an excuse to strike out. When he did, he would believe he was acting out of rage and honour, but he would be wrong. Impulsive rebellion in this terrible place was an act of despair. It had only one possible outcome.

I would not have it. There were so few left of the men who had come with me to Golgotha. And our mission was unfinished. Thraka still lived.

Bekket was a few metres ahead of me. Beyond the strain of pulling his cart, there was an extra tautness in his shoulder blades. He was on the verge. I tried to get closer. It was difficult. I only had one arm with which to pull the chain. My battle-claw was long gone, my trophy now Thraka's. And I wasn't a young man. All the same, I managed to draw within two metres before I risked speaking.

'Trooper Bekket.'

'Commissar?'

I had his attention, but then the man in front of him stumbled. He was another Guardsman, wearing the rags of a Mordian uniform. I didn't think he'd been with us on Golgotha. He looked like he'd been here for much longer. And still, he didn't fall or drop his chain. He just stumbled. That was enough for the nearest ork guard. The greenskin roared and lashed out with its whip. The weapon was a length of flexible metal cable embedded with jagged bits of blade. It wrapped around the Mordian's neck. The ork yanked hard. The coils tightened, constricting and severing. The man's head flew off. The ork roared again, this time with delighted laughter.

There was a heavy piece of piping in Bekket's cart. I had seen him eyeing it earlier. Now he grabbed it, letting his chain drop to the ground.

'Bekket, no,' I shouted, but he was already lunging at the ork, swinging the pipe at the monster's head. The ork swatted him down. The spikes on the back of its wrist-guard tore his cheek open, and I heard the crunch of his nose breaking. He spun as he fell. The ork put an iron boot on his chest. It stowed its whip and pulled a massive axe from its belt. It raised the blade high, the stupidly glowering eyes under its thick brow fixed on Bekket's skull.

I stepped forward. I locked gazes with the ork.

'No,' I said again, but I said it to the guard, I said it with ice and I said it in orkish. It disgusted me to use that obscene tongue, but it startled the guard. The ork hesitated.

I held the monster's eyes with my single one. I peered

up with my head tilted slightly down, so there would be more shadow, more mystery, in my empty socket. I was a one-armed, one-eyed human past his prime making direct eye contact with an ork. I should have been dead, my guts strewn all over the ground. But I was Yarrick, and I had the evil eye. I killed orks with a look. The brute in front of me knew this. At that moment, so did I. With Bekket's life dangling by a frayed thread, I channelled all of my faith in the Emperor and my hatred of the orks into the crystalline, adamantine belief that my gaze was a greenskin's doom. I was what they believed me to be.

The guard's axe wavered. The ork looked away from my eye and my dangerous socket, and glanced around, uncertain. It seemed to notice something on the gantries in the gloom high above our heads. Then it lowered the blade. It took its foot off Bekket, gave him a kick in the ribs, and stalked away down the line of slaves, snarling to itself.

As I helped Bekket up, the back of my neck prickled. I looked up into the shadows. I sensed the massive presence. *He* was up there, watching. *The* ork. Thraka.

I couldn't see him, but I hoped he saw the look in my eye.

I hoped he saw the lethal promise that lay within.

SARCOPHAGUS

DAVID ANNANDALE

The true measure of my enemy's threat isn't just in the brute force at his disposal. Nor is it fully captured in the tally of victories and defeats. What lies behind events? Why are some actions taken and others not? The answers to those questions can reveal a power even more deadly than armies of millions could imply. Ghazghkull Thraka had annihilated our forces on Golgotha. What that showed of his means and ability was bad enough, but that he released me had even worse implications.

Sometimes questions alone point to dark revelations.

I was in Anaon, south of Hive Tartarus. It was a smaller hive on the coast of the Tempest Ocean. I had come for two reasons. One was to inspect the maritime defences. The fate of Helsreach still hung in the balance, and we had to prepare against the possibility of a second invasion from the water. The other reason was symbolic. That had always been an integral part of my duties as a commissar: to represent something more important than the individual in the uniform.

I never meant to become an icon, but circumstances were circumstances. The Second War for Armageddon had changed the meaning of my name. 'Yarrick' now meant 'the Saviour of Armageddon'. My thoughts about the truth of the matter were irrelevant. The legend existed. And now the Third War had come. My duty was to use every weapon at my disposal against the enemy. So if my presence was enough to motivate a population to a greater effort, then I would make sure I was seen. The people of Anaon had to be willing to sacrifice everything, down to their lives. Every single one. No one person, group or hive was more important than Armageddon.

So I flew in from Tartarus. I made my inspection. I met with the commanders of the military forces charged with the hive's defence. I made myself visible. Anaon had suffered a few bombing raids, but had been spared a major assault. The people felt safe enough to take to the streets. I spoke to them. I exhorted. I made sure of their commitment to the war.

All was well and good, but the problems began when I had to return to Tartarus. A massive aerial battle was underway between the two hives. Air transport back to Tartarus was out of the question. I had to travel using terrestrial means.

I climbed out of my command car just inside the outer gate of Anaon, a massive configuration of entwined metal columns that resembled a fused manufactorum. I greeted Captain Veit Morena of the Steel Legion's 12th Company, 22nd Regiment. He was a short man and wiry. A good build for a tanker.

'Captain,' I said. 'I understand your squadron is being recalled to Hive Tartarus.'

'That's correct, commissar.'

'I would like to accompany you.'

He seemed taller suddenly. 'I would be honoured if you rode with me,' he said.

'Thank you.'

He led me to his Leman Russ Vanquisher, *Storm of the Wastes*. His driver, Alna Klaren, and gunner, Jaro Berne, snapped to attention. Like Morena, they were compact soldiers. They looked as if they had been born in the tank, their bodies shaped to its confines. Oil was so deep in their folds of their skin, it might as well have been pigmentation. The hull of *Storm* bore similar marks. It had been scored by centuries of exposure to the acidic rains of Armageddon.

The long line of tanks rolled out of Anaon at dusk with *Storm* at the head. The toxic cloud cover was heavy with the threat of rain. We made good time for the first few hours, rumbling along the pitted, cracked rockcrete route that linked Anaon to Tartarus. Morena and I alternated riding the hatch. At the northern horizon, in the direction of Tartarus, the night sky flashed and burned with reflected explosions. I saw the streaks of missiles, and the spiralling flame of stricken aircraft falling to earth. War's steady, pulsing thunder rolled over us, all the sounds of conflict melding into a muffled, arrhythmic, stuttering – *boom, b-boom-boom, b-b-boom*.

When I traded places with Morena, he looked into the distance. 'I make it another two hours before we're under the worst of the fighting,' he said.

'Agreed.'

I thought that would be the point of greatest vulnerability for the squadron, but I was wrong.

An hour later, when I was again at the hatch, the beat of the war drum changed. A layer detached itself from the rest. It was more regular, and sounded closer. It was slow, deep as a continent. Even over the rattling of the Vanquisher, I could feel the beat's vibrations in my chest. It came from north-east of our position.

I peered into the dark as points of light appeared. They confused me at first. They looked like stars, an impossible sight on Armageddon; the planet's polluted sludge of an atmosphere was impenetrable. Then I realised that the stars were moving. The ground shook at measured, relentless intervals. The stars drew nearer. They were in pairs and a red the colour of flames. I could make out massive shadows in the night as we came closer. Mountains were slouching toward the road to Tartarus.

I dropped back down the hatch. 'Gargants!' I warned.

Even in the red illumination of the tank's interior, I saw Morena turn pale. His fear was not cowardice. It was an entirely rational response to the presence of the ork monsters of war. 'We can't fight those,' he said. Those words weren't cowardice either. They were the judgement of a commander who knew the limits of his force's strength. War will call upon us to do the impossible. It will force us to fight when there is no chance of survival, let alone victory. But we were not in a position where choice had been taken away from us. Duty calls for sacrifice, not stupidity.

'Berne,' Morena told the gunner. 'Vox Tartarus Command. Warn them.'

I climbed out of the hatch entirely to make room for

Morena, riding on the turret and grasping the cupola with my power claw. We watched the progress of the Gargants. There were three of them, each a hundred metres high. They were still far from us, but we could see them more clearly now. They were lumbering, wide-bodied products of diseased invention; they had none of the majesty of Titans. But they provoked awe all the same. They gouted flame and smoke, towering over the landscape like brutal, shambolic gods. A single one could destroy a city. And they would reach the road long before we had passed them.

We looked further to the east. The land was dark, and there were no further sign of ork forces accompanying the Gargants.

'That way seems clear,' Morena said. 'I wish the terrain was better.'

We were in a region of bare, rocky hills. Perhaps at some point in Armageddon's distant, eroded past, they had been verdant. The millennia had stripped them of all vegetation and worn them down until they had the dead, rounded shapes of bone. The tanks could handle their slopes, but we wouldn't be able to see far ahead. Obstacles in the form of boulders would be common, and we'd be encountering them in the dark. Progress would be slow.

'We have no other option,' I said. If we stayed on the road, annihilation was a certainty. 'We'll need to make a wide sweep.' Even more time lost.

Morena nodded and disappeared inside the tank to issue the commands.

We turned off the road onto terrain that was uneven, broken, hostile to our passage. It was riddled with the cracks of dried stream beds. Forward visibility in the tanks' lamps shrank to the crest of the next hill. We headed east and did not turn until the earthquake rumble of the Gargants faded, their flames only pinpricks in the dark again. I guessed we were twenty kilometres off the road when Morena finally ordered a northward course again.

The hours passed. Dawn was still a long way off when the Gargants were finally to our south. Though we had been slowed, we were still faster than they were. I was so focused on the Gargants' position that I barely noticed how close we had come to the aerial battle.

It came to us with a high-pitched snarl. I looked up. More lights in the dark, a swarm of them racing in from the north-east: two ork bomber squadrons, and ten aircraft that I could count. There was no question of evasion – we had been spotted and the bombers were coming right for us.

They were still some distance away when they began to release their incendiary bombs. The land vanished in a billowing cloud of flame. The night burned, heat racing ahead of the fire. My face blistered. The holocaust marched toward us, and there would be no escape.

I went down into the tank again and sealed the hatch. The others were already reacting to the threat. Morena was at the vox, coordinating the response. Heavy bolter turrets along the entire line of the tank squadron were turning to fire at the enemy fliers. Klaren gunned the engine, pushing *Storm* to full speed, terrain be damned. We had little defence against what was coming. If we were lucky, heavy bolter-rounds or a miraculous cannon shot might bring down a couple of planes. Speed was a gesture more than a strategy. The weapons that were about to hit us did not require accuracy.

I braced, grasping the hatch ladder with my claw.

The booming voice of war had arrived and the bombs continued to fall. The light of sudden day burst though the driver's viewing block, bright enough the illuminate the full interior of *Storm*. Then the full force of the bombardment arrived and we drove into a high-explosive firestorm.

The vox exploded with cries. Morena was shouting into it. '*Tartarus Command, this is Scorched Earth Squadron, Twelfth of the Twenty-Second out of Anaon, transporting Commissar Yarrick. Our position–*'

The world erupted beneath *Storm of the Wastes*. For a moment, I had the impression of a gunship lifting off. Then we were turning end over end, and everything was violence and ruin.

And then everything was darkness.

Waking was a transition from one darkness to another. I left oblivion for pain and crushing pressure on my legs. Something was pushing my head and neck forward, forcing me into a harsh bend. The blackness swam with sparks, but they were all from behind my eye. I could hear metal ticking, creaking and settling. Somewhere, a circuit crackled and fell silent. I didn't know where I was or why I hurt.

Nothing moved. Nothing changed. There was only the pain, growing worse, and the weak muttering of wreckage. Then my head cleared and I knew what had happened.

It's not important, I told myself. *What's important is*

knowing what is happening now. Did I even know which way I was facing? No. Was I the only survivor?

'Captain Morena,' I called. 'Klaren. Berne.'

No answer.

I waited a minute before trying again, several more times, and louder. Nothing.

They're dead, then. What about the rest of the squadron? Learn the situation.

I kept quiet and listened. Beyond the groans of the dead tank, there were sounds from the outside world. The war thunder continued. It was distant once more. No combat in the immediate vicinity. I kept listening, straining to focus beyond my pain and interpret what I could hear and what I could not. There were no engines or guns. No hammering of tools. No sounds at all of any activity in the close proximity of the hull.

The conclusion was a simple one. The ork bombers had done their job well. The tank squadron had been destroyed.

A further conclusion: I was alone.

I confronted the temptation to close my eye and return to the deeper dark. I judged it unworthy. I had not earned the right to rest. Not yet. After Golgotha, when Thraka had taken me captive to his space hulk, he had thrown me into a pit. I had had every reason to believe I was about to die. During my fall, that was when I had known several seconds of rest. Those moments would still have to suffice. Perhaps, once Thraka was dead, I would win the reward of the truest sleep. Not now, though. My duty was far from discharged. Armageddon called.

Besides, I was very uncomfortable.

I tried to move. I could turn my head from side to side,

for all the good it did me. I was still hunched, my back protesting and darkness was everywhere. My legs were pinned. My left arm was blocked if it moved more than a few centimetres to my side. My right, though, had a good degree of range. I raised the claw up and down, left and right. I imagined that I was caught in a fold of the wreckage. My right arm reached into what had been the open space of the tank's interior.

Though my legs were trapped, I didn't think they were broken. They hurt, and I wasn't going anywhere. But I could feel and move my toes. When I struggled, there was no sudden burst of fresh agony.

You're intact. The Emperor protects. He truly does. So how will you use his blessing, old man? Show your gratitude. Get out.

I reached forward with the claw and struck crumpled metal right away. Keeping its digits closed, I brought it next to my side, then slid it up and down against the barrier. My legs were held, not pulped, so there had to be a gap, small though it was, in the wreckage that gripped me. It took me several attempts. I was trying to accomplish a task by touch with a hand that was not mine. At last, though, the claw slid forward a few centimetres. I worked it forward until it was wedged. Then I paused.

Are you sure you want to do this? You have no idea of the condition of the wreckage. You don't know what will happen if you disturb the present equilibrium.

True. I might contrive to crush myself properly. Then again, did I have a choice?

No. You don't.

I opened the claw as slowly as I could. Metal protested. I pried the three metal digits apart. The corpse of the

Vanquisher cried out. The pressure eased on my legs. I pulled. My feet moved. I lurched my torso to the right while keeping the claw in place. I was pivoting on my own arm, and now I did get some new bursts of agony.

I didn't stop. I risked opening the claw all the way. The wreckage shrieked. I heard snaps. I bent my legs and threw all my weight to the right, moving a bit further. I tested it, scrabbling with my feet until I found a purchase and making sure my boots wouldn't slip.

Ready?

I whispered, 'The Emperor protects.'

I shut the claw with a snap and propelled myself to the side, sliding out of the trap a second before it slammed shut.

I tumbled free through the space, landing on hard angles. I bought myself some new bruises.

I sat up, working the kinks out of my neck. Feeling around with my left hand, I learned the contours of my prison. Jagged angles and heavy masses pressed in on me. Not everything I found was metal. I discovered a leg that appeared to be sticking out of a solid mass of metal and broken bodies. My hand sank into something that felt like a broken sphere. It was very wet. I didn't know whose head it was.

I had room to crouch, but not stand. I could move a few steps in any direction. In the centre of the space, I found a cylindrical depression. This, I guessed, had been the turret hatch. The *Storm of the Wastes* was upside down. I would not be leaving that way.

I sat down on something level and rested, thinking. Trying to make my way up would mean going through the chassis. There was little hope there, unless it had already been split open. Was it night or day? I had no idea how long I'd been unconscious. A few more hours and I could assume there was daylight outside the tank. I'd know then if there were any tears in the armour I could exploit. I didn't feel any stirring of air, though. Upwards did not seem like a fruitful route.

The flanks, then. For the time being, I put aside considerations of where the armour was thickest or thinnest. I could punch through a lot with the claw. But not anything. And my leverage was limited.

I thought about the driver's compartment. The viewing block was too small to crawl through, but any gap might be something I could enlarge. I worked my way around the circumference of the space again and tried to orient myself. Where was the gunner's seat? Which way was the cannon? Which way were the engines?

I failed. The damage was too severe. Nothing was recognisable. Whatever direction I chose could lead me toward the engines, and I had no desire to start pounding at them. I was lucky that they had not exploded, and that I wasn't wading through promethium waiting for the first spark. I was already entombed. I was not ready to be cremated.

The thought of *Storm of the Wastes* as a coffin gave me pause. I stopped moving and made myself take the time to work through that possibility. The air smelled of grease and blood. There was a trace of smoke. I was not short of breath; the space was small. Enough time had passed, and I had exerted myself enough, that my lungs would be labouring if I were sealed in hermetically.

Air was getting in. That did not imply I would be getting out. It could mean that I would be able to breathe until I died of thirst.

What about rescue?

I chose not to work through those possibilities just yet. I would have to rely too much on outside circumstances. I was already at the mercy of plenty. Time enough to think about that later.

Up, then? I thought.

Yes. Up.

That was the only direction of which I had any certainty.

I felt above my head, looking for any hint of weakness. I found an area where the wreckage seemed a bit more sparse. I swiped at it with the claw. A metal tangle came down on me. I brushed it off, then began in earnest. I pulled my arm back as far as I could. The energy of the claw built up. I punched upward.

The bang shook the entire vehicle. I paused, waiting for the explosion or the final collapse. When neither occurred, I struck again. Then again. And again.

I settled into a rhythm. Each blow worked out a bit more frustration. For the first few minutes, I made progress. The decking buckled under my attacks. I had to reach higher. Soon I could straighten up.

That was the extent of my victories. Though I was tearing through layers of metal, I was also smashing the plating, mechanism and armour together to create a denser mass. A moment came when I could no longer reach my target. I tried to climb, but there was nothing I could perch on with enough stability to punch again. Even if I clung to the edge of the hole in the decking, there wasn't enough room to get the claw past my own arm.

I sat back down. I had gone as far as I could in this direction. My options had been reduced to one, and it was poor one: rescue.

I examined the facts. Remaining dispassionate was not difficult. Between the battering I had taken and the one I had just given, I was exhausted.

There would be a search for me, and to the degree that was possible in the middle of the worst ork assault in Armageddon's history. I had last been seen in Anaon, and it was known that I was travelling with the tanks of Sixth Company. Morena's route was known too.

But we had gone many kilometres off that route to avoid the Gargants towards the region of the air war. I could still hear the sounds of conflict, though I couldn't tell from that rumble how close the battle was to my position, nor its nature. Was the struggle for control of the airspace near Tartarus still ongoing? Or was I hearing the siege of the hive itself by the Gargants? I had no beacon. The vox was in fragments. There would be no transmission coming from the destroyed squadron.

So where did that leave me? I would have to count on the burned squadron being spotted by an overflight of this particular patch of hills. From the air, I doubted there would be anything to suggest the chance of a survivor. I was also having to count on *Storm of the Wastes* not having met its end so far from the rest of the squadron that it would be missed. How far had we rolled? How far had the others travelled? There was no way to know.

But *if* someone were to see the wrecks, and a land-based search followed, there would be nothing to say there was a survivor. Nothing to suggest that prying open the destroyed armour would be worthwhile. Unless there was an unmistakeable signal.

That was the one thing I could do. I couldn't reach high enough to strike and do any damage, but I could ring the hull like a bell. So I did. Three rhythmic blows. I stopped to listen, counting to twenty, then three more blows.

I fell into the new rhythm. I might very well not be able to hear searchers until they were actually working on the tank. For all I knew, I could be the last human on Armageddon, fruitlessly hitting the interior of his coffin. But I could not risk silence, in case there *was* help nearby. So I hit three times and listened. Hit three times, listened.

On and on. For hours. How many, I had no way of telling. My existence reduced itself to this one task of striking metal in pitch blackness, a task I had no reason to expect would be successful. I refused to accept the likelihood of failure. If I did, the temptation to rest would become overwhelming. I lived from second to second. I found the energy to strike the hull three times, and then again for another three. I tried to shut out all thoughts of the past and future. The eternal present was all that mattered. Despite my efforts, though, I could not ignore the irony of my situation. The Saviour of Armageddon, dead in an overturned tank. A glorious end, truly.

I did laugh a bit. That helped.

Time wore on, and my bursts of dry laughter died away. My throat was parched. I could barely move my arm. My body demanded sleep, but I refused. Then, quite suddenly, I heard noises outside. Engines. Loud, coughing, rattling engines. And over their din, closer to the hull, voices. Guttural. Savage.

Orks.

I had poor options. A choice of deaths, but the decision was an easy one. I would go down fighting. I smashed at my tomb with renewed force. After another three blows, I heard pounding from the other side. And then the unmistakeable grind of metal cutting metal. The green-skin voices sounded excited.

I reached to my belt and activated my shield generator. The air around me thrummed as the power field sprang into being. I drew my bolt pistol, building up the charge of my bale eye. I waited. I was eager to begin. The moment the orks broke through, the situation would change. I had no illusions about my chances, but I would make the best of them.

Sparks showered into my cell. The pitch of the grinding rose to a scream, and a chainblade broke through.

Still I waited for the enemy to free me and provide a clear shot at his bestial face.

The blade worked its way around in a rough circle about a metre wide. The cuts joined. The blade withdrew. A heavy blow from the other side knocked the sliced plating inside.

Armageddon's grey daylight was blinding after the hours of total darkness.

I fired my eye as the ork poked its head through the hole. The lasburst shot through the greenskin's right eye, incinerating its brain, and it fell away. There was a growl, and then another ork appeared. I blew its skull off with the pistol.

The orks roared with outrage. Fists pounded against the hull. For the moment I saw nothing except a circle of brown sky. Heavy booted feet thudded across the hull towards the hole. Firing again, I took off the brute's arm just as it began to aim.

The attack began in earnest now. They fired around the hole at every angle. Bullets ricocheted around the interior. My shield absorbed their kinetic energy and they fell.

A grenade arced in. I caught it and threw it back outside. It exploded in midair, and I was rewarded with roars of outrage that turned into roars of pain.

The orks kept coming and I kept shooting them. I was trapped, but they couldn't come at me where they could see me more than one at a time. I could hold them off indefinitely... until I ran out of clips for the pistol. Even then, I would take them apart with the power claw if they tried to come inside.

Indefinitely. Not infinitely.

I knew what the end was. I dismissed it. I would kill them one by one in the same eternal present as when I had banged my claw against the hull. They kept coming, wearing me down closer and closer to final exhaustion.

As I fought, and shot, and killed, I wondered why their attacks were so limited. I didn't hear any engines, so perhaps these orks were without heavy armour. But none of them tried to burn me out with flamers. A well-placed rocket would have ended the struggle in an instant. Instead, they appeared to be limiting themselves to shotguns and blades.

But in the end, they tired of the game, and decided to change the rules. The grinding started up again. When the blade poked through, it began to cut the outline of a much larger hole. I would lose my shelter. I would be cornered with no protection except my power field, and concentrated fire would overwhelm it.

I changed my bolt pistol's clip and waited for the endgame.

The huge roar of an approaching aircraft shook the air. I heard the shriek of launched missiles. Explosions. Howls from the orks. A confused stampede. The aircraft came closer. There was the blast of retro-rockets as it landed. And then the sounds of a perfect, cleansing slaughter.

I leapt and grabbed the edge of the gap with my claw. Hauling myself up, I climbed out of the coffin.

Storm of the Wastes had come to rest in a narrow plain between the hills. The wreck of one of the other tanks lay on the slope to my left. A dozen metres to my right, an obsidian Thunderhawk gunship sat on level ground. A squad of Space Marines marched through the battlefield. It was full day, but they looked like darkest thoughts of the night. They were horned monsters. Though they carried bolters, most of them were killing orks with blades that grew out of their forearms.

Black Dragons.

Judging from the number of bodies I saw, there had been a few hundred orks to start with. I had lost track of how many I had killed. In the initial moments of their attack, the Black Dragons had cut them down by half. The rest fought back, but not for long.

The massacre was over in just a few minutes.

The captain of the Black Dragons came to meet me as I jumped down from the Vanquisher's upturned hull. He towered over his battle-brothers. The adamantium edge of his crescent horn gleamed in the sun. The coating of his bone blades was dark with greenskin blood. His flesh seemed more reptilian than human. In appearance, the Space Marine approached the daemonic.

This being too, I reminded myself, had a role to play in service to the Emperor.

The Black Dragon nodded. 'Volos,' he said. 'Second Company. An honour, commissar.'

'My thanks, Captain Volos. I am greatly in your debt. How did you find me?'

'If we had flown through this area before you were attacked, I don't think we would have,' he said. 'We spotted the orks.'

I took in the bodies stretching away on all sides. 'So large a group in the middle of nowhere would have caught the eye,' I agreed.

'A large raiding party, yes,' he said. 'I am puzzled by their overall weakness, though. There are no warlords here. And their weapons...'

'...are very limited,' I finished.

He must have seen something on my face. 'Commissar?' he asked.

An ork force weak in strength but large in numbers. Easily spotted. One that could not simply blow up the tank they were attacking; one that would be just possible for a single human being to hold off. And why were the orks here? I had called them to the specific tank, pinpointing my location for any searching eyes, but I could not understand why this force had been in the area at all. After the bombers did the job, there was little to scavenge. There would have been no reason for any infantry to be diverted to this location.

Unless *I* was the reason.

I remembered Morena's last vox transmission, alerting Imperial forces to my presence. I wondered now if someone else had heard it, if my enemy had sent this force knowing I was here. If they had sent these orks, whose constant fire showed they were not trying to capture me and also did not have the means of an assured kill.

I had no answers, only possibilities. But the questions were enough.

They were their own revelations, and they gave me that much more of the measure of my enemy.

I finally answered Volos. 'I was just gathering my thoughts, Captain Volos,' I said. 'Learning what I must to win this war.'

STRAKEN:
A HERO'S DEATH

TOBY FROST

'Get down!' Colonel Straken yelled, and the charges det-onated. The Armageddon jungle seemed to burst apart, hurling itself at him. For a long second, foliage and chips of bark rained down on his bionics and his skin. The explosion rang in his ears. Then he shouted 'Smoke!'

There was a hollow pop of grenade launchers and a hiss of smoke. 'Move it, Catachans!' he called. 'Do I have to do everything myself?'

The platoon advanced: a rapid scurrying between rocks and fallen trees, ducked low with their lasguns raised. A few had slung their guns and pulled the long knives of their home world.

Straken took the centre. The orks would be dug in deep – the blast would have killed a few, but not enough. *You never can kill enough,* he thought.

'Captain Montara?' he called. 'Get up on the left flank.'
'On it,' she replied. He saw her briefly, a bulky shape

slipping through the smoke: her hair cut down to black stubble, an aquila shaved into it. Two men with shotguns followed her, one with a vox set lurching on his back. Straken plunged further into the smoke.

Ork heavy-weapons fire barked out of the swirling haze, a chattering pulse of light. Bullets hit tree trunks and tore them open, howling through the air over the Catachans.

'Move it,' Straken called. 'Shut that gun up!'

Broad, hulking figures appeared in the smoke ahead, half-obscured. Straken glimpsed red eyes and teeth like tusks under crude metal helmets. Las-fire caught one of the orks, spun it, and sent it to the ground. Straken raised his shotgun and fired at the other. It grunted and ducked out of view. Injured, but not dead.

They've left their camp, Straken thought. *They're in the trees.*

Doc Hollister appeared on Straken's right, medi-kit slung across his body, a big grin on his lined face. 'Got 'em scared now!' Hollister said.

Roars and grunts came from the undergrowth and flanks as well as from ahead.

'No, just angry,' Straken replied.

An ork burst out of the foliage on the right. It howled as if on fire, arms flailing, mouth swathed in foam. It wore a vest of grimy metal plates.

Straken blasted it in the thigh. The ork went down, cleaver bouncing out of its grip. Snarling, it reached for a pistol. Straken worked the slide of his shotgun and aimed, shooting it in the neck. The ork fell and Straken leaped after it. He stabbed down with his knife as the beast tried to rise, but the ork pulled a cleaver from its belt and blocked his blade. For a moment they strained against each other, a contest of sheer brute force, but the alien's strength seemed to break, and Straken's knife slid through its throat into the earth behind.

Gunfire roared from the left. Straken threw himself down and fired prone: he glimpsed a tusked face, and a body dropped into the undergrowth. Straken leaped up and rushed down the length of a huge fallen log, turned and saw Guardsman Hardec lying on the ground. Wooden spikes stuck out of his shoulder and a pack of scrawny creatures pinned him down, jabbering as they prodded the spikes.

Straken was on them before they could turn. His shotgun blasted the first three aliens apart. Their comrades turned, but too slowly, and Straken's metal fist clamped down on the biggest gretchin's head. Bone shattered. The others squealed and ran into the trees. Straken fired, and a thin scream answered him. He shouted for the medic to help Hardec and pushed on towards the ork camp.

In a clearing, just before the camp itself, an immense ork raged and bellowed. Half a dozen Guardsmen surrounded it, pouring las-fire into the ork's hide. It was riddled with wounds, kept alive, it seemed, by fury alone. Wild blows sent up a cloud of chopped foliage. 'Take it!' Straken cried, and he added his shotgun to the las-fire. Slowly, the brute sank down, grunting. It collapsed onto its knees, half-hidden by plants as if drowning beneath a green sea, then slumped onto all fours. For a moment, Straken could hear its hard, loud breathing. Then came the inevitable shot, and the sound of a huge body striking the earth.

Sudden quiet. Straken heard Hollister's voice – 'I'll just tie the bandage off' – and a groan of pain answered it.

Captain Montara looked over her shoulder and made a throat-cutting gesture. She meant that the enemy were all dead.

Straken said, 'Three squads. Montara, you check the area east of the bunker. Griersen?'

The lieutenant looked round. The left side of his face was mottled with scar tissue. 'Sir?'

'Take the west. I'll check the ork camp.'

Straken gestured to Cole, the demolitions expert, and Myers, the support gunner. Massive even by Catachan standards, Myers lumbered over and waited for the call to fight, holding his heavy bolter like a lasgun.

'Colonel?'

He turned: it was Lessky, the command squad's vox operator. The man squinted, pressing the comm-link to his ear. 'Sir, I've got a signal. It's on the special frequency, coded. I can almost make it out...'

'Get to higher ground. I'll cover you. Stokes,' he added, pointing at a corporal who wore nothing on his chest except dirt and a bandolier, 'take four men and come with us. Sergeant Tren, get the rest of the camp checked! Now move!'

'Alright, listen up. Previous orders are overridden.'

Straken stood on an outcrop of bare rock, as high as he could get. His officers watched from a little way down. Montara stood at the front of the group, arms folded. Lower down, a ring of Catachans watched the forest. The orders might be cancelled, but that didn't mean that the orks had gone away.

The outcrop just cleared the tops of the trees. They were only a few miles from the edge of the jungle, and the plant life was less dense here. Among the trees, visibility was down to a reasonable fifteen yards. Further in, you would be lucky to see three feet into the forest.

'There's a reason we're up here, and this is it.' Straken pointed to the east, his metal arm glinting in the sun. Miles away, a massive dark structure rose up from the ground, its base hidden by the forest. It was gigantic, but distance made its exact size hard to make out. The tip was wreathed in clouds: smoke billowed from the edges of the structure. It was roughly conical in shape, but bulged in places like a termite mound. It was, in some ways, the closest thing to a termite colony that the Imperium produced.

'Infernus Hive,' Straken said. 'A message has come through that the orks have been gaining ground inside the hive city. Looks like the front is stabilised – Emperor knows if that's good or bad news.'

A couple of Catachans nodded. Sergeant Halda spat over the side of the outcrop. The fight for the hive went in waves: not just forward and back, but up and down as different levels of the structure changed hands. It was confusing and vicious work, and Straken knew that his men had been pleased to be sent to fight orks in the jungle outside. The jungle might be no less deadly than the hive – probably more so – but it was a deadliness that they knew well.

'The vox says that in the last greenskin offensive, something called Perimeter Fifty-Six was overrun. It seems that General Beran of the Mordian One Hundred and Sixth had been believed dead along with his regiment. Turns out they've picked up a signal from them. The general is injured and they need extraction.'

There was a murmur. Someone said, 'Ah, hell.'

'And *we* will be extracting them. We move in on the location, taking out any opposition on the way. We locate this general and whatever's left of his men, then we get out and signal for extraction. Questions?'

Lessky raised his hand. It was missing a finger. 'Does that mean that we're going back into the hive, sir?'

'Yes, we are.' Straken looked them over. 'Alright then, what're you waiting for? Let's move!'

They slipped easily through the jungle, even as a multi-limbed and spider-like creature lunged at Straken. But he pinned its head to a trunk with his long knife, cleaning the blade as they kept walking.

Seventy years, nearly, he thought as he slipped the long blade back in its sheath. They made the fang-knives of Catachan well. Straken had never marked his kills on the blade the way some soldiers did – had he done so, he would have run out of metal decades ago.

'Colonel?' It was Hollister. The unit's medic was as tough as any of the rest of them, but there was something odd about the fellow, as if his mind was always half on other things.

The medic glanced at Straken, as if checking something. It made Straken think of the rejuvenat treatments that Hollister could provide. The thought of being kept going by some drug sent a flash of anger through him.

Seeing the colonel's expression, Hollister drew away, and Straken scowled at the path ahead.

They stopped at the edge of the jungle, spreading out at the treeline. Suddenly, there was no canopy to hide the Catachans. They had arrived at Infernus Hive.

Somewhere to the east, gunfire crackled and boomed as the front raged, but here it was quiet. Two hundred metres of barren ground stretched before them. It was dirt, grey-brown stuff, more like brick dust than compressed earth. Ruts criss-crossed the ground, a mass of scars laid down by tank tracks and huge wheels.

Ork vehicles lay wrecked before them: buggies, tanks, gun platforms, half-tracks, even a couple of flying machines covered in trophies and glyph-signs. They had that motley, thrown-together look common to ork machinery and lay among craters and chunks of rubble, some burned out, others blasted apart. Their pilots and crew were strewn around them, great green bodies torn and burned. All had been heading towards the same place, trying to swarm into the hive city when its defenders had opened fire.

Beyond the barren ground stood the wall of the hive. It rose into the sky, higher than any cliff. Gargoyles studded the wall. Friezes of Imperial heroes had been painted onto the rockcrete. The figures were taller than knight Titans, chipped and worn away by storms and explosions.

The scale of the wall was dizzying; it would have dwarfed a Capitol Imperialis. Beyond it, the next level of the hive city began, tapering slightly. High above, miles from ground level, the city vanished into the clouds.

Straken voxed the order down the line.

'Move up in squads,' he said. 'Use the ork armour for cover. And careful – just because a greenskin's lying down doesn't mean he's dead. If you don't know for sure, *make* sure. You've got your knives for a reason.'

Straken's command squad went first. They ran out, dashed across the open ground and ducked behind an armour-plated truck that had flipped onto its side. Straken peered around the edge of the truck and boosted the vision in his bionic eye. No lights shone on the wall, but he could see alcoves that looked like windows and firing-points. Maybe they were being watched. In a structure that big, it was impossible to tell. The only hope was that they would seem so tiny that no one would pay them any notice.

The snipers and heavy weapons teams hung back, hidden among the trees, covering the advance. Straken saw Serradus, the most experienced of the snipers, directing his crew to vantage points. Sellen and Ferricus, two men so alike that they seemed to share the same brain, set up their missile launcher.

Squads moved up behind Straken's, using one another's cover to advance. Straken kept to the front, as he always did. He ran alongside a stripped-down buggy, little more than a frame on wheels. A plasma gun had blasted straight though it, and the incinerated driver was as skeletal as his machine. The ork's mouth gaped open, the eye sockets turned to the wall as if awestruck by the size of the hive.

Sergeant Eiden gestured to get the colonel's attention. Eiden was on the far edge of the advance, crouching down behind a heap of ruined ork bikes. The white-haired sergeant wore a necklace of ork canines, each seven centimetres long.

'Hold position,' Straken told his squad. He broke cover, rushed across the ground and darted to Eiden's side. 'What've you got?'

'Entry point.' Eiden nodded at the wall. Straken looked, didn't see it for a moment, then realised what the sergeant meant.

Something, a vehicle or some kind of tunnelling

missile, had blown a hole in the bottom of the wall. It had cut along the ground, burning a trench as deep as a man was tall, before tearing into the rockcrete. Orks lay scattered around the hole, presumably killed as they had tried to rush into the breach.

But they still got in, Straken thought.

The hole in the wall was big enough for a Baneblade tank to pass through. It made him feel wary, a sense of being outside his natural hunting ground that no jungle, no matter how hostile, could give him.

'That's it,' he said, and motioned to the command squad to follow him.

They were forty-five metres from the hole when the orks opened fire.

Lights flared in the hole, bullets roared, and four men were cut down in half a second. Corporal Jenks was hit by some kind of mounted gun and blown to pieces. 'Take cover!' Straken bellowed, and threw himself down, reaching for a grenade with his steel hand.

Eiden's squad darted back behind a ruined truck. A great howl echoed from the wall and massive aliens rushed out of the hole, holding axes and machetes. Straken pulled the plasma pistol from his hip and snapped three shots into the first pair of orks.

An ork leaped onto a ruined buggy, heaving a machine gun up after it. Lasguns cracked, and its head burst. The alien toppled backwards, out of view. Straken risked a glance out of cover and saw more orks running down from the hole, a slavering gang of them. He raised the grenade to his mouth and paused a moment to let the aliens get closer.

Straken pulled the pin out with his teeth. He counted – one, two – and hurled the bomb with his metal arm. It hit the ground, bounced and exploded in midair. Several of the brutes were killed – but, more importantly, it made the rest of them pause.

'Come on,' Straken shouted, 'do I have to do everything myself?'

The Catachans rose up around him and charged in. Straken hacked down one ork and put a plasma blast straight through a second. His men brought the aliens down with knives and lasgun butts.

Gunfire rattled out of the hole, mowing down three men, but a missile streaked out of the Catachan line and burst in the gap, blasting orks out of cover. Enfilading fire came from the flank: Montara's squad ripped into the enemy from the side. A few orks ran back into the dark; most charged forward when they realised that their cover was no more use, and fell a few steps later.

Eiden approached. His knife was bloody and he held two long teeth in his other fist. 'Ambush,' he said.

Straken nodded. 'Let's go. They'll bring up others if they know we're here.'

The Catachans moved in silently, picking their way through the rubble and the wreckage that the orks had left behind. Straken sent out scouts to check the edges.

'Emperor!' Eiden said. 'Look at that.'

The explosion that had blasted through the wall had exposed several layers of the hive, as if the front had been ripped off a gigantic hotel, revealing the rooms and lives behind. Straken gazed upwards, seeing different levels: the narrow warrens of hab-zones, the halls that served as chapels and factories, canteens and recreation areas – even what looked like a mechanic's yard, crammed with dozens of armoured vehicles.

The entrance was daubed with dozens of ork symbols.

'Place looks infested,' Montara said. 'No wonder these Mordian guys are pinned down.'

'Keep moving,' Straken said. 'Go quietly. From here on, use your knives.'

One of the few good things about fighting orks was their disunity. In the decades that he'd been killing greenskins, Straken had never seen much organisation. They barely had ranks, and their groups were more like feral gangs than regiments. They came together to attack a common enemy, like animals preying on the same herd, and squabbled and bullied one another when there was no better enemy to be found. Straken had seen dozens of ork hordes, but never a true ork army.

Now, as he dragged a dead ork sentry into the shadows, he realised just how useful that was. The aliens considered it only natural that they would feud among themselves: if an ork went missing, he had probably just been killed by his fellow orks.

They pressed on, deeper into the hive, moving steadily closer to the Mordians. The hab-zones had been gang territory before the orks had taken them. The Catachans passed gang symbols on the walls and the corpses of the people who had once sprayed them there. Now various ork clans occupied the areas, and had added their own scrawl to the graffiti. The locals lay sprawled over barricades and across the narrow corridors, or wherever the orks had found it amusing to leave them. It seemed that the xenos had taken particular delight in throwing their enemies down the lift shafts.

The Catachans went quickly and quietly, fighting only

where they had to, and killing swiftly and silently when it could not be avoided. The scouts brought back reports of large alien gatherings to the east and west and Straken's men would be passing between them. Then they started to find dead orks.

'Las-fire,' Montara said, glancing at a huge green corpse. 'We must be near.'

Straken raised his metal hand. 'Wait.' He tilted his head, concentrating. 'You hear that?'

Montara cupped a scarred hand around her ear. 'Hear what? Wait, I–'

'Gunfire,' Straken said. 'Coming from the rendez-vous point. Listen!' he called. 'There's firing up ahead. Let's get down there and get stuck in. On the double, Guardsmen!'

They picked up the pace, running towards the sound. Only a few yards further, Straken began to hear the indi-vidual guns. A hundred yards on, and it was as though they were entering a storm of noise.

Straken led them down a staircase, towards the epicen-tre. Voices joined the gunfire: human shouts and screams, and the roars and grunts of aliens. Straken paused at the end of the corridor and checked his weapons. Then he turned to his men.

'Go!' Straken shouted, and he lunged around the corner.

They stood at the edge of an enormous hall. The ceiling, so high that it was almost lost to view, was criss-crossed by enormous pipes like metal intestines. Under them, in the centre of the hall, stood a singular slab-sided building covered in robed statues and symbols of the Adeptus Mechanicus. There was a hole in one corner, where something had blown the building open, and a barricade of junk, furniture and metal sheeting was piled around the hole like a scab on a wound.

Lasgun fire crackled from the barricade. Orks lay in heaps around the chamber, piles of xenos carcasses. Some were riddled with precise burn-holes, others blown limb from limb by grenades and mortar shells. As Straken entered, an ork eighteen metres away tried to rise, despite missing half of its head. Straken finished it with a shot-gun blast.

The Catachans tore into the remaining orks. The aliens were taken by surprise, hit from both sides. The las-fire from the Mordians and the knives of Straken's men made short work of the orks. Straken grabbed one alien from behind, broke its shoulder in his metal grip and yanked its chin back, snapping the alien's thick neck. Halda, the colour sergeant, knocked the legs of an ork out with his banner and drove it through its chest as if claiming the alien as Catachan territory. On the right, Montara grappled with a huge brute in yellow armour. Her arms strained as she pushed its head up and back, away from her. A Mordian on the barricade obligingly shot it through the brain, and it flopped down in a clatter of ramshackle armour.

Straken could just make out faces over the barricade. Most of them wore dark blue caps.

'Hey!' he called. 'Are you General Beran's men?'

'That's right!' a voice called back. A corporal stood up. His left arm was bandaged, most of the sleeve torn away.

'Colonel Straken, Second Catachan,' Straken replied. 'We came to get the general out.'

'Yes? You'd better come inside.'

* * *

'So,' the Mordian said, 'you've arrived.' Her name was Krall: she was about forty, pale, with light brown hair and hard, deep-set eyes. She dressed like the rest of them: blue tunic, trousers with a stripe down the side and a pillbox hat. Her insignia said that she was a lieutenant. She looked like a toy soldier, Straken thought. So did the rest of her men.

'Yep, we're here.' Straken walked into an entrance hall. Montara followed him. She looked grim and unimpressed. Behind them, Mordian soldiers were repairing the high barricade that they had half-dismantled to let the Catachans in. 'Where's General Beran?'

Lieutenant Krall pointed off into a doorway. 'He's over there. But... the general's dead.'

'Dead?'

Montara said, 'So what the hell did we hear?'

'Probably a recorded message. We got hold of one of High Command's servitors on the vox and told them to relay it. Then the orks attacked, and in the fight the set got smashed up. That's the last message we were able to send.'

'Great,' Montara said. 'So we came out here for nothing.'

Straken said, 'Sounds like there's not much to stay here for. How many of you are there?'

Krall paused. 'About a hundred and fifty. Forty of whom are wounded, fifteen seriously.'

'Get your troops ready to move out. You've got fifteen minutes. Put the injured on stretchers: we can rig up some sort of cart with the junk we passed on the way in.'

'We'd need to take the general. But–'

'Get him on a stretcher too.' After all this time, Straken still hadn't got used to the way some regiments dealt with the dead. On Catachan, it had always been the case that the body was left in the jungle, for the jungle to take. A man's knife and his bandanna were left to mark his passing – his corpse meant little once the life was gone.

'Colonel, you don't understand. We can't leave. I don't have the authority.'

Straken shrugged. 'Then tell your commander. What is he, a captain?'

'No. He's a commissar.'

Straken cursed under his breath. He paused a moment, thinking. 'Where is he?'

Krall said, 'At the other barricade. That's where we had the last big attack. You want me to take you?'

'No. Show the captain here what your set-up is. Montara, send two teams of scouts to check the area outside. I need you to find out what the defences are, how far the perimeter extends and where the exits are – all the usual stuff, but especially the exits.'

The Mordians had prepared for a siege, and once, Straken thought, they had been well-supplied. But now only a few ammunition boxes were stacked next to a couple of spare lasguns; the remaining medical gear and ration packs were guarded by broad, hard-eyed troopers. He passed an improvised hospital and saw a row of camp-beds filled by battered Guardsmen; their pain and senses blotted out with morphia. It was well-organised and neat. The only thing he couldn't see was a way out.

He walked past blue-uniformed men who looked as disapproving as they were wary of him. Thin grey dust was everywhere – Straken wondered how the hell the Mordians kept their gear so clean.

The room beyond was wide and long, like the nave of a church. A massive hole had been blown in the rear wall. Thirty yards down, furniture had been heaped around bulky machines to form another barricade almost twice the height of a man. Troopers stood on the barricade, watching for the orks. Every few seconds, there would be a sudden crackle of lasguns, and a grunt or bellow from beyond the barricade. Beside the soldiers was a man in a long leather coat.

'Commissar!'

The man turned from his watch, stared at Straken, and then clambered down the heap of furniture.

'Who are you?' he demanded. 'Where's your uniform?'

'Colonel Straken, Second Catachan. We picked up your distress message. I'm here to get you out. And this *is* my uniform.'

The commissar was old, Straken saw, long-limbed and quick. He looked strong without being bulky.

'Welcome,' he said. 'Commissar Redmund Verryn. I assumed command here when General Beran was killed, and after Major Adamik showed himself incapable of facing up to the situation.'

Which probably means that he got nervous and you shot him, Straken thought. *All the same, commissars.*

Verryn took off his cap and stashed it under his arm. His hair looked as if it had been glued to his scalp in strips. 'I don't know how you got down here, but I'm afraid that the time for rescue is long-gone. We're surrounded by the xenos.'

'I've brought my men. We reckon we can get out of here. Probably take the wounded back, too. And the general.'

'Appreciated, colonel.' The commissar glanced back at

the barricade. 'But the orks will be too many. One way or another, we're hemmed in. Emperor only knows how you got in – we barely managed it, too – but believe me, the way out will be closed by now.'

'What do you mean?'

'I mean, colonel, that we are surrounded.' He gestured around the hall. 'This is it.' Verryn smiled. 'I always wondered what a last stand would feel like. It's surprisingly bearable.'

Straken felt a strong urge to knock that smile off the man's face. 'So we die here, is that it?'

'Like heroes of the Imperium, colonel.' Verryn sighed. 'I've been with the Mordians all my life, you know. A lot of that time, I had the honour to serve with General Beran. Believe me, you'd have had the honour of fighting beside one of the great soldiers of the Imperial Guard.'

'Too bad he's a corpse. I'd have asked for his autograph otherwise.'

'That's enough of that attitude! You are in the presence of great men here, Straken. Great men. You should consider yourself lucky to be in such company.'

'You should consider *yourself* lucky that I'm in a good mood.'

Something seemed to snap in Verryn. His head darted forward, as if to bite Straken. His eyes were wild and as round and hard as spotlights. 'What the hell does that mean?'

'It means that I'm getting these people out of here before you get them killed,' Straken growled.

'I'm not "getting them killed"! Didn't you see how many orks there were? Or have your bionics rusted up?'

'Yes, I saw. And I fought my way through 'em! Listen – I

saw the state of your supplies. You don't have long, commissar. Once you're out of heavy weapon ammo, the orks
will take two minutes to get over your defences and one
minute to take your men apart. If we want to get out of
this, we need to stick together and get out of here. *Now.*'

'That's enough! You will man the barricades and fight
like a soldier of the Guard. And if you don't...' Verryn
glanced over Straken's shoulder. 'Believe me, you won't
be on the barricade – you'll be in front of it.'

At the edge of Straken's vision, a Mordian soldier stopped
and glared at him. Straken wondered if there were others
standing around, listening. He felt eyes on his back. He
lowered his voice as much as his anger would allow.

'Commissar, my men got here and they can get out
again. We can get you, and the others, out. And then you
can bury the general, come back and blow the hell out
of as many orks as you want. Nobody has to die – not
penned up in here, not on the way back.'

Verryn's teeth were clenched. 'Your opinion is noted,
colonel.' He took a deep breath. 'We will hold our ground.
We can inflict far heavier casualties upon the enemy here
than we could do on some hopeless escape attempt. The
general's body has to be protected. Consider it an honour guard.'

'I consider it a waste of time,' Straken said, turning
away.

'I don't know what your customs are on Catachan, colonel, but the Mordians don't abandon their dead,' Verryn
said, coldly.

'Catachans don't abandon the living, commissar,' said
Straken as he walked back towards his men.

* * *

'They've tried to rush us more times than I can count,' Lieutenant Krall was saying, 'but the barricades hold up.' She patted the heap of furniture. 'We had some mines rigged, but the orks sent gretchin over them. Thing is, we're short of ammo. Short of pretty much everything, really. Two, three, more good attacks and they'll be inside.'

'Right,' Montara replied. She held a battered cup, a third full of low-grade recaff. It was the best that Krall had been able to provide. 'Right.'

Straken approached as Krall turned back to the barricade. Montara stepped back and walked over to him. 'How's the commissar?'

Straken grimaced. 'Well, he's either crazy or just a mean bastard,' he replied. 'Either way, this is his last stand.'

'What?'

'He means to die here. With these men.'

The captain glanced around. 'Are you serious? And they're going to let him do that?'

'Maybe. I told him otherwise. They didn't look happy. These guys are used to following orders.'

'So? *I* follow orders. I just don't follow crazy orders from a lunatic.' She glanced round. 'To hell with this place. I say we just leave and write off the whole damn thing. If they want to waste their lives playing soldier–'

Straken raised his flesh-and-blood hand. 'Captain,' he said, 'what do you know about this hive?'

Montara shrugged. 'Not much more than you, sir. The lieutenant said that it goes down much deeper than this, into the ground. She said the lower levels are full of mutants, and most of the upper floors are overrun by orks. I never liked these places–'

'Colonel!'

It was Krall. She pointed behind them, to the way that Straken had arrived.

A man scrambled over the barricade, helped in by the defenders. He wore a combat vest and a Catachan sniper's cloak. *Trouble,* Straken thought. *As if I need more of that.*

The man was Strom, one of the scouting team. 'Sir, we've got a problem. The orks are coming back, closing on our position.'

'How many?'

'A few thousand, perhaps more. Heavy armour, flamers, rocket launchers, all kinds of stuff.'

Straken thought of his team, outside, facing a horde. He glanced at the barricades and then at Montara, seeing that she understood the decision he was taking.

'Get your team inside the perimeter.'

'Sir, once they're inside–' Montara protested.

'Do it.'

A voice bellowed, 'Orks!' Men gripped their weapons, soldiers resting at the base of the barricade scrambled up to man the parapet.

'Orks to the east!'

Straken ran to the barricade, shotgun in hand. He leaped up, caught a protruding chair leg and hauled himself up. He took up position beside his men, waiting as the sound rose from beyond the defences: roaring ork voices and the pounding of hundreds of pairs of heavy boots.

The aliens ran into sight but the Guardsmen cut them down. The ground beyond the barricade was like a tunnel down to hell: packed with hulking bodies and faces that were little more than glittering eyes and fangs. Mobs of ork infantry surged towards the humans, grunting and roaring, and within moments the hall was half-choked with alien dead.

They kept coming. They trampled their wounded, tripping on them, and were shot full of las-fire before they could rise. Straken used his shotgun on those that threatened to get close, but the great majority were killed within a few moments of coming into view. Some of the orks carried crude shields, but grenades and plasma fire took care of them.

The Mordians weren't bad fighters, Straken thought. They lacked the natural fury of the Catachans, the hunger for combat, but their cold discipline nearly made up for it. Lieutenant Krall never seemed to stop barking commands, as if to rival those yelled by Straken and his men.

Suddenly, the orks stopped coming. Nobody fired: the corridor seemed incredibly quiet. Somewhere far off, an alien groaned. Straken glimpsed a few shapes in the distance, hidden by smoke and dust, pulling back. The attack was over, for now.

The defenders checked their wounds. Six Mordians and four Catachans had been killed, all victims of lucky ork gunfire. Another man had slipped down the barricade and broken his arm. Overall, it wasn't bad.

But as he climbed down from his firing-point, Straken saw the real problem. One of Krall's men handed his comrade a new magazine. Another put his grenade launcher down and drew a laspistol instead. Power packs that should have been charged from a generator were placed on a metal rack over a fire, like barbecued meat.

First, they would run out of grenades and support weapons, and then their lasguns would run dry.

Straken gestured to Lieutenant Krall. 'I need to talk to you,' he said. 'Quietly.'

'The orks come maybe once, twice a day – sometimes more,' the lieutenant said. 'Maybe they have orders from above, maybe they're like small gangs. Perhaps they just smell a fight.' They stood at once side of the building, in the shadows near empty hab-quarters that had been used by the soldiers to doss down. A Mordian sat on a stool, cleaning his lasgun. He leaped up and saluted; Krall motioned him back at ease. 'I don't know what makes them keep coming.'

'They're orks,' Straken said. 'It's what they do.' He stepped into one of the hab-quarters, satisfied that they would not be overheard.

'You wanted to talk privately, sir,' Krall said.

'Yes. Your commissar expects you all to die here. He thinks the ship's sinking, and he wants everyone to go down with it. Mark of respect for the general or something.'

'I know.'

'You going to do something about that?'

'Like what?' Krall asked. 'I've got orders to follow, sir.'

'Too bad those orders are going to get you, and the people you command, killed.'

For all her discipline, Krall couldn't prevent the anger that flashed in her eyes. Then it was gone.

Straken sighed. 'That's the trouble with the Guard. Too many people making last stands, getting medals, settling scores, rubbish like that. Not enough winning wars.

You're a good soldier: you must be, to keep this mess together.' He glanced around the room. It seemed tiny compared to his high-gravity physique, as if he'd strayed into a doll's house. 'What would happen if Verryn wasn't in charge?'

'I'd take command, sir. Or rather, command would transfer to you, as ranking officer. But – but the commissar would never go. And people are loyal to him. Well, not to him personally, but to the uniform. It's how we are, sir. Every soldier is part of the unit, and the unit obeys the officer. On your own, you die.'

That's the difference, Straken thought. On Catachan, you were always on your own. You grew up tough and self-sufficient. The people who died were the ones who couldn't manage on their own.

'So if the commissar happened to get himself killed, you'd be in charge. And the others would obey you.'

A strand of sandy hair slipped out of Krall's cap and hung across her eyes. 'I am uncomfortable with this line of conversation, sir.'

'Captain Montara said that you mentioned something strange,' Straken said. 'Something about mutants on the lower levels. Thing is, I've seen a lot of orks... but no mutants.'

'The under-levels,' Krall replied. 'Look, there's levels under here, loads of them. I don't know much about them, but I saw some on the way in here, and they weren't nice. They have workshops down there, where they keep these mutants – slaves, I suppose. But with the war all the people, the normal people, took off. And the mutants took over.' She shrugged. 'Maybe some of them were loose before, feral, but they're all free now.

I don't know whether the orks go down there. Probably not much to take if they did.'

'So these mutants control the levels below us?'

'I think so. I didn't stay too long. It makes this dump look like a noble's palace: no power, no light, half the place flooded...'

Straken nodded and smiled. 'Sounds great.' Had Krall known him better, she would have realised that trouble was coming. 'How do I get there?'

The manufactorum had a cellar, where the workers had stashed things that they did not need. Rolls of cable hung from pegs on the walls. A deactivated servitor stood in a corner, head drooping. Along the far wall was a row of alcoves.

Krall led Straken to the alcoves. One had a square grating in the floor. Straken heaved the cover up, without difficulty, and set it aside.

'Close it after me,' he said.

Straken loaded his weapons and descended. He dropped down and heard Krall push the lid back into place as quietly as she could.

It was dark, pitch black. There was no sound, not even that of boots overhead. The air smelled of dust. Straken pulled his bandanna up over his nose and mouth and activated the image enhancement in his bionic eye. Then he started walking.

His vision made the world look bleached: a dead, washed-out world. He passed the inevitable gang signs, insults and threats scrawled on the walls and advanced. At points, the graffiti was so dense, and the walls so high, he felt like an insect on a printed page. The place seemed deserted, but he did not lower his guard.

The floor had collapsed up ahead: the sloping rockcrete made a ramp down to the next level. He descended into what had once been a scholam. A faded mural showed children greeting saints and heroes. He began to sense that he was being followed. Good.

Straken found metal stairs that could still bear weight and went down. The air was damp now. Condensation clung to the walls and patches of fungi gave off a soft, blue glow. There were shallow puddles under his boots.

The corridor opened out onto what might have been a loading bay, sunk into the ground. It was full of water now. Jury-rigged machines stood around the reservoir: pipes channelled the water away to be filtered and piped into cans. The walls were covered in lichen.

In the centre of the pool, bobbing on a wooden raft, stood an effigy of some kind of god, perhaps the Emperor. Arms open, face in a broad and empty smile, it greeted him.

Straken took a step forward. Half a dozen guns clattered as they were raised.

They came from the shadows, like animals at feeding time – the monsters, the discarded people, the genetic heretics. Hunched, wide-eyed, as pale as the bellies of fish, the mutants advanced on him. Some held crossbows, others clutched looted guns. One skinny creature raised a spear like a tribal fisherman.

A slight, long-necked person walked from the far end of the room. Smooth-skinned, huge-eyed, it wore a robe made from old sacks. Straken wondered if the thing was male or female. It looked very old.

'You are lost,' the elder said.

Straken shook his head. 'I want to talk to you.'

'No,' said the elder. 'You are lost. Your kind, the soldiers with their guns, the overseers with their whips, as soon as they come here, they are lost. The orks as well. They drown as easily as men.'

Straken looked around. They were, in their own way, adapted to this place. 'I kill orks too.'

The smooth face frowned. 'Lucky you. And then, when all the orks are dead, your lords will send you after us. This place is ours.'

'Yes. That's why we want to leave.'

'Leave? To go?'

'I want to get some people out of here, through your territory. Once we're gone, we'll never come back.'

To Straken's right, one of the mutants gave a low, gurgling laugh. Straken heard the contempt in it.

'The orks want to kill us all,' he said. 'They don't care that you're mutants. They don't give a damn about what you think of the Imperium. You're just another kind of human to them. More people to kill – that's how they see you.'

The elder smiled, without pleasure. 'And how do *you* see us?'

'As someone who can help. Once we're gone, you can do whatever you like. Stay here, if you think you'll live – I won't tell anyone, that's for sure. Run away, if you like. Just let us out, and we'll leave you alone. That's a promise.'

The elder folded its arms. 'And why should I believe you?'

'Because I keep my word.'

Myers and Eiden were on lookout when Straken returned. He pushed the hatch up, and Eiden's lined face glared back at him. The sergeant stuck out a hand, but Straken didn't take it. He could manage fine on his own – and his metal fingers could crush a man's bones.

Straken crouched down and put the hatch back in place. 'Anyone miss me?'

Sergeant Eiden shook his head. His white hair was dusted with grime. 'We told 'em you were busy. And that you wouldn't like being interrupted.' He smiled, revealing chipped and uneven teeth. 'They didn't bother us after that.'

Myers nodded keenly. 'I didn't see nobody,' he said. 'Honest.'

Straken believed him. The gunner might be simple, but he obeyed every order to the letter. 'We're good to go,' he told Eiden. 'Let the others know.'

They climbed the stairs. Straken opened the door, checked that nobody was there, and slipped out. In a side room, Hollister and a Mordian orderly were checking several wounded troopers. The medic looked up as Straken passed. Straken gave him a quick nod, watching as Hollister responded with a grin before getting back to work.

Getting the injured ready to go, Straken realised.

The centre of the building was empty: most soldiers were manning the barricades at either end. Someone had pinned a devotional poster to the wall. The saint gazed out, stern but not angry, sword held out in both hands for the viewer to take.

Montara came to find him, striding across the stone floor. Her combat jacket and trousers, both originally green, were now grey. Even her red bandanna was dusty. 'Any luck, sir?'

'Yes. There's a way through. Any news on the orks?'

She shook her head. 'We've been watching. I sent a few scouts forward. There's no mines, but we've wired up a few tripwires and grenades. Should give us some warning.'

'Good. They'll come.' Straken sighed. 'Seventy years fighting for the Guard. Even after all that time, I'm still sticking the same knife into a bunch of orks.'

'You're complaining, right?'

Straken snorted, amused. 'When the time comes, we'll move out by squad. You take the lead. Head straight down and follow the marks on the walls. In case I'm not with you, you're looking for sub-level Sixty-Eight Gamma. If you see anyone down there – gangs, even mutants – do not open fire. Anyone except orks, of course. Understand?'

'Sure.'

'Good. Take the Catachans first. The Mordians should realise that it's time to head off once we're gone. I'll hang back and make sure they all get out.'

The captain leaned closer. 'Listen, colonel. What are we going to do with the commissar?'

'I'll take care of him.'

Montara's face hardened. 'I'll do it if you want. The way Captain Tanner would have done.' She ran a finger across her throat. 'Commissars.'

He taught you well, Straken thought, and he felt a stab of sadness. Tanner had been a good officer – a great one, even – and a friend. For a second Straken wished that Tanner was still with him, fighting at his side – but then again he didn't, because Tanner was somewhere much better now.

'Get back to the men,' he said. 'Watch for orks. I'll talk

to Commissar Verryn once I've checked my weapons. Last thing I need is my plasma pistol cooking off in the middle of battle.'

The commissar stood on the western barricade, a bolt-gun held ready across his chest. He looked hard and ancient, a man from whom the flesh had withered away. The commissar's profile reminded Straken of a face he'd seen moulded into the cutting edge of an axe. A Chaos cultist had wielded it on a world whose name Straken had long since forgotten.

'Commissar!'

Verryn climbed down to meet Straken.

'Ah, colonel. I was wondering where you'd got to.'

'I was manning the other barricade.'

'Of course. I hear that you did good work repelling the last attack. Your men are a welcome addition.'

Straken hadn't expected that. 'Thanks.'

Verryn smiled. 'It's a pleasure to be fighting beside an expert. Two veterans against the tide, eh?'

Suddenly, Straken understood him. *We are the same, in a way*, Straken thought. *No shrines or statues to remember us, not even children and wives. Once we're dead, all that will remain will be other people's memories.*

Verryn didn't want to die fighting because he was a great commissar, but because his stubbornness had overcome him. To the commissar, retreat, surrender and failure had become the same thing. Anything less than a heroic death would be a defeat.

Straken almost pitied the man. Then he remembered that Verryn's great deed would take hundreds of people down with him.

He said, 'There's still a way out of here, commissar. I found a way down, through the hive–'

'Through the mutants?' Verryn scowled. 'No. A man risks not only his life, but his very soul down there. The place is tainted, colonel. Tainted.' The commissar looked curiously pleased with himself. 'The creatures down there are insane. The touch of Chaos has driven them mad.'

'Chaos? I don't think so. I reckon they just stuck around here too long, commissar.' Straken flexed the fingers of his metal hand. 'Listen. One way or another, we're getting out of here. You can have your last stand, you can go down in all the history books you like, but you're doing it alone.'

'Not alone,' Verryn said. He glanced over Straken's shoulder. Figures moved, not quickly, but coming closer. Big men in dark blue uniforms.

Straken knew that he could take them. But it would be mad to set Catachan against Mordian. The Mordians already regarded Straken's men as wild and ill-disciplined, and that would be proof of their worst suspicions. The Catachans would look like nothing more than bandits to them – and whatever happened then, it would help the orks.

'You see, colonel–' Verryn said, a cruel smile creeping across his lean face, but a voice drowned him out.

'Orks!' a Guardsman screamed from the top of the barricade. 'Orks!'

Straken spun round, away from the commissar. 'To your positions!' he shouted. 'Full alert! Commissar? I'll take the east barricade.'

Yells tore the air. Straken ran back towards his men. Hollister stood in the doorway of the makeshift infirmary, lasgun in his hands. 'Get ready to go,' Straken barked. 'If anyone asks, tell them I said so.' He ran on, weaving down corridors, past soldiers scrambling to man the lines. 'Get moving, Guardsmen! Do I have to do everything myself?'

Orks, he thought, and anger rose in him, fired him like a dog on a scent.

He saw the barricade. Two troopers crouched beside a mortar, ready to lob shells over the wall. Sellen had propped his missile launcher on the parapet. Ferricus crouched next to him, ready to load.

From far away, Straken heard roars and the thumping of heavy boots. Dust trickled from the roof.

Men leaned over the edge of the barricade and pulled up several Catachan scouts.

Straken strode towards them. 'You!' he shouted, pointing. 'How many are there?'

'Hundreds, sir,' the scout replied. 'A whole legion of 'em. They've got big guns, and heavy armour as well.'

'Get ready, then.' Straken climbed up the barricade, over broken furniture and sheets of dented metal. Around him, soldiers checked their guns, loosened their knives in their sheaths. 'Listen! I want none of these scumbags anywhere near this barricade. If you can't hit 'em in the head, take their legs out. Heavy weapons, pick your targets. Shoot the big ones and any special gear they've got. Take out anything that's too thick for a lasgun to go through. Make those shots count, Catachans!'

He paused. The acoustics were bad; it was hard to make out where the orks were, let alone how close they might be.

I could live a thousand years, he thought, *and there would still be orks to kill.*

'I see 'em!' a woman yelled at the far end of the balcony.

'Then what are you waiting for?' Straken roared back. 'Kill them! Kill them all!'

Shadows moved in the dark and the wall came alive in gunfire. For a moment, the dust obscured the orks, and Straken couldn't quite make them out. Then he saw that they were covered in chunks of armour, square plates like paving-slabs. Las-shots ricocheted off the metal. A Mordian blew a hole in the mass of orks, killing one of the beasts, but another alien scrambled over its fallen comrade and advanced. A missile blasted two of the great orks apart in a shower of torn metal and alien flesh, but others rushed to take their place.

This time, the orks didn't sprint at the barricade. Gunfire came from gaps between the armoured bodies: fat bullets ripped through the barricade. A long barrel, drilled with rows of ventilation holes, was thrust between the rows of orks, and high-calibre shells scythed across the parapet. One Mordian was cut in half; a Catachan toppled back, his scalp suddenly red. Worse, soldiers took cover, and as they ducked, the orks closed in.

'Frag grenades!' Straken shouted. 'Aim low!'

His men pulled out their bombs, yanked the pins and hurled them over the parapet. The grenades looked tiny as they hit the walls and ork armour, disappearing from view.

A moment later, he heard the muffled boom of grenades. Orks still roared, but with pain as well as rage. 'Now!' Straken yelled.

They sprang up. The orks had paused; several had fallen. As one, the Guardsmen poured las-fire into the aliens. The corridor strobed with light and drummed with explosions. Orks fell by the dozen. Human voices shouted, cursed and screamed.

Suddenly, there were no more orks to kill. The alien advance was stalled. From beyond, out of view, ork voices called and bellowed.

Other orks answered, and, under them, other creatures. They sounded like grox.

A swarm of bodies dashed around the corner. Red things ran between the orks, no higher than the aliens' knees. They looked the heads of monsters: round creatures that seemed to be nothing but snarling teeth and scrabbling legs.

Squigs, Straken realised, as the lasguns cracked out.

The squigs were much faster than their masters and harder to hit. Straken used his shotgun, brought one down, then another, but a third slipped through. One of the squigs reached the barricade and tried to jump up. Others joined it, and then Straken saw the packs strapped to some of them, the wads of explosive and wires–

'Down!' he cried, and the bomb-squigs detonated.

The barricade burst. Men and women were thrown in all directions. Bodies were ripped apart, soldiers smashed against the roof and walls, Guardsmen stabbed and lacerated by debris. Something crashed into Straken's metal arm and he fell, tumbling down, pieces of the barricade hitting his hip and side like the blows of a club. He struck the ground, rolled onto his front, clambered upright with his ears ringing. He heard snarls from behind, and turned back to see the first ork soldiers tearing through the barricade.

'Fall back!' Straken roared. 'The orks are inside! Fall back!'

They pulled back. The orks swarmed over the barricade. Straken saw Doc Hollister helping two Mordian orderlies carry a wounded Catachan. Myers, the gunner, shouted wordlessly and fired his heavy bolter, blasting orks apart.

Men ran in, Mordians and Catachans. They saw the orks and began firing, using doorways and support joists as cover. Lieutenant Krall was among them, yelling orders and encouragement.

'Montara!' Straken shouted. 'Help the Mordians.'

'What about you?'

Straken drew his plasma pistol. 'I'm getting the commissar.'

The boltgun bucked and shook in Verryn's gloved hands as it punched shells into the ork horde. The aliens had reached the west barricade – partly through covering fire, partly through force of numbers – and they were climbing up faster than they could be shot down. Behind him, someone shouted about the eastern barricade going down. The boltgun ran dry.

This is it, Verryn thought, tearing the magazine out and slapping the last one into place.

'For the saints!' he cried.

Then something huge ran at the barricade, and he knew that this was indeed the end.

It was an ork warboss, twice man-height and wider again, its chest bare, its left leg and lower jaw replaced by crude bionics. It had a chainaxe in one hand and a whirring, oversized buzzsaw in the other.

Lasgun shots hit its warty hide: those that penetrated did not slow it. A grenade blew a hole in the beast's shoulder-armour, revealing pistons inside. The monster waded over and through the barricade, its weight snapping and twisting the defences. Every sweep of its weapons threw soldiers into the air, a bowing wave of mangled bodies.

Verryn sighted the ork and fired.

It threw its arm up, and the bolter shells burst against metal. Stray shells caught the ork's body, wounding and enraging it. The ork's chainaxe clipped a man and threw blood across the ceiling.

'Hold your ground!' Verryn shouted, over the screaming. 'To the death, Guardsmen! Together we–'

His gun ran out. The warboss towered over him, its shadow entirely eclipsing the commissar. The words stopped in his throat.

'Verryn!'

He spun round. Straken ran forward, out of the mayhem behind him, and drew his arm back. He lobbed something – not a grenade, but a gun. 'Use it!'

Verryn snatched the plasma pistol out of the air. The warboss pulled itself over the parapet of the barricade, and then ork and commissar were eye-to-eye.

'Die, filth,' Verryn said, and he pushed the barrel against the ork's forehead.

He pulled the trigger. The gun exploded.

The plasma gun liquefied both the commissar and the warboss's head. The ork toppled forward, collapsed limb by limb, keeling over onto its front. It crashed onto the remains of the barricade. Of Commissar Verryn, there was no recognisable trace.

The battle was over.

Orks lay in heaps and wreckage covered the floor. Amid

the aliens, perhaps one to every seven orks, lay soldiers of the Guard. Some wore blue uniforms, others combat vests and red bandannas. Already the dust was settling on them all.

'They'll be back soon,' Captain Montara said. Her face was grey with dirt.

Straken could taste blood. There was a steady ache in his side that rose and fell with each breath. As he walked it became a sharp pain, jabbing him with every step. He'd felt worse. 'Move out,' he said.

Montara said, 'I'll go and check my team,' and she strode off into the cloud of dust.

A small group of Mordians approached with Lieutenant Krall at the front.

'You're the commanding officer now, colonel,' Krall said. 'I'll have my people ready in ten minutes.'

'Five,' Straken replied. 'We need to move.'

'Yes, sir. I saw what happened back there. To the commissar.' She looked straight at him, but he couldn't read her expression.

Montara took a deep breath. 'Best get moving, then.'

'Yes,' Straken said.

They picked their way through the underhive, boots sloshing through brackish, oil-slicked water, the blue light cold and soft around their faces. Protected by scouts, the Guardsmen carried their wounded, and General Beran, home.

Fresh signs had been painted on the walls, to show the way, but they saw nobody else. The Mordians did not go as quickly as Straken would have hoped, but they were tough and uncomplaining. He glanced back to make sure that no one had lagged behind, and Hollister came hurrying up to talk.

'Damn shame about your plasma pistol, eh?' the medic said, grinning.

'Yeah.'

'An honest mistake,' Hollister replied. 'How were you to know? Some of these plasma weapons are terribly unreliable, I've heard. The machine-spirits, you know.' He peered at Straken, frowning. 'Are you feeling all right, colonel?'

'Fine,' Straken said. 'Let's go.'

BLOODLORD

BRADEN CAMPBELL

The cultists were like an oncoming wall. There must have been two hundred of them. They were armed mostly with laspistols and whatever heavy tools they had scrounged from the city's now abandoned manufactoria. Still, through my magnoculars I could see some scavenged weapons of military grade – grenade launchers and flamers – and the ogryns too. I've always found them revolting, even when they were fighting on our side. These corrupted brutes were even worse. They led the attack, screaming and bellowing like possessed animals, waving axes, hammers and picks. On their heads they wore hoods made of sackcloth with evil sigils painted onto them.

We poured lasfire into them as they came, but it didn't seem to affect them in the least. Even the shells of our heavy autocannons did little to slow them. For the thousandth time since coming to this planet, I wished that we still had at least one operational tank.

To my right, Velez, our primaris psyker, had his eyes squeezed shut and fingers planted forcefully against the side of his head. Tiny arcs of electricity danced across his brow as he surveyed all the possible futures that stemmed from this moment – he didn't look particularly reassured by any of them. On my left, the priest, Lantz, had his arms extended before him, palms open. He chanted loudly for all to hear, crying out for divine deliverance from both the lightning and the tempest. Both of them were Cadians, like myself, and therefore upstanding and capable men in their own right.

'Options?' I barked.

Velez answered first. He opened his eyes and stared at the oncoming mass of corrupted flesh that had once been the good people of the city of Rycklor. 'I recommend we fall back,' he said in his raspy voice.

I agreed completely. Behind us was the bridge, and if we regrouped on the far side then the enemy would be channelled into a compact column which would allow us to concentrate our firepower to greater effect, or failing that, blow the structure out from under them and send the whole lot into the flowing, corrosive acid of the Solray River.

However, before I could open my mouth to order a retreat, Major Leclair appeared by my side. Like the rest of Zhenya's natives, he was pale and blond. His moustache, an affectation worn by all the men on this planet, was so thick that it covered the entirety of his upper lip. His sword was drawn.

'I'm certain I didn't hear that correctly, Captain Kervis,' he said to me. 'We must seize the initiative by charging the enemy ourselves.'

Glancing over my shoulder, I saw that Leclair had assembled all of the remaining members of the Zhen-yan defence force. They had affixed bayonets to the ends of their lasrifles, and their red and blue uniforms stood out in sharp contrast to the bleak emptiness of the surrounding countryside.

'No,' I replied. 'We need to pull back to better ground.' I didn't have time to go over this argument again. On paper Leclair outranked me and oversaw the local militia, whereas I was in charge of an actual regiment of the Astra Militarum. That alone gave me seniority. It had been a contention between us since the day we first arrived on their world. Leclair had expected that we would fill the gaps in his depleted force and not usurp control of it completely.

The major, who had been trained in a comfortable local academy rather than a Whiteshield youth auxiliary program, quoted a passage from the Tactica Imperium: '*The offensive alone can give victory, but the defensive gives only defeat and shame.*'

The Zhenyans nodded, and I heard at least one 'hur-rah' from somewhere nearby.

But I too was familiar with the Astra Militarum's encyclopedia of sage advice: '*If the enemy comes on in a great horde, try to direct them into a narrow defile or enclosed space, so that their numbers work against them...*'

'Yes, yes. I'm familiar with that one,' he replied.

'Then you agree that our priority is to defend this point.'

The corner of Leclair's right eye twitched with disappointment. 'Yes, sir.'

Without another word, and considering the matter closed, I turned and began running down the length of the bridge. Lantz remained almost joined to me at the elbow, and Velez fell in as fast as his left leg would allow. He had broken it during our first campaign together, and the knee joint had never been quite right afterwards. On the far side, behind sandbag barricades, my Cadian brothers and sisters were standing with their weapons at the ready.

'Firing line,' I shouted. 'Form a firing line, on the double!'

The rearguard scrambled into two ranks. Lasgun safeties clicked off in unison. Only when the psyker, the priest and I were safely behind the barricades, did I realize that Leclair and the Zhenyans had failed to follow us.

At the far end of the bridge, Leclair raised his sword towards the cultists. 'For glory and honour!' he cried.

'For Zhenya!' the soldiers yelled, their spirits buoyed up immeasurably by the major's infectious bravado.

They sprinted forwards, blades and rifles held up like spears, with Leclair in the lead, and plowed into the foe. For a moment it seemed as if their exuberance alone would carry the day. They stabbed the ogryns again and again, and pummelled them with the butts of their rifles. Sprays of blood formed a red mist in the air. Then, the hulking creatures roared and struck back. Things went very badly after that.

These ogryns were like nothing I'd ever encountered. Not only did they seem to ignore the multiple, gaping wounds inflicted upon them, but also their already formidable strength seemed to have increased. The ogryns lashed out with their weapons and the bodies of Leclair's men crumpled and fell in an instant. Limbs went cartwheeling through the air, and cries, which moments before had been patriotic, turned bloodcurdling.

Velez gripped his long psyker staff with both hands. The cultists were surging around the ogryns now. They hit Leclair and his men on their flanks, chanting and screaming in tortured tones. Blood drooled from their mouths and turned their eyeballs red, covering their clothing and dripping on the ground.

'Damned fool!' I spat. The major had doomed not only himself but all of his men with his rashness.

I dropped to one knee and unlocked a nearby metal storage box. Inside were a selection of frag grenades, satchel charges and a remote detonator. I withdrew this last item, extended a stubby antenna and let my thumb hover over the single, red button on its side. With the smallest of motions, the explosive compounds wired into the bridge's support structures several months previously were ready to be activated – a contingency against a situation just like this.

Eight months ago, everything in this star system had suddenly fallen apart. Blood-thirsty cults had swept through the cities, and there had been daily mass murders in the agricultural areas. It was an insurrection on a massive scale, and local forces, like Major Leclair's, were quickly overwhelmed. As a result, we, the sons and daughters of Cadia, had been brought in to help restore order. Still, with every battle we fought, the chaos only became compounded. The system's infrastructure had broken down to almost nothing and interplanetary communications were virtually non-existent. We hadn't actually received orders from anyone in system command since last summer, but the commands we did receive had been quite clear. We were told to establish a containment perimeter around the Rycklor manufactorum district, to protect all bridges and roadways leading into and out of said district, to annihilate anything from within the city that attempted to stage a breakout, and to wait for further reinforcements.

Now it was early winter – the ground was hard and jagged and the wind was damp and cold. Thick banks of unnatural, rust-coloured fog roiled in the skies and obscured the city. Reinforcements had yet to appear and supplies were running dangerously low. Still, we held our position as we had been told to do, trusting that a column of Leman Russes would come trundling down the road to lead us to victory. If this bridge disappeared by the time they arrived, our heavy armour could end up stranded on the wrong side of the Solray. More than that, the eventual recapture of the city of Rycklor might be crippled by the loss of a major thoroughfare.

I looked up at Velez. 'Maybe it won't come to this,' I said quietly.

Looking down the bridge once more, I saw that Leclair's men were still alive and fighting valiantly. An impressive number of bodies lay sprawled on the ground at their feet, but it was obvious to me that their cause was lost. They were outnumbered nearly three to one and, what's more, the cultists seemed enraged beyond mortal understanding.

I searched the whirling melee and at last caught a glimpse of a silver sabre as it was thrust through the chest of one of the ogryns. The hulking corpse toppled forward to reveal the major. The hem of his greatcoat was soaked in the blood of traitors and he had taken a nasty wound to his left shoulder, to which he seemed to pay no mind.

I was impressed. Again, he was no Cadian, but his

valour couldn't be denied. It was possible, I thought, that in the years to come his actions here, during the Siege of Rycklor, might find their way into the teaching manuals of the Departmento Munitorum.

Another of the ogryns rose up behind him, its face covered by some kind of metal plate or welder's mask, and in its hands it carried what appeared to be the bottom half of a street sign or lamppost with a chunky wad of rockcrete at one end. He hefted this impromptu club over one shoulder and swung it with all his might, striking Major Leclair in the side of the head. The handsome face was obliterated, and his body fountained blood before it collapsed to the ground.

The Zhenyans had failed. Now, it was up to us.

'When they funnel down the deck of that bridge,' I shouted, 'open fire and don't stop until I say so. First rank, take aim. Second rank, at the ready.'

Our priest unchained a thick tome from his belt, opened its yellowed pages and began to read aloud. I recognised the passage at once as being taken from the Book of Saint Ollanius, the patron saint of the Astra Militarum.

'Let me preach His name!' he cried out. 'Praise be to the Emperor, who trains my hands for war, my fingers for battle.'

At the end of the bridge, the last of Leclair's men cried out and fell in a heap. The cultists cheered and began to surge towards us. The remaining ogryns were in the lead, once more acting as living shields for the rest. I watched them rush headlong towards us, becoming dimly aware of a high-pitched howling in the distance.

'Part the heavens, Lord, and come down. Touch the mountains, so that they smoke. Send forth lightning and scatter our enemy.'

I raised my free hand and clutched the detonator tightly with the other. 'First rank, fire!'

With a loud crack, twenty-five beams of searing light struck the brutes. Two of the monsters stumbled and fell face first onto the bridge deck plating. The cultists scrambled over their dead bodies.

'Reach down your hand from on high...'

'Second rank, fire!'

Twenty-five more shots struck the oncoming foe. Another ogryn went down, steam escaping from the holes in his chest. Still, the horde kept coming and the howling sound grew louder.

'Intercede on our behalf...'

'Fire at will!'

My soldiers loosed a last, desperate volley that felled one more of the ogryn. By my count there were still nine left, and behind them perhaps three times our number in cultists. We were about to be overrun.

I put my thumb on the detonator.

'And from the deadly peril, deliver us,' Lantz concluded.

'Look!' Velez cried. He was pointing at something in the sky behind me. I whirled around.

A transport ship, resembling nothing so much as a flying brick, had broken through the sickly-coloured clouds and descended towards us. Its wings spanned nearly thirty meters and its hull was painted flat black. It had massive, twin engines mounted on each side, and at the back sprouted a stubby tail with dual stabilizers. As it grew closer, the screaming sound became a thunderous roar, and I could just make out white panels on its sides. Another, smaller brick was fastened to its underbelly, secured in place by six, segmented, mechanical arms.

Realization hit, leaving me speechless – you hear stories about such things, but you never really expect it to happen. Yet, there it was: a Thunderhawk. The Space Marines were coming to save us.

The transport suddenly tilted its nose up, and a blast of heated air washed over the land. Clumps of frozen dirt and debris swirled everywhere. I threw an arm across my eyes, struggling to watch as the titanic machine glided overhead, covering us with its shadow. The thing nestled underneath it was a wide, tracked vehicle with weapon mountings on either side. I blinked as I realised that it could only be a Land Raider.

Velez was just as dumbstruck as I, and Lantz had dropped his book of sacred verse and stood with arms spread wide. He grinned like an idiot, mouthing words that were impossible to hear over the Thunderhawk's turbines.

I tore my attention away and glanced down the bridge. At the sight of this incredible intervention, the cultists had finally stopped their murderous charge. They stood frozen near the midpoint of the bridge and watched as the transport's six mechanical arms suddenly flicked open. The Land Raider dropped onto the deck, its mass so great that the rockcrete beneath its treads cracked and splintered. Then, its engine came to life and it began to rumble forwards. With its role complete, the Thunderhawk rocketed back into the rusty clouds, leaving twisted contrails in its wake.

The mass of former factory workers began to back away from the Land Raider's implacable advance, but the ogryns showed a stunning lack of fear. The brute that had killed Major Leclair raised his massive cudgel.

'Blood for the Blood God,' he cried, and struck the tank's forward hull.

There was a resounding clang, and I saw the rockcrete at the base of the pole shatter into powder. Unaffected, the Land Raider repaid the fellow's heresy by grinding him into mush beneath its treads. The other five were bowled over the guardrails where they splashed into the green sludge of the river.

The Space Marines had replaced their tank's lascan-nons with an assembly of boltguns, rigged to fire in unison. The sound was indescribable, and it roused not only myself, but also Lantz, Velez and the others out of our stupor. I took my thumb away from the detonator button and put the device back into the lock box. The sight of the Land Raider effortlessly pushing back the cultists brought on a heady enthusiasm.

'Fall in behind that tank,' I shouted. 'Re-establish the line at the other end of the bridge. Support for the Space Marines on my order.'

'Onward!' Lantz shouted. He leapt over the sandbag wall with the agility of a man half his age and began run-ning madly after the Land Raider. 'Lend assistance to the Emperor's Angels of Death!'

The massive machine was nearly across the bridge by the time we caught up to it. The cultists, whose numbers had been greatly thinned by the firepower of the Space Marines, were once again on open ground. They were about to break and flee back into Rycklor, when the Land Raider suddenly stopped.

For a split second the world was still. Then, the front of the machine opened up, dropping its assault ramp amidst the bodies of the slain. Panels on either side of the entryway exploded outwards, spraying the cultists with jagged shards of shrapnel, and from the inside of the cavity, Space Marines strode out into the pale, morning light.

There were sixteen of them. Like their tank, the armour they wore was primarily black with patches of white, but there appeared to be different styles between them. Their leader clad in a baroque suit with a high collar and a long, flowing cloak carried a shield the size of a dinner table, and a hammer that crackled with a nimbus of destructive energy. Behind him were eight who wore the iconic power armour of the Adeptus Astartes – impossibly heavy and with massive, rounded shoulder plates. They carried boltguns festooned with purity seals and strips of parchment. And then, crouched low, came seven burly men in a lighter kind of combat dress that was not too different from my carapace armour. They too wielded boltguns.

Did this indicate differing levels of rank or achievement? Were we looking at a single unit, or some kind of mixed formation? I had no way of knowing for certain; the doctrines of the Space Marines are unknown and inscrutable to persons such as myself. In truth, it mattered very little.

The corrupted citizens rallied and charged. I don't know why – they might have been suddenly encouraged by their superior numbers, or perhaps their so-called blood god spurred them on. My guess is the latter, because within a few seconds, there was blood everywhere.

The Space Marines received the charge by firing their boltguns. Explosive shells tore limbs from torsos, heads from necks and cut some of the cultists clean in half. Their leader used his shield to smash three of the burly men into heaps of meat and broken bone before swinging his hammer in a wide horizontal arc to decapitate two others. The ground was covered in crimson, too frozen to soak up even the smallest amount of gore. It pooled around the Space Marines' feet and sprayed across the white patches of their armour.

Through it all, the mob fought back, refusing to flee even when it became apparent that they were going to lose. It seemed their god had sent them on a suicide mission.

The five ogryns that had fallen off the bridge hauled themselves up from out of the river. Their massive weapons remained intact, even though their cloth hoods and ragged clothing had all dissolved in the toxic sludge. Their skin was now a sickly green colour in the places where it was not falling off entirely. How they were still alive, let alone hungry for combat, was a miracle.

The Space Marines whirled around to face this new threat. Boltguns were of no use at such close range, so they slashed and stabbed their attackers with knives the size of short swords. I saw one of the ogryn lifelessly slide beneath the surface of the river. The others, however, refused to die and struck back with fury.

Their blows were harmlessly absorbed or deflected by the Space Marines' armour, save for an enormous pick-axe that flew up and shattered the helmet of one of the suits. I saw the Space Marine stumble backwards from the force of the blow, falling onto his back in a puddle of blood.

The Space Marines had their backs to the mob of cultists and now faced a battle on two fronts, something wholly unacceptable. I ordered my shock troops to join in the fray and they happily obliged. Frustrated, cold and hungry, they unleashed all their pent-up frustration on the cultists, using the butts of their lasguns to knock out teeth and break noses. When one of the enemy fell or doubled over, they finished the wretch with the steel toes of their boots. It was a brutal, horrible scene that had more in common with a street brawl than a military counter-attack.

At once I fell back into familiar motions of cut, thrust, and parry. Several of the cultists I killed were nondescript, their features lost in a blur of kill-or-be-killed. I do recall a middle-aged man with a scraggly beard though, only because his neck geysered like a waterfall as I dragged my blade across it. As he went down, I caught a glimpse of the Space Marines' leader.

He was using his shield to protect the fallen, helmetless comrade, while beating at the ogryn with his unwieldy hammer; there was a sound like thunder and a flash of light every time the weapon found its mark. The ogryn took three blows to the chest – the last of which sent him flying backwards into the river once and for all. The remaining ogryns blinked as if blinded, shaking their heads, and the Space Marines finished them with no further incident to themselves.

Likewise, our fight against the cultists drew to a hasty conclusion. From somewhere on my left, a young woman drove a club into my ribs. My armour dulled most of the pain, but the impact left me gasping for breath. Spinning around, I kicked her legs out from under her and thrust my sword through her heart before she could get back up. I sprang back and searched for another target, only to find none.

Of the fifty soldiers I had started with, I counted

thirty-two still alive. We were surrounded by a sea of destroyed bodies and congealing gore. Velez was a slight distance away, leaning heavily against one of the bridge's support columns, and several dead cultists were heaped before him.

'It's a sign,' he said, as if reading my thoughts.

My boots made squishing sounds as I approached him. 'Velez, don't be paranoid. There's a lot of it, sure, but it's just blood.'

'Is it, Olen? Is it?' Forgoing both my rank and last name, he tapped his staff against one of the corpses at his feet. The chest was covered by a pair of circles, nearly inter-twined, that appeared to have been burned directly onto the skin.

'A brand of some kind?'

Velez seemed to consider how to reply. He was sweat-ing despite the cold, his gaze drifting over the scene and coming to rest on the Space Marines. 'I can't yet say for certain. But they didn't arrive just to help us, I promise you that.'

The Space Marine leader was kneeling beside the one who had taken the severe blow to the head. He set his hammer and shield down and removed the helmet of his armour, revealing skin the colour of old leather. His nose was his most prominent feature – wide and flat, as if it had been broken and reset innumerable times – and his brow was creased with worry.

The scene was an oil painting come to life, worthy of immortalization in the stained glass or vaulted ceiling of any cathedral. Lantz must have thought so as well.

'Would that I had the means to capture this moment,' he said loudly.

The faces of all sixteen Space Marines shot up to glare at him in unison. Velez closed his eyes and sighed as I darted forwards.

'I think what he means is that we are very, very grateful for your help. Isn't that right, Lantz?' I replied.

'To have the Emperor's Angels of Death stand with us, to be allowed to fight at their side, is an honour none here deserve,' Lantz continued, even louder this time.

The leader rose. 'Angels of Death,' he repeated. His face showed no emotion, but the tone of his voice held a hint of amusement. Reaching down, he helped the fallen Space Marine to his feet. Two of the others retrieved his shield, hammer and helmet. He took the helmet first and passed it to the man who no longer had one, then calmly rearmed himself. 'I am looking for Captain Olen Kervis, Cadian Guard, Twenty-Eighth Regiment.'

I instinctively snapped to attention. 'Reporting... Sir, my lord? I'm sorry, I have no idea how I'm supposed to address you.'

'I am Isaias, Castellan of the Black Templars.' His rank meant nothing to me, but it sounded very impressive. 'Captain, you are currently overseeing the command of a number of native Zhenyans.'

'A local force regiment, yes.'

'I require use of them,' he said.

One of my junior officers, a sergeant named Crowell, stepped forward. Her violet-coloured eyes darted nervously at the Templars before she shook her head at me. Leclair's sword rested across her outstretched arms.

'Castellan, I regret to inform you the last of the local soldiers have all died in combat against the enemy.'

Isaias frowned in silent tableau for a moment. Sickly

clouds swallowed the sun once more, and the wind picked up, whistling through the superstructure of the bridge. 'Then, you and your men will come with us. Now.'

'Castellan,' I said cautiously, 'we have orders to protect this bridge and to keep the enemy bottled up in Rycklor until a relief force arrives. Are you that force?'

'We are not.'

'Then, I'm sorry, but I cannot abandon this post.'

He blinked several times, which I presume is the reaction a Space Marine makes when he is confused or in a state of disbelief.

'Yes?' I finally asked.

'One does not say no to the Angels of Death, Kervis,' Lantz hissed.

'I'm not going before a court martial for dereliction of duty,' I said. 'No one here is.'

Isaias raised his chin. 'Your commitment is well placed, captain, but you mistake a command for a request.'

Velez had been correct. There was an agenda at work here and we were to play some part in it.

'Why? What could Space Marines possibly need our help with?'

Again, there was a moment of strained silence punctuated only by the winter wind.

'We are going into Rycklor,' Isaias finally said.

This statement caused a stir. No one had gone into the city for months. It was firmly in the hold of renegades, cultists and, it was whispered, horrific monsters that could strip the flesh from a man in seconds.

'Normally,' Isaias continued, 'we would use teleport homing beacons or orbital drop pods in a situation such as this. However, Rycklor is blanketed by a fell miasma.'

I didn't recognize the term. It sounded arcane and otherworldly. 'By a what?'

Isaias turned towards the city. From here it appeared as a jumbled collection of dark shapes through thick fog that hung over it like a death shroud.

'Ah, yes, that. It's been there ever since we arrived,' I said. 'The forces couldn't maintain their hold and had to abandon it. They told us that not long after, this... fog... billowed up and smothered it. It's spreading across the countryside now, but we've never been able to formerly identify it. Maybe a nerve agent or chemical weapon?'

'Nothing so mundane. It does, however render the city-scape immune to our augur arrays. Without accurate targeting data, we must instead enter the city by using *Integuma*,' he said, casting a glance at the Land Raider.

Thinking that I knew what the Space Marines were after, I snapped my fingers and held out a hand. Crowell read the gesture intuitively, handed Leclair's sword to Lantz and produced a field map from her kit. She unfolded the wrinkled paper and gave it to me, revealing a rough map of Rycklor compiled from the descriptions of local soldiers.

'I can offer you this,' I said, holding the map towards Isais. 'We made it for the day long-range artillery would arrive. I can't vouch for it entirely, though. It's based on a lot of conjecture and is likely months out of date.'

'We have no need for your maps,' Isaias said. 'You will guide us safely to our destination.'

'Which is?' I asked.

'The Verevya Basilica.'

I removed my hat and vigorously scratched the top of my head. On the map, Verevya Basilica was located near the centre of the city on an artificial island created by several intersecting canals. What the Templars were asking us – telling us – to do was reasonable from a tactical standpoint. Even a machine as impenetrable as the Land Raider could find itself crippled by a single well-placed explosive device, especially since the mysterious fog rendered augurs all but unusable. Our job would be to clear a path for it by finding and eliminating such potential traps, as well as any enemies that might be lying in wait. The journey would not be long, but it would be fraught with danger.

I put my hat back on and called to the sergeant. As she snapped a salute, her eyes darted nervously toward Isaias. 'Sir?'

'Sergeant, I want you to gather up twelve men and form a squad. Repair our barricades, and get the autocannons cleaned and reloaded. You're in charge of defending this bridge now.'

Crowell nodded. 'And the bodies, sir?'

'Gather up the ones that are ours and form a burial detail. Burn the rest.'

Crowell saluted once again and left to carry out her orders. I turned back to Isaias.

'I'll leave a token force here,' I said. 'That means I can give you two full squads of shock troops, plus myself, the priest and our psyker. Will that be enough?'

'It will suffice.'

I called Velez to come up. There were weapons and lasgun powerpacks scattered among the dead cultists that we could put to use, and I intended him to oversee this unpleasant duty. But the second he limped to my side, I saw Isaias' face tighten and give Velez a burning, hate-filled stare. He actually growled at him.

Velez kept his eyes on the ground and began chewing on his lower lip. His mysterious abilities had always been an issue within our regiment. Everyone made certain to steer clear of him, and no one besides myself placed any real amount of trust in him. He was given the same regard that one might give an unexploded bomb: it was safe for the time being but could go off at any time, and when that happened it was best to be at a safe distance.

This was something more, though. Isaias's eyes burned with enmity, not suspicion. Velez withered under the Templar's gaze as I gave him orders to secure any extra weapons and ammunition he could find.

'Especially flamers,' I said. 'I know I saw a few.'

'Yes, sir,' he muttered.

'I can give you fifteen minutes, at most. Get whatever you need and meet back here.'

'No,' Isaias said. '*It* is not coming with us.'

I caught the full implication of the impersonal pronoun. 'I wouldn't dare go into the city without him,' I replied. 'He's a diviner. He's our help in avoiding traps and ambushes, just as he's always been.'

'A psyker is a gateway to things and powers that you could not begin to comprehend. Margh will easily tempt him into destruction.'

I had no idea who or what Isaias was referring to, but I was determined to take Velez with us into Rycklor. 'He bears the symbols of Imperial conditioning and carries the staff of a registered psyker. That's not assurance enough for you?'

Isaias stared at me for a moment, and I did my best not to whither beneath his icy gaze. 'If time were not against us, I would leave the lot of you here and find others to guide us,' he said, plodding back into the gaping maw of the Land Raider. The other Templars fell in behind him without so much as a word.

Lantz scowled at me. 'You forget yourself, captain. We are all servants of the Emperor, but the Angels of Death are closer to His divinity than mortal men. They are to be obeyed, not argued with.'

'Sir,' Velez said quietly, 'I agree. You should have let it go.'

'Probably. But if we're going into the city, then I want every possible protection.'

On the horizon, the dark spires of Rycklor looked like the jagged teeth of a colossal monster lying in wait to swallow us whole.

The journey down the highway was uneventful. The sky remained threatening and sickly, and the wind blew steadily across the empty plain. Lantz, Velez, and I walked along together while *Integuma* rumbled a short distance behind us. Up ahead, my men moved in a loose formation across the width of the road. Two of them carried flame throwers they had ripped from the dead hands of the cultists. Trooper Medrano, the youngest member of our platoon, had been entrusted with a vox-caster, one of only two communication arrays we had left. I considered taking the three grenade launchers we had discovered, but in the end left them with Sergeant Crowell. If our mission into Rycklor succeeded only in stirring up the crazed and mutated inhabitants, allowing them to stream out of the ruins like a swarm of angry hornets, she would need them more than me in order to keep that bridge in Imperial hands.

As we neared the city, the dark orange mist – the miasma, Isaias had called it – thickened. It pooled in low places, such as the bomb craters and wrecked vehicles that littered the roadside, and clung to our ankles with wispy tendrils. It smelled of copper and made our eyes water and turn bloodshot. The backs of our throats swelled until it became painful to swallow. Three of the troopers developed nosebleeds, while others began to sporadically cough. Worst of all, it reduced our visibility greatly.

We came to the outermost defence wall. Huge pieces of rockcrete had fallen from its top or been blown out of Rycklor's external facing. The highway dipped downward into a wide tunnel, filled with swirling banks of gas. We closed up the distance between ourselves and began to head under the wall. Four of the men lit flares that bathed the tunnel with wavering orange light and phantom shapes. The security checkpoints were empty, the gun emplacements were rusted and abandoned – it was a perfect spot for an ambush, and sure enough, within moments we encountered our first trap.

It was what we Cadians call an EFP – an explosively formed penetrator – and was little more than a sheet of plasteel lying on the ground. Underneath it was a canister tightly packed with explosives. If *Integuma* had gone over the plate the detonator would have been triggered, and the plasteel sheet would have rocketed upwards into the tank at several times the speed of sound. Sergeant Ingram, who had the steadiest nerves of any man I'd ever known, disarmed the device and placed the canister into his shoulder bag for safekeeping.

The road pitched upward and we emerged on the other

side of the wall. The wind had vanished and a light snow fell, stained an awful colour by the miasma. Before us lay an open area, filled with abandoned vehicles, and beyond that a cluster of dead trees. We made our way carefully between the vehicles, scanning for tripwires or pressure plates. *Integuma* emerged from the mouth of the tunnel exit and lurched forward, loudly crushing a dozen groundcars beneath its tread as it went.

I rubbed my burning eyes. 'You know, at first I was overjoyed at the thought of having a tank on our side – an honest-to-Terra tank – but this is ridiculous.'

'Every wretched soul in this city is going hear us coming for miles,' Ingram replied.

I fully agreed. The Land Raider was an immensely powerful weapon to have on one's side, but it was also a fire magnet. We had to increase our distance from it without completely isolating it either.

Although I hated to reduce our small number any further, I ordered Ingram to take half the men to form a scout unit. Composed of the fastest runners, I made certain that they travelled light and leave the excess gear to the rest of us.

I unfolded our hand drawn map and smoothed it across the hood of the groundcar. Ingram and I studied it for several minutes, tracing paths through the maze of streets with our fingers. We discounted several possibilities before deciding on a tentative route. Ingram took the paper and left with the scouts.

Slowly we crept towards the cathedral at the centre of Rycklor, and the orange fog grew worse. Crumbled buildings and heaps of rubble leapt into clarity as we came upon them, fading into nonexistence as soon as we passed. We could see no more than half a block in any direction. For the most part, the only sounds were our footsteps as we made our way through the deepening drifts and the distant thrum of *Integuma*'s engine. Sometimes a sudden screech or the grinding of metal on metal would break the silence, but we could never find its source.

We were passing by a shattered storefront when we heard the sound of crunching glass and boots scrabbling over stones. All of the Guardsmen pulled their lasguns up into firing position, and I drew my pistol. Around the corner, came one of the forward scouts. At the sight of our weapons, he skidded to a halt. Wide-eyed and gasping for breath, he made a flailing gesture, pointing towards something down an adjacent street.

I understood at once. Lighting a flare, I dropped it into the intersection to show the Space Marines our whereabouts and gestured to the scout. 'Show us,' I said.

He led us back around the corner and down a narrow, two-laned side street. When this opened up into a circular area, he stopped, bent over with his hands on his knees, and gulped for air. The other members of the scouting party stood nearby. Their faces were pale.

'We thought you should see this, sir,' one of them said to me.

In the middle of the roundabout was a fluted column three metres tall, atop which the image of some long-dead Imperial nobleman had once stood. The statue now lay toppled in the street, face down and partially buried in the snow. In his place, someone or something had built a pyramid of corpses. In the heap, I could make out men and women, young and old, dark skinned and fair. Once citizens of Rycklor, loyal servants of the Imperium, they were now a grotesque monument to evil. Their arms, legs and bodies were held together by the frozen blood of a thousand wounds. Crimson icicles stretched down to the ground and fused into pools. But that wasn't the worst part.

'They... they have no...Where are the heads?' I finally managed to say.

'Not here, sir,' Sergeant Ingram said through a clenched jaw. 'We looked.'

Lantz began to pray softly that the Emperor would take the souls of these unfortunates into His care. A few others began to join him.

'Velez,' I said, my gaze still locked on the obscenity before me, 'does this mean anything to you?'

The psyker limped to the base of the column, slipped on a pool of frozen blood, regained his balance and gripped the frigid stone. He closed his eyes and the muscles in his cheeks twitched.

Velez yanked his hand away from the column. 'Captain, we are in critical danger here.'

Before he could elaborate, we were bathed in a brilliant light. The Land Raider had turned the corner, and was slowly crawling towards us. Lamps mounted above its track assemblies cast everything in shades of white. The machine ground to a halt, and the forward ramp dropped open with a loud clang.

Castellan Isaias came clomping toward us. I wanted to ask him if the Space Marines knew anything of being subtle or inconspicuous, but decided against it. The Templar leader was still helmetless, and his eyes narrowed as he surveyed the hideous monument.

'Emperor as my witness, I will repay Samnang Margh for this a hundred-fold,' he said, breathing thick clouds in the frigid air. Then, he raised his voice to address us. 'There is no time for rest. We will soon lose what little daylight we have. How close are we to the basilica?'

Ingram answered. 'It's not far now. To the west there's a canal. We go over that, then cut through Bivin Park. The church is across the street from there.'

Velez touched my sleeve. 'Captain, I still have to advise against going any farther.'

'Keep your intuitions to yourself, psyker!' Isaias barked. 'We've no need of them here. To abandon us in this mission is to admit defeat, and to admit defeat is to blaspheme against the Emperor.'

Lantz apparently agreed with the Space Marine leader, and wanted him to know so. 'Indeed, captain. If there is a weakening of morale here, it is because of your undermining opinions, Velez. We have our faith and the Emperor's own angels to watch over us. With those two things, we shall not want.'

At these words, the men regained some of their fortitude. A few of them even nodded grimly. Medrano cracked his knuckles, like a brawler spoiling for a fight. I had no doubt that a great danger lay ahead of us, just as Velez had said.

I motioned to the two men carrying flamers to set the headless pile ablaze. Streams of burning promethium shot forth and filled the plaza with the stink of roasting flesh.

'Let's move out,' I said.

Satisfied, Isaias began to walk back to his transport. Velez, used to being a pariah, silently endured the scowls and whispers directed at him and headed down the street.

'We'll just finish this and get the hell out of here,' I said to him, meaning it to be conciliatory.

Three times we found our path blocked by collapsed buildings and heaps of impassable rubble, and four times we encountered explosive traps designed to gut the belly of any troop transport. We were forced to backtrack and search for alternate routes. I grew more and more frustrated as the hours slipped past and the shadows grew longer. Finally, we passed through a massive manufactorum that had been gutted by fire. The roof was completely gone, save for a blackened, skeletal support beam and sagging catwalks. Snow covered the silent hulks of machines, whose purposes I could not even guess, and the sound of *Integuma*'s engine reverberated off of the bare brick walls.

The forward squad stopped. Sergeant Ingram waved for me to come join them. Next to a conveyor belt, where the wind was unable to disturb them, a series of footprints were pressed into a snowdrift. They had two large front toes and one behind. From the depth of them, the creature that made them was very heavy.

'Could be dogs,' Ingram said hopefully.

'Have you heard any wild dogs since we've been here?' I scowled.

Ingram muttered something insubordinate in reply that I didn't catch. We each peered about. Nothing moved in the shadows or the clinging fog, and yet the feeling that we were being watched was unshakable.

Outside the building was a neighbourhood of narrow hab-blocks separated by alleyways. The street contracted to the point where the Land Raider's tracks crumpled the pavement and its side sponsons scraped against the fronts of the buildings. We were forced to alter our formation into a long column.

Three blocks remained until we came to the canal, and the cold was increasing as the afternoon waned. Trooper Medrano was walking not more than five steps ahead of me, his shoulders hunched and head down. Many of the men, Medrano included, had insufficient winter gear, and were having to make do with multiple layers of clothing beneath their flak armour. As an officer I was slightly better off, and thought about offering him the use of my gloves, when something hulking and red shot out of the tiny side street to my right. There was a hot rush of foul-smelling air. Medrano made a sharp gasp, and then he was gone. Something had snagged him and then vanished down the alleyway on the left, trailing blood as it went. The tracks it had made in the snow were the same as those I had seen in the manufactorum.

Ingram broke formation and ran to the mouth of the alley. It was pitch black, but he was determined to charge in, regardless. I caught his arm before he could go any farther.

'No, don't!' I barked.

'Medrano!' Ingram shouted. Additional hands clasped his shoulders, dragging him back towards the street.

'He's gone, trooper,' I yelled. 'And if you go charging after him, you will be too. What were you thinking?'

There was a scream from somewhere nearby, followed by a baleful, undulating howl.

Then silence.

The men holding Ingram back tentatively released their

grasp. He let out a long exhalation and said, 'Sir, he had the vox-caster.'

It took a moment for this to sink in. There could now be no contact with Sergeant Crowell back at the bridge and no calling for aid or reinforcements. We were completely cut off from the outside world. My hands balled themselves into fists, and before I knew it, I was cursing Medrano's name. How could he be so stupid as to let himself be snatched away like that? How could he have let his guard down?

'Captain!' Lantz shouted.

But as quickly as the rage had came over me, it suddenly passed.

Everyone was staring. I removed my hat and squeezed my eyes shut. What was happening? We were Cadians, damn it. We didn't suffer fits of rage, shaken nerves, and internal squabbling that so often plagued other, less-disciplined regiments. If we were going to survive whatever it was that the Space Marines had dragged us into, we would have to stay united and strong. We would also have to get out of the city before we ended up turning on each other.

'Did anyone see it?' I asked.

'I did,' one of the men said. 'It had four legs, captain, and red skin.'

'It was... terrible,' said another.

Lantz had opened his tome of sacred writings and read from it in a subdued voice. 'Where the Ruinous Powers are made manifest, there are the nightmares of men given form. When you find yourself in such a place, pilgrim, cling steadfast to the Emperor's light, for truly you walk among daemons.'

He closed the book with a dramatic thunk and no one spoke for several seconds. What more was there to say? *Integuma* drew steadily closer. I put my hat back on, and we continued once more. With every pace, every shadow that wavered, we expected the creature to return. But it didn't.

Moments later, we entered onto a broad avenue hedged by low, rockcrete security barriers. A canal ran parallel to it. There was a curved stone bridge nearby, and a small forest of ashen, barren trees beyond it. Whatever lay past it was lost in drifting curtains of snow and fog.

I stopped dead in my tracks. On the far side of avenue was a pair of Chimeras painted in the colours of the Zhen-yan militia, fitted for urban combat with extra armour mounted on their hulls and a dozer blade attached to the front. One had smashed through part of the retaining wall and come to rest at a sharp incline, never to move again. The other was simply stopped in the middle of the street. Their hulls bore dozens of dents and burn marks and their rear access doors were open to the elements. Nearly two dozen headless bodies lay nearby. Their weapons were nowhere to be seen.

I signalled my men to crouch down. It had all the hallmarks of being a trap, and yet there was a very real possibility that the two abandoned personnel carriers contained vital supplies. My stomach growled at the thought of ration packs, candied energy bars or grox jerky. They might contain medi-packs, pain killers and healing elixirs, and there was still a cosmically remote chance that the Chimera sat in the open was still operational.

Sergeant Ingram was crouched down on my left and Velez was behind me on the same side.

'Thoughts?' I asked.

'Bit too good to be true,' Ingram said, 'but there might some materiel inside we could use.'

'Officer thinking, Ingram. Velez?'

'I don't know.'

They were three words that I'd never heard from him. 'What do you mean, you don't know? You can see the future.'

The pupils of his eyes had reduced to tiny circles of black. 'All I see is an unholy man standing in a once holy place. There is nothing except for him and all probability is drowned out by his rage.'

'What... what are you talking about?' I recalled the whispered name that Isaias had sworn his hundred-fold vengeance upon. 'Samnang Margh. Does that mean anything to you?'

Velez didn't have an answer. He seemed lost, taken hostage by something only he was privy to. I actually thought, however brief, that I would have to perform a commissar's work right then and there, shooting Velez through the temple for his own good.

The Land Raider was a block behind us. I realised something was waiting for us up ahead; something so terrible that it required the attention of the Space Marines. My self-preservation instincts kicked into overdrive and, suddenly, I had never wanted so badly to be ensconced behind walls of plasteel. I drew my laspistol.

'Ingram, you see that Chimera closest to us, the one in the middle of the street?'

'Yes, sir.'

'I want it. Pick a small team to check out the other one. Everyone else, stay here and provide cover.'

The sergeant brought three of his scouts, and together we dashed across the wide street. Ingram and I stepped around the decapitated, frozen bodies and entered the first transport. The hatch leading up into the top-mounted turret hung open, its insides painted with blood. The tiny storage lockers along the walls had been thoroughly ransacked. The floor of the rear section was littered with empty food tins, drained lasgun power packs and crumpled pieces of paper. I picked one of the pages up; it was from an Imperial Infantryman's Uplifting Primer, a copy of which I hadn't seen since leaving Cadia. The 'Prayer for the Lost and Endangered' stared back at me. I crumpled it back up and stuffed it in my coat pocket.

In times of trial, some men find their convictions increase. Others see them crushed beneath a weight of suffering. Lantz was one of the former. I was not.

Sergeant Ingram had gone into the pilot's compartment. After a moment he returned, shaking his head. 'The controls seem fine, sir, but the fuel reserves are dry. I'd guess that's why it stopped here in the first place.'

'No medical supplies, either,' I grumbled, kicking one of the empty tins out into the street. 'No food. No help.'

As we exited the Chimera, I looked down at the nearest corpse. It was sitting upright with something metallic clenched in its right hand. I knelt down and discovered that it was a silver igniter. I yanked it free, noting with satisfaction that it was finely engraved with the crest of the Zhenyan forces, and wondered if the dead soldier might have tabac or perhaps a pipe on his person. Throne, it had been seasons since I'd had a good smoke. Having disturbed it, the body slowly tipped over. Something made a distinct pinging sound. Ingram shouted and grabbed me by the shoulders, flinging me to the side just as something exploded.

I had worried that the depraved occupiers of Rycklor would trap the vehicles. I should have known that they would instead, trap the corpses of the fallen. It's what we Cadians informally call a 'road kill bomb'.

I felt the wave of heat that pushed me through the air. Skidding across the frozen pavement, I struck something. Filthy snowflakes were falling into my eyes. I wanted to brush them away, but my arms refused to obey. My ears were ringing and my cry for help came out as little more than a croak.

I felt frantic hands reach under me, carrying me somewhere, and then just as quickly, set me down again. A face swam in front of mine. After what felt like an eternity, I recognized it as belonging to one of Sergeant Ingram's scouts. He was mouthing words, looking very concerned. The scout tore open a square paper package and pressed a field compress to my forehead. The sharp tang of medical elixirs filled my nose.

'Where did you find this?' I finally slurred, but my would-be physician was gone. I looked around and discovered that I was alone inside one of the Chimeras. I began to make out the sounds of shouting and lasgun fire. After two tries, I managed to get up onto my feet and remain vertical. Stumbling to the rear hatch, I looked outside.

Eight creatures were attacking my men. They looked like giant, hairless dogs with red, blistered skin and pale horns protruding from their backs. Thick brass collars were cinched around their powerful necks, and their eyes glowed with supernatural hate.

They had charged towards the Chimeras in a tightly-formed pack, only to be intercepted by Velez, Lantz and the others. A stream of promethium set one of the monsters on fire, but it remained undeterred. I saw the psyker and the priest fighting side by side, their differences momentarily put aside in the face of this shared danger.

There was a flurry of teeth and claws, then six Guardsmen lay dead, their blood staining the freshly fallen snow. Velez motioned for the men to fall back and regroup closer to the Chimeras. The daemonic hounds charged again, but this time Velez was ready for them. The two flamers played back and forth, creating a wall the creatures had no choice but to move through. They leapt through the fires, their skin blackening, and were hit with a point-blank volley of lasfire. Three of the hounds appeared to explode in a shower of bone fragments and quivering chunks of flesh. The remaining five tore into their targets with teeth the size of my hand.

Before I understood what was happening I was running out into the melee, weapons drawn. Lantz belonged more in an abattoir than a pulpit as he used a massive chainsword to carve up any of the creatures that came within his reach.

I helped the priest dispatch the last two monsters. Like all the others, they detonated into gristly pieces as soon as the twisted life force that drove them was extinguished. Small shards of bone embedded themselves in our armoured chest plates.

We stood triumphant, but the skirmish had taken the lives of six more of Cadia's finest. 'Ingram!' I called. The effort made my head pound.

Lantz looked grim. 'Taken into the Emperor's glory,' he said.

'The bodies of the Zhenyans,' I said. 'They were trapped.'

'We saw,' Velez added. 'He pushed you aside and took the brunt of the blast. He might have been all right still if he hadn't had that canister of explosives in his pack.'

'We moved you to safety, but the noise brought these daemons out of hiding,' Lantz said.

'Where the hell are the Space Marines?' I shouted.

As if in reply, *Integuma* slowly turned the corner.

One of Ingram's scouts stepped forward. 'If there's any good news in this, sir, it's that we found a medi-kit stashed under the pilot's seat in the other Chimera.'

'The spirit of the Emperor is with us,' Lantz said. All around him, the men nodded. 'He provides for those who remain fervent in his service.'

I wiped my mouth on the back of my glove, which came away covered with blood. Leaning over, I spat a long stream of it onto the ground. As much as I found his constant sermonising an annoyance, I had to admit that Lantz was excellent for morale.

'I want to try and get one these Chimeras up and running. Someone should inform Castellan Isaias. Lantz, I can't think of a better messenger than you.'

The priest smiled. 'Indeed, captain. I should be glad to.'

He was halfway across the avenue when the three riders came charging out of the mist.

They shared the same red, blistered skin as the daemonic hounds, but were more humanoid in appearance. Curving, black horns stretched above the crown of their heads, and each one carried a jagged sword that seemed to glow with heat as if pulled from some terrible forge.

The creatures that bore them were squat and powerful, covered entirely in heavy plates of armour, and their hooves melted the surface of the street as they galloped.

Lantz spun around and faced them, even as I cried out in warning. Fearlessly he raised his chainsword, but the weapon was so unwieldy that it had barely come up to his chest before the daemons struck him down. The molten swords of the riders slashed downwards, leaving smoking trails in their wake, and then they were past him. I saw the priest's armour opened up in half a dozen places. He spun slightly, a look of dismay on his face as his entrails spilled out onto the street. Finally he fell face down into his own organs, his hands twitching.

The daemonic riders, now half a block down the avenue, spun and headed directly for us.

There were only a dozen of us left and, whatever these things were, something told me that we would prove no match for them if we remained out in the open.

'Embark!' I ordered.

We scattered as quickly as we could, clambering into the abandoned Chimeras, but I could still hear the dying wails of at least two more Guardsmen as I slammed the access door behind me.

Velez, myself and eight others had made it into the transport intended for the remainder of our stay in Rycklor.

'One of you fire this thing up. I need power!' I yelled.

The floor pitched upwards at a steep angle, and it was with great effort that I managed to get to the turret hatch. As I swung it open, I could hear the riders slam into the other transport. I pulled myself up into the gunner's position just in time to see the daemons knock the other Chimera over on its side. One of the riders and his mount leapt on top of it. The other two plunged their swords into its vulnerable undercarriage again and again. Ceramite plating began to glow and melt with infernal heat. If anyone was still alive in there, they didn't have long to remain so.

A little further away, *Integuma's* assault ramp had opened. The Templars were striding towards the battle as quickly as they could with Isaias leading the charge.

So, I thought bitterly, *only when things are about as bad as they're going to get do you bother to help us?*

The Chimera came to life, and the indicator lights before me turned green. Determined not to let the Templars take all the glory, I seized the controls and spun the turret. The multilaser fired, striking one of the riders, but it seemed unaffected by the trio of holes that had been burned into it. Below me, some of the men manned the lasgun emplacements built into either side of the vehicle. The beams bounced harmlessly off the iron hide of one of the riding beasts.

Something inside of the overturned Chimera burst, and black smoke began to billow out of every seam. Satisfied, the three riders turned their attention to the Space Marines and pounced. I managed to fire the multilaser one more time, but the daemons took no notice of the holes I burned into them.

I had been too busy fighting for my life to fully appreciate the combat prowess and fortitude of the Templars back at the bridge. Now, I had a perfect seat to take it in.

The three riders crashed into the Templars with hurricane force, swinging their swords in sweeping, limb-removing arcs. The mounts reared up and lashed out with their front legs. Yet, the same attacks that had been enough to easily destroy a military transport couldn't do much more to the Space Marines than scratch the paint from their armoured suits. Boltguns fired, fists pummelled, daemonic flesh and metal were rent open and steaming gouts of dark liquid poured everywhere. The hulking beasts screamed and collapsed, and once they fell into the snow, the Templars proceeded to slaughter their riders.

One daemon and his mount remained, and it fell to Isaias to deliver the coup de grace. His hammer swung and struck the creature in the neck. There was a blinding flash of light and sound like artillery being detonated. The rider sailed backwards through the air and landed half a block down the avenue. His riding beast lay dead at the Castellan's feet, its chest completely ruptured.

Isaias pointed his hammer at the daemonic rider and slowly walked towards it. To my utter disbelief, the daemon was still alive. It picked itself up from where it had landed, sword raised above its head. It gave an ear-piercing scream of defiance and then flew apart, painting the snow with bloody gore and pieces of jagged yellow bone.

Dizzily, I climbed down from the turret. The eight troopers were trying their best to remain composed. 'Sir,' one of them said quietly, 'without the priest...'

I cut him off with a raised hand, opened the rear hatch of the Chimera and walked outside. There was no need to examine the overturned transport for survivors; it was obvious that any occupants were dead from the fire raging within its perforated shell. There were ten of us left now, including Velez and myself. Half my troopers had died in a single day, and we hadn't yet arrived at our destination. At this rate, the only ones to enter Verevya Basilica would be the Black Templars.

Isaias approached. He considered the burning Chimera and the fallen bodies. His face showed all the emotion of a carved statue as he offered us what sounded like congratulations. 'Your people fought well against the flesh hounds, and it was wise to utilize cover against the bloodcrushers. They can prove to be fearsome cavalry if encountered in the open.'

'Who is Samnang Margh?' I challenged.

Ah, how to describe the perverse joy I felt as I finally saw the Castellan's impassive exterior crack. His eyes widened by the tiniest amount and his jaw, for the briefest of moments, slackened. I had privileged information, he realised, and he had been one to let it slip.

I crossed my arms and waited for an answer. Behind me, Velez and the others exited the Chimera and stood silently.

Isaias regained his icy composure at once. 'You do not need to know,' he said.

'I think we do.'

'Perhaps I should have said it is better for you if you do not know.' He began to turn away.

'An unholy man, standing in a once holy place.'

Isaias whirled. His mouth twisted with indignation and he levelled his hammer toward Velez. 'Psyker! You have been using your damned witchcraft to peer into my thoughts!'

'No,' Velez pleaded. 'No, I swear.'

'Has he spoken to you? Have you been listening to his foul whispers? Tell me true, or I will kill you where you stand!'

'No, nothing like that. I just... I can see him. I can feel his power.' Velez lowered his eyes and his voice dropped to whisper. 'He frightens me.'

Isaias lowered his hammer. 'He should.'

The snowfall began to abate. The daylight was nearly gone. I shivered, and plunged my hands into my coat pockets.

'Samnang Margh is one of the bloodlords,' Isaias said. 'A long time ago he was one of humanity's champions, a Space Marine, but he has since fallen into darkness.'

I felt the blood drain from my face. One often heard stories of the Space Marines and their heroic, superhuman exploits, and one also heard about the traitorous Space Marines. They were ones who had renounced their oaths to the Emperor millennia ago to embrace the Ruinous Powers: brutal, cunning and utterly inhuman monsters. They had attacked Cadia many times over for the past ten thousand years, though never in my lifetime, but to encounter them was to court certain death. As we were leaving for the Krandor System, there had been rumours that one of their massive invasions – a so-called Black Crusade – was preparing to attack once more.

'A Chaos Space Marine,' I breathed.

Isaias nodded. 'One with all the powers of the warp at his disposal.'

'And he's here? On Zhenya?'

'Only recently. We believe that he has been active in this system for decades, beginning with the capital world. Once it fell, his minions spread throughout the other Krandorian planets, including this one.'

'So, he's the cause for all of this?' I swept my arm across the ruined cityscape. Suddenly, I was having trouble catching my breath. 'One man. One man is able to completely destroy an entire civilization?'

'Hardly a "man", Isaias said.

'How are we supposed to kill such a... thing, then?'

'You cannot. That is for us to do.' Isaias said, setting his hammer down and leaning on it slightly. 'You are ambitious, men of Cadia, and you admittedly do not lack for courage. However, to face one as great as Samnang Margh requires a third thing that you, regrettably, no longer have.'

'And what is that?' I asked, as the last rays of the sun dipped behind the ruined plaza.

'Weapons, vehicles, armour. These things are important, yes, but in the end they are only tools. Faith in the Emperor is what lends power and permanence to our actions. Your priest is dead, and without another such as him to focus and strengthen your resolve I do not believe you have the endurance to face what is otherwise unbearable. Captain Kervis, you and your troopers are dismissed. We will continue alone from this point.'

He picked up his hammer and walked away. We stood there, my men and I, feeling abandoned as babes. We had endured eight months of siege warfare, weeks of cold and starvation and, now, a day of unrelenting loss. To be told we would not be allowed to see things through, to make the suffering and sacrifice actually count for something, was unthinkable.

My hand curled around the crumpled page from the Infantry Primer, recalling Lantz's penultimate words. 'He provides for those who remain fervent in his service,' I muttered.

Unfolding the tattered page, I began to read aloud.

'Most powerful and glorious Emperor, Who commands the winds and eddies of the galaxy, we are miserable men adrift in peril. We cry unto thee for help, save us or we will perish.'

Isaias stopped and slowly turned back to face us. He cocked his head slightly.

'We see how great and terrible Thou art. We fear you, and offer You our awe. We fear naught but Your wrath, and beg a chance to prove ourselves...' The remainder of the prayer had been torn away, but my point was sufficiently made.

'The Prayer for the Lost and Endangered,' Isaias said to himself.

'I will stand for these men. I will be their spiritual centre.'

Verevya Basilica had once been beautiful, a sweeping structure of white-washed rockcrete and stained glass windows, but now it was a monument to evil. Blood dripped from the eaves and ran down the walls in rivers, staining everything red. The colourful scenes of Verevya's life had all been smashed to pieces. Torches and bonfires burned in their place. We also discovered where the severed heads of Rycklor's citizens had been taken. The skin and flesh had been removed from each and every one, leaving only a gleaming white skull. The stairs leading up to the enormous double doors were littered with them. They were clustered in piles along the window sills and hung on brass wires from the corners of the bell tower. It was defilement on a scale that none of us had ever seen.

Our part in the mission was largely complete. We had, despite the losses, guided the Templars to their destination with their precious Land Raider completely unscathed. Now, it was their turn to take the lead.

Before the church was a spacious courtyard, paved with flagstones and lined by statues of Zhenyan saints and religious leaders. The heads had all been lopped off and replaced by piles of burning coals. Cultists filled the space – it seemed as if the entire population of Ryklor was concentrated in this one spot. They gathered around roaring bonfires and piles of salvaged equipment, gibbering and moaning. They gouged at themselves, or one another, with pieces of rusted metal and branded their chests with twin circles of iron.

Integuma surged forward, leaving us behind as its bolter racks unleashed a hurricane of shells into the assembly. The cultists fell in droves, and many who were not shot were ground to a pulp beneath the Land Raider's treads as it mounted the cathedral stairs and plowed through the entryway.

We ran to catch up, taking the steps two at a time. Through the smashed doors lay a narthex filled with yet more skulls. Ahead of us, the Land Raider continued into the nave, its weapons mowing down cultists with impunity. It pitched forward as it descended down a flight of steps into the main sanctuary. Pews, handcarved and made of polished Zhenyan pine, utterly priceless, were ground to splinters beneath it until it finally came to rest.

We came to a stop at the top of the landing as a horde of cultists suddenly began to pour out of every doorway. Like those who had attacked us on the bridge, their eyes were filled with blood and their bodies bore signs of mutilation. They screamed incoherently as they tried to attack *Integuma*. The machine responded by powering up its assault cannons to thin the horde. Chunks of flesh filled the air and the floor of the basilica became awash with blood. Steam rose as it cooled in the winter air.

We did our part by adding lasbeams to the fray, but this moment truly belonged to the Space Marines. Minutes went by and still the people came. Spent shell casings piled in drifts around the base of the Land Raider, and I smiled to think that *Integuma* carried more ammunition than I had seen in the past year.

Suddenly the tank's assault ramp dropped open and the Black Templars poured out with their Castellan in the lead. They no longer bothered to fire their boltguns, but threw themselves immediately into close combat, pummelling the enemy with short and precise movements, breaking bones and caving in skulls with every blow.

At last, the tide slowed to a trickle and stopped. *Integuma*'s weapons ceased their din and came to rest. Smoke drifted up like incense towards the vaulted ceiling.

Isaias nodded to me, signalling our position to be secure. Now, we had to begin the search for Samnang Margh, a lengthy and exhausting endeavour.

Or so we thought.

All at once, the space was filled with peals of laughter and Lantz's face went pale. Somewhere in the shadows came a voice.

'Isaias, Isaias. It certainly took you long enough.'

The Templars looked every which way. *Integuma*'s weapons moved back and forth, unable to identify a target.

'Show yourself, Margh!' Isaias roared. 'Come within my reach, and I may grant you a quick death.'

A figure stepped forward from the shadows of a choir

loft set high into the wall above the central altar. It was a man, huge across the chest and shoulders, and dressed in power armour, much as Isaias, but in shades of reddish-brown. Spikes jutted out from his shoulders, elbows, and knees. And his misshapen face was dominated by a black, cross-shaped tattoo that covered his left eye and cheek.

'Clever of you to conscript a psyker, Isaias,' he said. 'I didn't think you would be able to get over your prejudices so easily. No, my old adversary, it is you who should surrender. For you see, Zhenya is set to fall, along with the seven other planets in this system. And once they belong wholly to the Blood God, the false emperor will have no power here. Real space will give way to the immaterium, and the full fury of my lord's daemonic will be unleashed upon your precious Imperium.' The Traitor Space Marine laughed. 'In the years to come, they will say that the great tide of blood began here and that the eight worlds of the Krandor System were the undoing of all that you hold holy.'

'Fire!' Isaias cried, but the machine-spirit within *Integuma* was already in motion. The hurricane bolter racks swivelled to the right, elevated in unison, and destroyed the place where Samnang Margh was standing. The choir loft exploded into chunks of wood and stone and tumbled to the floor in a cloud of dust.

I had difficulty seeing past Isaias and the Templars as they converged on the place where the Chaos Space Marine had fallen, but I could hear him cough and sputter. Isaias gestured to his men, granting them some kind of permission, and they descended on Margh. Each of them was eager to land at least one blow against this renowned enemy, exorcising his traitorous spirit by beating his body into a pulp.

Finally, Isaias raised his hammer high above his head and the Templars cleared out of the way. I caught a glimpse of Samnang Margh as he struggled to stand. Emperor help me, he was not only still alive, but sporting a smile despite the bloody ruin of his face.

'In the name of the God-Emperor of mankind,' Isaias proclaimed, 'to whom every knee shall bow and every sin be revealed, I condemn you, Samnang Margh, to an eternity in torment and darkness.'

'No pity! No remorse!' the Templars cried.

The hammer began its final, crushing, death blow, but it somehow never arrived. I'm not sure what Margh did in those last few seconds, but there was a flash of light and a concussion wave that tossed the Templars backward. I threw an arm across my face to shield it from a hail of tiny stones and splinters. When I looked again, Margh was surrounded by a swirling cloud the same rusted-blood colour as the miasma. Noises emerged from it: awful sounds that brought to mind images of snapping bones and tearing skin.

The Space Marines fired their boltguns into the cloud to no effect that I could see. Isaias launched himself towards it, only to be thrown back once more the moment he made contact. He smashed through a row of pews and leapt back to his feet just as the cloud dispersed.

Samnang Margh was gone, but he had transformed into – or perhaps, been replaced by – a towering daemon.

To describe it was nearly impossible. It had the general shape of a man, but was colossal in stature. Its head was like that of a snarling dog, and brass plating covered its chest, shoulders and upper legs. In one hand, it held an axe, whose edge was composed of jagged teeth. In the other hand was a whip made of living fire. It shook the building with its birth cry, and as it spread wide its leathery, bat-like wings, pieces of masonry plummeted from above and crashed around its hooved feet.

It radiated such evil, such hatred, that my eyes began to water. It took every ounce of strength I had to stop my knees from giving out. Behind me, I was certain that I heard at least one man whimper. I didn't blame him one bit.

The first thing it did was to stomp *Integuma* with all its might and its assault cannons crumpled and split.

The Templars were back on their feet, charging fearlessly towards the daemon who swept its axe into their midst. Two Space Marines were immediately decapitated, and a third was sliced cleanly in half.

I was stunned. After seeing their armour take more punishment in a day then some tanks endure in a month, I had begun to think of the Templars as being nearly indestructible.

The surviving Space Marines unleashed a fury of blows upon it, but were given no reward for their efforts. The thing that had been Samnang Margh was completely unharmed.

Then, Isaias leapt into the air and drove his hammer into the daemon's chest plate. In the confined space of the basilica, the sound of the impact was enough to crack the very walls. The Castellan landed heavily, crouching low, and spun around for another attack. This time the hammer caught a leg, and a hunk of daemonic flesh tore free. The daemon howled, stumbled and fell against the back of the church, turning two support columns into powder.

Isaias's men regrouped and brought up their bolters. Explosive shells rained into the creature, but failed to find any purchase. The daemon screamed and sent the pommel of its axe through the helmet of the nearest Templar, tearing him in half. Its whip lashed out, wrapping itself around four of the Templars with lighter armour. The ceramite plates instantly liquefied and gave way, tearing the four Space Marines in two. The flaming halves of their corpses filled the space with a sickening stench.

Isaias swung his hammer in a horizontal arc, catching the daemon across the face. It should have been a killing blow, but instead of collapsing, the monster rose up again to its full height.

A cold, unnatural terror had nested beneath my ribs, stopping my breath and freezing my heart. This creature was simply beyond anything that I had ever encountered or been trained to face.

I turned my head as a hand came to rest on my shoulder. Velez and other troopers were gathered behind me. I saw in their faces the same fear and grim resolve as they fixed their bayonets for a charge. We said nothing. There was no need. Our duty in this matter was clear. With its attention focused singularly on the Templars, the daemon seemed certain to emerge victorious from this fight. Though, if its attention could be divided, then perhaps the Space Marines could destroy it.

I gripped the rosarius that I had taken from Lantz's corpse and held it up for the others to see. The golden pendant, worn only by the Emperor's ministers, felt warm in my hand. The men nodded with reassurance. Behind us, part of the ceiling began to shift, and a huge plascrete beam came crashing down.

Velez raised a palm towards the daemon, and then curled his fingers inward. I had no idea what he was doing, but it caught the attention of the beast. Its head whipped around, and it roared.

I suddenly recalled one of Lantz's favourite inspirational quotes. 'Fear not, men! We go to the Emperor's side to fight at the end of time!' At that moment we hurled ourselves down the steps, leaping over broken pews and shattered pieces of masonry. The daemon's axe barely missed me and to my left there came a collection of stifled cries. A wash of hot liquid flowed across my legs, and I knew without looking that half of those behind me were dead.

The whip of fire descended towards us like an infernal judgement. I dropped and slid down the last few stairs, but Velez was not so fast. He screamed horribly as his skin burst into flame, and his right arm was severed. Then, the daemon kicked him across the room. Velez struck one of the upper balconies and plummeted like a discarded doll into a heap of tumbled rockcrete.

The last four of my men and I joined Isaias and his surviving Templars who once again tried to defeat their foe in a melee. We cut and stabbed, slashed and pounded, but to no avail. The axe swung again and, in a single motion, caught myself and those beside me with its tooth-lined edge. Their flimsy armour did nothing to protect them, and they were torn apart in a wash of red. But I had something they did not: the rosarius. Built into the pendant was a conversion field, a personal energy barrier powerful enough to stop me from being instantly killed. Even so, the impact of the blow sent me reeling.

I fell against the steps. My ribs ached, and my mouth had started bleeding again. Through a gathering haze of agony, I saw Isaias' hammer finally punch through the daemon's brass armour. Its face flashed from confusion, to realization and then fury. Deep cracks appeared across its body, widening to pour forth both a sickly red light and rivers of steaming blood. It howled with an infinite rage and collapsed in on itself. There was an explosion from somewhere inside its chest, and then it was raining on us. Bone and flesh flew out in all directions, and an ocean of blood came crashing down into the once sacred space of the basilica.

After some time, I pulled myself into a sitting position. The daemon was gone, sent back at last to whatever netherworld it had come from. I was suddenly more tired than I had ever been in my life. I watched as the Templars gathered their dead and carried them back into *Integuma*'s hold. Though damaged, the Land Raider was apparently still quite operational. Finally, Isaias came and stood before me as I struggled to get back up on my feet.

'Captain Kervis, our mission is complete. We will now take our leave of you.'

I continued to grip my sword. 'How will you get safely out of the city? There's no one left to guide you.'

'There is no need now that Samnang Margh is dead.' He gestured upwards. Half of the basilica's roof had caved in during the battle. In the cold sky above, the miasma clouds were beginning to thin and break apart. 'Our Thunderhawk is already on its way to rendezvous with us in an open area nearby.'

I leaned forward and spat bloody saliva from my mouth.

I wanted to ask if I could trouble him for a ride, either back to my original post or perhaps even off-world, but I couldn't think of how to do so without sounding like some lost child. Besides, Space Marines surely had more important things to concern themselves with than the welfare of a single Cadian shock trooper.

'Where will you go now?'

'Margh was not the last of the bloodlords,' Isaias said without further elaboration.

'Of course. My condolences about your men,' I said.

Isaias looked puzzled. Did Space Marines even have a concept of what sympathy was? I had no idea.

'They have earned the rest and peace that only death in the Emperor's service can bring,' he said at last. 'There can be no greater achievement. Did you not learn this during your childhood seminary studies?'

'Never mind,' I sighed.

Isaias placed his fist over the place where his heart presumably lay. It took me a moment to understand that he was saluting me. I returned the gesture of respect in the traditional, Cadian way, fingers pressed against my temple and palm facing forwards.

Just then, the gulf between Space Marine and shock trooper was not quite so vast. Isaias dropped his arm and turned to board the Land Raider. The front ramp slowly closed behind him as the engine rumbled to life, and the machine made an exit through a gaping hole in the west wall.

I stood alone for a moment. There was nothing to hear but my own breathing.

No, there was something else. A faint groaning. I followed the sound, carefully picking my way over piles of rubble until I came upon Velez. It was obvious from the way in which he was lying that his back had been broken. He looked at me with glazed eyes.

'I heard... what he said. About the Emperor's peace. Do you... do you think I've earned it, abomination though I am?'

It was a good question. I wasn't sure.

'Of course you have,' I said softly.

Velez shut his eyes, and smiled weakly. 'Then, give it to me.'

'What?'

He opened his eyes again. 'Give me the Emperor's Peace. I mean, you're qualified now, yes?'

I looked down at my sword. The rosarius gave a pale glow.

'Or weren't you serious about taking on Lantz's mantle?'

I paused for a moment. 'I was serious.'

Relief washed over Velez's face, and he once again shut his eyes. I impaled him through the heart in a single motion and did not remove my blade until I was certain that he was gone.

'Emperor,' I whispered, 'this man was a fine soldier and a trusted friend. I hope that counts for something in Your eyes.'

I sheathed my sword, adjusted my hat, and shoved my hands into my coat pockets. The crumpled prayer from the Infantryman's Primer was my only companion as I began to forge a path back out of the city.

I sincerely prayed that I would make it.

LAST STEP BACKWARDS

JUSTIN D HILL

The aircraft came out of nowhere, roaring from the skies on super-charged engines, making the world shake. Major Luka ducked. They were so low he thought they might take off his head. Then they wheeled over the causeway, spewing white contrails from their wing-slung rocket pods, the side gunners raking the ground with heavy bolter-rounds. Salvos of missiles exploded in the air, shredding the lead squads of blood-maddened Anckorites, stemming the tide for a brief moment.

'Valkyries!' Major Luka shouted as the lead craft swung to the right, while three others pulled to a halt about ninety metres back from the Aegis defence line, their thrumming engines sending up clouds of blue dust. He had a brief glimpse of troops rappelling in pairs from either side, before they were lost in dust.

The lead Valkyries came in again. One sparked a

half-track that was pushing up between the burning wrecks of the lead tanks. It gouted black promethium smoke. Then the flyers peeled off. The din of their engines faded. The world seemed quiet for a moment. Major Luka paused. 'Do you hear that?'

Cadet Slander looked at him.

'Do you hear it?'

Slander shook his head, but then over the din of men shouting and dying and the rattle of gunfire and las-rounds, came the strains of music. Not the dull chanting of the enemy, but *music*. And not just any music. 'It sounds like... Flower of Cadia...'

Major Luka jumped up. 'Sing, man! Sing!'

The sound came clear and distinctive. It was getting louder. Major Luka walked out into the causeway, ignoring the las-shots that stitched the air about him. The swirling dust began to settle. Four squads of elite Cadian kasrkin appeared, coming in at a half run.

Major Luka remembered being a young boy in the choir at the cathedral in Kasr Ferrox. Yes, he thought, the sight of those kasrkin was more beautiful than even the chapel mural of Saint Beatine. The music grew louder. 'For Cadia!' the major shouted, answering shouts coming from all across the ridge. Then he stopped.

In the middle of the kasrkin came a bear of a man: officer's greatcoat thrown over his shoulders, bull neck, head low, thrust forward, an air of defiant resolution, irresistible willpower, and the strength, courage and determination to resist.

'Creed,' shouted Luka. 'It's Creed!'

* * *

Earlier...

War is the heart that pumps life through the Imperium of Man. Cadet Fesk had learned that in basic training. *War is the heart of the Imperium, and the Astra Militarum is the blood.* What did that make the men he was watching? he wondered.

The Cadian Cadet – known as a Whiteshield for the broad white stripe on their helmets – was standing by the side of a six-lane rockcrete slabway watching files of weary troopers fleeing back towards the planet's only major habitation, Starport. The men were from a planet called Ephalia, and they were mysterious to him in their manners, food, speech, customs. Two weeks before, these troops had been speeding the opposite way down into the Long Dry, waving and whistling as they clung onto their lasrifles and velvet shakos. Now there was no cheering. They looked weary, exhausted and wounded. Even worse, Fesk thought, they looked *defeated*.

Major Luka always told them there was no defeat for a Cadian Shock Trooper, only tactical withdrawal, counterstrike and, ultimately, a hero's death.

Fesk's attention was caught by a gunner who sat half in the turret of his Chimera. His right arm was in a sling and he had lost his shako, his mouth rimmed with dried blue dust.

'They're coming!' the man shouted in heavily accented Gothic. He pointed back to the lowlands of the Long Dry. 'They'll kill you all!'

He held out a hand to Fesk, as if willing him and the other cadets up, but Fesk turned his back. 'The Anckorites are coming!' the man shouted again, but Fesk was already walking away. He was a Cadian.

* * *

Major Luka was in the communications bunker. There was a steady crackle of static from the vox. He kicked the unit with his good foot and Slander, the vox-operator, as well, in his frustration. 'What do you mean you can't get through?' he demanded.

Whiteshield Slander shrugged. He'd been a petty thief on Cadia, and he had been lucky to escape the penal legions of St Josmane's Hope. He was good with the vox-unit. It was just like picking locks, he said. But not even Slander could get through to headquarters. 'It's this planet,' he said. 'It frags the comms.'

Major Luka gave the vox-unit another kick, this time with his bionic foot. The steady crackle of static was unchanged. He let out a long sigh and took out his order strip, written in the neat penmanship of a Administratum servo-scribe, stared at it for a moment, then sighed and slipped it back into his breast flap pocket.

'What is that, sir?'

'Our orders,' he said after a while. 'Fortify and hold the Incardine Ridge against Luciver Anckor's cult forces.'

'But those orders are three weeks old,' Slander said. 'When we were on the offensive–'

'What are you saying, cadet?'

'Well, I thought that maybe we've been overlooked. We're only...'

'Only what, Cadet Slander?'

Slander gulped. 'Only Whiteshields.'

Major Luka bent down. Slander could smell sweat, stale lho-sticks, and the morning meal of fried grox patties as the major roared at him. 'There are half a million Anckorites down in the Long Dry who want to get to Starport, and it's the only geographical feature this

Throne-forsaken planet has. This is the only place we have a hope of stopping him. Sometimes it falls on the weak and defenceless. But that is the job of a Guardsman, do you understand? To die so that others might live.

'If we abandon our position, what then? Once Luciver Anckor gets up the ridge it's a straight drive to Starport. Understand? He'll be on your back before you can fight your way through this rabble onto a lander. And it will be a fight. Every one of those men will knife you rather than let you on a lander before him. I've seen evacuations. They're not pretty.'

'So we stay here?' Slander said.

'Yes, damn it! Dig in. We hold the Incardine Ridge! And we shall show those cowards what it means to stand and fight.'

Major Luka had survived thirty years in the Cadian Eighth and had taken up the mantle of training the next generation of Shock Troopers. He shouted everything, especially when communicating with Slander.

'You're a stupid, know-it-all fool!' he bellowed as Slander dug a fire support trench. 'Dig deeper, understand?'

'But the dust,' Slander said, patting his sleeves, which were thick with the flour-fine blue dust of Besana.

'To the Eye with the dust!' Major Luka's veins stood out, he was shouting so hard. 'If you don't dig deeper we'll be burying you in it!'

Slander dug till the dust choked him. They all dug – Lina, Slander, Yetske, Darkins, Garonne – as Major Luka laid out the defence, drawing lines in the blue sand with his good foot.

'Fire support here, reserves here. Comms here,

command and control bunker here. I want the foxholes man-deep with grenade sumps dug at the bottom of each one at thirty degrees precisely. Do I make myself clear?'

'Yes, sir!' they all called back.

Fesk was with Lina, holding the empty flour sack while she filled it with spoil.

Lina was seventeen. A hard little nut with a shaved head and big green eyes, and she was good with a blade. Most of the others found the rings that pierced her lower lip and the aquila tattoo on her left cheek a little off-putting. Not Fesk. He rather liked her. But she didn't seem to appreciate the fact.

'What are you looking at,' she said. It didn't sound like a question.

'Nothing.'

She kept digging. Her shoulders were lean and hard in her standard issue green tank top. Her back was wet with sweat, and it made the fabric cling to her lean contours. 'I heard you're to be stationed in this hole,' she said.

'With you?'

'No fragging way. Me and Darkins. You're getting that loser Yetske.' She laughed. 'You never know, the way he handles his lasrifle, you might be his first kill.'

Fesk hefted the sandbag into place. He paused for a moment to look across at the long rubble causeway, up which the enemy would be coming. It stretched out for almost half a kilometre, lifting the road three hundred metres up from the Long Dry to the rocky summit of Incardine Ridge. 'What if they don't come up that road?'

Lina paused, and wiped her forehead with the back of her arm, leaving dirty blue smears.

'Have you been down there? Slipsand pools as deep as a man. They'll drown anyone who tries to come off the road. And armour will never make it. Now, it's your turn to shovel.'

Ryse sent his own shuttle to pick them up: a stately barge suitable for a Warmaster, with brass fittings and an axelwood panelled mess with more fine types of luxury amasec than Jarran Kell had ever seen before. The colour sergeant spent a few minutes smelling each one and laughed when he picked out one from the back. 'Look at this!' he said to his companion, lifting up the gold-stoppered bottle. 'Arcady Pride!'

It seemed a shame to waste this stuff on pen pushers and Administratum consuls. 'Bring it along,' said Ursakar Creed. 'We'll celebrate later.'

The officer who met them at the landing bay blast gates was a major of the Cadian 345th. He was in his grey dress uniform with peaked cap and black leather glove. His other sleeve was neatly folded up at the elbow, and pinned in place. He saluted smartly.

'General Creed,' he said. Men always tried to say 'General Creed' without showing their excitement. It was impossible of course, like saying 'Ah! Commissar Yarrick!' or 'Commander Pask, I presume.'

Creed nodded. 'Where did you lose it?' he asked. The man looked confused. 'Your hand,' Creed said.

The man laughed. 'Oh, on Rellion Five.'

'Traitor Ridge?'

'No.' The major's cheeks coloured a little. 'My company were seconded to the Forty-Fifth.'

'You helped to clear the Shima Forest.'

The major nodded. He said nothing more. No need, Kell thought. Shima Forest had been a waste of good men.

'I told Grask not to go in there,' Creed said. 'But I was only a colonel then, and Grask had stripes, a hundred years more experience than me and, well, let's just say an arrogance problem. You were lucky to only lose a hand.'

'Thank you, sir,' the man said.

Creed paused. 'What's your name?'

'Major Freight,' he said.

'Tell me, Freight, this recall. It's got to be something bad. How deep in it is Warmaster Ryse?'

'Not for me to say, sir.'

'Ah,' smiled Creed. 'Look, Kell. Here we have a man of tact, as pure as the driven snow.'

The major's mouth opened and then shut again. Kell smiled. It was always like this when men met Creed. They expected the Emperor Resplendent in flak armour and a greatcoat, with glowing halo and the aura of an Imperial saint, speaking beatitudes. *Blessed are the battle-worthy, for they shall stand firm. Blessed are the chaste, for their faith shall be ceramite.*

What they got was Ursarkar E. Creed.

'Show me in then, Freight. I'll see for myself.'

Warmaster Ryse was so deep in thought that he did not hear the door open. Creed. It had to be Creed. It had been Ryse who had pushed for him. Two years before, at a seven course planning dinner, he had softened up the generals with vintage claret from Lethe Eleven, then made his pitch.

'For the next push I want Major Creed to lead the right flank.'

'Who?' General Vishron had said.

'Ursarkar Creed.'

'Never heard of him.'

'I have.' That had been Lord General Gerder, a white-haired veteran with impeccable military pedigree and a bionic monocle. 'He is an *Utsider*.'

Utsider's were those folk who lived in the bleak moors and wastes of Cadia, outside the bastion cities that dotted the landscape. Who lived always under the baleful gleam of the Eye of Terror and who retained something of the wild about them.

Ryse had set them straight with a few facts. Rexus IX, the Dreen Salient, Kasr Fuul and the Kamalang Bridge Campaign.

Lord General Gerder had not been impressed. 'But he's only thirty-six.'

'Thirty-seven,' Ryse had corrected.

'Never mind. This Creed chap has got to serve his *time*.'

'Time? *Time?*' Ryse had slammed his hand onto the polished axelwood table. The officers had looked stunned and the waiters had shifted uncomfortably around the edges of the chamber. Even the clock had ticked slower. 'You could give me twenty generals with a hundred times his experience, but I want Creed. He's a *winner*. And he's good. Damn good. *Macharius* good!'

There was a collective air of disapproval at the name Macharius. His conquests had been admirable, but he was remembered as a maverick. Loners, peacocks, demagogues and mavericks were the antithesis of disciplined, organised warfare.

They hadn't liked it, but they had agreed. He was the warmaster, after all. 'On your head be it,' Lord General Gerder said later, in private conference, a threat he had never been able to make good on.

That meeting replayed through Warmaster Ryse's mind as he paced up and down the bay windows in the feast hall of the governor of Hare. Creed had not let him down. Yet. But when – *if* – he did, Ryse knew that the high command would be waiting.

Freight stood smartly aside and announced, 'General Creed, sir.'

Creed swept in and Ryse turned. 'Throne, Ursakar, what took you so long? Listen, it's that damned fool Travis,' he said. 'He's been covering up a rebellion in the Gort System.'

Creed silently held out an igniter and the Warmaster sucked the flame into the end of a lho-stub – one, two, three puffs, before it lit.

'I gave him a safe job and he's screwed it up royally,' growled the warmaster, as Creed lit up one of his own. 'Look!' Ryse held out a sheaf of reports and puffed furiously as Creed flicked through them. The last one was stamped with the sigil of the Inquisition. Creed bit his stub.

'That bad?' he asked.

Ryse exhaled slowly. 'Yes,' he said. 'It's threatening the whole crusade. I need you to fix it!'

'When do I leave?'

'Your ship is waiting now. I've given you three companies.'

'Will that be enough?'

'It'll have to be.' Creed said nothing, so Ryse continued. 'But they're Cadians.'

'Which regiment?'

'The Eighth.'

'That's very thoughtful of you, sir.'

Ryse ground his stub into the porcelain ashtray. 'Don't let me down here, Creed.'

'This way, please.' Captain Avery, a smartly dressed officer of Battlefleet Scarus, stood aside to let Creed and Sergeant Kell through the blast door ahead of him.

He had insisted on taking them on a tour of the more interesting parts of his three and a half kilometre-long ship, the *Magister Thine*, though Kell would rather have been drinking with the five hundred Cadian Shock Troopers billeted in one of the empty cargo stores, as would Creed if he knew him at all. But this was the captain's first command.

'I am sure you will be impressed by this viewing chamber,' the captain said. 'Some fine ornamental detailing.'

They stepped inside an arched chamber, with vast stained glass windows that were dark and indecipherable with the blackness of void behind them. Kell dutifully lifted his face to admire the mural of the Emperor Resplendent directing the Great Crusade in golden armour and halo. It covered most of the ceiling.

'Very good,' Kell said.

Creed walked across to the viewport. Even through the thick armourglass, it radiated cold.

Captain Avery coughed politely. 'Perhaps I might interest you in something more... *military*. The gun decks perhaps? The Avenger-class has a most remarkable lance array. Far above her class.'

'No, thank you,' Creed said. It was the first thing he'd

said for half an hour. The captain caught Kell's eye and the sergeant shrugged. Creed was Creed.

'Apparently the captain has spent some time on Besana,' Kell said at last.

'Oh yes?' Creed turned quite suddenly. His manner was so intense that Captain Avery took an involuntary step back.

'Well,' the captain said. 'Only three days planetside. There's nothing particular about the place. All the usual for this sector. Stowers, geishons, enough stimms to blow a servitor's cortex. Oh, yes, and of course cad-ore.'

'Cad-ore. What's that?' Creed asked.

'Who knows,' the captain said. 'All I know is that it's what gives the soil its blue colour and that the Adeptus Mechanicus ship it out by the gigaton.'

'Anything else?'

'Well... nothing grows on Besana. And the soil is poisonous. Don't inhale when you're there.' Captain Avery laughed briefly, then quickly added, 'Not a problem for a week or two, but cumulative exposure will lead to rapid degenerative disease. Not a place for a protracted campaign.'

'How long until we can go planetside?'

'Seven hours.'

Creed nodded. 'I am sure you have much to do, captain.'

He shook the man's hand and turned back to the viewport. He stood with his arms behind his back, clutching a data-slate, staring at the blue planet as if it were an intricate puzzle that only he could solve.

Night was falling on the planet as Colour Sergeant Jarran Kell stared through the dust-pocked viewports of the Aquila lander. Besana looked bleak, even viewed from far above. He'd read that fierce winds heralded each dawn and dusk as temperature variations sent ferocious dust storms whipping across the arid, featureless expanses. Dust storms, heretics and war.

An hour passed. Maybe more. Kell stared out into the dark haze. He was lost in thought as the ground slowly approached. 'We're coming in to land.' The navigator's green screen underlit his face as the intercoms crackled. 'That's Starport,' he said, pointing down to the left.

Below them, Starport was lit up with glowing strings of yellow sodium lumens, revealing sprawling complexes of warehouses, habs, bunkers and the evacuation camps of Imperial Guard regiments.

'How long?'

'Ten minutes.'

Kell nodded and made his way to the back of the lander with one hand on the side to keep his balance. His power fist was stowed away in cargo, but he re-checked the charge of his power sword and slammed home a fresh battery pack into his hotshot laspistol. You never knew.

Starport changed from strings of lights to roads, runways, landing zones, lines of parked landers and the disorganised mess of abandoned Chimeras and Taurox. Kell could see a crashed Arvus, then individual figures on the ground.

There was a crackle of static. 'It's a hell of a mess down there,' the copilot said. The roar of descent returned. Kell flipped his vox-bead to 'on'. 'Bring it down where you can,' he said. 'Are we announced?'

There was a long pause as the lander banked slowly to bleed off entry speed. 'I can't get through,' the pilot said. 'Apparently it's the cad-ore. Frekks the comms.'

The ground was rushing up now, and as it did so a rabble of Guardsmen climbed the barriers. 'They're storming the landing zone!' the pilot's panicked voice said.

Creed had not spoken the whole trip. He sometimes reminded Kell of an actor, sitting in the shadows, waiting to play his part. Now his time was fast approaching.

Creed clicked on the vox. 'Just put it down,' he said. 'The bright ones will work it out.'

The engines flared one last time, driving the rabble back, before the landing gear scraped down and the back ramp thumped open and the hot desert air of Besana rushed in.

Commander Nel, of the Leman Russ tank *Pride of Aquaria,* hit the fuel gauge and cursed.

'Can't you get her to go faster?' he yelled through the hatch.

'I'm praying as hard as you!' Jenks yelled back.

Night was falling and the lead hunters of the Anckorites were a kilometre or two behind. The image of them kept appearing in his mind: hooded, scarred faces wrapped close with black rags, blood-red eyes rimmed with kohl, scraps of flak armour, laspistols in one hand and sickle cult blades in the other. Each time those eyes stared at him, a shiver went through him. He did not want to be caught alive. He'd seen what they did to men they caught. Faster, he urged. They'd been gaining all day and now they were at the ridge, but he didn't know if they had enough fuel – or time – to get up it.

'We're slowing!' Nel said as the engine started to judder.

'I'm trying,' said Jenks.

Nel had never been much of a shrine man, but he

prayed then, every catechism he knew, as the fuel tanks bled down to the dregs and the exhaust began to vent thick black fumes.

They were on the causeway that lifted the road from the Long Dry to the top of the Incardine Ridge. Whoever had laid the road had decided not to zigzag up the slope but to stick to straight lines and build a three kilometre causeway to lift the road the three hundred meters to the plateau.

The engine coughed and the Russ jerked. Nel rocked back and forth, as if he could will the tank faster. Dust started to whip up about him. The evening storms. He screened his mouth with his arm and squinted forward, but it soon became impossible. The winds blew fine blue crystalline dust straight up the hillside. He ducked down and slammed the hatch closed.

'How are the filters?'

'I emptied them this morning,' Jenks said. 'They *should* last.'

The way he said 'should' did not fill Nel with confidence.

Slowly, too slowly, they chugged up the last half kilometre and crested the top. Suddenly they slammed to a halt and the engine wheezed.

'I don't know what it is,' Jenks said, as he rammed the pedals. 'We're stuck.'

'Throne!' Nel cursed, spinning the hatch lock and pushing it open.

Dust swirled inside as he pushed himself up. It took him a moment to see what they had hit. 'It's a frekking Aegis,' he said. 'Someone's left a defence line across the road.' Nel shouted down to Jenks. 'Swing us around this thing.'

At that moment there was a whine from the engines.

'Jenks!' Nel shouted. 'Filters!'

Jenks cut the engine and pulled himself up.

Nel was shouting at Jenks when a light came towards them through the blizzard. It was a man with a portable luminator. He acted as if he were a traffic officer on some military base. He had bushy grey eyebrows and a sweat patch where his belly strained against his fatigues. Nel stared at him in disbelief.

'I am Major Luka of the Cadian–' the officer started.

'I don't care who you are,' Nel shouted back, his mouth full of cad-ore. 'Get out the way!'

'We have our orders to hold this ridge.'

'And I have my orders to get off this planet,' Nel told him, but then he looked about, and saw, in the light of the Russ's searchlights, the dazed faces of soldiers appearing from foxholes dug on either side of the ridge.

No, not soldiers. Boys. The white bands on their helmets marked them clearly out.

'Gun-babies?' Nel said and slapped the top of his tank. 'You're holding this line with gun-babies? Oh, Throne, I've seen everything now!'

Creed marched down the rockcrete bunker corridor, wiping cad-ore dust from his hands. He paused at the half open ceramite blast door, spray-stencilled 'Starport: Command and Control', and stiffened as he heard the note of panic from inside.

'Gentlemen,' Creed said as he stepped inside. There were a handful of hereditaries in the trim velvet dress jackets of various Mordax Prime regiments, a pair of sallow-faced officers from the Gudrunite Rifles with polished black webbing and boots, a couple of other minor planetary officers, an officer of Saint Percival's Cavalry in full dress uniform and a couple of officers with the cap badges of the Aquarian Guard, 17th Armoured Company.

'I am Lord General Ursarkar E. Creed. Who is in command here?'

One of the Mordaxians stepped forward. He was a tall affable looking fellow with short-cropped hair and a golden cog symbol on his gold-trimmed jacket. He cleared his throat. 'Lord General Travis–' he started.

Creed cut him off. 'I have put General Travis into the custody of the Commissariat, on the orders of Warmaster Ryse. What I asked was who is in charge here in his absence?'

'I am, sir. My name is General Stretto Balc.' His manner was stiff and defensive. No doubt he resented a Cadian officer dropping in and pulling rank. Creed didn't care what he thought, but stood before the man, waiting for him to finish. 'No doubt you want a full briefing, but time is short. The Anckorites outnumber us ten to one, perhaps more. They are closing rapidly on Starport. Our situation is untenable. Evacuation will start as soon as the landers are loaded.'

'No, it won't,' Creed said. He felt the officers bristle. Regiments of lesser reputation resented Cadians turning up and telling everyone else how to do their jobs. 'General Balc,' Creed said. 'Seventeenth Steward of the Mordax Cuirassiers. A hereditary position. You are... the fourth to hold the post, and the great grandson of a Marcharian Cross winner. Am I correct?'

Balc nodded.

'General Balc, did you become a general in the Astra Militarum of the Imperium of Mankind to cede planets to the enemy?'

'No, sire, but...'

'Good. On this we are agreed. The Imperial Guard has taken its last step backwards. I expect you to lead your men with exemplary courage and recklessness. Reckless courage, I tell you, underlined three times.'

Balc's voice quivered. 'It would be suicide.'

'Perhaps.' Creed was impassive. 'But at least we shall go down with honour.' Balc put up a hand but Creed cut him off. 'You have shown extreme cowardice and incompetence in the defence of this planet. If you do not do as I ask then I shall report you to the commissars, who will lead you to the nearest wall and put a bolt-round through your head. Your family will lose their position, and they will curse your name for evermore. Now, which is it?'

General Balc straightened up. 'Fight, sir!'

'Good.' Creed looked each officer in the eye, one by one. 'The Emperor is watching us all. There is to be no evacuation. We are holding this planet, gentlemen. Or we are dying here. Understood?'

Creed swept his greatcoat over the back of a pearlwood chair. The fringes of the map had been weighted down with las-packs, an aide's spent watch, a Gudrunite's black helmet and a pair of matt-green scanners. 'This is the Incardine Ridge, yes?' Creed asked.

A lean woman with close-cropped hair and an aquila tattoo across her left cheek stepped forward and put out a hand. 'I'm Kemala,' she said. 'Besana militia. Yes. There are two causeways that lift the highway from the Long

Dry to the Highlands. The ridge is the best place to stop the attack on Starport. Well, the only place really.'

Creed took a long drag of his stub and let the smoke curl from his mouth and nostrils. 'And that is being fortified and defended?'

Kamala frowned. 'I think so.'

'By who?'

'I don't know.'

'Find out,' he said.

It took Kamala five minutes to find someone who knew. 'I have the answer,' she said. 'But you won't like it.'

The dawn storm came just as predictably as the evening one, except the dawn storm blew in the opposite direction. It was whipping into the faces of the Anckorite vanguard as they came up the causeway, their crews squinting forward as the cad-ore crystals blinded them.

They were halfway up the slope when Nel's *Pride of Aquaria* broke the brow of the ridge, a little to the left of Fesk's dugout. The loader was muttering the Blessing of the Righteous. Nel added the Rite of Destruction as well, just for good measure, as the first enemy vehicle appeared through the sheets of blizzard dust.

'Half track soft-skin,' Nel said. 'Register gunner?'

'Aye.'

'Frag round,' he said.

'Frag round,' the gunner repeated.

There was a pause.

'Ready?'

'Ready.'

Sheeting dust hid the tanks for a moment, then the *Pride* fired. They speared the first, and the second slewed off-road, over the lip of the causeway, and turned over three times, throwing out bodies and crushing them in turn. A burning crewman was still screaming when the next vehicle – trying to ram its way through the wrecks – exploded. Then something larger rumbled up behind them.

'They've got a Chimera,' said Nel. 'Register?'

'Register,' the gunner said. There was a clunk as he slid back the blast door of the top ammo crates. 'Armour-piercing round.'

'Acknowledged,' said Nel. There was a long pause, then the *Pride of Aquaria* fired again, and blew the troops inside the Chimera out of the back door in a bloody spray of charred human remains.

'Good shot,' Nel said, a few moments later. 'Two more incoming.'

Lina touched the aquila tattoo on her left cheek for luck, then leaned into the rifle stock. She had been lying all night in her foxhole: sleepless, tense, ready and excited. She aimed as an open-topped half track revved between the wrecks. Lina let her breath out and saw the black-wrapped face of the driver through her scope. His eyes were black-rimmed and bloodshot. She felt instant revulsion and fired three shots in rapid succession.

Two rounds knocked the driver's head back. He didn't move after that. His engine slewed to a halt. 'I've done it,' she said and turned to Darkins. 'I killed one.'

'I thought to prove you killed one you had to get his ear or something,' Darkins said.

'Yeah. You go get his ear. I tell you I shot him. He's dead, no matter how many ears he's still got.'

'Lina's got one!' Darkins called out. There were scattered cheers.

Lina closed her eyes and said a prayer. If she survived this, she would be a Cadian Shock Trooper.

On the other side of the causeway, Fesk heard the news, and wanted to slap Lina on the back.

'Let's hope she lives long enough to be promoted,' Yetske said as return fire slammed into the hillside. A storm of las, grenades and heavier rounds that threw up choking clouds of cad-ore. There were screams from the next dug-out. 'Booth's hit!' one of them shouted. There was panic in the voice, and then Fesk heard, 'Oh sh–' and the voice stopped.

After what seemed like an age, the Anckorites, black-wrapped shapes wielding sickle knives and lasrifles, fell back under cover of the storm.

For that first hour after dawn the causeway was silent. Major Luka went from position to position, doling out water, ammo and medical supplies. Five Whiteshields had been killed. Three were badly wounded.

As the storm cleared, Fesk pulled out a monocular. A dark line of vehicles and desert cavalry stretched back as far as the monocular would focus. They were all moving towards them, the lead units milling about in confusion at the bottom of the causeway.

'Are there more?' Yetske asked.

'Oh yes,' Fesk said.

'Funny,' Yetske said. 'I thought for a minute that we'd beaten them.'

Fesk watched as the hunched shapes of Anckorites

began to part, and through the mobs came a file of Leman Russ. Fesk put the monocular down. He felt sick. He did not tell Yetske what he had seen hanging from the sides of the lead battle tank. He wasn't going to die that way. No chance. No way.

Fesk checked his grenade pack. He'd keep a frag for the end, he thought.

The sound of revving engines drifted up to them, along with wild chanting voices and the background whine of chainblades in eager fists, and then, over it all, the voice of a demagogue shouting and raging in an unknown tongue.

'What the hell is that?' Yetske said.

From below came a great shout. A thousand – or it could have been ten thousand – voices lifted as one and then, with the roar of engines and gunning chain-blades, the Anckorites started up the slope: a mess of tanks; half-tracks; mounted raiders with long charged lances, loping forward on shaggy, two-legged bighorns; four-wheeled assault speeders; bikers with revving chain-blades; and hooded foot-sloggers scrambling up in their eagerness to spill Imperial blood.

The *Pride of Aquaria* had the range on them. She took out the lead Russ with a lucky shot on the mounting that spun the turret ten metres into the air. Three more here-tic tanks pushed past and began to fire back.

The first shot missed, and then there was a sudden *whoosh*. Fesk pressed himself flat and shouted a curse as a shower of soil fell on his helmet and hands. He dusted himself off and looked up, watching a flash and the tank bucking backwards before he heard the boom of another round. He held his hands over his ears and prayed.

The lead Anckorites were dodging up through the rock fields. Hundreds of them, low to the ground, zig-zagging, firing up at them and chanting over and over. Fesk stepped up onto the firing step. Five shots and he got one, a skinny little thing – not much older than himself – with a chainsword who went down like a sack.

There were sudden tears on his cheeks. 'I did it,' he said to no one in particular.

And then from around the tanks came a charge of horsemen, and he could see the lance tips as they bobbed towards him.

Major Luka ducked down behind the defence line, ejected the magazine from his pistol and jammed ten rounds in. Prendervil and Holden's positions had been overrun already, and their heads were trophies in the hands of the lead horsemen. Major Luka cursed. His lads were being murdered and there was nothing he could do. 'Nel!' he shouted, but the tank had stalled again and Jenks was out kicking the filter casing open.

Major Luka took up a new firing position, firing wildly at the mass of riders who were howling as they hacked down his lads. He saw one horseman go down, saw another punched from the saddle and dragged along by the stirrup. Then he saw one with a Whiteshield's head in his fist and he emptied the magazine.

'Nel!' he shouted, gesticulating wildly.

The tank commander seemed to understand. He shouted at Jenks and the *Pride of Aquaria* bucked suddenly forward. There was a moment's pause before the heavy bolter sponsors opened up. The deep clatter of bolt shells made the defence line vibrate. Major Luka put up his head to watch the ruin of the Anckorite horsemen. Mount and rider alike were ripped apart by exploding bolts. It was over in moments. The causeway was a charnel house of feebly kicking horses and men lifting a hand to salute their Dark Gods.

Then the heretic tanks fired back. One round hit the *Pride of Aquaria* in the soft spot on the underside of her hull, and she went up like a firecracker, roaring flames and black smoke.

No one climbed out. *The Pride of Aquaria* burned like a torch.

'Frekk!' Luka said simply. 'Fix bayonets!'

Fesk fired wildly. Rock by rock the Anckorites were coming closer, and their low chanting grew louder. 'They're all around us,' Yetske said in panic, as he fumbled with his battery pack. He spun round, but above them was Kernigg's firing pit, and Kernigg was still firing.

There was an Anckorite hiding behind a rock about fifteen metres down and to the right. Fesk waited for him to come out, his barrel ready to nail him, but he didn't appear.

The sound of chanting grew louder and more insistent. Yetske started crying. 'I can't do it,' he said.

'Yes, you can,' Fesk said, stealing a glance over to where he stood with the power pack in his hands. 'Yetske, push the button and put it in, front catch first.'

Yetske looked down at his rifle as if he was staring at some kind of strange puzzle. He started engaging the catch when he dropped to the ground.

'Get up!' Fesk said.

Yetske lay on the floor. He was gurgling horribly.

'Yetske,' Fesk said, kneeling down. There was barely room in the firing pit. Yetske's eyes rolled up to stare at him, begging for help. Foam and blood poured out of a hole in his neck. Fesk put his hand over the wound, as if he could hold back the flow.

A shadow fell across them and Fesk realised his mistake: Yetske hadn't been asking for help – he was trying to warn him. He grabbed for his rifle, but he was too late. The shadow wanted his life.

All he felt was stabbing pain.

Fesk was dying. He knew the signs from his basic medicae training. He was bleeding out, adding his life-blood to this dry hellhole and staining the cad-ore red. Frekk this planet.

He tried to speak, but he slipped away for a moment, into dreams. A Cadian snowfall. Standing under a pylon on night-exercise, listening to it sing. Putting his ear to the cool rock, and hearing the melody as the wind blew through the honeycomb holes, and the structure hummed as if alive. Pulling his pack onto his back and turning to the cadet next to him in the embarkation parade. It was Lina. 'So where we going?' he asked.

'Throne knows,' she said.

He blinked back to consciousness for a moment. 'Yetske,' he said, before he remembered. He put out a hand, and pulled Yetske back. The cadet's eyes had rolled up white into their sockets. His head lolled loose on his neck. Dead.

You'll be joining him soon, a voice in his head said. Fesk shut his eyes.

He was on Cadia again, rubbing bare hands against

the cold, fumbling with his las-rifle, cursing the cold.
In his dreams there was a roar of aircraft. He looked
up into the night sky and saw only the purple stain of
the Eye of Terror, rising high into the sky. He thought
of Lina's sweat-soaked top, her lop-sided smile, and the
blue aquila on her cheek.

Then there was singing. That was when Fesk knew he
was a goner. These were the companies of souls welcom-
ing him to the Emperor's Blessing. He closed his eyes.
He said his last prayer, fixed in his mind the vision of the
Golden Throne. The singing grew louder. The angels were
singing *Flower of Cadia*. Fesk's mouth moved weakly as
he joined in.

Creed. The word came to him in his delirium. It stalled
his dreams for a moment.

'Creed!' an ecstatic voice shouted from the top of the
ridge. 'It's frekking Creed!'

Creed swept Major Luka up with him as he barked out
orders and the kasrkin manned the Aegis, unfolded
their heavy bolter stands, piled crates of missiles up and
flipped the catches open. 'Luka!' the general shouted. 'It's
been a while. I see they made you a major.'

'It was in exchange for the foot.' Luka lifted his bionic
foot as if for proof.

Creed laughed briefly. 'How are your lads?'

'Well, we've no heavy weaponry and it looks like Anckor
has launched his entire army against us. Business as
usual,' he said.

They made their way between the dugouts. 'I've got
reinforcements on the way,' Creed said. 'But we're going
to have to hold out until then. It's just us and whatever

the Valkyries can ferry in. How many Whiteshields do you have?'

'I had two hundred this morning,' Luka said. 'We've lost thirty, I'd say. The cavalry overawed them. And this is the first time they've seen heresy.'

Creed nodded. He knew all about that. Knew exactly the terror your first cultist brought. 'Well, I've brought some bolters, and lots of ammo. I need the ridge to hold. I know it's a big thing to ask, but it has to be done. We have to stop them here.'

'For how long?'

'A day,' Creed said.

Luka puffed out his cheeks. It didn't look optimistic. Creed laughed again and slapped him on the arm. 'I know. It looks a little tight, but the whole crusade is resting on our shoulders here, and I had no one else to send, so I had to come myself!'

Jasper Fesk was wandering.

He was still wandering in dreams – and Jasper Fesk's dreams were not a pleasant place to be.

He was eight and frightened, hiding under a bed. There were explosions and screaming, and the screams were getting closer. Ingri, his sister, was with him. In one hand she clutched her rag doll. It was dressed in a scrap of old desert camo. The doll was called Sabine after a saint her aunt had told them about, and Ingri loved it more than anything. Her other hand was clamped over Fesk's mouth. It was clamped so tight he couldn't breathe. He kicked and struggled.

'Shut up,' his sister breathed in his ear. '*They're* coming!'

There was wild laughter. The door was kicked open. Footsteps came closer. A shadow fell over him and...

...Fesk struggled to consciousness. It was coming back to him. Fire, flames, pain. He would not be taken alive. His fingers scrabbled for that grenade. A foot pinned his hand to the floor. A gloved hand reached down and grasped him. It lifted him up.

There was a face close to his. The face was speaking, but not to him.

'He's still alive,' it said. 'One gun-baby still alive. One dead.'

His vox crackled. The man spoke slowly and loudly. 'I'm getting you out. Understand? Can you walk?'

'What is that?' Darkins said as Lina fell back into their pit. Lina bent down and pulled at the straps. There was a black Munitorum canister inside. 'Look what the Valkyries brought us!'

She flipped back the clasps and pushed the lid back. Inside lay a compact heavy bolter, brand-spanking-fresh-from-the-Munitorum-new.

'Holy throne! Think you can handle it?'

'Sure I can,' she said.

They scrambled to get it up on its tripod, remembering their drills. But they had trained with Godwyn-pattern bolters... Darkins cursed as the coils of shells slipped through his hands. 'How do you get the bolts in?'

Lina tried one way then another. In the end she looked at the inside lid of the air-drop canister. 'Accatran Vd,' the label said, then simple cartoon instructions, with a neat-looking Guardsman. 'Oh I see,' she said. 'You've got to pull the bolt back first.'

Lina set the tripod down on top of the sandbags, pulled the bolt back, and felt the first round engage. 'Here goes!' she said.

She aimed down the hill. *Thud thud thud*. It was like holding onto a wild dog. She took her finger off the trigger for a moment, and then fired again, panning wildly from side to side as the bands of Anckorites scrambled towards them. *Thud thud thud. Thud thud thud.*

'Did you hit anything?' a voice shouted.

'I don't know,' Lina shouted back.

Darkins nudged her and she looked back at the man standing over her pit.

She almost dropped the bolter in surprise. 'Frekk. Is that...?'

'Yes it is,' General Creed said. 'Now, there's more than one heretic for each of those bolt shells. Make sure you find each one an owner.'

'Yes, sir!' she shouted, and kept firing until her boots were buried beneath bright brass bolter shells.

It was a battle of immovable object and unstoppable force; the Anckorite army massed on the Route Equatorial trying to squeeze up the causeway in the face of defiant resistance. Creed paced back and forth, shouting orders, bolstering men's courage when it was lacking and fighting when killing was needed. With him came Kell, power fist crackling with energy, and the colours of the Cadian Eighth held high.

'That's it lads!' he called out. 'We're showing these heretics what it means to rebel against the Imperium of Mankind!'

There was a sudden wail and an artillery shell landed about thirty metres beyond them. Creed didn't even duck. He paced up and down, smoking and firing, and laughed. 'I've missed this,' he said.

* * *

Every hour the six Valkyries returned on their ferrying mission, kasrkin rappelling, dump canisters being shoved out of the side hatches. They barely replaced the men killed, but they were Cadians, and they made their numbers tell three times over.

In their desperation the Anckorites sought a route around the sides of the causeway, but the slip-sands swallowed them, drowning them in deep pools of blue cad-ore.

The day was failing at last. The wind picked up, this time blasting dust into the eyes of the defenders. The Valkyries would not be flying in these conditions. Their vents would be clogged in seconds. 'Pull back!' Creed ordered, and they stumbled up through the dark and dust to the defence line.

The Anckorite armour tried to force a passage. It was a terrifying stand off as tank shells hammered the Aegis and the heavy weapons teams returned the hatred. There was a brief and furious exchange of lascannon bursts, bolter shells and missiles.

Cadians fell in droves as shells exploded about them. Creed roared to the gun crews, and suddenly the surviving tanks clicked into reverse and this time the Anckorite infantry charged. They were met with a blizzard of las and bolter shells.

The battle was impossibly savage and impossibly brutal, close-quarters, incessant, terrifying. Creed was everywhere. Kell's power fist crackled furiously, punching holes in any Anckorites that managed to clamber over the Aegis line, pulling their spines out of the front of their chests.

Then they fell back one last time.

'How are you men doing?' Creed asked Luka.

Luka's top was dark with sweat and splattered blood. He had lost his helmet somewhere. 'As you'd expect,' he gasped.

'Time for a smoke,' Creed said and pulled out a half smoked lho-stub from his breast flap pocket. They fell back to the communications bunker. There was a kasr-kin manning it now.

'Got that thing working yet?' Creed said.

'Not yet,' he said.

'Keep trying.' Creed puffed slowly. Luka thought he could see concern in the general's eyes.

'Need it?' he asked.

Creed looked thoughtful. 'The vox? Well, possibly. It would certainly make things easier. Perhaps when this storm has passed.'

Darkness fell. The wind dropped. The air cleared.

The hours passed quietly and Creed sent out scouts. 'I want to know when they're coming back before they do.'

It was an hour after nightfall. Slander was fifty metres back from the front line, standing at the water butt with six bottles to fill. Throne knew how they had held on so far. The funny thing was that all that training they had done was starting to make sense now. Fire drills, fixing bayonets and charging. It all made sense. He was going to tell that to Major Luka.

The thought made him smile as he turned to fill the bottles he had slung about his neck. He filled one, put it to the side, was opening the second when someone tapped him on the helmet.

'Wait your turn!' he snapped. 'I've got a whole load to fill up here.'

The tap came again.

'Is that Lina?' he asked. Frekking Lina, he thought. They all had had to listen to how much better a shot she was than all the rest of them.

There was another tap, a little harder this time. 'Throne!' he said, turning to see which idiot was doing this. The face that looked down on him was wrapped in the black of the Anckorite Brotherhood, red eyes staring down at him, ritual scars criss-crossing the face.

'They're behind us!' Slander yelled. Except there was a hand clamped over his mouth and pain, terrible pain then hot gushing liquid that was his blood. He would never be able to tell Major Luka now.

Creed was alone in the command bunker studying maps of Besana. The wind blew the curtain open. He heard men laughing not far off. The curtain wafted again. Creed smelled fresh blood. It was all the warning he needed. A blade seared a line along his shoulder. It snagged on his carapace plating.

He heard the hiss of his foe and twisted, ramming his forearm up under the Anckorite's neck. Creed saw a face wound round and round with strips of black cloth, red eyes, and a mouth slick with blood. He drove the heretic back against the sandbagged walls and heard a satisfying grunt of pain.

The serrated sickle blade stabbed for a chink in his carapace armour. Creed drove it deep into the groin of his enemy, keeping the foe pinned to the wall, stabbing until the Anckorite's guts slipped out of the tattered wreck of his abdomen and his struggles weakened and failed.

Creed pulled his arm away and let the body slop to the floor amongst its own guts. He fell to one knee, unholstered his pistol and fired from a kneeling position. The hotshot las seared a hole through a second Anckorite's face as he came through the door. Three more shots punched the figure back. Creed stepped towards the exit and his boot slipped. The cadet sentry lay sprawled against the back of the bunker, the floor slick with blood. 'Kell!' Creed bellowed. He could hear his colour sergeant's vox-amplified voice shouting orders.

Two more shadows were outside. Creed stepped in close. He had been fighting ever since he could remember. Since his days with his father, sparring in the yard outside their cabin. Afterwards, in Kasr Gallan, he had boxed in the street until his knuckles were raw and bloody, and he soaked them in surgical spirit, despite the pain. The years as an orphan when he had to prove himself, not to others but to himself. He gloried in the danger, the thrill, the joy of fixing the throat of a foe, and then punching his face to mush.

It was almost a relief to get in close like this. Not to be thinking positions, reinforcements, counter-attacks, logistics – to just be thinking about life and death, the next blow his enemy would throw, and how he was going to kill him.

Creed hammered the enemy's wrist, a short hard strike that knocked the blade from his hand while the other hand, clenched into a blunt bull fist, punched the heretic's windpipe. There was a gasp of pain. Creed stamped on the man's foot, came in close, caught his head and twisted it to the side, brought it down on his rapidly rising knee. Either could have killed. Both were a surety. There was a crunch. Neck, skull, Creed didn't care. He pulled a pistol out, fired it point-blank into the Anckorite's face.

'This takes me back,' he muttered. 'Where the frekk is Kell?'

Jarran Kell causally tore the head from the last of the Anckorite Brotherhood, then deactivated his power fist and let the steaming head drop to the floor with a wet thud.

Creed was standing with his back to the sandbag wall, breathing hard. The cloth at his shoulder was ripped, blood flowing freely.

Kell stopped. 'You all right?' he said.

'I've been better.'

Kell nodded. 'We'll get it stitched up.'

'Find out where they came up and cover the rat hole.'

Kell nodded.

Half an hour later, Kell appeared through the darkness, his eyebrows singed. He had lost seven men.

'Did you find it?' Creed asked.

'There'll be no more coming that way.'

Creed nodded. There was nothing more offputting for a soldier than to have the enemy in unexpected places. 'They'll get around us again. Make sure everyone knows that. I don't want anyone surprised. We should expect them to surround us. That doesn't matter. All we have to do is hold on.'

Kell nodded.

'Have they got through to the *Magister Thine* yet?'

Kell's voice sounded the way it did when he wanted to appear calm. 'Not yet.'

Creed thumped the table. 'Damn it,' he said. The two men shared a brief glance. Creed was already thinking five steps ahead. 'I'm going to have to go. You'll have to stay.'

Kell stiffened. He had sworn to protect Creed and he hated being put in an impossible position like this. 'No,' Kell said. 'I come with you.'

'Jarran,' Creed said. 'I need you here.'

'No.'

'Friend,' Creed said. 'I'll be fine. You will be the one in danger. Don't get yourself killed.'

'Of course not.'

'Good. Think you can hold the line?'

Kell waited a long time before answering. But when he did his tone had changed. 'How long for?'

'I don't know.'

'You really need this?'

'I do. This planet needs it. Warmaster Ryse needs it.' Creed gave his friend a wink.

Kell looked away, but he nodded. 'We'll hold,' he said. Creed smiled briefly. He put his hand to his friend's arm and they exchanged a brief look. He didn't need to say more.

'Vox officer!' Creed shouted. 'Get me a flight back to Spaceport. I need to have some words with the head-quarter staff.'

'I'm trying.'

'Don't try, *do*.'

'Yes, sir!'

Fesk woke with a start.

'You're up.' Darkins was crouching over him. The night

was black about them. Fesk pushed himself up. They'd put a bag of fluid into his veins, and he felt odd with the stimms in the mix. An unpleasant mix of queasy and hyper alert. He winced. The ground was strewn with sleeping men, rolled sandbags used as pillows, lasrifles held in their arms. Fesk yawned, wincing from the pain of his wound, and picked up his own lasrifle. He was on third watch.

He made his way over the sleeping bodies. From the Long Dry there was the occasional growl of a chainblade, and the sound of chanting that rose and fell. Fesk tried not to listen to it.

He was on the second point at the middle of the Aegis. Far below, at the bottom of the long causeway, he could see their lights in the lowlands. Camp fires, torches. One man seemingly on patrol, walking up and down in lines. There were hundreds, perhaps thousands, of them and yet more vehicles streaming up along the Route Equatorial.

How could they hold back such numbers?

Fesk looked up. The stars burned white. He did not recognise them. He was very far from home. 'Dear Ingri,' Fesk said aloud, imagining writing to his sister. 'We held out against the enemy for as long as we could. You, Sharla and Oleg would have been proud of us. We did Cadia proud. We are her sons. I was not afraid when I died. I have taken many enemies of mankind with me.'

'Cadet,' a voice said suddenly. 'Do you have faith in the Emperor?'

Fesk started. He reached for his gun. 'Do you have faith?' the large figure asked, stepping close. It was a bear of a man. The glow of a stub lit his fingers and face as he inhaled.

'L-lord General?'

'Do you have faith in the Emperor?'

'Y-yes, sir!'

'At ease. Here. Smoke?'

Fesk didn't but he took a lho-stick and inhaled.

'I have to get back to Spaceport,' mused General Creed. 'But I should think another six hours.'

'Is that how long we have left?' Fesk stammered.

Creed grinned in the light cast by his stub. 'I think so,' he said. There was a long pause. 'You did well today. All of you.'

'I feel like we took a hell of a beating.'

Creed seemed amused.

'I mean, look at how few of us are left,' Fesk continued.

Creed looked around. 'You think we're done?' He savoured a long drag. '*They* are the ones who're trapped, cadet. They're bottled up with the quicksand on either side of them, with us in front, and soon we'll send them howling back to the warp. They are about to face the wrath of the Astra Militarum.'

Fesk said nothing. He didn't quite believe it.

'Where are you from?' Creed said after a while.

'Kasr Ferrox.'

'Ah. There's a fine minster there. My mother took me there once.' Creed paused. 'I must have been six years old. I had never seen such a bastion. Great spires and gun emplacements, and statues of saints at every loophole. I was an Utsider. My father was a hunter in the Gallan Highlands. I think Kasr Ferrox was the first city I ever saw. It would be good to go and see it again.'

'It would,' Fesk said.

'We should go there when this war is over, when Anckor

and his men are dead.' Creed slipped a lho-stick behind
Fesk's ear. 'Save that for tomorrow,' he said, walking off.
'When this is all over.'

When Fesk finished his watch he stumbled back to the
camp.

Lina was sitting, smoking a lho-stick. 'I saw him talking to you too,' she said.

He nodded and rolled his jacket up as a pillow.

'What did he talk about?'

'The minster at Kasr Ferrox.'

She laughed. 'You're kidding.'

'No.'

She pulled out her knife, wiped it on her thigh and
slammed it back into its sheath. 'He's something else, isn't
he? Did you ever think you would meet someone like that?'

'No.'

'I hope they come again tomorrow.'

'I'm sure they will.'

They stood staring out into the night, watching Creed
moving slowly around the sentries. Every once in a while
they could hear his low bass chuckle, or see the red glow
of his stub.

Fesk started as Lina suddenly stepped towards him.
He could smell her proximity, and then without warning she leaned in close and kissed him. A firm, wet kiss.

Fesk was lucky there was a line of sandbags for him to
lean against. He put a hand on the small of her back, and
she pulled away out of reach. 'Tomorrow, let's kill them all.'

It was an hour before dawn when Fesk woke with a start.
Valkyries were approaching. He sat up and squinted as
they landed and kicked up a blizzard of cad-ore. The wind

was starting to stir. He smelled stub smoke and sat up. The gunships paused for a minute, and then they veered up and wheeled away. Fesk pushed himself up with his rifle butt and limped along the sandbacks. He felt deflated suddenly. As if hope had blown away on the wind.

'What happened?' Fesk said when he saw Major Luka standing over him, running a hand over the stubble on his head.

'He's gone.'

'Creed? He's left us?' Fesk felt panic quicken his heartbeat. 'Why?'

'He's a commander. Now he has to command.'

'So what's going to happen here?'

'I have no idea, cadet. And nor, I bet, do the Anckorites.'

Major Luka started away, but he turned and put out a hand. 'You fought well, Cadet Fesk. This should all be over soon. Get some more sleep. We should have a few hours yet. Have faith in General Creed. If anyone can pull this off, he can.'

Creed jumped from the Valkyrie as it fired its landing jets.

Kamala, the wiry commander of the local militia, ran in to greet him. 'We thought you were lost!' she said.

'Well, I'm here now,' he shouted over the roar of the engines. 'What's the situation?'

'The commissars have rallied the retreating columns. They're heading to the coordinates you provided. They'll be in position by 0600.'

'And did you get through to the fleet?'

'Yes, sir.'

'At last.'

* * *

Creed stood over the maps at headquarters. Kamala had never seen an officer who thought so quickly and in such detail. He made rapid calculations of movements, deployments, unit strengths. An air of quiet intensity filled the place as he shuffled through the maps, checked his timepiece and then looked up.

'Get me the *Magister Thine*,' he said. 'I want to speak to the captain personally. Now.'

Creed drummed his fingers as he waited. When the link was established he took the handset. 'Captain Avery,' he said. 'I need those lance batteries of yours. The future of this campaign lies on your shoulders. I am going to give you coordinates. You will position your craft above the target and strike them at 0600 hours local time. You will bombard that point for exactly three minutes.'

He put his thumb on the map, and picked out a series of points below the Incardine Ridge, asked Captain Avery to repeat them and then nodded.

'Good. You have the thanks of the Astra Militarum and of Warmaster Ryse himself, captain.'

At 0553 hours the order went through *Magister Thine* to open gunports for 'collective and concentrated fire'. For kilometres along the length of the grand cruiser, batteries opened, colossal turrets turned to face the planet, vast black gun barrels slowly pointing towards the Incardine Ridge and lances powered up. Gunnery crews, hundreds strong, hoisted vast kilotonne ordnance; power lines hummed as the gantries shook with power lifts slowly slamming the shells into firing position.

At 0558 silence fell. The gantries and loading decks were strangely still. The clocks ticked down. The order to 'ready weapons' came, and dull clicks rang through the ancient linebreaker as firing mechanisms engaged.

At three seconds after 0600 hours the bombardment was announced. The *Magister Thine* lurched suddenly in orbit.

A sudden storm raged in the skies above Besana. The planet trembled. Fissures began to form in the crust of the world as the *Magister Thine*'s linear accelerators threw magma warheads with adamantine cores deep into the base of the Incardine Ridge. The firing picked out the coordinates, boxing the massed Anckorites in then smashing into their massed ranks with horrible precision. Volcanic eruptions threw up dust storms of cad-ore that would last for months after. Along the Incardine Ridge men threw themselves to the bottom of their dugouts. They shouted to the Golden Throne and could not hear themselves.

Below them the hordes of Anckorites died, their screams unheard in the maelstrom. The massed ranks were incinerated, the reinforcements turning and fleeing back into the Long Dry, where the escape was blocked by disciplined companies of Cadian Eighth, Ephanlian Hussars, the brightly coloured lances of Saint Percival's Cavalry and, ranked in echelon formation, the massed grey armour of the 17th Company of the Aquarian Guard.

The Anckorites stopped and pulled the black rags from their scarred faces and stared in shock at the thousands of muzzles – lasrifle, bolter, autocannon and battlecannon – all trained on them.

Then a single voice gave the order – 'Fire!' – and the Anckorites howled in fury and frustration as they were slaughtered.

* * *

Fesk's nightmare was of thunder and flame.

It was later that day when he woke in the back of a Chimera, while the medic injected more stimms into his arm. There was cad-ore in his mouth, his ears, and it gummed his eyes closed.

There was a brief sting, the odd sensation of the syringe being emptied into his vein, and then the stimms hit and he let out a sigh. There were voices all about. Calm, professional voices, hurrying back and forth. The medic was busy. He put a wad of cotton on the place he had injected.

It took an age for Fesk to unglue his lips to speak. When it came, his voice was a dry croak. 'Did we win?'

'Not yet,' the man said through his white mask.

The sound of an autocannon started up somewhere nearby. Then two, and eventually a chorus of them.

Fesk sat up with a start. He wanted his rifle. He wasn't going to get caught again. 'Are we going to die?'

The medic spoke between clenched teeth. 'Will you sit still?' He breathed slowly and Fesk could feel the tug of skin as the needle went in and pulled the wound tight. 'Creed's shown them.'

What had he shown them? Fesk wondered. The drugs took hold again and he lay back and dreamed of Creed, and of Lina and the sudden kiss. Fesk started laughing. He wiped his eyes. He couldn't help it. He sniffed and shook his head. He felt someone next to him and looked up. It was Yetske. He was staring at the lho-stick behind Fesk's ear.

'I'd give it to you, but you're dead,' Fesk said.

Yetske didn't go away. But his face turned into Lina's.

'Oh, you too?' he said. 'You're dead too?'

'You're crying,' she said. 'Fesk blubbing like a baby?'

'No,' Fesk said, wiping his cheeks again.

It was a week later that Fesk – still a little giddy with stimms – slung his kitbag over his shoulder and limped forward to join the file of men waiting to exit Starport Medicac Facility. There were ships out there; he had heard their engines as they landed. Maybe he'd get to write that letter, he thought as he shuffled forward, but now he didn't really know what to say. He was still alive. That was enough.

The line was slow. At last he came to the front. A short-tempered Munitorum quartermaster stood behind a high wooden counter. He had a clipboard before him. 'Name and number?'

'C20004.346. Whiteshield Jasper Fesk.'

The man flipped a number of pages back and looked up. He found the right spot. 'Fesk. Uniform, helmet. Yes?'

Fesk nodded. Whatever they said. The quartermaster walked off and came back a minute later with a neatly folded pile of clothes, with a fresh helmet on. Fesk took it, signed and then moved to the side before realising he'd been given the wrong pile.

'Excuse me,' he called out, but the quartermaster was already serving the next man. He gave Fesk a fixed look.

'Yes?'

'You gave me the wrong pile.'

The quartermaster came forward. He looked like he was going to strike him.

'Fesk. Whiteshield. 20004th Cadet Group. ident number 346. Correct?'

Fesk nodded.

The quartermaster put out a hand and lifted the materials. 'These are correct,' he said. 'What is the problem?'

Fesk held up his helmet. There was no white stripe. The quartermaster was busy and waved him away. 'Did no one tell you?' he said. 'You're a Shock Trooper now. Cadian Eighth.'

Fesk looked at the icon on the helmet. A silver skull and Cadian Gate badge, underneath the number eight and a wreath of laurels.

Fesk looked around. He didn't know the men about him. They were a mix of all the wounded from the fighting: Mordax Dragoons, Crinan Fourth, Aquarians and a Vostroyan Firstborn with a grey moustache and a white bandage over one eye.

'Are you all right, lad?' he asked.

'I'm a Shock Trooper,' Fesk said dumbly.

The Vostroyan had no idea what he was talking about.

'I'm a Shock Trooper,' he said again, holding up the badge.

'Eighth?' the Vostroyan asked.

Fesk nodded.

'Never heard of them,' the man said, and stalked off towards the landers where files of troops, transports, freshly washed armour and gun barrels in their tarpaulin sheathes were waiting to board.

Fesk found Lina and they stood together. Lina had her jacket thrown over a fresh tank top. 'Not dead then?' he asked. He didn't know what to expect in response.

All she said was: 'Eighth?'

Fesk nodded.

'Me too,' Lina said. There was a long pause. 'He got away.'

'Who?'

'Luciver Anckorite. He let his men die and ran. We're going after him.'

'Are we?'

Lina gave him a look. 'Don't you listen to anything?'

Fesk shook his head. 'I've been in the medicae.'

'Oh. How is it?' She looked down. His stitches pulled, but they were healing. He said nothing. The ground shook as a lander took off about a mile away.

'I hear they got Darkins,' Fesk said.

Lina looked away for a moment. When she looked back at him there were tears in her eyes, but they did not fall and the look she gave him dared him to notice them.

'Yeah,' she said. 'Pultin. Yetske. Shanner. Brantsk. All the poor frekkers. They got Garonne too. Skinned him.' Lina paused. She nodded as she scratched a symbol in the dirt with her toe. 'Well,' she said. 'We should get to the lander.'

It took a day to load the lander. Fesk and Lina and the other new Shock Troopers bunched together. Major Luka came to say farewell.

'I'm proud of you all!' he said. 'Now go out there and kill each and every one of them.'

'What will you do now?' Fesk asked.

'Teach more gun-babies like you how to survive.'

'That was a tough straw we pulled, yeah?'

Major Luka looked him in the eye. 'One of the toughest I've ever seen. But you made it. And you held Luciver back. And now you're Shock Troopers!'

The crowd drifted off in twos and threes. Fesk lingered. 'What happened, major?' he said. 'I was wounded, and I don't really remember what was going on around us. Last thing I remember is you telling me to go back to sleep. The rest seems like a dream.'

Major Luka stopped. 'You don't remember the bombardment?'

'Oh, yeah. I remember that.'

'Well, our position was critical. We had to hold the causeway. Once Creed had the Anckorites bunched up along the Route Equatorial he had the Navy boys fire on it. I've never felt a planet shake before. Besana trembled before the fury of the *Magister Thine*. The very ground shook. It was the only way we could beat the Anckorites. They outnumbered us ten or more to one.'

'So why didn't they just flee?' Fesk asked.

'Ah well. They tried that. But remember all those troops who were sitting on landers waiting to evacuate? Creed landed in the Long Dry behind the Anckorites. He put belief back into them. The enemy were trapped. Desert. Causeway. Imperial armour.' Major Luka held out an open palm, and slowly closed it. 'He crushed them.'

Fesk was numb as he filed up the lander ramps. The Cadians were quartered in container Alpha-Six. He passed containers full of parked tanks and Chimeras, and a gallery of Sentinels, like ranks of giant warriors, eerily still.

Fesk looked about him. Each Shock Trooper found a bunk. He pictured one in the corner under a massive steel girder. He was quiet and thoughtful, looking about the vast hangar. This was his regiment now and his family. This was his world.

An hour after boarding, a klaxon rang. No one seemed

to take any notice. Then the engines lit and the whole craft began to vibrate, and then they were taking off.

His stomach always lurched when the landers took off. He shut his eyes and prayed that this time he didn't vomit. Suddenly, Fesk smelled something. He pushed himself off his bunk and walked towards a crowd of men. None of them knew him, but they saw a young face and they let him in. They were all Cadians. Someone in the middle was telling jokes.

Fesk pushed to the front. There was a long table of men. In the middle was a bear of a man, three days of stubble, a greatcoat over his shoulder, a stub in his fingers, empty bottle on the table.

'Ah!' he said. Creed put his hand out to the table to steady himself. 'Gentlemen! Meet one of our newest recruits...'

'Jasper Fesk,' Fesk said.

'Drink with me, Fesk.' Creed poured an amasec and held it out to him. 'Arcady Pride!' he said. 'Straight from the warmaster's table!'

Fesk took the glass. The liquid smelled sweet and strong. He held it up and took in the men about him: young, old, wary, wounded, fierce and friendly. He lifted it to his mouth and drank.

Creed winked. 'Just for luck.'

LOST HOPE

JUSTIN D HILL

It had been ten minutes since the astropathic message had reached him, and Ursarkar Creed was still cursing. Colour Sergeant Jarran Kell watched as Creed strode towards the drinks table, picked up a bottle of green spirit and read the label.

'What is this?' Creed growled.

Kell stepped up. '*Zub-rod-ka*. It's amasec, or something like it. Fleet Captain Avery sent it, with his regards. I think he finds having you on board easier when you have good drink around you.'

Creed grunted, unscrewed the brass cap, poured a measure of the green liquid into a cut crystal glass and knocked it back. From his expression Kell guessed it wasn't bad. Creed offered the bottle to Kell.

'No, thank you,' he said.

'Not when on duty, eh?' said Creed. 'You're always such a stickler for those kinds of things.' The general poured himself another drink, rested both fists on the map table and stared down at the spread of system charts. Scarus, Belis Corona, Chinchare, Agripinaa. In the centre was a chart of the Cadian system. Every region was covered with crosses, each one marking an uprising, a rebellion, a lost contact.

'Look at it!' Creed snapped. 'It's clear!'

Kell looked. It wasn't clear to him, and he told Creed so.

'Look!' Creed shouted. 'Here! Here! Here! Supply routes to Cadia. That's what this all about. It's not random – it's war, and it's about *Cadia*. About the Imperium itself. And Warmaster Ryse is so far up his own backside that he thinks his little campaign is all that is going on. Damn him! Damn the lot of them!'

The lot of them were the officers of Cadian High Command. They hadn't taken to Creed any more than he had to them. He was too *rough*, was how they phrased it as they passed the amasec to the left. Too successful, more like.

Creed slammed an open palm down again. Neither of them spoke. The silence was marked only by the scratch of the seated data-servitor's blunt metal quill writing out more reports of uprisings and more attacks by Anckorite forces – more mess for them to clean up.

'And now Ryse tells me we need to end this campaign before I can get back to Cadia and High Command.'

Creed knocked his drink back, sat down and lit his lho-stub. He stared at the glowing data screen on the wall above the servitor's head, which scrolled with unpunctuated lines of data: names of places, officers, reports, automated reminders, ship-to-ship transmissions. All the petty white noise of Imperial communications. Kell picked up a plan for a mooted defensive trench system on a planet named Atelier-888 and studied it.

Creed had the air about him of a man who was beaten, and Kell didn't know what to say. Warmaster Ryse's message had been clear. Defeat Luciver Anckor, with no more reinforcements.

'What's that?' Creed said suddenly.

Kell looked up but the line of data had already scrolled down out of sight. Creed moved over to the dataport. He pressed buttons and cursed. 'How do you work this thing?'

Kell gingerly turned a brass dial three clicks to the left, but nothing happened.

'Servitor,' Creed snapped. 'There was a report of a ship just arriving in-system. Is it a military craft? Reserves, perhaps?'

Stranger things had happened. Ships got lost, delayed, diverted. Perhaps this was one of those. Cogs whirred in the metal parts of the servitor's brain as its speech function warmed up.

'Negative,' it said.

'Hostiles?' Kell asked, his mind beginning to organise boarding parties, strongpoints, layers of defence.

'Negative,' the servitor responded. 'Vessel is the *Justicae Eternas*. Prison barge. Crew, one thousand three hundred and seven. Indentured population at outset from Scarus Sector, twenty-five thousand, six hundred and eighty-three. Attrition rate estimated at 4.3 per cent per month of travel. Due to dock at Lost Hope–'

'Impossible,' Creed muttered, leafing through the pile of maps. He slapped the one he wanted with an air of triumph. 'Lost Hope. Ice world. Uninhabited!'

Creed impressed Kell at moments like these. The knowledge he had was phenomenal. The cogs behind the screen whirred again as the servitor accessed its data banks. 'Data incorrect. Penal colony on Lost Hope for one hundred and fifty years–'

'A penal colony?'

'Correct, servicing a promethium drilling station at the pole,' the servitor said. 'Administrators of House Kasky tithed to the Administratum...' It droned on, reeling through lists of information that were no longer pertinent. Creed had what he wanted. He clapped his hands and laughed. 'A penal colony!'

Kell didn't know what was so amusing.

'Jarran,' Creed said, a grin on his face, 'we've got an army!' Kell's expression must have spoken volumes. 'Don't worry,' Creed said as he swept up the bottle of zubrodka. He swept Kell up as he thrust the bottle into his greatcoat pocket. 'Come on, there's no time to waste. And stop looking at me like that. I won't put you in charge of training them. We need to see Captain Avery.'

Kell spat, and his spit froze in the air before it hit the ice.

'Frekk, it's cold,' he muttered as he strode to the bottom of the landing ramp and looked around at the ball of ice and rock that was Lost Hope.

The landing zone was deserted. All Kell could see was a row of six vast rusted promethium tanks, wide puddles of oily slush where Adeptus Mechanicus tankers had landed to refill, and behind and about it all a bleak vision of white tundra, marked only by a few patches of dark pine forest where terraforming had achieved limited levels of success. He rolled his head back into his high jacket collar. He wore hostile environment thermals, but still the chill was like icy water on his scalp.

Creed appeared at the head of his honour guard as the landers' engines powered down. 'This is it?' he asked.

Kell nodded. 'Yes. This is it.'

Creed rubbed his gloved hands together and watched the first Chimera began to reverse down the landing ramp. He seemed unduly cheerful. 'It's not so bad.'

Kell had a sense of doom about this whole endeavour. He saw no point in putting polish on the proverbial. 'This planet is a class-A frekkhole,' he said sourly.

Creed took a deep breath and stalked off. 'It smells just like Kasr Partox,' he called back.

'Kasr Partox is a frekkhole,' Kell muttered, as he followed his commander.

There was no need for signposts. A single track led off through the plateau of dull grey ice. The place was deserted. Creed climbed into the lead Chimera with his personal guard.

'Let's go,' Kell called out to the remaining troopers. 'No point getting cold.'

Kell was the last to embark, and he stood on top of the Chimera, scanned one last time for stragglers then waved to the lander pilot preparing for take-off. He dropped into the Chimera turret, closed the hatch above him and shimmied into the front gunner's seat, next to the driver, Blendal. He tapped the heavy flamer fuel canisters and nodded in approval. They were full.

'Let's go,' he said. His tone conveying in no uncertain terms that Colour Sergeant Jarran Kell was in a bad mood.

'It's cold,' Blendal tried after a few minutes.

'Tell me something I don't know,' Kell said. He reached back and tried to loosen the ache in his shoulder, but beneath the hostile environment jacket he was wearing his carapace armour and he couldn't get to it. 'Is the heat on?'

Bendal flipped a couple of switches for show. 'It's at maximum, sir.'

Kell cursed silently and tried rolling his shoulder instead.

Trooper Agemmon crawled in from the back cabin. 'So what are we doing here, sergeant?' he asked.

'We're picking up penal troopers,' Kell said.

'How many?'

'Ten thousand.'

'You're not serious,' Agemmon said.

'Yes, trooper, I most certainly am.'

'We're that short?'

Yes, Kell thought, and Creed's got it into his head that Cadia is in danger. But his jaw remained shut and his face gave nothing away. He didn't comment on things like that.

Agemmon puffed out his cheeks. 'Think they'll be any good? The penals?'

He withered under the look Kell gave him.

The prison governor's residence was set in a low valley which offered a little shelter from the gales that plagued the planet. A simple barricade of ice and ditches formed a square about the prefabricated complex. From a single watchtower flew an aquila flag, and the banner of House Kasky: two white hands clasped in friendship. The metal struts of the watchtower had not been cleared of icicles for a month or more. The only sign of life was a flickering strip light and a plume of sooty black smoke coming from a heating duct. Kell had seen a number of complexes like this on far-flung worlds. They were all the same, designed to support life in the worst of conditions: a tiny top floor of hab units, with a vast system below the ice comprising of heating and ventilation works, store rooms, freezers and bunkers that could keep the inhabitants alive for decades.

Blendal pulled his Chimera up behind Creed's. Kell was first out and into the biting air. He dropped onto the ice with a dull crunch, laspistol ready, while the other Cadians formed a semicircle about Creed as he strode down his vehicle's ramp. The general seemed oblivious to the precision of the troops, but Kell was not. He watched each man and he was pleased, though he didn't show it. They were, after all, men of his own Cadian Eighth.

'They should be expecting us,' Creed said, pulling his greatcoat closed and starting up the broad rockcrete steps to the prefab doorway. As they approached, the blast doors gave a low sneeze of hydraulics and began to slide open. A tall woman stepped out. She wore a long coat of purple silk-velvet astrakhan shako. Behind her stood four penal guards dressed in heavy black greatcoats, with rebreathers and pump-action short-barrelled shotguns. Not very friendly, Kell thought, but he kept his mouth closed. The galaxy was full of populations who had spent too long in isolation.

'Welcome to Lost Hope,' the woman called out in an imperious voice. 'I am Governor Irena Kasky, of the House Kasky.'

Kell saluted. He'd overheard enough of Creed's communications to know that the Kaskys claimed to be descended from an ancient family of rogue traders. The sector was full of their scions. They bought up hereditary positions by the system-load. Why any of them would want to run a penal colony, Kell had no idea.

Creed saluted. 'I am General Creed of the Cadian Eighth, commander of the Imperial forces in this sector.'

'It is an honour, General Creed. Come inside.' She stood aside to let the Cadians enter. Kell counted them all in, then looked up and realized she was staring at him. Or rather at his equipment. 'Are all of those *entirely* necessary?' she asked.

Kell never went anywhere without his power fist, laspistol and a brace of grenades. He shrugged. 'The galaxy is a dangerous place.'

'Clearly,' she said. 'This way please.'

Agemmon gave Kell a wink as if to say he had caught the eye of the local lady. The sergeant's broad jaw betrayed nothing in return. He gave a slight inclination of his head.

'Inside, trooper,' he growled.

Kell kept his arms behind his back as they followed Governor Kasky down the corridor. The complex had the shabby, lived-in air of an Imperial troop carrier after a long warp jump. There was dust in the corners, water stains down the walls, and an old notice board with yellowed signs, long since out of date.

They stopped at what appeared to be Kasky's office. Outside was a roster list, a poster of an Imperial Guardsman with the words *Stay Alert, Stay Alive* printed underneath, and a picture of Saint Celestine, which appeared, blasphemously, to have been used as a target for darts.

Kell sniffed, and Kasky's cheeks coloured.

'Shall we go inside?' she said. 'We can talk there.'

'A good idea,' Creed said. 'Kell, with me.'

Kasky gave him a look. 'Does he follow you everywhere?'

'Yes,' said Creed. 'Yes, he does.'

The walls of Kasky's chambers were hung with rich carpets, the floor was strewn with cushions, and one end of the room was given over to a vast bed. There was a silver ewer of water. She poured each of them a glass and handed them out. 'It's fresh,' she said.

Creed waited for her to drink first. She did, ostentatiously. Kell refused, and stood smartly by the door as Creed pulled up an ornate velvet chair and started to talk in a low voice. It took about thirty seconds for Kasky's voice to rise. 'You want what? No. It is unacceptable!'

Kell couldn't hear what Creed was saying clearly, but he could guess.

'There are always problems!' Kasky said. There was a long pause. 'General Creed, my family has invested...' she stopped and looked for the right words. 'I... I have tithes to deliver. You cannot just come here and take my prisoners. I have my superiors too, you know.'

The general, evidently, was not budging. Kasky stood up and tried a different tack. 'Can you even fit ten thousand prisoners on your ship? Oh.' At last she said, 'Not all the prisoners are fit. Some have gone, well, mad, during their incarceration. Maybe you should go to check on them. You would not want to take some of them on board any ship.'

Creed nodded and stood up, raising his voice for Kell to hear. 'I understand. I am in a hurry, so I think the best thing is for us to go and sort through them. We would not want anything untoward to happen on ship, after all.' He turned away from Kasky and winked at Kell.

'Coats on,' Kell said as he strode out. 'We're going to see the new recruits!'

There was a palpable air of disappointment as the men knocked back their cups of fresh water, but within a moment they had slung their lasguns and were stand-ing ready at the door.

'You will understand if I do not join you,' Kasky said as they assembled just inside the entrance doors. 'I need to communicate this information urgently to my family.'

'Of course,' Creed said. He gave Kell a look that implied that the less time they had to spend with Kasky the better.

'There are guards at the hangars, about five kilometres away. They will meet you down there. They won't be hard to find – there are only two roads on Lost Hope. Adel!' she called. 'Can you go with our guests and make sure they reach the hangars?'

Adel was a skinny man with patches of ginger stubble and pale blue eyes. He seemed a little giddy with the prospect of someone new to talk to. 'Yes, ma'am.'

'Take them to the prison camp,' ordered Kasky. 'They want to sort through the prisoners for those suitable.'

The man put out a hand. 'I'm Adel. I'm the plant chief.' He nodded towards their Chimeras as the blast doors shut behind them. The vehicles were still wearing their mottled brown and beige desert camouflage from the Besana cam-paign. 'Didn't have time to whitewash them, eh?'

Kell had the suspicion that he was talking to an idiot. 'No,' he said slowly. 'But then, we're not expecting trouble.'

Adel laughed, 'No, and why should you?' He rubbed his hands together. 'Well, let's get going.'

The prison camp was situated next to the promethium fields, where derricks were black against the sky and long, low hangars were half-buried with snow. Work seemed to have stopped for the day, and a company of about twenty guards were waiting around a burning barrel, hands outstretched or thrust deep into pockets. They were a hard-faced bunch with long knives, a variety of shotgun patterns, autopistols, rebreathers, and black shakos, which must have been a House Kasky thing. They gave their hands a last rub as they left the barrel and walked across to where the Chimeras were idling. Adel waved a brief greeting. He did not speak to them, but stamped his feet as he led them down the broad rockcrete steps to the first hangar doors and stopped before the interlocking steel blast doors. The black spray-painted lettering was flaking with the cold. *Grubhut 01*, it read.

'You sure want to see them?' he asked.

Kell nodded. 'That's why we're here.' He turned to the troopers. 'Safeties off. Just in case.'

The doors rolled slowly back. The hangar stretched into darkness. There was no sign of the convicts. Adel banged on the doors with his electro-goad. There was a hollow metallic ring.

'Up, dogs!' he shouted.

There was no response.

Kell and Creed exchanged looks and together they

strode into the hangar. The deeper they went the stronger the stench of sour, sweaty, unwashed bodies became. Someone behind them flicked a switch and lumen strips flickered to life overhead. The harsh light revealed a crowd of hundreds, crouching together for warmth. 'They've come again,' a voice said.

'Shhh!' said another.

'Are those Guardsmen?' asked a third. 'Listen!'

Kell felt disgust. *They're barely worth shooting,* he thought.

Creed stopped, hands on hips, and stared at them. His disappointment was palpable. He needed killers, not whipped dogs.

'Look at you,' Creed called out. 'You have sunk as low as men can sink. And you will die here on Lost Hope, sooner or later. Like this. On this Emperor-forsaken hole. But I offer you a chance of redemption.'

There was a muted response. 'Shh!' one of the men said. 'Listen!'

Creed called out again. 'I am offering you something very precious, a chance few men get. Do you want to make your peace with the Emperor?'

The heap of bodies began to break apart. One man came forward on his knees, tears streaking his face. 'Take me from this hell!' he hissed reaching for Creed. Kell drew his pistol, but Creed raised a hand. 'Give me a gun and I will atone for my sins!'

Soon all those that could were coming forward on their knees. They were like animated corpses, shuffling forward into the light. They were not desperate, Kell thought, they were *thankful*. He felt his skin tingle. He'd seen Creed do this before, turn fleeing cowards into men who would take a las-round to the heart and still keep fighting. But always before it had been in the madness of defeat, with the ordnance exploding about them and the mad flare of las-fire strobing Creed's ash-streaked face. But here, in this dark, cold, forsaken pit, men – starved, broken, inhuman – were lifting their hands up to thank him for the chance to die a glorious death. A death worth having.

Despite everything, Sergeant Kell felt pride.

Creed gave Kell a curt nod and lowered his voice. 'We'll take them all. Any who can hold a gun. Keep them here until the lander arrives. I'll see what transports they have to get them all up to the space port. We'll pack them in as tight as we need to. Burn their clothes, shave their heads, delouse them all. We'll make sure they get a good meal.' He paused. 'I don't like the way they've been treated here. I have a bad feeling about this place.'

Kell saluted.

'Adel,' Creed said as he marched out. 'I'm going straight back to call my ship. Take Sergeant Kell to the other hangars. He will finish up here.'

They took the hangars in threes to get through them more quickly.

'Make it look like you're sorting through them,' Kell said to Sergeant Tarloc, 'but we'll take the lot, unless they're really mad. Don't leave any here with these scum.'

Tarloc nodded, and led his two men off to see the last batch.

'This is the Corrections unit,' Adel said as he led them to the last structure, much like the others but about half the size. There was a single door, set into the blast shutters. Adel tapped a code into a datapad and the door unlocked. He motioned the Guardsmen to go in. Troopers Hesk and Luord went first, and Tarloc followed.

Hesk hit the lumen switch, and the lights came on from the back, revealing a long chamber of cages. 'They're all empty,' Tarloc said, turning back.

Adel was standing in the doorway, leaning casually against the doorpost. 'Yes,' he said. 'Funny that.'

'Where are the penals?'

Adel grinned. 'I think you killed them,' he said. 'On Besana.'

Tarloc glanced at Hesk and stepped forward to shove Adel out the way, but Adel lowered his shotgun from his shoulder to point straight at Tarloc's face.

'Quit frekking around,' Tarloc said.

'Don't give me orders,' Adel said, and fired. Point blank, both barrels.

Sergeant Tarloc was dead before he hit the ground. Trooper Luord left a long red smear down the hangar door. Hesk lay on the ground, moaning in pain. He had been hit in the side of the face. Adel walked casually up and kicked him hard in the ribs. Hesk glared up at the man, his one good eye filled with anger and hatred. He tried to reach for his fallen lasgun, but Adel kicked it away.

'No, no, no,' he said as if he were scolding a naughty child. He put the barrel of his gun to the side of the Cadian's head and fired.

Adel was whistling as he arrived at Grubhut 07. His men were wiping their long knives clean.

'Done?' he called out. They pointed down to the floor where three Cadians lay, freshly butchered. Their blood was bright against the snow, the red puddles already freezing. 'Good work,' Adel said, and climbed up towards Grubhut 06. He hummed as he went, resting his shotgun on his shoulder and reliving the moment he had shot the Guardsman in the face, relishing the look on his stupid face when he knew he was about to die. He grinned. He liked killing.

'Got them?' he called out as he rounded the corner. There were five dead bodies lying on the ground. They were laid out as they had been killed, arms and bodies twisted and bloody and broken. Adel looked again. The dead men were not Cadians. He barely had a moment to curse before a hand clasped his shoulder and spun him around.

His attacker headbutted him, slammed him against a wall, kneed him in the crotch, then slammed him against the wall again, a hand so tight about his throat he could barely breath. His nose felt broken, and he gagged on blood as he spat out two teeth. As he blinked away tears, he looked into the indigo-blue eyes of a Cadian. And not just any Cadian, but Colour Sergeant Jarran Kell.

The Cadian ground out the words between clenched teeth. 'What the frekk is happening here?' He let the pressure off a fraction. 'Do you know what happens when I turn this thing on?'

Adel looked down and saw that it wasn't just a hand clamped about his throat, but Kell's power fist. He kicked out at his attacker and then felt a sudden searing pain as the power fist's energy field was activated and his neck fried and came apart.

The stench of cooked skin and blood filled Kell's nostrils. He let Adel's smoking body drop to the floor.

Drusus and Odwin had secured the open hangar doors. 'Anything?' Drusus said.

Kell shook his head and wiped the gore from his face onto his sleeve. His carapace armour had saved him but the shotgun blasts had torn holes through his extreme hostile environment suit and he was losing heat fast.

'Here they come,' Agemmon hissed. Kell could hear the prison guards laughing and chatting as they ambled up the slope. 'Lots of them.'

Kell and his men exchanged glances. 'Come!' the sergeant said. 'To the Chimeras.'

As the prison guards came around the corner, Drusus slammed the Chimera into full forward and Odwin, in the front gunner's seat, mumbled the prayer of Righteous Flaming and squeezed the trigger. A great gout of burning promethium blazed towards the traitors. They didn't stand a chance. The Chimera rumbled over their burning bodies, and Kell, in the turret, tracked those few who had escaped.

The multi-laser whined as the batteries charged. Kell was almost casual about it. He sniffed, aimed, fired. Fist-sized holes were seared through each fleeing man.

'Got them,' Kell voxed. 'I'm going to check on the others.'

Kell's face was grim when he returned.

'All dead,' he said, pulling a less damaged hostile environment jacket on. He dropped down through the turret. 'Right, let's get the hell out of here and find out what's really happening on Lost Hope.'

* * *

They found the remains of Creed's Chimera at the top of the slope. It had fallen into the ditch at the side of the road and tipped onto its side. It had been shot up badly, by an autocannon judging from the damage.

Kell knew what happened when heavy calibre rounds penetrated armour like this. They filled the cabin with molten shards of metal and toxic smoke. It got messy. He peered in through the open top hatch. Jeorg and Fresk had been torn apart. Their blood and guts had frozen to the metal. Poor frekkers. They hadn't stood a chance.

Blendal was in the front. His head had been shot away. Resko had crawled clear. His throat had been cut, and he had bled out into the snow. There was no sign of Creed. Kell looked about him. The white tundra was blank, silent and empty.

Odwin called out, 'Sir. I found this.'

It was a thin piece of cloth scrawled with glyphs. Kell recognised them.

'Anckorites,' he cursed.

'The general?' Agemmon said.

Kell shook his head. 'He's not dead,' he said. 'He must be over there,' he said and strode towards the Chimera. There was only one 'there' to speak of.

Drusus climbed back into the driver's seat.

'So, we attack the governor's residence? Just the four of us?'

'Yes,' Kell said, closing the top hatch. 'Just the four of us. They won't know what hit them.'

Ursarkar E. Creed shivered. He was a child again, sitting by the fireside on Cadia, inside his father's sheiling. Winter had come. The auroks were grunting in their pens as they chewed through the loads of leaf-hay he had helped his father cut in the summer. There was not enough to feed the herd. His father blamed the weather, his mother the spirits that howled through the pylons. His sister said nothing. Ursarkar was seven and he shivered. He didn't know who to blame.

'Son, come!' his father said. His sister gave him a look, but Ursarkar did not need the warning. He had seen how much his father had drunk. He followed the old man's gaze. Above them, the vast, dark purple and green bruise of the Eye of Terror had risen high in the sky. He did not need to point, but gripped his son's shoulders too hard, and said simply, 'I fought there.'

Ursarkar bit his lip to stop himself wincing. He looked up. It did not seem possible to leave the world and travel into the stars and fight.

'I fought in the stars. I was a Cadian Shock Trooper.'

Ursarkar turned and looked up into his father's eyes. Dark and unsure, almost guilty, they brimmed with tears for a moment. He wiped the tears away before they could betray him.

Ursarkar put his hand up and touched his father's face. 'I will fight there too,' he said.

'Good,' his father said, but he sounded distant. The world went dark and there was a scream. His father and the shieling were gone. The screaming went on. It was his own voice, calling on the shooting to stop.

He was lying under a bed, rockcrete dust in his nose, his mouth, his eyes. He gagged and coughed. His ears were ringing from the explosions. He could not move. There was a weight on his leg. It was his sister. Her eyes were open and staring. Blood trickled from her nostrils.

The sight of her dead face shocked him back into understanding, with a sudden terror, that he was eight again, in Kasr Gallan.

The realisation clutched him like a cold hand. Cultists were padding through the ruins, sniffing for survivors, mumbling their prayers, their sacrificial knives dripping blood. He knew he must not move. He must make no sound. He could not help his sister.

He did not know how long he lay there before he heard the crunch of a footstep entering what remained of the room. A heavy footstep. He held his breath and squeezed his eyes shut. Step by gritty step, the footsteps crossed the room towards him. Great black-booted feet, larger than seemed possible for a human. He did not dare even breathe as the metal frame of the bed was lifted back. He risked a glance.

Above him stood a giant, dressed in gleaming black power armour and swathed in cream-coloured robes that hid his face. He held a pistol in one hand. He reached down and pressed the pistol into Creed's hand. It was a laspistol. Then the warrior spoke to him in a voice that was deep, ancient and lonely...

Creed woke with a start before he heard the words. Not that he had ever forgotten them. He looked around. It was dark and cold, and deathly still. He was at the bottom of a crude shelter, a rough roof of pine branches above his head. His hands were bound. His head ached.

A man squatted over him. Not the armoured warrior of his dream, but a common man: skinny, shaggily bearded, thin, curious. The distinctive blue number of a convict was tattooed across his forehead. The man motioned Creed to silence with his finger.

Creed nodded and looked about him. There were twenty more men, shaggy, crouching low to the ground, three of them carrying lasguns.

He pulled himself up into a seated position and remembered what had happened. He had been sitting in the front of the Chimera, smoking and looking forward to planning the next campaign against Luciver Anckor's fortress on Grettel, when the cabin was suddenly full of smoke and ice and bits of what turned out to be Blendal's head.

Creed had kicked open the Chimera's top hatches, and hauled Gismar out. He was moaning, and it was clear from the bone sticking through his fatigues that his shin had been broken in the crash. Creed was about to start cutting the cloth away to set it straight when he saw dark shapes loping over the ice, shaggy fur capes and prayer strips flapping behind them. Harsh voices whooped and called out to their gods.

Trooper Gismar was solid, reliable. Creed had seen him lose a hand on Besos Nine and still hold a gun emplacement against the greenskins. 'If this is the end, Gismar, there's no one I'd rather have by my side,' Creed said.

Gismar had laughed. 'Don't let Sergeant Kell hear you saying that, sir,' he had croaked. Together they'd put up a stout resistance, but it was clear they were trapped and outnumbered. Creed fired three shots off behind them. They were returned. The Anckorites were working their way around them. There was nothing else for it. He had to think of Cadia, and if he was going to go he'd have to go now. Creed looked about. If he ran along the ditch he might just make that stand of trees.

'Go!' Gismar hissed as he reloaded. 'I'll hold them off.'

'See you on Cadia,' Creed said, looking into Gismar's face. Another one he would always remember.

Gismar looked up and smiled. His spirit was going home first, faster than any starship. He saluted with his bionic hand. 'See you on Cadia, general.'

The Anckorites shouted to one another as Creed burst from the ditch fifty yards away and dashed hard and low for the trees. The cold was raw in his throat. His legs pumped. Las-rounds lanced about him. One went through his greatcoat wings. They fizzed in the cold air about him. But he had grown up on the frigid moors of Cadia, and this felt like his home turf as he outpaced the Anckorites. He threw himself into the trees and rolled to the side, keeping the trunks between him and his pursuers.

He had easily outpaced them, and when he was clear Creed started looking for a way of surviving the night. He had been making this shelter when he had heard a footstep, and turned just in time to see a club descend towards his head. And now here he was, trussed up like a beast ready for slaughter. His captors were a gang of escaped convicts, each with a blue tattoo across their foreheads. The man who squatted next to him stared at his uniform and the name badge sewn into his left breast: Creed.

'You're not one of them,' the man said finally.

Creed shook his head. 'I am not.'

'When did you come to this planet?'

'Last night.'

'I saw your lander. It was a blue star in the sky. Two hours before darkness.'

'That's it.'

'Were the other landers yours as well?'

Creed's mind raced. What other landers?

'No,' he said.

There was a pause. The man had been through Creed's pockets: the contents lay on the ice between them. Ration packs, lho-sticks, a folded map, and his whiteshield cap badge. Creed's pistols were missing.

The man followed Creed's eyes. 'You are a Guardsman,' he said.

Creed nodded.

'Which regiment?'

'Cadian Eighth.'

'Never heard of them.' The man took one of the ration bars and took a bite. He chewed slowly, savouring the flavour. 'I was Guardsman once.'

'Which regiment?'

'Vostroyan Firstborn.'

'Never heard of them,' Creed smiled.

The man gave a low laugh. 'I like you. Are there more of you?'

'More of me? I hope not. I landed with twenty men though. My ship is in orbit and I have thousands there. If I can talk to them I can help you all.'

The man put up a hand. All Creed could hear was the low moan of the wind through the trees, the lonely howl of some hunting beast, and then the distant crack of exploding sap. The mans seemed satisfied.

'Who are you?' Creed whispered.

'I am a dead man to my people, my planet, my regiment. Here I am Convict 92497759. But once men called me Sergeant Leder. You think you can help us?'

Creed nodded.

The man held Creed's gaze. He seemed to be thinking. At last he took out his knife and bent over Creed to cut his ties. He helped Creed stand. 'Come,' he said. 'You should meet the others.'

Darkness thickened about them as they trekked through the forest. They walked for nearly an hour. The only sound was the scrape of boots on ice and low voices as they checked the way. Creed was shivering despite his hostile environment suit. The cold was so intense it went straight through to the bone marrow. Leder suddenly stopped at the base of a fallen pine. 'In here,' he said.

The opening was dark and damp. Pine roots brushing against his face. Creed bent down and as he pushed along the short passageway a fine sprinkle of dirt fell down the back of his collar. At last he stepped out into an open chamber and straightened. A smoky tallow flame burnt in the centre of the ice cave.

Creed smelt hot broth, stale sweat and heat.

Leder stood up. 'I have brought someone,' he announced. 'He comes from the Imperium. He wishes to speak to us all.'

They abandoned the Chimera two kilometres from the governor's palace. Kell led Agemmon, Odwin and Drusus across the ice fields. They were quiet, determined. When they sighted the hab complex Kell squatted down, laid out the plan, then said simply, 'Understand?'

The three shock troopers nodded.

'Right,' Kell said. 'Move out.'

The watch tower still appeared to be deserted. They moved with a quiet discipline, covering each other, kneeling, checking they had not been spotted, hurrying on. They dashed across the last stretch of open ground and slid down behind the perimeter bank. Kell peered over the top. He was tormented by the idea that Creed was in there and was pushing them along at a ruthless pace.

All clear, he motioned. They scrambled up, crossing the last thirty feet and ducking down by the side of the buildings. Kell led them along the walls to a hooped metal ladder. He kept his power fist beneath his jacket to stop the batteries from seizing up with the cold. In a moment they were up amongst the lumps, vents and chimney stacks of the hab-complex. At last Kell found what he was looking for. He knelt down, used his hostile environment mitten to dust off the snow and grinned.

Generatorium.

He had to take off the mitten to clamp a melta bomb in place and set the timer.

'Right,' he said, leading them a little way off. He took out his chronometer and counted down quietly. 'Five, four, three, two...' The melta bomb blew.

He pulled his power fist out of his jacket. It fizzed ineffectively. The battery had run low. Odwin shot Drusus a worried look.

'Frekk!' Kell counted to ten and tried once more. The power unit sparked one, two, three times, and at last the fist was coated in a crackling blue light. He plunged it down through the melted hole and peeled back the frozen sheets of metal, widening the breach. He kicked the last panel out. 'Ready?' he asked.

They nodded.

Kell went first, dropping down through the hole.

* * *

'Why should we help you?'

The voice rang out through the ice cave. A figure strode towards Creed. His fingers were black with frost bite, one of his eyes was a mess of scar tissue and an ugly scar ran from forehead to jaw. The other eye burned with hatred as he spat out words.

'I was sent to this hell for the sins of our commanders, who were cowards. Do you know what they did to us here, the House of Kasky? Their men cut symbols into our flesh. They fed us on our own raw dead. The things they did to us were inhuman. Look at my brother.' He pointed to one man in the corner of the room. His eyes had been torn out, and his face had been carved with grotesque glyphs and symbols. '*That* is what they did to us. So why should we help the Imperium who put us here?'

Creed's greatcoat hung from his shoulders. He was impassive as the man paced towards him. When he spoke his voice was low and resonant. 'Because I need you. Because the Imperium needs you... and because I can free you.'

'Free us from what, greatcoat?'

'I can free you from *fear*.' He paused, and let his words sink in. 'Your struggle here is part of a larger conflict. Great forces are moving. War is coming.'

'War is always here!' the other man laughed.

'This is war on a scale that we have never seen,' Creed said. 'What do you know of Luciver Anckor? He is a heretic. An enemy of the Imperium of Mankind. *He* is the man who had this done to your brother. His forces are on this planet. They are desperate and broken and I need your help to finish them. My ship is in orbit. If I can communicate with it, I can call my men down.'

'How can you call them? The only comms on the planet are at the Governor's residence.'

'Then we take it.'

The man snorted derisively. 'And what do *we* get from helping you?'

'When the battle is done I will take you with me. From this planet.'

'For what? To die as penal troopers?'

Creed smiled. 'We all die,' he said. 'But when you do, at least the Golden Throne will shine on you. You will die knowing that the Emperor has forgiven you.'

The man looked at him. His stare was long and hard. 'Keep your forgiveness. I want only revenge.' He walked forward and saluted. 'I am Major Darr Vel.'

Governor Kasky closed the door to her chambers. She was starting to panic.

'We have to get out of here,' she said. Her men nodded. She was right, but none of them wanted to go and none of them wanted to stay.

At that moment the complex shook. The lights flickered and went out, and klaxons began to wail as the secondary generatorium kick-started. '*Environmental breach,*' a voice announced. '*Environmental breach.*'

'Throne!' she hissed as the door flew from the hinges.

Sergeant Kell shot the two men on either side of Governor Kasky, grabbed her and put the gun to her head. 'Don't you dare blaspheme,' he hissed. 'Where is he?'

'Who?'

'General Creed. You have him. I want him back.'

He had her held tight. 'He's dead,' she hissed. She spoke quickly. 'I tried to warn you all, but you wouldn't listen.

My men found his body and brought it back. They were attacked by escaped convicts.'

'Show me!'

Two guards brought a black body bag forward and untied the fastenings. Kell kept his pistol trained on the governor. He looked down for a moment.

'That's not him–' he started, and Kasky turned out of his grasp.

As she twisted free, a giant roared into the room. It was clad in red power armour and the symbol on its shoulder was a black claw. Small horns protruded from its forehead, and its eyes were red flames, its smile a gruesome line of needle sharp teeth. At the Chaos Space Marine's belt hung five heads, one of them dripping thick blood down his left leg. In his left hand he carried a giant bolter that tracked about the room. Kell started moving. The bolter bucked one, two, three times and with each one a prison guard jumped and danced as the bolt rounds exploded within him, spraying the room with gore.

'Down!' Kell shouted.

Odwin was too slow. A bolt round hit him square in the chest and punched him from his feet. A second later his chest exploded. Kell was already throwing himself behind Kasky's desk. The bolter rounds followed them across the floor, tearing gaping holes into the desk panels. One bolter round went straight through the desk and Drusus alike.

Kell tried to activate his power fist, but the battery was dead again, and the power field fizzled uselessly. 'Frekk,' he muttered and fired wildly over the top of the desk as Agemmon lobbed a grenade.

There was a deafening thud. Agemmon kicked a

ventilation grate in the wall free. 'Go!' Kell hissed as the Space Marine thudded closer. It leered down at him as he pushed Agemmon through the hole and jumped after him.

The roar of bolter shells followed him as he twisted down and round, fell over and over, then suddenly there was open air and he was flying through it. He landed on top of Agemmon, who grunted. It was pitch black. Whatever room they had fallen into had the feel of a wide open space. In the distance he could hear the hum of a generator turning over quietly. The note changed, as if the thing had sensed them. Kell's skin suddenly prickled. A shape began to form in the darkness.

'Sarge...' said Agemmon warily.

Kell looked up and as his eyes accustomed themselves to the darkness he started to make out a vast metallic shadow rearing over them. Agemmon's hand clutched at his sleeve.

'What in the name of the Golden Throne is *that*?'

'We have what we steal,' Sergeant Leder said as he threw back the tarpaulin. 'It's not much.'

Creed inspected their cache of weapons. They had a few autoguns, carbines, an antique las-lock and an assortment of knives, clubs and fire-hardened spears. Leder handed the weapons out. One between two. That was all they had. The last man lifted a battered old lasgun from the pile and held it up.

'Not bad. Mars pattern,' he declared, then checked the ammo pack. 'Thirty shots left.' It would have to do.

'Make them count,' Creed told him and turned to Leder. The scouts had come back from the hangars. 'Any word of my men?'

'Yes. But there was a strange tale to tell. The prison guards were dead. All dead, and seven of your men. The Chimera you spoke of was gone. The scouts who are watching the compound say it was abandoned a few kilometres north of the Kasky Compound.'

'No sign of any survivors?'

Leder shook his head.

Creed nodded and tried to make sense of it all. He put his hand on Leder's shoulder and spoke confidentially. 'Sergeant Leder. Your men took my pistols when I came into your company.'

Leder lifted his coat. In his belt were two pistols. 'Which do you want?'

'Both.'

'Both?'

'Yes,' Creed said.

'You need two when men are lacking?'

'I need them both,' Creed repeated. There was a moment's pause. 'They are my weapons. They have value to me.'

Leder pulled out the more ornate of the two, a fine piece, designed for an officer, with brass fittings to the handle and an aquila on the barrel.

'And the other,' Creed said.

The other was an old Mars-pattern model, battered and scratched. A faded serial number was stencilled in small white letters across one side. 'This one?' Leder said.

'Yes. That one.' Creed did not wait but took it from his hand. 'I've had it a very long time,' he said as he checked the grip and the battery pack, and that the barrel was clear, and then thrust it back into his right holster. 'And it has saved my life more times than I can remember. Today it might save yours.' He turned to the men. 'All ready?'

They were ready. He could see it in their eyes.

'Leder, will you lead us on the right path. Remember, men,' Creed said as they filed out of the ice cave, 'the Emperor is watching.'

They climbed for two hours through the scattered pine forests, picking their way as the sun slowly lifted from the horizon and grew bright enough to cast long shadows over the snow. At one point Leder put his hands up and stopped. Creed was at his shoulder. 'Something ahead,' he said. He crouched down and seemed to sniff the air. 'I will go forward and see.'

Creed took out his battered old pistol just in case, but a few minutes later Leder came back with Darr Vel.

The one-eyed warrior had lost none of his anger. 'I have brought as many men as I could. You have seen those in the hangars. They all wanted to come, but they are too weak. They would have died of exposure. I brought only the strongest. There are a hundred of them. They have called themselves the Lost Hopers, though you have given them hope. They have no weapons, but their hands. No fear, but of failure. No cause, but yours.'

Creed squatted in the snow with Darr Vel and Leder as he planned the attack. They did not have the troops, the intelligence or the equipment he needed. They did not have time to lose. It felt good putting plans together.

'They are few and we are many,' he told the huddled men. They nodded. 'Have faith in the Emperor and He will protect. Our numbers are our chief weapon.' He grinned and they grinned back at him. 'Remember. Forwards, men, always forwards!'

Creed took Darr Vel aside and gave him quick

instructions on his diversionary attack. At the end he had the one-eyed warrior repeat them to him.

'Right,' he said. 'Do you think you can do that?'

Darr Vel nodded. 'Of course we can.'

Creed clasped his hands. He spoke in a low urgent voice. 'I need you there.'

Darr Vel gripped his hands back just as hard. 'Then we shall be there.'

They picked their way down the slopes. At last they came to rest half a kilometre from the compound perimeter. Creed was tense as he waited for the appointed time. There was fifteen kilometres still to go when there was a dull, distinctive explosion.

'Damn!' Creed cursed. He threw himself down. Smoke rose from the compound. But all was eerily silent. There was no sign of Darr Vel's men. Whatever had happened was not linked to the Lost Hopers. Creed could not stand the tension of waiting. It was as good a distraction as any.

'Up!' Creed commanded. 'Up!' The men leapt to their feet, clutching their weapons, and scrambled to the lip of the ditch. Plans never survived contact with the enemy. It was in the chaos of battle that Creed was at his best.

He was fast, decisive, and most importantly, he thought, touching his pistol butt, he was lucky.

'What is the madman doing?' Darr Vel said as he saw Creed's greatcoated figure launching the attack from the heights. 'Lost Hopers forward!' They were with him in a moment, scrambling to the lip of the hollow.

It was a desperate charge across the ice flats. They were halfway across when a heavy stubber opened up. Men grunted as they were hit. Creed could hear their bodies slamming into the ice like dumped sacks. He kept running. The ground was treacherous.

Creed's men had weapons. They took the stubber out as Darr Vel's Lost Hopers stormed the compound. The defenders were a handful of prison guards. They seemed scared and witless as the tortured men gave vent to years of pain and tore them apart with their bare hands.

'Here!' Creed said, as they met at the compound gates. He tossed him a fresh battery pack. 'Keep moving,' he said. 'We have to get inside.'

Darr Vel and Leder shouted to their men to gather whatever they could from the dead.

'You have the bomb?' Darr Vel shouted.

Creed handed him a melta bomb. The cold metal stuck to Vel's hands. The convict ignored the pain as he slammed the bomb home and ducked back behind the entranceway. When the smoke had cleared the blast doors looked like a giant fist had punched them through.

Inside the corridor a squad of Anckorites put up a stout resistance, but the Lost Hopers outnumbered them ten to one. They took the facility by weight of numbers, storming each room, moving forward, always forward. As they cleared a storeroom, five Anckorites ran round a corner, and barely had a moment to react before Creed shot one clean through the forehead and then struck down the next two with repeated shots to the chest.

'Guard chamber!' Darr Vel shouted.

A frag grenade bounced down the corridor. It blew short, but Darr Vel was out and sprinting down the corridor. He clubbed the foe. The second had a belly full of shrapnel and was trying to reach his las-rifle. Darr Vel kicked him so hard his neck snapped. The third swung at him, and the major ducked and shoulder barged him. There was the whizz of an autogun round ricocheting off the wall as he plunged his knife into the Anckorite's warm belly and sawed his guts open.

The Lost Hopers hit the compound from every direction, and took each level, room by room. They blasted routes in where there were none, kept moving forward despite the opposition. At the top of a long metal staircase bolter rounds exploded about Creed. Shrapnel grazed his cheek.

Leder ducked back behind the bulkhead. 'There is *something* there. Something I have not seen before.'

Creed nodded. There was always something more to kill. 'Forward,' he commanded.

'We can't!' Leder shouted over the bark of more bolter fire. 'Have you seen the size of it?'

Creed nodded. He had seen Space Marines before, and this was one, twisted and tainted and deadly, a monster in transhuman form.

'It is evil,' he said. 'We must destroy it.'

'They won't follow me.'

'They will,' Creed told him, but he could see that Leder had lost his nerve. Fear overcame many men in the face of such unnatural horror. Creed turned to look the survivors in the eye. His look offered death and pain, but also victory over the enemies of mankind. 'Men of the Imperium, will you join me?' he asked, his voice hoarse.

Darr Vel stepped forward. The survivors about him nodded. They were bloodied, weary, fearless. Leder swallowed and nodded.

'Right,' Creed said, and flipped the setting of his laspistols to full power.

Darr Vel ripped a frag grenade's pin out with his teeth, tossed it along the corridor and held up his fingers ready for the charge.

'For Cadia!' Creed shouted. As the grenade exploded Darr Vel was up and running, the Lost Hopers behind him.

Darr Vel's leg gave way in a bloody mess and he roared with frustration. A bolt round struck Leder's chest and tore a gaping hole as it exited his back. The Lost Hopers raced forward as the bolter spat fire, and they danced a macabre dance as each took a bolt round. They fell almost as fast as they came forward, and the Traitor Space Marine laughed as he slammed another magazine home. He was half way through the second magazine when his laughter began to fail. There were too many of the Lost Hopers and he was not killing them fast enough.

Creed was amongst the crowd of charging men. His voice was pushing them all on, raging against the heresy. 'Forward in the name of the Emperor of Mankind!'

Men were screaming to either side of him. The stock of his ornate pistol was hard in his hand. One eye was closed. The world was just the small circle of his pistol's target. Wherever it went it was filled by the size of his foe. His first shot fizzled against the thing's breast plate. The second left a pale scar on the power armour. He fired with such speed that the laspistol grew warm in his hand. The Lost Hopers fell away about him. But still the rage drove him and those about him on.

The Space Marine recognised this and singled him out. The wide black barrel of the bolter trailed smoke as it pointed at him. Creed wondered about the expression behind the Chaos Space Marine's visor – doubt? Joy? Amusement?

Creed pulled his trigger again, but the pistol did not fire. His mouth went dry. The creature laughed.

'I was counting the shots,' it said, the voice harsh and metallic.

Fear clutched at Creed. For a moment he was a boy again, in the ruins of Kasr Gallan, blood on his cheeks, dead bodies lying all about him, and a power-armoured figure reaching down.

Pure rage flared within him, divine, white, incandescent rage, and he drew his combat knife and charged. The space marine laughed and stepped forward to swat him away. He backhanded Creed with a blow of such force that the Cadian was thrown violently against the wall.

Creed ducked back as the Chaos Space Marine activated a whining chainblade and swept it down. It opened his face up from his brow to his jaw. Blood blinded him. Creed reached down and pulled his battered old pistol from its holster. *Cadia*, he kept thinking.

'Your head will hang from my belt, Cadian,' the metallic voice rumbled. The chainblade whined and Creed braced as the blade came closer to sever his head.

'Cadia!' Creed spat, and pointed his pistol and fired.

The thing that held him laughed as it tore the pistol from his hand.

'Too late, Cadian,' it hissed.

He smiled. 'My name is–'

'Creed!' Jarran Kell crashed through the wall, roaring his friend's name. He seized the Chaos Space Marine's chainsword hand, power fist-wreathed fingers driving inexorably through armour, flesh and bone.

He tore the hand from the arm, and the towering thing snarled, swinging with the other hand. Kell caught the other hand in his power fist. He could barely hold it still, even as he crushed the limb into another mess of blood and gore and burning power armour. It was like struggling with a statue. With a final effort Kell closed his fingers and tore the ruined arm free with a screech of power armour servos snapping and flailing. The thing swung its stump at Kell, and he ducked as he punched low through its power armour, grabbed whatever organs he could find, and pulled them out the front. The creature shuddered and fell to its knees.

Jarran Kell was panting heavily as he stood almost face to face with the thing. He pulled out his laspistol. He was formal about these things. He put his pistol to the thing's head and said, 'In the Name of the Holy Emperor of Mankind.'

Then he fired.

Agemmon stooped low over Creed.

'Sir!' he shouted. 'It's the general.'

Creed's could feel blood running down his face, but he lived. He cursed as he tried to push Agemmon's hands off, but his movements were feeble. At last he struggled to his feet and cast about for support.

'Jarran, is that you?'

Kell gripped his friend's hands. 'What happened?' he asked.

Creed waved a hand at the Chaos Space Marine's brutalised corpse. 'That. Thank you, Jarran. Come, we have much to do. Cadia is at risk. I have to stop Anckor, and then get back there and make them see.'

'You could have been killed!' Kell said.

Creed forced a smile. 'We all die in the service of the Emperor eventually. Listen to me, Jarran, he's here. I'm sure of it. Luciver Anckor is here. It's where he was drawing his troops from. He had the same idea as me. He's clever. Very clever. And he clearly has help.'

Kell held up a finger, which still bore the traces of the distinctive blue cad-ore dust of Besana. 'We found his ship down below. I tore out the controls. If he's here, he's trapped.'

Creed laughed. 'Good work, my friend! But we *must* get him. We must know what is going on. With me.'

The temperature was dropping rapidly as they pushed through to the back of the complex. The female voice kept repeating, '*Environmental breach. Environmental breach.*' Ice was starting to form on the walls and ceiling.

The few remaining Anckorites were quickly overwhelmed by the tide of Lost Hopers, who laughed as they killed their foes. They came to a door, which opened up to the ice.

'This way.' Kell called, venturing out into the cold air.

A hundred paces before them, five giants in red power armour stood in a circle and at the centre of that ring, like a sacrifice, stood a man.

He was robed in a cape of white fur, great brass bells hanging from his shoulders.

A hood was drawn low over his face and as Kell approached, he turned his face towards them. Kell stopped dead. It was not the face of a man, but a crude imitation with heavy brows, deep-set eyes, an aquiline nose and a mouth wide open as if in a long cry of grief.

His hair was alive, like serpents. His eyes burned in the shadows of the face like two points of red fire. But the light was not angry. It was almost sad, longing, melancholy.

Creed arrived.

'It's over, Anckor,' he said. He shouted back to the men. 'Kill him, quickly.'

Agemmon put his rifle to his cheek and aimed, but the heretical Space Marines stepped close and shielded Anckor with their bodies. As Kell started forward there was a sudden roar from above. The ground shook and the air was full of flames. There was a bright flash and an explosion.

'Down!' Kell pushed Creed back as the air turned hot on their cheeks.

When the fire had passed, Kell saw a metal craft, a pod on insectoid legs, had landed above the circle of figures. Like a spider, the thing lowered its belly over the enemy, and as the legs straightened the Space Marines and Anckor were gone, swallowed up within the vessel.

Kell fired las-rounds as the pod's rockets reignited and it launched into the air. It rose slowly at first, and then was just a bright spark in the sky, rising out of sight. Kell stopped shooting.

Calm returned to Lost Hope, the night broken by the coughs of the men, and the insistent klaxons within the complex. Creed sighed. 'He is gone. Again.'

Kell turned, furious and disbelieving, but Creed had taken out his lho-stub, and was tapping the charred unlit end into his palm.

'Is that all you can say?' Kell shouted.

Creed lit his stub and puffed. He seemed pleased.

'It's not all bad, Jarran. We have our penal legion, and

we've tested their mettle. We've closed off the Anckorites' troop supply. And we know that we are close on his tail.'

The surviving Lost Hopers marched four abreast up the lander's wide rear-ramps. In the two days since Anckor's escape, their clothes had been burned, their heads shaved and they had been dressed in uniforms of penal legion blue.

Creed had just come from inspecting the lander that Kell had found deep in the vaults of the compound. His head had been bandaged and one eye – bruised and discoloured – peered out. Still he puffed slowly on a lho-stick. A fire was started nearby as men poured oil on the bodies of Kasky and her guards, and the Anckorites. Thick black smoke drifted skywards as the oil caught light.

'What will you tell House Kasky?' asked Kell.

Creed lit the end of his lho-stub with long slow puffs. 'I will suggest to them that they ought to provide me with more resources, or I will report their niece's activities here. It won't take them long to decide, I'm sure.'

As they stood some of the Lost Hopers broke off and started towards Creed.

There was a brief scuffle. 'Back!' their wardens shouted, brandishing their electro-goads.

'Stop!' Creed called across. 'Let them through.' He walked over to meet them.

'So, this is it. You're shipping us all out,' Darr Vel called out. He was on crutches.

'I am bringing you aboard my ship,' Creed said.

'Do you know how few of us are left?'

'I do, but there are plenty more men here to join you.'

'Are you going to free us?'

'I cannot do that, Major Darr Vel. I promised to free you from fear. I promised to take you from this planet. I promised you all a death worth living for. I keep my word.'

'That's it, then?'

'For now. I will make sure you are all well cared for. As for your sentences, I'm afraid I cannot change them. You will die. But in the Emperor's service you can choose how you die, and how you are remembered.'

Darr Vel saluted. It was an awkward gesture.

Creed saluted back.

'What will you tell Warmaster Ryse?' Kell said as they watched the last of the Lost Hopers file up into the lander.

'That I have located Luciver Anckor, and have raised three regiments of a penal legion, and expect to conclude the campaign within, say, two Terran months.'

There was a long pause. Kell couldn't stop himself. He drew in a deep breath, and said, 'What was that thing, sir?'

'What thing?'

'You know. That thing I killed.' There was a long pause. Creed did not answer. 'It looked like a Space Marine.'

There was a long pause. 'It was, after a fashion.'

'So why...'

Creed's look stopped him. Creed took a puff of his lho-stub. 'Jarran,' he said. 'You do not want to know. That you have been this long in the Astra Militarum and not encountered such horrors before is a wonder, but please believe me when I say that *you do not want to know*.'

'Why?'

Creed stopped and looked at Kell. His face seemed strained. He looked tired again, sleepless. 'Because my friend, sometimes ignorance is strength. And I need you strong for the storm that is coming.'

The lander started its engines, and they walked a little way back as the ripples of heat began to spill out towards them. It lifted from the ground, and the two of them stood as the roar of it faded, and it dwindled to being just a bright star in the morning sky. Creed offered him a lho-stub. Kell shook his head.

'You did well, Colour Sergeant Kell. You almost trapped them, just as they trapped us. We will pour vengeance on them, you and I. We will clear up this mess, then I can speak to High Command. Personally.'

'You really think Cadia is in danger?'

Creed's eye was deep Cadian indigo. It stared out from a face discoloured: purple, blue, yellow. It gave Kell an odd feeling, as if he were looking into the swirling bilious maelstrom of the Eye of Terror.

'I am sure of it,' Creed said. 'And I have to be there.'

THE BATTLE OF
TYROK FIELDS

JUSTIN D HILL

'Damn it, Creed!' Major Janka of the Cadian 840th was angry. 'There's no point being right if no one listens to you!'

Janka and his companion reached the flight deck of the *Excubitoi Castellum*. The pride of Cadia, the Capitol Imperialis was a behemoth of steel and brass, and had been the governor of Cadia's personal transport since – well, for as long as anyone could remember.

Ursarkar E. Creed – Lord General of the Cadian Eighth regiment of the Astra Militarum and newly-appointed Castellan of Kasr Rorzann – stopped as a flight of eight heavy Thunderbolt fighters, in Cadian field grey, roared overhead. They tipped their wings in a salute and the vast bronze horns of the *Excubitoi Castellum* blasted in response. About them came the answering horns of the seven escorting Leviathans. From their lofty position, the sounds seemed distant and tinny in comparison.

The breeze tugged at Creed's greatcoat. He stared out across the vast flats of the Tyrok Fields where they faded into the fens, a misty green line obscuring the southern horizon. On the landing fields were neat squares and columns of men, armour, tented camps: the preparations for warfare on a planetary scale. His mind drifted back to the briefing hours before, and how he had interrupted General Gruber as the governor's strategy was laid out. It had been neat, precise and too damn predictable, and Creed hadn't minced his words. General Gruber had peered through his monocle and sneered. 'What do you know, *Castellan* Creed?'

Creed slammed the guard rail with an open palm. 'They're idiots!'

'They're following Governor Porelska's orders.'

'Porelska is an idiot! Look at this place. He's packed the *Excubitoi* with bean counters. Have you ever seen so many equerries? All horsehair plumes and lines of medals for wars they never fought in. Damn it. They're sitting in the corridors. You can't go anywhere without some middle-ranking clerk trailing his calculations in your face. They wouldn't know a bayonet from a fish knife.'

He slammed the rail twice more in his fury.

'Well, you didn't have to tell the governor quite so bluntly,' Janka said, absent-mindedly polishing the steel part of his skull with his cuff. The major had taken a head wound putting down a rebellion on Enceladus. The steel replacement was supposed to have been temporary, but that was seven years ago. Janka had been in the field ever since. 'What could the rest of them do but shut you down?'

Creed turned to his friend. 'Janka,' he said quietly,

'this is too serious. This is *Cadia*.' The centre of the landing zone was still being cleared for tomorrow. It was a smudge of smoke and activity. 'We – the men and women of Cadia – we are the only thing that holds the enemy back.' Creed turned away, slammed the rail again and cursed into the wind.

'You have to be politic,' said Janka.

'Not even Ryse would support me in public. I've been telling him for three years now and all he's been fussing about is his crusade. Now look at it! Deucalia has fallen, we've lost Besana. Luciver Anckor has not been caught. The whole thing is,' he paused, then said, '*chaos*.'

Janka gave him a warning look. It wasn't a word that should be spoken.

'Sorry.' Creed put a hand to his head. 'But no one gives a damn about Warmaster Ryse's precious legacy, because the whole Imperium is now creaking. On Cadia we get shipments regularly, but remember Deucalia? We used to get supplies every two months. Then it was three. These little changes add up on the front line. You know that! Porelska is out of his depth. He's been governor so long he's gone soft.'

Another warning look. Soft was not something often said of a Cadian.

Creed sighed. 'Well. Not soft. Just... out of touch.'

Janka inspected his cuff.

'Did you hear about Belisar?' Creed asked.

Janka shook his head.

'It's bad.'

'How bad?'

'Bad,' Creed said.

* * *

An hour later, Creed and Colour Sergeant Jarran Kell were sitting in the back of an Arvus lander. It had recently been ferrying recaff, judging by the smell and the fine black dust on the floor. It was hardly the kind of transport that the governor of Cadia normally bestowed upon his generals. But then these were clearly not normal times.

Kell sniffed. 'So,' he said, 'what did you do to deserve this?'

Creed said nothing.

Kell mimicked Warmaster Ryse's baritone boom, something he usually only did to entertain the junior officers. 'Young Creed, you're an arrogant whippersnapper. As punishment, you'll deliver a shipment of recaff for me.'

Creed shook his head. 'I told Governor Porelska that his plans were pathetically incompetent. And I told Lord General Maximus Gruber that his strategy was so needlessly precise that a single broken down battle tank could throw it off course. And I told them that we are facing an onslaught that has been years, decades, perhaps centuries in the planning.'

Kell said nothing.

Creed closed his eyes as he recalled the details. 'The Malin's Reach uprising. The Guild cultists. Morten Quay. Aurent. Moab.'

Kell had never heard of any of these places. But it didn't matter, events had an odd way of proving Creed right. But still... he'd been predicting a major attack on the Cadian Gate for years now. Kell sniffed again. There were a lot of pressures on Creed. In the last years of the Deucalion Crusade, Warmaster Ryse had kept the general close by his side. The warmaster had leant heavily on the younger commander, putting much of the crusade under his direct command. Some of the junior officers had even whispered that Creed should be in charge, not Ryse.

Creed had put a stop to that talk.

The Arvus bucked as it encountered some turbulence, but Creed didn't seem to notice. The general lay back, rolled up an empty sack and used it as a pillow.

'Wake me when we get home,' he said.

Home was Kasr Rorzann, a spear of rockcrete, ceramite, gun-gargoyles and laser defence batteries. Set on granite crags surrounding landing fields, the foundations of its central tower were as deep as those of the mountain itself. The ancient ramparts were buttressed with gun-turrets, vaulted landing zones and sally-ports with armoured blast doors wide enough for three Leman Russ battle tanks to drive out, guns blazing.

It was one of the twelve cathedrals of war that guarded the landing fields of Kasr Tyrok, the seat of one of the twelve castellans of Cadia. Each fortress was the home of one of the founding regiments of Cadian shock troops.

Kasr Rorzann was the citadel of the Cadian Eighth, the Warmongers.

A vast V-shaped redoubt had been thrown about the base of the tower, and it was on top of the central gate that the Arvus came to rest with a clang of landing gear and the rusty scrape and thud of its ramp.

Kell was first out. *Clear*, he signalled.

They crossed the empty flagstones towards the gates of the tower. A squad of kasrkin in green, white and black camo carapace armour came smartly to attention. Creed was expected. His equerry, Castor, was waiting just inside the foot-thick ceramite gates. Castor was dressed in the same simple camo pattern. Creed was not one to waste men's time on polishing brass buttons and shining boots. As long as they stood firm and could shoot and reload faster than their comrades he was happy.

Castor's breath steamed in the vast empty space as he handed Creed the latest reports, sealed inside the official red leather folders. Creed pulled the sheaf of papers out without comment. His lho-stub was unlit in his fingers as he flicked through the top pages.

Kell tried to read the two men's faces.

'Anything important?' Creed asked.

'More of the same,' Castor said.

Creed studied the sheaf of reports. They were all stamped Code Vermillion. Everything was Utmost Secrecy these days.

'I'll be in my office,' Creed said.

'What is it?' Kell said as he heard a tentative knock on his door.

One of his junior sergeants came in. 'Sergeant Fesk,' the young man saluted. 'Seventh Company.'

Kell stared at him for a moment. 'Ah yes! Fesk. Come in. Besana, wasn't it?'

'That's right, sir,' Fesk said and saluted again. He'd earnt his promotion from Whiteshield on Besana three years earlier. Fesk had done well. Now he had sergeant's stripes, an augmetic eye, and the look of a shock trooper: scarred, tough, fearless.

'You're in the sentinels now?' Kell could tell from the crossed lascannon cap badge. 'Tank hunter?'

Fesk grinned. 'Yes sir! Achilles Squadron.' It was a dangerous and deadly job. Fesk clearly excelled to have risen so quickly to the rank of sergeant. 'I know you're busy, sir. But the men are talking.'

Kell sighed. 'Sit down,' he said. 'Tell me what they're saying.'

He let Fesk talk. It was all the same. As Colour Sergeant of the Cadian Eighth, the care of the regiment was his responsibility. He spent each evening like this, reassuring sergeants, captains, even some of the more senior officers of the Eighth. The problem was that there had been squads and units all over the sector, adding a bit of steel to the boot of the Imperium, a bit of iron into their fist. And then they had all been recalled, every Cadian unit within three months of warp travel.

Fesk said it before Kell. 'They say it's coming... The last great battle for Cadia.'

Kell leaned forward. 'Listen,' he said, in a quiet voice. 'In this system alone there are the three fortress worlds of Sonnen, Holn and Partox, all the hive scum of Macharia, training grounds on Prosan and Vigilatum, and if we need more bodies then there's the prison world of St Josmane's Hope. Who could come against us without us knowing? And even if they got through all the orbital defences, battleships and cruisers and they actually land here, on Cadia...' He sat back. 'Then they come up against men like you and me. The finest soldiers in the Imperium of Mankind. There are ten thousand of us in *this* citadel. Eleven more citadels about Tyrok Fields. Hundreds more across the planet. We are the shock troopers of Cadia. We crush the enemies of mankind under boot and tread.' He smiled. 'Do not spread the words of the enemy. Do not let the words of the enemy weaken your resolve. Do not doubt yourself, your brothers, your leaders. Understand?'

Fesk's cheeks were coloured. He stood smartly and saluted. 'Thank you, sir!'

It was midnight before Kell's last meeting was done. His head ached and his shoulders were tight as he padded through the windowless rockcrete corridors towards the officer's habs in the heart of the tower. The walls of Kasr Rorzann were so thick you could be a mile underground and not know. Nothing was signposted – you had to know your way. Each kasr was unique, and each fortress kept its own secrets. It was one of the first things recruits from the Whiteshields were taught.

All he could hear were his own bootsteps. All along the walls black marble plaques marked the graves of soldiers from the Cadian Eighth whose exemplary service had earned them this great honour: to be interred in the very fabric of their home fortress.

Some of them were old beyond memory. Creed claimed to know them all, to have learned each name, each award, each victory, as he wandered the corridors when he was a foundling, the company mascot, just another of Cadia's many orphans. Kell claimed no such memory, but he knew the way back to his billet.

He passed Major Galan, M36, Gold Aquila, Lost on Zaga IV, turned left at the gold-edged plaque of Colonel Jerami, Ward of Cadia, Urdesh Reclamation, 771.M41, and gave a brief nod to the long bas-relief with inset candles, which declared in High Gothic that it housed the 207 skulls of the 17th Company, 'Firebrands', Merit of Terra – 'Each Man Gave His All. We Left None Behind.'

The newest grave was barely a year old. Major S. Shaw-Hedin, Armageddon, M41.998. Kell and Creed had served with Shaw when they were both fresh recruits. They remembered him fondly. He was a tough, mean bastard of a commander, but he knew how to win battles. Whatever it took, he gave it.

There were kasrkin at each intersection now. They saluted as Kell marched past, all alert, awake and unafraid.

Kell almost walked past Creed's office, but he saw the light was on and listened for a moment before knocking quietly. There was no answer.

He knocked again. 'General Creed?' he called out.

The door was unlocked. The room seemed empty. Creed's reports lay scattered across the table. One lay at the top from the prison world of St Josmane's Hope. There was a long report, and a blurred pict-image of a hooded man, a giant, standing amongst a crowd of convicts. The sight made Kell shiver. He looked about. There was a murmur from behind the desk. Kell drew his laspistol.

He saw the feet first. It was Creed, lying face down, hand raised as if to ward off a blow.

'Ursarkar!' Kell hissed as he turned the general over. He smelled amasec, and in his irritation he let Creed drop. He straightened and ran a hand through his hair. 'You idiot!' he said.

'Drink this,' Kell said, when he had finally got Creed into bed. He kept a flask of stimms and triple shot recaff for times like this, and those times were getting more and more frequent these days.

'Jarran?' Creed slurred.

'Drink!' Kell said.

'They're idiots!' Creed said.

'Yes,' Kell said.

'It's him,' Creed said. 'He's on St Josmane. He's come back for me.'

Kell said nothing this time. Creed finished the flask and fell back.

Kell left a full glass of water by his commander's bed, and went to the door. A dark shape in the doorway made him start. He reached for his pistol and stopped himself, thinking it would be Castor. But it was not. Commissar Aldrad stepped into the light, his young face lean and unscarred.

Aldrad had been with them six months, and he'd spent half of that on a troop transport. He'd been with the Crinan 93rd before joining the Cadian Eighth. The Crinan regiments were drawn from the thick asteroid belts on the spinward edges of Deadhenge. They were tough puritanical mining types that had to be held back from the enemy. Not much call for a commissar there. Not much call for one in the Cadian Eighth either, Kell thought. Aldrad hadn't shot anyone yet, and Kell was happy for it to stay that way.

The commissar had proved his worth on the fortress moon on Helicus Rex. Kell didn't mind him normally, but he didn't like him being *here*. Not now.

'Commissar Aldrad. Can I help you, sir?'

Aldrad looked over at Creed. 'Is he alright?'

'He'll be fine,' Kell said.

Kell had the suspicion that Aldrad had petitioned for an appointment to the Cadian Eighth so that he could serve under Creed. From Aldrad's expression it seemed Creed was turning out to be something of a disappointment.

'Has he been...'

'Leave him with me.' Kell was tense. Too tense. He sighed. 'It happens.'

Aldrad looked almost hurt. 'But tonight of all nights? Will he be fit?'

'What for?'

'Tomorrow.'

Kell didn't know what he was talking about, and said so.

'The landings,' Aldrad said. 'We're part of the honour guard.'

Kell closed his eyes and sighed. All the pomp and meetings and brass band stuff wasn't his style.

Aldrad paused in the doorway.

'Creed didn't tell you?' he asked.

'No,' Kell said. 'He didn't tell me. Who is landing tomorrow?'

'The Volscani Cataphracts,' Aldrad said.

'Never heard of them,' Kell said. He gently pulled the door to, heard the click of the lock falling shut, let out a sigh. 'I'll sort it out.'

Dawn was throwing a thin light down through the ventilation shafts as Archivist Orsani Rudvald looked up from the leather-bound tome on the carved rosewood stand in front of him.

The footsteps came slowly, and without any pretence at silence, down the long rockcrete staircase. He knew the tread of those feet and waited till they had almost reached the bottom of the stairs.

'Ursarkar!' He was one of the only men who was allowed to call Creed by his first name. The general came forward into the light. He knew his old mentor would be here. Orsani found consolation in the vaults, amongst the carefully inscribed journals, battle diaries and commanders' letters. It was so early that the kasr lumens were still set at half-light. One of them, a long way down the stacks of shelves and rolled vellum data sheets, flickered as it tried to light.

'Have you slept?' Orsani said. 'You look terrible.'

'I slept.' Creed winced. He could not remember being this hungover, since, well, the last time. 'I think. Passed out might be closer to the truth.'

Creed looked over Orsani's shoulder. He was reading *A Shorter History of the Scarus Sector, Volume III*. 'Good?' he asked.

Orsani frowned. 'There are inconsistencies,' he said, 'with what is written in the journals of our commander in those days.'

'Valens?' Creed said.

Orsani gave an almost imperceptible tut. He had been teaching and testing Creed since he had found him, under a bed, in the blood-splattered ruins of Kasr Gallan. 'Wulfic,' he said.

Creed slumped down in a leather chair, closed his eyes, and weakly waved a hand. His head hurt too much for history. He thought he might still be a little drunk. He rubbed his face with both hands and looked almost imploringly up at the frail old man. Orsani had taken to growing long military moustaches. They weren't a Cadian fashion, but something he had picked up fighting alongside the Vostroyans, and now took a perverse delight in. But take away the augmetic eye, the battle-scarring, the long white moustaches, and it was the same gaunt face that had looked down on Ursarkar as a child.

'They're screwing it up,' Creed said. 'I just know it. The top brass. They're not up to the job.'

Orsani carefully lifted a red silk ribbon, laid it gently down the middle of the book, and closed it. He sat, letting his augmetic legs wheeze slowly as they lowered him into his cradle.

'Look at the data,' he said.

'Everything is about data to Porelska. So many millions of troops. So many tanks. So much ordnance. He has a team of pen-pushers running about HQ. There's not a warrior among them.' Orsani gave him a look. 'Well,' Creed said, 'not a *real* warrior. They've been on Cadia too long.'

'So they need someone like you?'

'Someone like Ryse. Someone. Anyone who has fought in a battle recently. Porelska must be four hundred years old! When was the last time he held field command?'

'938.M41,' Orsani said. 'Hydator Prime.'

Creed gestured. 'Exactly! Porelska and his like are honourable men. But this is a crisis.'

'Crisis,' Orsani said, and nodded. 'There used to be a special title, for times of crisis on Cadia.' He wheezed across to the bookshelf, reached high to bring a tome down, laid it onto the table and gently turned the illuminated pages. 'It was a special rank. It allowed the bearer to put the governing councils aside and rule Cadia as a general.'

Creed puffed out his cheeks. 'One man in command?'

'Ah! There. The bearers were called 'Lord Castellan'. To answer your question, yes. One man ruling Cadia, answerable only to Terra.'

Creed rubbed his jaw. He ought to shave. 'That is how we weather this storm. A commander commanding!'

'It is a serious measure.'

'We should make Ryse the Lord Castellan. How does it happen?'

'I don't know. This book doesn't say.'

There was a long silence. Creed shut his eyes again. He seemed deflated.

'You think a storm is coming?' Orsani said.

Creed looked at him. His jowls were heavy, his eyes pink, his cheeks heavily stubbled. 'I've known it for years,' he said. 'And I've had dreams.'

The air in the room seemed to grow cold.

'He's back,' Creed said. 'I saw a pict-slate from St Josmane's Hope. He's calling himself "The Voice".'

'You think he is coming for you?'

'I don't know what to think,' Creed snapped. He stood up, and paced back and forth. 'I'm sorry. My head is killing me. I think the stimms are wearing off.'

High up above, a bell rang. It was the sixth hour of the day. The guard shifts were changing.

'Throne,' Creed said. 'We're on parade today. The Volscani are landing.' He paused. 'I'll try and see Ryse.'

Creed stood and looked at the frail remains of the man who saved him so many years before. He was the last surviving man of that company, and war had ravaged him. Only his mind was as sharp as ever.

Creed was half way across the room when Orsani called out, 'I found this yesterday.'

He opened a drawer on his reading stand, and pulled out a book. It was the size and shape of the Uplifting Primer, and bound in red leather, such as the kind of book a line officer might keep in his pocket. The spine was unmarked and the marbled boards held the hand-written title *De Gloria Macharius*.

He held it out and Creed turned the book over in his hands. This had been his favourite book as a lad. How the men had laughed, all through the Gallan campaign, as the eight-year-old Creed sat barefoot in the corner during bombardments, reading *De Gloria Macharius*.

Creed felt tears coming and shook his head. If that boy had known what he would grow up to do, he would have been amazed. So why was it that he had a sense of his life being wasted? He was meant for more than this. He offered it back to Orsani.

'Keep it,' Orsani said.

Creed smiled, despite his headache.

'I will,' he said. 'Thank you.'

'Ursarkar.'

Creed paused at the door.

'Do you think Ryse would make a good Lord Castellan?'

Creed paused. 'No.'

'You could ask for it yourself?' Orsani said.

Creed laughed and held up the book. 'Thank you for this.'

'That's a damned fine entrance,' Ryse said as the shrill blasts of saluting Leviathans drowned out the cheers of ranks of men, horns of Leman Russ battle tanks, and even the honour salute from the 190th and 210th Artillery Regiments. Creed nodded. It certainly was. The whole parade was. Ryse's Leviathan, *Sacramentum,* was right next to the Governor's *Excubitoi Castellum.* Ryse was suitably proud of the honour and was speaking in a loud, expansive manner.

The last Leviathans were reversing into position as the landers slowed their descent on full retro burners, touched down, and came to rest before the honour guard of Major Janka's 840th. The assault ramps slammed down. Volscani armoured companies swarmed out, and from the central lander came a command Baneblade, with two more super-heavies flanking.

'Magnificent!' Ryse said. He was flush with the pomp and display. Creed looked away, uncomfortable with something, some detail. He was distracted by a flash from somewhere in the fens. He stood at Ryse's shoulder, shielded his eyes, and wondered what it was. Then it hit him.

'The banner...' he muttered. No one heard. He took his magnoculars and focussed on the banner that flew from the lead Baneblade. He gagged. It was covered in glyphs that seemed to be moving. He gagged harder. For a moment he almost put it down to his hangover. Then the Baneblade's turret began to slowly move.

'Back!' Creed roared. 'Back!' The officials in their smart dress uniforms looked as if he had gone mad.

Void shields down, the Cadian Leviathans were sitting targets. The Volscani tank turrets all swivelled to face the *Excubitoi Castellum*. Battlecannons, demolisher cannons, lascannons. It was a firing squad. An execution. Kell dragged Ryse away from the edge and Creed fell backwards as *Sacramentum* rocked with impacts, and suddenly all about him was flames.

Gunner Lina was sitting in the cramped Executioner-class Leman Russ *Pride of Cadia III*, playing Black Five with her fellow gunners. She had three blacks, a blue and a red heart, and a pile of cash. She was about to clean Callen out. He was sweating. Linday had a cocksure look. He was bluffing. The tank's commander, 'Hot Hands' Ibsic, was wistfully inspecting the unlit stub of his lho-stick. Gannesh, their driver, was sulking about something.

The tank rattled as the distant Leviathans sounded off. Engines roared. Linday was trying to peek. Lina curled her cards in, sniffed nonchalantly. 'Have they landed yet?'

Gannesh looked up from the prayer logs through the driver's vision slit.

'Yes,' he sniffed. 'They're unloading.'

'Regent,' Linday said, putting his first card down. 'Sure you want to keep going?'

'Yes,' Lina said. She held his eyes the whole time she put her first card down. He had been flirting with her ever since she had got this promotion to sponson gunner on the *Pride of Cadia III*. The last person in this position had let his gun overheat, and hadn't survived the experience.

'Gotta say the prayers right,' Ibric had told her when she joined the crew. 'And you got to be lucky,' he said. 'Because every so often the plasma tanks just blow up in your face.' Both his hands were augmetic. He hadn't been lucky once, though lucky enough to survive.

She felt the vibrations as the ramps of the landers came down. The tank shook, and fine dust rained down from the plasma reactor. She swept it off and looked to Callen.

'You can quit you know,' she said.

Callen bit his lip, picked a card and laid it down almost reluctantly. 'Black Ace,' he said.

Lina swore. The *Pride of Cadia III* shook more violently. Gannesh slammed the prayer logs closed.

'What is it?' she asked. Ibsic stuck his head out the top. They could see flashes in the sky through the hatch.

'They're frekking shooting!' he said, and ducked down. He had a way of speaking quietly when things got scary. 'Gun stations. This is for real.'

Ibsic and Callen went through the routine with practised speed. They pulled the dust covers off the plasma destroyer, slammed the emergency vents open and locked the heat shield in place as the photonic fuel cells began to wine.

'Fuel cells.'

'Check.'

'Secondary vents.'

'Check.'

'Power her up!'

'Check.'

The space in Lina's plasma cannon sponson was tight, and it was already getting warm. She sniffed as she locked the heat shield down.

'Port sponson primed,' she called, and felt a thrill as she beat Callen to it by half a second.

'Starboard sponson primed,' he said and made a rude gesture.

She returned it.

'Say your prayers,' Ibsic called.

They intoned the Rituals of Plasma as Ibsic pulled the activation switch. There was a whine as pure energy boiled in the tanks about them. 'Right, Gannesh, get this baby moving.'

Gannesh let the throttle out, and the ancient battle tank rumbled forward.

'Reporting in,' Ibsic called on the vox. It answered with a roar of static. 'This is *Pride of Cadia III*! Active. On duty.'

* * *

Sergeant Fesk of Achilles Squadron had left his vox-unit on broadcast so he could shut his eyes and listen to the comms-traffic. It was lonely in the sentinels, especially the armoured tank hunters. It took a certain mentality, which suited him fine. Disconnected voices in a vox-unit gave him just the right amount of company.

As the Volscani landers came down he was sitting, hunched forward, hand pressed to the side of his skull. His augmetic eye was still embedding. He kept seeing motes of light that weren't there, and they made his head ache after a while. He had his good eye shut when a cacophony of voices filled his cabin.

He slammed the volume down on the vox-unit and stood on the seat just in time to see a Leviathan war machine's plasma core overheat. It filled the sky with fire. He slid down into his seat and flipped his lascannon to live. His augmetic eye blinked for a moment as it connected with the lascannon's systems. The motes of light were still there, but a blue target eclipsed his vision.

Searching, the systems reported.

He started forward, not really sure which way to go.

At the command post, Aldrad had his pistol out and primed. He was looking for someone to shoot, as the men put it.

'What the hell is happening?' Aldrad roared. 'Where is Creed?'

'He went to speak to Warmaster Ryse,' Castor shouted. They both looked at the plumes of smoke and fire around the Leviathans.

'Damn it!' Aldrad said. 'Find him! His position is here. Any failure to return will be a dereliction of his duty!'

'Yes, sir!' Castor saluted as another Leviathan began to

explode. He picked the headset up again. 'I'm looking for General Creed,' he shouted. 'No, I don't know where your company is!' He slammed the hand piece down. 'I'll find him. If he's alive.'

Aldrad ran through Imperial doctrine. Dereliction of duty deserved the most stringent punishment. He could hear his Schola Progenium master beating the blackboard with the butt of his bolt pistol. *Command without doubt. Obey without question. Punish without hesitation.*

'Who's second in charge?' he asked.

'Major Troilus.'

There was the roar of an incoming squadron. Aldrad guessed they were Thunderbolts, from the deep note of their twin engines.

'Are those friendlies?' he shouted, but he could tell from the way they came in on the attack run that they were not.

'Fire!' he shouted, but the men manning the auto-cannons were too slow in responding. The ground erupted about him as the fighters opened up with their nose-mounted quad autocannons. All about him were the shouts of wounded men. He stood alone, defiant, his black leather stormcoat flapping angrily about his legs.

He cursed. Where the hell was Creed?

Sacramentum's void shields finally fizzed into place and Creed felt the hair on the back of his neck stand. A table had overturned, spilling bottles of Arcady Pride and pre-filled crystal shot glasses across the viewing platform. They crunched underfoot as he waded through the uniformed administrative staff, thrusting them aside as they gaped. He parted the squads of masked kasrkin who rushed along the corridors.

'We have to reach the flight deck!' Kell shouted.

Kell was right behind him, but he could barely hear what he was saying.

'Brace for boarding!' the command sirens blared. Creed shoved his way through the panic, up to the top deck. Smoke filled the corridors. The whole Leviathan shook.

The last flight of metal stairs brought them at last to the armoured roof batteries. There was pandemonium. Gunnery sergeants were bawling into the comms for the ordnance bays to be manned and the ammo lifts loaded, while pilots were rushing to their craft, still shoving their arms into their flight jackets, pulling their comms sets over their heads.

Creed grabbed a naval officer by his flying jacket.

'I need a Valkyrie,' he said and thrust him towards one of the waiting craft.

'We've got to get her loaded!' a gunnery officer shouted, but Creed shoved the loading servitors out of the way and as soon as the pilot's hatch closed, he climbed up and banged on the inside panels. 'Up! Up! Up!'

Within moments the engines fired up, the missile cradles fell away, and the world tilted and banked. 'Take me up high!' Creed shouted into the comms bead. 'I need to see what the hell is happening!'

The Valkyrie corkscrewed above the battlefield.

Creed felt sick. Sick from last night. Sick from the stimms, and sick at the sight of the destruction below. Companies were pouring out of the Volscani vehicles – already one of the Cadian war machines was gone, and another was smoking dangerously.

* * *

'I've got him!' Castor shouted triumphantly as artillery shells starting raining dangerously close to their left flank. The Cadian Eighth's tanks had formed a protective barrier to the left and sentinel squadrons were scouting forward. One of the tanks was hit. It burned. No one came out alive.

Aldrad seized the comms as another Thunderbolt roared overhead. Its quad autocannons rattled as it wheeled after an enemy fighter.

'Creed!' Commissar Aldrad shouted. 'Creed! Where are you?' He had been full of fury and frustration, but now, as he heard Creed's voice – calm, assured, confident – he felt his panic lessen.

'Good,' he said at last. 'Yes. I will. As quick as you can. Your place is here. We need you *here!*'

There was another pause.

'I shall,' Commissar Aldrad said, and returned the comms set to Castor. His training reasserted itself. *Command without doubt. Obey without question.*

'One last time,' Creed shouted.

'Roger,' the pilot said, and they swung round for a third time.

Creed had to see it with his own eyes. Heresy on Cadia.

Kell stood at Creed's shoulder, his hand on the door-rail above his head. The wind was full of cordite, ozone and thick black promethium smoke. All they could hear was the roar of the engine and the wind in their ears. Neither of them spoke. They were the still centre of a raging inferno. A battle of titanic proportions, fought here, on the most sacred soil in the segmentum.

All about them, fighters of the Imperial Navy – loyalist

and heretic alike – were strafing, diving, pitching, rolling, dying. On the ground, the Volscani landers released ravening hordes of traitors as their Leviathans and companies of hardened veterans charged towards the Cadian lines.

Willelm Dux was already being boarded. *Sacramentum*'s weapons were the first to return fire, crippling one of the enemy Baneblades. Volscani armour had been landing for days. A division was already swinging about their left flank. The fens, where penal legions had been camped, were aflame.

Here and there, as individual Cadian units regrouped, the ground was lit with ferocious las-battles: the criss-cross stitching of searing bolts created almost continual light. A flight of Vendettas made a desperate attack on the lead Volscani Leviathan. The last one was still firing as its wings were torn away by flak batteries mounted on the brass beast's sides. Void shields flared as its carcass crashed in a ball of flaming promethium. A heretic Thunderbolt, rolling in for another attack on *Excubitoi Castellum,* misjudged and hit *Claves* in the exposed upper deck, just as the crew had brought an earlier blaze under control.

The fireball disappeared behind them as the Valkyrie banked. The earth below exploded as an artillery battery opened fire.

All across the battlefield Creed could see similar vignettes. Tank squadrons blundered forward, firing on friendly forces, artillery captains shouted for a position, and infantry fixed bayonets and charged. Brave but futile, uncoordinated and easily crushed. Confusion – that ragged imposter – reigned on Cadia. The men looked to the

Excubitoi Castellum for leadership, but there was none. The ancient warhorse of Cadia was burning. The governor of Cadia was silent.

'Take us down,' ordered Creed. 'I've seen enough. It's time to turn the tide.'

'Creed!'

Aldrad strode towards the Valkyrie as it touched down, nose first. Castor was right behind him. 'Creed!' Aldrad shouted. His head was lowered, his cap pulled low, his bolt pistol drawn.

'Later!' Creed told him. He took Aldrad's rehearsed words away. 'Castor, get the comms teams to me now!'

'Sir!' Sergeant Agemmon came forward, vox-caster in hand. 'Major Barker.'

Creed made a face. 'Barker? Listen. Cadia's survival depends on you. Get through to the 190th. Creeping barrage. My man will give you the coordinates. As soon as you start I will strike straight forwards. We must throw the enemy off balance.'

Creed stood with a vox in each hand, relaying orders, giving instructions, keeping control, spreading calm through the Cadian officers. 'Are the 210th near you? Well tell Klude to get his men firing. At what? At the Volscani!'

One by one Creed gave commands, picking up the scattered regicide pieces and starting a fresh game.

'They're coming,' Kell shouted. Creed looked up. He could see a dark line of Volscani making their way towards them, sentinels at the fore, crimson banners marking the commander of this assault.

'Right. Let's go!'

Agemmon shouldered the vox-unit as Creed strode

forward to where the Cadian Eighth had formed up in battle lines. Six thousand Guardsmen with tanks, sentinels and heavy weapons teams, all ready, all looking to Creed as the dark mass of heretics slowly took shape, moving towards them at assault speed.

Creed looked back at them. His men, his brothers. He had no words, but took them all in with a steely glance, knelt, and pressed an open palm to the ground. His planet, his home soil. Cadia. It spoke to him. It shook like a weeping body. He could feel the vibrations of shells exploding, the dull rumble of the Volscani Leviathans as they pressed forward. The hateful press of the traitors' landers on her soil. The bloody tramp of heretical feet. The spiked tracks of their armour.

Each shell that landed, each footstep on Cadian soil, was like his own body was being torn, plundered, violated.

'We are Cadia,' he said quietly. 'Cadia is us.'

'They're coming,' Kell hissed.

Creed stood abruptly. 'Fix bayonets!'

'Fix bayonets!' Kell repeated through his parade-speaker. In a magnificent display of dress discipline, the Cadian Eighth moved as one. Their banner was brought forward and presented to Kell. He took it in his power-fisted hand and raised it high.

'For the Eighth! For Cadia!' Creed shouted.

'For Cadia!' the roar came back, and the Cadian Eighth turned together. A loudspeaker started up the tune *Imperium Gloriam*, and the men all started to sing as one. Sentinels leading, tanks on either wing, they plunged into the smoke and fire of battle.

* * *

In the distance, Lina could see massive war machines knocking chunks of burning armour off each other. But here, where it was kill or be killed, she couldn't see anything but smoke and wreckage.

'Still no damn targets,' she reported.

On the other side, Callen's plasma cannon was close to overheating. There was no shortage of targets on his side. He was cursing Gannesh's driving.

'Stay calm,' Ibsic said.

'Yes, sir!'

Something went just over their heads. It whined as it passed and they could all hear the air being sucked through the vents.

'What was that?' Callen hissed.

Gannesh and Linday spoke at the same time: 'Krak round.' 'Contact!'

'Where did that come from?' Ibsic hissed.

Lina felt a wave of fear as the others scrambled to get the main weapon charged. Something hit the tank on her left. It was a Vanquisher, *Imperialis X*. Lina knew the crew. They were a tight bunch. The commander, Jovian, had looked out for her since she joined the company.

'They're hit,' she hissed. 'It's smoking.'

She willed them to disembark. 'Yes!' she shouted as a sponson hatch was thrown open and Oleg and Luord fell out. Luord was burning. 'Come on. Get out!' she croaked. 'Get out!'

Luord rolled on the ground. Oleg bent to pick him up. He ran back to the hatch. Jovian was still inside. *Come on! Just get the frekk out.*

Imperialis exploded and Lina slammed the front of her sponson hatch. The Vanquisher's turret spiralled up into the air. Vents blew out and roared with furnace flames as the ordnance chambers ignited within the confines of the tank. She slammed the inside of her sponson again. 'Damn it!'

'No survivors,' Ibsic reported a few moments later.

Lina slammed the panel before her again. She wanted to kill now. 'Swing me round,' she said. 'I want to get whatever killed them.'

'No time,' Ibsic said. 'Main gun. Charge.'

'I want to kill it,' she said.

'No time. Charge!'

Lina slammed the heat shield down and pulled her sponson about as far as it would go, straining for a target. They chanted the prayers together, and then Ibsic fired the main gun. Lina turned her head as the enemy tank gouted flames and the glare washed her screens out. Gannesh slewed the tank round. Lina saw a line of Volscani armour, track to track, battlecannons flaring.

'I'll take the cannon,' said Linday. He dropped into the front gunner seat and charged the lascannon. It sapped energy from the plasma destroyer, but this needed something with a bit more penetration, as Linday liked to say.

'Need heavy support,' Ibsic reported back to whoever was commanding this mess.

'Got one!' Linday laughed. He turned to Lina. She winked.

'Good work,' Ibsic said. 'They're bringing in fire support. Tank hunter heavy weapons. Lascannons.' There was a pause as Gannesh pulled them round. Ibsic whistled through his teeth. 'Fire at will,' he said.

Lina was already recharging her plasma cannon. She could see a group of Taurox transports trying to outflank them. She sighted, prayed, slammed the heat shield down and fired. The plasma shot went straight through the transport's driver's slit. It lit up from the inside, liquid plasma shooting out of the top hatch and the side vision ports.

Gannesh pushed forward. Lina lost count of how many times she had fired. Suddenly there were troops all about them. Friendlies. Lina saw them setting down their lascannon tripods. Someone climbed onto the back of the *Pride of Cadia III* and rapped the Eighth's motto on the hull: three short taps, two long. Ibsic unlocked the turret. A head blocked out the light. He wore the uniform of the Cadian Eighth.

'Creed says we can't stop. Push forward,' he said. 'Keep outflanking them.'

Gannesh let out a long breath.

'You heard him,' Ibsic said.

Gannesh slammed the gears and they started forward again. 'Say your prayers,' he muttered.

Fesk's sentinel was hidden in the fringes of the fens, the thick sorghum heads brushing gently against his cabin. He risked a brief look up, and his augmetic retina flashed red as his lascannon locked on: five squadrons of sentinels pacing along the fen margins, looking in the other direction.

He fired a short burst of lascannon shots. One kill, he noted as his mount's left foot dragged out of the mud and lurched forward. His retina flashed red again.

Two more shots. Two more kills.

'Forward!' Fesk said, his sentinel lurching again. 'Achilles Squad forward. Keep in the fens. We'll keep pounding anything we see.'

It had been a few minutes since he had had any response from Achilles Squad, and he had the feeling that there was no one else left, but it reassured him to still be giving orders.

A warning ping made him look up as a Leman Russ in field brown appeared through the smoke on his right, autocannons blasting. The vox erupted as a sentinel that had strayed too close to the dry land exploded.

'I'm hit!' someone shouted. Fesk was too busy staying alive to notice who. Everyone was talking. The leg gears crunched as he swung his sentinel round, searching for better cover. The rough landscape was funnelling the enemy into a tight mass so dense that everything was a target.

Fesk listened. He couldn't tell what the hell was happening. He counted to twenty then moved his sentinel forward. He could feel his walker's legs sinking deep into the mud. The sentinel swayed dangerously as the leg mechanisms laboured.

'I've gone over,' someone reported over the vox. He thought it was Garret, from the Kasr Gallan accent.

Fesk kept moving. He could feel the rumble of the approaching Volscani armour. They were getting dangerously close.

'I can see them,' Macrinus said.

The shooting started and the vox chatter was like a sudden storm. Someone was whooping. Someone was dying. 'Leave some for me,' another voice called out. Fesk kept contact with his own squadron, screened the others out. He kept moving. He could feel the ground grow firmer. He could smell the ozone now. Stray rounds whizzed overhead.

'Heading out, Achilles Squad. Cover me if you can,' he called out.

The vox unit crackled back.

Searching, his targeter read.

He came out near a burning Chimera. A rough picket of tank hunter sentinels were moving through the margins of the water, ducking into cover, positioning to get rear and flank shots, picking off Volscani armour. From the chevrons on the hatches it looked like Trewin, Karma and Longe Squadrons.

As the smoke cleared he caught a glimpse of a Leman Russ, its rear to him. His targeter blinked red.

Fesk fired as the turret swung towards him. He missed, swore and felt his palms slip as he gripped the joystick trying to get a targeting fix. He stepped to the right as the tank opened up and the autocannon rounds whistled through the sorghum stalks. Fesk ducked his sentinel down and could not believe that he was still alive.

Fesk flicked a switch and engaged his auxiliary weapon before standing the walker up again. His system pinged: *lock on.* The sentinel's cabin rattled as the hunter-killer missile ignited and launched. It seared a white spot in his retina as it wound out from the tall stalks towards the tank. He blinked too late and cursed as his vision flared white with the explosion. He reversed his sentinel and felt the left leg plunge deep into the one of the sink holes. His fingers scrabbled for the smoke launchers.

Rounds rattled against his front armour. He kept the smoke launchers pumping and started to pray.

The Cadian Eighth were drawn up in ranks: there was a skirmish line flat on the ground, behind them were special weapon squads, their tank-busting plasma and grenade launchers primed and ready, then came the massed body of heavy weapons and infantry squads. In the middle of the formation, black stormcoat flapping, Commissar Aldrad stood with Major Troilus.

Tracers lanced out. Explosions ripped through the enemy lines as the Eighth opened up with multi-lasers, spitting out streams of livid red light. Sergeants shouted, pointed, slapped men's backs, and urged them to fire faster. The air was thick with grunts and the click of magazines being fixed into place, with empty clips being discarded and new ones brought forward.

'More ammo!' someone shouted.

'Get it here!' came a sergeant's voice. 'What are you waiting for? The Emperor himself?'

Aldrad marched up and down, exhorting the men with texts that inspired them. Each regiment had their favourites.

'*Be strong in your ignorance!*' he shouted. '*By your death shall we know you. Soldier, you and I are sons of one faith, and it is the lasgun, the ammo pack, the dead heretic.*'

Commissar Aldrad stopped, held firm his faith against the foe. The ground was thick with brass autocannon cartridges. Similar piles showed where the heavy weapons teams had fired and moved forward. Constantly forward. '*A sitting duck is a dead duck,*' as Creed liked to say.

The general was off to the right along the banks of the fens, taking personal control where the fighting was fiercest. Troilus kept looking that way.

'Will they hold?' Aldrad shouted.

'They'll hold,' Troilus said. 'Creed will make sure of that.'

* * *

Fesk was lost. His head ached, the white motes kept dancing even when he closed his eyes, and when he opened them he was still lost.

He locked the sentinel's legs, threw open the top hatch and stood on the back of his seat. Smoke was billowing up from all around him. The whole planet seemed to be on fire.

He dropped back into his seat and flicked on his auxiliary battery. It blinked red. He'd fired both missiles, and seemed to be the only sentinel from his squadron still standing.

'Well,' he said to no one in particular, 'best keep going.'

He unbraked the walker's legs and turned towards what he guessed was the main battle. The sorghum was thinning. He lurched up out of the mud onto the ridge. A regiment was moving up ahead of him. They were dressed in the plain blue drab of penal legionaries. A group was sitting down, eating a meal.

Of all the times, he thought. Didn't they know there was a war on?

The troops turned. They dropped what they were eating. He stopped. There was blood on their lips. They were hunched over a dead body. A human body. One of them pointed and shouted and suddenly the whole ridge seemed to sprout with standing men. A thousand faces were staring at him. Someone fired a lasgun but the beam fizzed overhead. Fesk desperately turned his sentinel around. It lurched dangerously as it splashed back into the mud.

There was a thud and his walker swayed. The hatch was wrenched open. A heretic stared down at him, cheeks had been carved with sickening symbols. Fesk fumbled for his laspistol and fired. The heretic fell from the sentinel, but two more took his place. One grabbed Fesk by the chin, and a blade stabbed down.

Blood poured down Fesk's front. It was his own.

With his last thought, he wished he'd managed to warn his fellows.

Lina watched as Ibsic tore off his protective jacket and stood naked to the waist, head pressed to the targeting array. The *Pride of Cadia III* was hull down in a crater shell. The main body of Volscani were charging towards the centre. He wound the targeting wheel round a few turns.

'Got them,' he said quietly.

'Pushing forward to engage,' Gannesh said. The tank lurched as it came out of the crater.

Ibsic focussed the view-port. 'Charge the guns.'

Their squadron was on the extreme left of the Cadian lines, facing back across the battlefield, fens in the far distance. Lina swung her sponson gun around, looking for a target, but all she saw was the centre tank of their impromptu squadron moving cautiously forward. *Rex Augustus* was Commander Erick's Punisher. On the far side of her was the Demolisher, *Celestine Inferno*.

'Keep flanking,' Ibsic said.

Gannesh cursed as a shell landed too close. 'Taking us into another crater,' he said, and Lina braced herself as the tank tilted forward and down.

Callen cursed. 'Have you seen how many there are?'

'I can't see them,' Lina said.

'Oh, you will,' Callen laughed.

As Gannesh brought the tank round to face the enemy,

Lina whistled. 'Holy Throne!' she said, slamming her charge lever to full.

Ibsic had his face still pressed to the targeting array. 'Can't miss,' he said.

'Tell that to Callen!' Lina said. *Rex Augustus*'s gatling cannon span as it fired off a few short bursts to warm the mechanisms up. Ibsic had his eyes pressed to the range finder, comms unit on one ear. He counted down.

'Let the frying commence,' he said, and then the squadron opened up.

Superheated globs of incandescent blue plasma arched towards more Chimeras than Lina had ever seen. They melted puncture holes through the turrets and side armour. Superheated shot fused the tracks, dripped through exhaust vents and filled engine mechanisms with liquid metal. Cramped driver cabins filled with poisonous fumes as plasma globules sprayed through stifling troop compartments and cooked the troops inside. Lina could see the *Celestine Inferno* from the corner of her eye. The gaping black demolisher cannon fired a rocket-propelled shell that tore holes in the enemy, while the air about her quivered with heat as its multi-meltas seared holes through man, metal and tank alike.

She blasted a Chimera in the flank as it spewed las-bolts towards them. She hit a second, and watched it slew to a halt and the back ramp slam down. A heavily armoured Volscani squad came out at a run. She fired at them again, missed and cursed.

'Meltas. Port side. Twenty degrees,' she said. 'Need me up top?'

Ibsic didn't look up from the targeter. 'Not yet. Erick,' he called across the vox. 'See them?'

She could hear the tinny crackle of Erick's voice answering. *Rex Augustus'* Punisher gatling cannon started up: thousands of metal slugs shredded the traitors, leaving a red mist hanging where they had once stood. She could picture Erick bracing himself against the back of the turret as he fired. Lina laughed. There was nothing like a Punisher gatling to strike fear into the enemy, except maybe a squad of Space Marines.

Something exploded to her left. She threw back the vision slit.

Black smoke billowed into the sky. The *Celestine Inferno* was a burning wreck. Callen threw the top hatch open to see. 'Demolitions squad,' he shouted down as he dropped back into the cabin. He dragged the heavy stubber out, and pushed it up through the cupola, slamming it into its mounting. He threw his body round. Something metallic hit the hull and Lina felt a sudden chill.

'I can't see them,' she said.

'Get them!'

'I can't *see* them.'

'Gannesh?'

There was an explosion. Callen was shouting. Everyone was shouting.

'Shut up!' Ibsic yelled as Gannesh reversed them out of the crater. 'Lina, to the front!'

She scrambled into the nose gunner seat and charged up the lascannon. She saw the demo squad and cursed as she panned the cannon round and opened fire.

'Got 'em!' she shouted, as she fried the last. 'Where did they come from?'

'Let's get out of here.' Gannesh slammed the tracks into reverse.

'Stop!' Ibsic said. 'Keep pushing forward.'

'Have you seen how many there are?'

'Creed's orders!' Ibsic said.

Gannesh swallowed and nodded.

Pride of Cadia and two more squadrons kept firing and outflanking on the right. Firing, outflanking. Lina's world narrowed to the view along her lascannon. Some time later – though she had no idea how long – the *Pride of Cadia III* was still pushing forward. They were all firing so fast there was no time for prayers. The plasma destroyer was glowing. The tank was like a sauna.

Gannesh's nerves were shot. 'It's going to blow,' he shouted as they sighted more enemy armour.

'Tanks,' Callen said.

Lina cursed silently.

Ibsic found them. 'Charge,' he said. Linday locked the heat shields down.

'It's going to blow. You'll kill us all!' Gannesh shouted as the main gun fired again. The lights flickered.

They were still alive. Lina grinned as she detonated an ammo container with a pinpoint shot and took a squad of Volscani out.

'Good shooting, Lina,' Ibsic said.

She risked a glance. He'd taken a plasma burn to his shoulder. The flesh was raw and bloody. Sweat was running like a stream down his back. He started another cycle.

Gannesh turned in his seat. 'Let it cool!'

Ibsic panned the turret for another target. 'Ready,' he said.

Gannesh made the sign of the aquila and cursed as steam vented into the cabin. 'Shut it down! It's overheating.'

Ibsic threw levers, pressed buttons and shut down the main gun. He counted to three, then charged it up again.

'Don't! It's too soon!' Gannesh squealed, pulling at his restraints.

'Have you seen what's out there?' Ibsic said quietly. 'We keep going. Either we fry them or we fry ourselves before they can kill us.'

He panned the turret round again. Lina puffed her hair out of her face. The reactor wound up for another shot. Ibsic zeroed in on his target. 'Say your prayers,' he said. Lina did so. The lights went out.

Someone screamed.

Field commanders had given up trying to reach *Excubitoi Castellum*. They were all calling Creed directly now. He had seven vox-operators trailing after him as he gave out orders. He looked over at Kell.

'Are you alright?'

Kell's face was pale. He nodded. His neck had been grazed by a las-bolt meant for Creed. Targeted air strikes had silenced the Volscani snipers after that.

'It's nothing,' Kell said, rubbing the blood from his fingers onto his webbing.

'Sure?'

'Sure,' Kell said.

Creed climbed up on a ruined sentinel and looked about. To the north, the Leviathans had moved into a great melee of monstrous behemoths. The air fizzed with void shields and ordnance. The Volscani landers loomed overhead and the legions were now dark on the plains before him.

He looked behind their formation at another mass of Cadian troops. 'That's the Seventh?'

Castor nodded. 'Yes, sir!'

'Get me Xander,' he said.

'Xander's dead.'

'Who's their second?'

'They've lost four of their commanders, sir.'

'Careless,' Creed said. 'Well, get me someone who can speak for them.'

'Yes, sir!'

He gave them orders. One by one, Creed spoke to the leaders of fragmented and confused units, and gave them direction and purpose. He made contact with a major named Benedict, of the Cadian 101st, an armoured company with a Stormsword super-heavy tank.

'The *Hammer of Mezanoid*?' Creed said. He started chuckling as he spoke. 'Good! Bring her up, man! Bring her up with all speed! We need her holy strength with the enemy before us! Repeat,' he shouted down the comms. 'All speed!'

Creed handed back the comms and lit his lho-stub. He looked about him and nodded, took a few puffs and stepped down from the Volscani sentinel. He felt his boot slip on something soft. He did not look down. Kell steadied him.

Creed looked about at the faces of his men. Half an hour before they had been white and stunned. Now they were bloodied and dirty, but the fear and the shock had gone. They were staring at him, grim, determined, fearless. He looked each of them in the eye and gave them a brief nod.

On the right, the Volscani armour was pinned down and being steadily picked and pounded along the fens. The division on the left was burning and being driven back towards the bulging central line. The Volscani Chimeras were running almost track to track. Cadian heavy weapon squads, dug into craters and behind wrecks, were already throwing the front runners back. On the right, Waylon's siege breakers were advancing behind the barrage of Medusa shells; on the left a squadron of the 71st's Hydras had lowered their quad-guns and were using them to hose high velocity autocannon rounds into the Volscani Chimeras.

Creed's grip was tightening on this corner of the battle. He could feel it. Piece by piece he was putting the fragments of the Cadian army together to form a workable defence.

'Troilus!' Castor said, handing him a vox.

'What is it?'

'Creed!' Troilus shouted. 'Penals. From the fens. Thousands of them.'

'Can you hold them?'

'Maybe,' Troilus said. Creed heard his orders being relayed. His right wing was castling up in a tight defensive formation.

'Do your best. I'll find something.' Creed closed the link. 'Castor!' he shouted. His equerry ran over. 'We need ordnance. Got someone?'

'Yes!' He handed Creed a vox unit. 'The 810th.'

'This is General Creed. Cadian Eighth. Yes. I need fire support. Urgently.' He cupped the comms unit with his hands. 'Castor, what are our coordinates?'

Creed repeated them down the vox. 'Right. Ready. Give me a ranging shot.'

From far back, a single Basilisk fired. The shell landed in the fens and a great gout of water sprayed up.

'Too far to the left,' Creed shouted. 'Bring it back five hundred meters and go for it. Creeping barrage forward.'

'Roger,' the response came.

'Troilus!' Creed shouted. 'Keep your heads down. We're carpeting all about you, then we're going ahead.'

'Roger,' Troilus said.

Creed was already pointing and shouting. 'Artillery!' Castor handed him a vox link. 'Right. Start moving forward from that position!'

Commissar Aldrad paused to savour the moment as the drum roll of artillery started gathering pace till it was continuous roar, a single sound of terrible ferocity. He watched as the ground came to life, hundreds of flowers of earth blooming before him. It was a maelstrom of high explosives that tore the massed formations to shreds.

The barrage began to creep forward. The Cadian 190th started pounding a division of Volscani armour that appeared on their extreme right. Creed re-established contact with six units of the 210th, whose Manticores were over forty kilometres behind the lines, and had their weapons zoning onto the foe. Their storm eagle warheads streaked the sky with white contrails that split and divided as they angled down, and then the ground exploded with great white puffs of smoke. The warheads plunged through the lighter top armour, and the crews inside were vaporised in the explosions.

'Battle is all about the application of overwhelming force,' Creed said to Kell and Aldrad. 'We've hammered the Volscani wing into oblivion. Now a hole is opening up. And we're about to tear it wide open.'

* * *

The earth was still steaming as Creed led them forward. It stank of ash and high explosives. All about them were disordered shells of ruined armour, dead men, burning pools of oil and melted rubber. Rank upon rank of ruined Chimeras were joined by dead and dying Volscani, their bodies thrown about by the ferocity of the bombardment, crumpled, torn, ripped to shreds of meat that hung, still dripping blood, from the wrecks of their transports.

As they came through the field of the dead, the Cadians sighted the stunned heretic survivors, forming a desperate circle around their banner.

'There are the men who brought this hell to our planet!' Kell raged, breaking into a run as he led the charge. Creed was beside him. A tight knot of kasrkin guards paused, aimed, fired.

A wedge of Cadian ochre and green punched deep into the mob of Volscani. A flamer roared. Men screamed. Aldrad ran to keep up. His bolt pistol bucked as he emptied the magazine, punching the Cataphracts back off their booted feet. He pistol whipped one Volscani, shattering the man's blast visor. Shards of plastek and sharpened teeth sprayed into the air. He plunged his power sword into the heretic's chest and pulled it out to parry a serrated battle axe, then twisted the blade to slash open the attacker's guts, spilling them in a stinking pink mess.

The Volscani officer kept fighting, even as he stepped on his own insides, his fury knocking Aldrad back for a moment. The commissar ducked the first swing and the second, sidestepped a third and beheaded his foe. He shot another through the chest and strode on, hacking and cutting.

Volscani berserkers threw themselves at Kell. The Cadian shock troopers surged around him like a wall of bodies. Creed fired both pistols as fast as he could pump the triggers, hotshot rounds searing holes through foe after foe. Stimms, heresy, hatred and madness drove the Volscani forward. The Cadians knelt and fired until their lasguns glowed red, until the dead were piled one upon the other, a wall of twitching flesh.

Through the confusion came a phalanx of armoured vehicles, the red banner of the Volscani flapping wetly from the lead Chimera, wet human scalps and faces hanging off it.

One of the Chimeras spewed out a great gout of flame. Creed tumbled back as the nearest men took the full brunt of the torrent. A plasma shot from the Cadian ranks knocked out the tracks and the transport slewed to a halt before a meltagun shot tore the turret and flamer apart, and the promethium tanks exploded.

The rear ramp slammed down and Volscani Cataphracts stumbled out, prayer cloths wrapped close about their faces. Behind them came a giant of a man, tall with a cape of white about his shoulders, his hood thrown back to reveal a hideous mask, his scalp crawling like snakes. He pointed towards Creed, his red eyes burning like fires.

'Luciver Anckor!' Creed hissed. He shoved Aldrad aside and stepped towards the enemy's bodyguard. He raised his pistol to shoot the foe he had hunted for three years.

Luciver Anckor lifted a hand and the air turned cold.

'He's a psyker!' Creed gasped. He strained to fire, but his hand was turning back on himself. He felt his guts contract as the air was crushed out of him. Ice rimed the Chimera's hull as the temperature dropped. Creed fell to his knees. He reached out with his other hand to pull the laspistol down, but it wouldn't move. He could feel the cold circle of steel at his temple. Around him, he heard his men engage the Volscani, and felt pride.

+Fire,+ a voice in his head commanded, but his finger would not pull the trigger. Anckor's eyes burned with hatred as he strode through his men towards Creed. At the edge of his perceptions, he heard Kell calling his name.

Snow began to fall.

+Fire.+ The command came again. His finger tightened on the trigger as he desperately fought to drop the pistol.

'For Cadia!' a strangled voice called out. Commissar Aldrad pushed forward and sliced at Anckor with his blade, driving him back. The Chaos psyker hit Aldrad in the chest with a single thrust of his clawed hand and the force of the blow crumpled the commissar's breastplate, flinging him ten feet back. He slammed against a ruined Leman Russ.

The spell broke.

Creed snarled and dragged the pistol from his forehead. He staggered to his feet. Too late, he thought, as Luciver Anckor stepped towards him, claws outstretched.

Jarran Kell's power fist sizzled as he back-handed a Volscani, obliterating his chest. The stench of super-heated flesh filled the air as he messily decapitated another. He drew his power sword and executed two more of the enemy as he pushed through the melee towards Creed.

'For Cadia!' Kell shouted. Luciver Anckor turned. Kell kicked him in the chest, sending him reeling, then stepped forward, power fist blazing with energy. Anckor's black-masked face came towards him. The stench of his breath was overpowering and his hair was alive with writhing blue worms.

'You don't understand,' the psyker hissed.

Kell knew better than to engage servants of the enemy in conversation.

He punched Anckor in the chest with his power fist, feeling it hit the man's spine. Luciver Anckor shrieked as he fell with a wet slap onto the frost-covered ground.

Kell turned to see Creed stumbling over towards him. 'Is he dead?'

Kell raised an eyebrow.

Creed laughed weakly. 'Thank you, Jarran,' he said. He leant on Kell's arm as the colour sergeant took the banner of the Eighth from its bearer and thrust it high.

'Is it over?' Castor asked, as a flight of Vendettas swept in from the west, strafing the fleeing Volscani.

There was a clap of thunder. Great gouts of burning soil were flung high into the air. Burning objects fell from the sky.

'It's not over,' Creed said quietly.

Aldrad joined them, limping slightly. Kell glanced at him, and he nodded.

'What is that?' the commissar asked.

Creed was looking up. 'The real attack,' he said simply.

Pride of Cadia III was full of fumes. The plasma destroyer had overheated and sprayed liquid coolant through the cabin. Linday lay on the floor, groaning. Ibsic held his augmetic hands out. They were fused and smoking. He started laughing.

'Shut it down,' Lina said. There was no answer, so she

clambered out and did it herself while Callen hosed Ibsic's hands down with flame retardant. The steel tendons hissed.

'Can you move?' Lina asked. 'Come on.' She opened the top hatch and looked out. Before her was a scene of utter devastation; smoke, death, ruin.

She ducked back down. Gannesh lay over his drive controls. Guts, blood and body fluids oozed from where a globule of plasma had burned a fist-wide hole straight through him.

Lina put a hand to his neck and checked for a pulse, then let his head fall back onto the control panels and dragged Linday off the floor.

'Let's get out of here,' she said.

Ibsic nodded, still holding his fused metal hands out.

Lina threw her hatch open. She slid through and helped Linday out. He was moaning. 'You'll be fine,' she told him. His left leg had been seared to a shard of bone, blackened and blistered. The red marrow showed. She gagged. 'Don't look,' she said.

Something roared overhead and they ducked, but it wasn't ordnance. It didn't explode. It *landed*.

It was like a metal flower. Petals opened, slamming down into the ground, and power armoured figures emerged. Callen stopped. He laughed and stood up. 'Space Marines!' he said, awe in his voice. 'Space Marines!'

Lina had never seen warriors of the Adeptus Astartes before. She stared in wonder as eight giants in ornate black power armour chased with bronze stepped towards them. Linday leant on Lina as Callen ran forward, waving his arms over his head.

'Here!' he shouted. 'Here!' Ibsic stumbled after him. One of the giants turned towards them. There was a noise and a flare from the huge boxy weapon he carried.

Callen's head exploded.

Ibsic grunted as he flew backwards, his ribs exploding out of his body. Linday threw himself sideways, grunting in pain. Lina fell with him, and saw the black-armoured Space Marines turning away, moving towards the distant banner of the Cadian Eighth.

'Traitors!' she tried to shout, but Linday was on top of her, and her voice was muffled, and no one heard.

Commissar Aldrad ducked down behind the wreck of a Chimera as Cadians were torn apart by bolter rounds.

'Heretics!' Kell shouted, the first to react. 'Open fire!'

The Cadians dropped to their knees, put their lasguns to their shoulders and fired, but the treacherous Space Marines were already in the maze of ruined armour.

A black armoured giant turned the corner of a burning tank, roared, and ran towards the commissar, a chain-axe whirring in its hand. Aldrad knew this was his death and he stood alone, defiant, bolt pistol bucking. His shells only chipped the ornate ceramite.

The teeth of the Space Marine's chain-axe blurred as the engine revved and droplets of blood sprayed off in a fine red mist. Aldrad felt fear, but years of schooling had left their mark. He stood firm. He would not yield. He would not fail.

'Faith in the Emperor,' he said quietly. 'By their deaths shall we know them.'

'Fire!' someone behind him shouted, and the air was suddenly bright with massed las-fire. The power-armoured figure came on in slow motion. The bright beams had no more effect than rain.

Aldrad could smell the stench of blood, old and new. His bolt pistol bucked three, four times.

He half-acknowledged a squad of kasrkin who moved up, knelt beside him and added their hotshot rounds to the fusillade.

The traitor Space Marine slowed. One leg dragged, then the figure stumbled. It slammed into the ground at Aldrad's black-booted feet. He fired into the back of its helmet and heard the dull wet thud as the explosive round went off within the skull, throwing up a spray of blood, brain matter and scalp.

Aldrad turned to face the kasrkin. The men about him met his gaze. No one spoke. Together they had killed it. Aldrad drew in a deep breath to say something profound. He felt a hand grasp his foot.

'For the Emperor!' he roared, and fired again.

Four Chaos Space Marines hit the group of Cadians clustered around Creed. The Cadians fell back as the giants strode amongst them. Jarran Kell made sure Creed was safe, surrounded by a kasrkin guard, then led the counter-attack, power sword sizzling with traitor blood. Around him, men died bravely, throwing themselves at the massive warriors, firing point-blank las-rounds into armour joints, smashing at them with rifle butts, stabbing the weak points in their armour.

The Cadian dead were two deep, but the living did not falter and numbers were on their side. One by one the enemy slowed, stopped, and began to fall back. Kell crushed a bolter with his power fist and ducked as the weapon exploded in its bearer's hand. He spun and drove his power sword through a Space Marine's chest. The massive warrior fell, before another was brought down by two squads of Cadians working together.

The last two traitors made a stand, back to back, their bolter shells ripping men apart, but they were surrounded in a sea of ochre and green. Hotshot rounds burned neat holes through their power armour. Steel blades found the joints of their armour. The cost in Cadian lives was great, but eventually only one traitor still stood, its right arm useless.

It pulled off its helmet to reveal a pale, hairless face, knitted with scars. It glared at Kell, hatred in its eyes. Its lipless mouth hissed, 'Death to the False Emperor!' as Kell charged.

Kell drew his power sword from the fallen giant's chest. He looked up over the dead body of the Space Marine, and his eyes turned towards the fens. There was fighting going on there as well.

The earth started to shake.

Creed looked around as one of the Volscani landing craft in the distance started to rock. Armour plates buckled and bent. The metal contorted like a living thing as it birthed something terrible. Creed watched in horror as a hulking, twisted Warhound Titan stalked out onto Cadia with a baying howl.

A Reaver Titan burst from another lander and started forward. Two more Warhounds joined it.

'Titans,' Creed hissed. As he spoke the sky went dark. More drop pods rained down upon Tyrok Fields. The true assault had begun.

'Raise the crew of the *Hammer of Mezanoid*!' Creed shouted. His hand was trembling, but his voice was steady.

One of the Titans sighted something a kilometre to their left, and fired three stabbing pulses of bright energy. Creed put his arm up to shield his eyes. He felt the earth tremble and grabbed a vox-unit to start giving orders. The situation had changed and the plan had to as well.

A signals officer stood next to him with magnoculars pressed to his eyes. He was giving Creed a running commentary and his voice was tense with thrill and expectation as an armoured column moved up in tight order about the *Hammer of Mezanoid*, shielding the Stormsword from fire.

One of the Warhounds charged forward and crushed a tank with a stamp of its three-clawed foot. The remaining tanks turned their turrets onto it as it thundered towards them, the focal point of a hundred threads of tracer and weapons fire. Its void shields began to glow, then flared blue lightning as they approached overload.

Creed's knuckles were white about the vox-unit as he spoke calmly and quietly.

The Warhound's shields flickered once, twice and then popped with a dull boom that made the whole battle-field shake.

At that moment the Stormsword surged forward, engines whining. The Titan came to meet it with all the swagger of a street brawler. Its giant gatling gun whirled. The hail of rounds thudded into the Stormsword's forward armour.

The massive tank paused and its siege cannon fired. It was built for levelling whole blocks in the tight and furious confines of urban warfare. As the round shot forward, its rocket fuel ignited and it accelerated. Its fire hit the Titan low in the belly, where legs and torso connected. It rocked the thing back, and then detonated with concussive force. The explosion tore through armour plating and mechanisms, and blew the Warhound Titan apart. The Warhound hung in the air for a moment then collapsed.

There was a brief moment of joy, then almost casually the Reaver's weapon stabbed down – a searing bolt of red – and the *Hammer of Mezanoid* exploded.

A hail of drop pods fell onto Tyrok Fields and Chaos Space Marines stamped onto Cadia's soil. Attack craft swooped down. Tracers arced up into the sky. The Leviathans – Cadian and Volscani – remained locked together in a stalemate. Along the fens, a battered and bloodied Cadian coalition stood about Creed.

Commissar Aldrad looked to Creed to see what he would do. The general was standing and gesticulating wildly as he shouted into a vox unit. Aldrad felt the earth tremble again and looked up.

A shadow fell over the battlefield. Creed looked up and dropped the vox-unit. Through the fens a shape appeared. Another maniple of Titans, dark against the sky. Around their feet swarmed a horde of blue-clad penal troopers.

Aldrad pushed his way through the men to Creed in time to hear the general speaking to Kell in a low voice.

'We're doomed,' Creed was saying. 'How can the foe land such forces here, on Cadia itself, unless our own have turned against us?'

Kell gripped his commander's shoulder. 'We shall fight here together. And die together.'

'Well said, Colour Sergeant,' said Aldrad. 'If we are to die, we will die with our heads held high.'

Creed looked at them both and nodded. 'So it ends here,' he said. He raised his voice. 'Castle up!' he ordered. The Cadians obeyed, forming a series of gunlines facing both the threat from the landing fields and the new arrivals as the first of the penal legionnaires broke the fens.

All along the line officers gave orders and hefted their weapons. 'Take aim!' they shouted.

Weapons were readied and the world seemed to pause in anticipation of the slaughter to come.

'Hold fire. We need them massed out in the open,' Creed said.

More and more of the enemy broke the cover of the fens.

'Hold fire,' Creed said again, then after a moment, he started to push forward towards the approaching men. 'Hold fire!' Something in his voice was different. Aldrad followed him, trying to see what had caught Creed's attention.

At the head of the penal legionnaires strode a single warrior, carrying a banner. It didn't bear the sigils of Chaos but the symbol of the Imperium: the aquila.

'Darr Vel!' Kell whispered from behind him.

Creed stopped and raised his arms. 'It's Darr Vel!' He laughed. 'Damn me, Kell. It's the Lost Hopers!'

The man approached and planted the banner into the blood-soaked ground. He saluted Creed, who pulled him into an embrace and laughed as he slapped his back.

'Darr Vel!' Creed said. 'We were about to cut you all down! What the hell is happening out there?'

'I was going to ask you the same, sir. We woke this morning and there were heretics rampaging through the camp. The guards wouldn't give us weapons. The whole place is swarming with them. We had to fight our way out. The guards wouldn't give us weapons. We only have what we could capture. It was just enough.'

'See what you can gather from the fallen.' Creed had to shout to be heard over the thunderous footfalls of the approaching Titans. 'What about your friends here?'

Darr Vel looked up as an officer shouldered his way through the crowd of confused Cadians and handed a vox-unit to Creed.

'Sir,' the man said, awe in his voice, 'Princeps Nakatana of the Legio Ignatum wants to talk to you.'

Creed took the handset and as he started to speak the lead Titan turned towards him and dipped its head. Aldrad smiled at the odd image of Creed standing talking to this monstrous lord of war.

'Princeps, yes, it is Lord General Creed. I do remember you indeed, from the Dreen Salient,' said Creed. 'Yes. I need two things from you, my old friend. Destroy their Titans and stop more of their troops from landing. If you can do that, we will do the rest.'

The Titan dipped its head again, and then turned to look across across the battlefield to the enemy. It blasted its loudhailer and started forward, opening fire on the drop pods that were still falling.

Aldrad turned his attention back towards the heart of the battle. The enemy were landing all about the *Excubitoi Castellum*.

'The governor,' he said. 'They're trying to kill Porelska. General Creed, we have to do something.'

Creed nodded. 'We are, commissar. Castor, get me a link to Admiral Elen.'

It took almost a minute to raise the fleet. 'Give it to me,' Creed said as the men regrouped. He pressed the vox-unit to his ear. 'Who is this?'

He listened for a moment.

'I am General Ursarkar E. Creed of the Cadian Eighth. I need to speak to Admiral Elen.' There was another pause. 'Admiral. There are heretics among us. You have to stop anything else from landing on Cadia. I repeat. We are under attack. Nothing must land.'

His face became grim as he listened to the admiral. 'I understand you have your own battle to fight, Admiral. But it is imperative that any more landings be prevented. On whose authority? On the authority of Warmaster Ryse.' Creed spoke quickly. 'Yes, of course you can speak to the warmaster.' His face was pale as he turned to Kell, 'Warmaster Ryse,' he said. 'The admiral would like you to confirm your orders.'

Kell held out a hesitant hand. Creed nodded towards him and thrust the vox-unit into his hand. He took it, closed his eyes, drew himself up in the slightly pompous way Ryse had, and began to impersonate the warmaster.

'I must protest!' Aldrad said.

Creed shook his head. 'Commissar Aldrad, you are not hearing or seeing this.'

'But I am,' the commissar said, hand on his bolt pistol holster.

'Commissar, look about you. There is nothing between us and defeat here. If you think we have stopped the attack on Cadia, you are wrong. This is just the beginning. A decapitation assault, designed to cripple our resolve before the battle has begun. What did they teach you of Imperial History in the Schola Progenium? Did you ever hear of Horus?'

'Yes,' Aldrad said, but he sounded hesitant.

'What did you hear?'

'He was a traitor and nearly tore the Imperium in two. What has this to do with anything?'

Creed stepped in close. His voice was low and deadly serious. 'It has *everything* to do with what is happening now. Horus was the Warmaster. He was the primarch of a Space Marine Legion. The Emperor slew him. But his favourite son survived. His name is Abaddon, and you *have* heard of him. Yes, the Despoiler. He is twisted, evil, Chaos. This is *his* work. As we argue his forces are wiping out Cadian High Command. We must stop him! Now.'

Aldrad took a deep breath and stepped back, taking his hand off the holster. He nodded.

'Yes, sir.'

The battle raged across the landing fields as heretic and loyalist alike fought and died. At its heart were the vast Leviathans, locked together. It was like the swirling vortex of a vast storm, the crack and flash of explosions like lightning and thunder on a summer's day.

It was into this dreadful conflagration that Creed led his men in a growing convoy of armour and transports. Creed himself stood on the back of a Cadian Chimera with Kell by his side, the banner of the Eighth flapping in the wind. All men who saw them flocked to their side, and soon he led a great army of scattered regiments across the battlefield.

Creed was orchestrating the whole strength of the Imperium on Cadia to work as one. The last few heretic landers careened dangerously towards the earth as Imperial Navy vessels sped into low orbit, their batteries and lance platforms flaring in the heavens as they sealed the skies above the landing fields. The landers split apart under the sustained fire.

'We have them!' Creed roared. He was filled with a virtuous fire. It didn't seem so clear to Kell at that moment. 'We have them now!'

Lina and Linday had been swept up. They had caught a ride on a Chimera. Troops clung to it. They were all saying that victory was at hand, that Creed was going to save the day. They saw him standing tall at their fore and believed.

Cadia was waking and recoiling at the touch of heresy on her soil. She had more to give. Creed could feel it. He felt her fury, and as the wind whipped up, he heard the distant moan of the pylons urging them all on. The ground shook as the Titans engaged.

He sang the sacred words as Lightning fighters wove and soared, chasing the steaming contrails of invading drop pods. Thunderbolt squadrons swirled around the heads of the heretic Titans. Flights of Vendettas, wing to wing, came in low to the ground and tore into the Chaos forces. Elite kasrkin airborne regiments deployed on grav-chutes, firing on rampaging warbands as they landed.

And through the maelstrom, Creed led his men. Scattered squads swelled his numbers. Among them was the familiar figure of Major Luka, who was leading an honour guard of five hundred handpicked Whiteshields.

'Luka!' Creed yelled as the old man saluted him.

'Ursarkar, I'm glad to see you. Where do you need us?'

Creed did not pause. 'We have to save the governor.'

They smashed through a picket line of heavy weapons, then outflanked a Volscani Baneblade, luring it out from its support units and hitting it on both flanks as a company of Hydras kept the skies above them clear.

But the closer Creed's army got to the centre of the storm, the tougher the resistance became – and soon they were no longer fighting Volscani heretics, but power-armoured warriors.

The traitor Space Marines were few in number – fewer than the quantity of drop pods would have suggested – but they were tough. Creed cracked them nonetheless, outflanking, outnumbering, out-shooting. Always on the move, the Cadians were soon within the smoke cloud cast by the burning Leviathans.

Creed pointed towards the *Excubitoi Castellum*, which rose above the carnage. It was beset, besieged, but still standing defiantly.

'Keep moving!' he roared. 'We are not too late!'

But the enemy had taken note.

Through the choking black smoke stalked a huge, hunched figure, black smoke billowing about its baroque brass armour, which dripped with the blood of the corpses chained to its carapace. It snorted fire from its nostrils and stamped a clawed foot. There were cries of panic.

Darr Vel's Chimera appeared through the smoke and slewed to a halt. The former prisoner had a plasma pistol thrust into his belt and a harness of melta bombs over one shoulder.

'Darr Vel!' Creed shouted. 'It's time to make your peace with the Emperor. I promised you that chance. I need you to slow that Titan down!'

The man nodded solemnly and turned to issue orders to his troops.

* * *

It was like hunting for food on Lost Hope. Just... bigger. Darr Vel's skin prickled. The air roared. Fire blasted behind him and he shouted a warning, too late. He pressed himself against the hull of his Chimera. His hair caught fire, but he barely noticed, as the roar of the flame drowned out most of the screams of his Lost Hopers. Most. Not all.

He patted out the fire and prepared to move. 'With me!' he shouted.

The remaining Lost Hopers charged forward, heads down, Darr Vel at their fore. The flamer flared again.

More screams in the darkness of billowing smoke. Somehow Darr Vel's small group, lying flat in a crater, were still alive. They jumped up and sprinted forward. To the left, Jovet's mob was almost in range.

'Go!' Darr Vel indicated them forward. A meltagun fired. An explosive went off. The Titan stamped down. As the foot lifted, Darr Vel glimpsed the glistening remains of Jovet's men before the swirling smoke hid them all.

He looked up. Only six men were still with him. He laughed, realising that this was how he would end.

'Damn you, Creed,' he shouted. 'From ice world to a fiery death! Let's get it!'

He started running. He heard the roar of another flamer blast, then all there was was his own breath, labouring as he gripped the bandolier of melta bombs in his right fist. Within seconds he was in the shadow of the Titan.

'I've got you now!' he screamed.

A three-toed metal foot swung forward through the gloom. He could smell lubricants and taste the plasma boiling furiously. The foot crunched down twenty feet to his left, the toes, each larger than him, pressing into the earth as the Titan's weight shifted forward. He was alone. It was up to him. Creed was depending on it. He made his break and felt the other foot swing over his head.

He could see pistons the size of tanks. The inhuman toes, bending and flexing, the metal creaking as it took the full weight of the Titan. Darr Vel caught one of them. It almost threw him as it lifted up for another ponderous stride. He clung on with both arms. The piston dragged him down and up as the toe flexed. He lost sight of the ground, did not know how much longer he could hold on. He got one hand onto a melta bomb, and set the charge.

The warning light flashed, slow at first, then more rapidly.

'The Emperor Protects.' Darr Vel closed his eyes as the melta bombs detonated.

Creed watched as a foot was torn off the Titan. The behemoth stumbled forward on its ruined leg, metal superstructure groaning as it lost balance and fell nose-forward into the earth. Its machine-spirit wailed as explosions tore through the superstructure, and then its plasma reactor overheated, and one last cataclysmic explosion threw debris spinning across the battlefield.

Creed hoped Darr Vel was with the Emperor now.

'Keep moving!' he yelled.

The ground was thick with empty enemy landers, their armoured ramps open and still. The *Excubitoi Castellum* rose up like a cliff face before them. Her bottom decks were ruined and broken. Pipes leaked bloody fluids, small fires burned and there were dead Cadians everywhere – shot, disembowelled, decapitated, hanging from windows, slumped against broken blast heads, drowning in their own blood. Hatches lay open.

'Inside!' he shouted. 'We take it back.'

Kell strode through the corpse-choked corridors behind Creed.

They turned a corner to see a grotesquely armoured Space Marine lying amongst a heap of human dead. 'Do not look at it!' Creed warned in a low voice, but Kell could not help himself. The sickening symbols made his head spin. The spiked armour was studded with fresh heads. He gagged and turned away, up a ruined staircase that was slick with blood, keeping to Creed's side.

As they rose the din of battle grew louder.

'Quicker!' Creed urged them as they mounted the ornate stairs.

They heard a howl and turned. Three traitor Space Marines sprinted towards them, chainswords buzzing.

Kell stepped before Creed and gestured towards the foe. A bodyguard of kasrkin ran forward, firing from the hip. Hotshot las-rounds punched through power armour with puffs of bloody steam. They riddled the enemy, and one by one they fell.

The carapace-armoured shock troops took each corridor, each staircase, each room, and the rest of the force followed, securing the chambers and holding them against enemy counter-attack.

Creed drove the Cadians forward. '*Save the governor!*' became their war cry as Kell carried the banner of the Cadian Eighth into the very heart of the *Excubitoi Castellum*.

'Closer!' Creed urged them as they reached the bridge antechamber. 'Forward!'

The damage to the ancient artefact was terrible to behold. Ancient banners, some from the founding of Cadia itself, lay torn and ruined on the floor. Relic caskets had been shattered. The bones of saints and Imperial heroes had been slashed and broken and vellum leaves swirled in the breeze from the open bridge doorway. The floor was slick with blood.

Creed marched across the antechamber and stopped on the threshold to the bridge. He turned away, face pale, and Kell stepped up to see what was inside.

Shreds of flesh, guts, dress uniform and gold braid hung from the walls. A pile of fresh heads filled the room. Kell knew many of them. Staff officers. Colonels. Equerries. Even the distinctive white-bearded face of Lord General Jaquias.

A power armoured giant stepped into the opposite doorway. In one hand, a chain-axe revved. In the other it held the bloody head of Governor Marus Porelska. Its voice came through its vox grilles: inhumanly deep and impossibly ancient and hate-filled.

'I knew you would come,' the creature laughed as it tossed Porelska's head towards them. It landed with a splash in a puddle of blood. The chain-axe revved again as the Chaos Space Marine strode towards them. 'But you're too late.'

'Who are you?' Creed demanded.

'I am the future,' the thing said. 'I am war. I am death. I am carnage.'

'You are dead, traitor,' Kell roared.

The Chaos Space Marine laughed. Its chain-axe buzzed in its hand as it roared and charged, fast and furious. Kell lashed out and caught the axe in his power fist as it swung down. There was a screech of tearing metal and the weapon exploded, hot metal teeth scything through the chamber. The traitor Space Marine staggered back and Kell swung and stabbed low. His power sword sheared through armour and flesh to hit bone, but his foe seemed to feel no pain. It roared again and kicked Kell aside, sending him thudding into the wall. The colour sergeant's power sword fell and hit the ground, the energy that wreathed it extinguishing.

The Space Marine turned on Creed and swiped at him with gauntleted hands. Creed ducked once, twice, and then threw himself backwards.

'The sword,' Kell moaned as he tried to push himself up from the floor.

Creed's looked around and threw himself in the direction of the blade. He fumbled, and then his fingers closed around it. He saw movement and brought the sword up to parry, but it wasn't his enemy that approached. He looked up into the face of Commissar Aldrad. The commissar was ragged and bloodied and a rough bandage was tied around a stump where his left hand had been. In his right was his bolt pistol, and it was pointed at the traitor Space Marine.

'Aim!' Aldrad spat. The Cadians behind him levelled their lasguns. Creed pulled himself to his feet and held up a hand.

'No!' he said. 'This one is mine. Let me send it back to the hell from whence it came.'

It had been a long time since he had handled a sword in battle, but the old training came back to him. He held the sword two handed. It was a standard pattern, with familiar balance and familiar weight. He thumbed the activation stud and it leapt into life. It was good to feel the static in the air as blue light flickered along the blade. He began to drive the Chaos Space Marine back with sweeps of crackling energy.

His opponent bulled forward and Creed parried a punch, relishing the growl of pain as the glowing blade sliced through the Space Marine's gauntlet and bit flesh. The traitor pulled back again and Creed pushed in. His first stroke tore a spike from its armour. The second failed to connect. The third opened a wide gash in the chest-plate. Creed ducked a fist, sidestepped, and made a wild stab that went through armour, belly, and armour again. He dragged the blade out, and a flood of black blood and bile poured out of the wound as the traitor Space Marine fell to its knees.

'You cannot win,' it said.

'Then we shall die trying!' Creed snarled.

He swung once more. The head of the traitor tumbled from its shoulders. The headless torso swayed and Creed gave it a contemptuous kick backwards.

'Here!' he said, and helped Kell pick himself up from the floor. The colour sergeant's face was pale and his right arm hung useless by his side. Together they limped through the bridge. The carnage was appalling. Creed could feel the horror of the last battle here.

'Hundreds of men...' he said, visualising what must have happened. 'They tried to barricade the blast doors... When the traitors broke through they protected Gover-nor Porelska with their own bodies...'

'And they all died,' said Kell. 'Bravely. Like heroes.'

Creed put a hand against the wall to steady himself, but touched blood, wet and warm. He pulled his hand away and wiped it clean on his fatigues. 'Cover them up,' he said.

'By their deaths shall we know them,' Kell said and made the sign of the aquila.

Creed was spent. 'I need fresh air,' he said. 'If there's any out there.'

He picked his way over the body of a dead kasrkin to the balcony doors, where the gold-worked red velvet curtains hung in strips. He pushed them aside and stepped over the threshold.

All across the Landing Fields, heretics were making their last stands.

'The battle is won, but the killing never ends,' said Creed bitterly. He walked over to the railings and looked down. He saw devastation and ruin – wrecked armour, the slag of burning Titans, wounded and dying men.

He watched as a Legio Ignatum Reaver casually pumped three shots from its volcano cannon into the last intact Volscani Leviathan. On the third hit the Leviathan exploded. The blast of heat was so intense it warmed his face.

But Ursarkar E. Creed felt nothing. All he could see before him was defeat, death, disaster.

Kell stopped on the threshold and looked out at Creed. The general looked small, broken. Kell turned to go back inside.

'Stay, Jarran,' Creed said.

Kell stepped forward. He heard a noise behind him and looked round to see Aldrad, pale from blood loss. The colour sergeant motioned him forward. Together, the three men looked out at the ruin of Tyrok Fields.

'We failed,' Creed said. 'We won the day, but we failed.'

Kell took in a deep breath. He tasted blood and smoke

and burning flesh. He had nothing to say. In the distance, one of the last traitor ships fired into the clouds.

'Why are they fleeing?' Aldrad asked.

Creed shrugged. 'Their job was done.'

There was a cough behind them. Kell turned to see Castor carrying a vox-unit. 'General, you should take this,' he said. Creed took it and listened intently.

There was a moment's pause, then Creed said, 'No. Governor Porelska is dead. I am Castellan Creed of the Cadian Eighth. I led the counter-attack on the *Excubitoi Castellum*. We... were too late.'

There was another pause.

Kell looked out. Far below a flamer flared. He could not tell whose it was. A Valkyrie hovered and fired off a salvo of anti-personnel rockets. They were so distant the flashes came almost a second before the firecracker patter of explosions.

'Yes, Warmaster Ryse,' said Creed. 'I will secure the *Excubitoi Castellum* and establish who is still alive, then await your arrival.'

Creed handed the vox-unit back to Castor and waited until the trooper had gone back inside.

'Jarran, Aldrad,' Creed said. 'Ryse told me that the Governor Secundus is also feared lost. All attempts to contact him at Kasr Vazan have failed.' He gripped the railings with both hands. 'They have struck the Imperium at our most defiant citadel, and found us lacking.'

The sun was setting. It was a dull red disk through the smoke and dust of battle.

Creed's face was grim. 'Look. Day has ended on Cadia. The long night has begun.'

* * *

The Eye of Terror filled the sky with a sickening bruise of purple light.

Baleful red fires still burned across Tyrok Fields, and the moaning of wounded men drifted on the air as medicae teams did their best to find and treat survivors.

It was two hours after sunset when Creed arrived at the warmaster's Leviathan, *Sacramentum*, with Kell and Commissar Aldrad in attendance. The battle had been so intense that it felt strange to be walking down unruined corridors to stand in an intact room amongst men who were not the enemy.

Creed limped as he climbed the steps. A thumb-sized piece of shrapnel had been removed from his thigh. He hadn't felt it until the battle was over, but now every muscle in his body ached. He had eaten nothing and drunk only a flask of water all day. His hangover was returning with a vengeance.

'See if you can find something to drink,' he muttered to Kell as they saluted the two kasrkin who stood at the entrance to the *Sacramentum*'s feast hall.

The room echoed as Creed strode in. Some of the fresher looking officers had flown in from the more distant kasr. They looked almost panicked and unsure. They had not been in the battle. They had not seen it. Creed could tell from their eyes that they hated not having been there.

The survivors had a weary look about them. Warmaster Ryse was trying to be jocular with his left arm in a sling, and a lump torn off his left ear. *Sacramentum*'s crew had repelled boarders. The warmaster had fought with great bravery, so his staff reported.

Creed had heard all about it, but he had been too weary

to take it in. Everyone on Tyrok Fields that day had a tale to tell. *Everyone* had been through hell. Some had been lucky enough to survive.

Too many had not.

Around Warmaster Ryse stood the few surviving members of the Cadian governing council, retired generals and castellans. Lord General Gruber was there, his head bandaged, but his monocle unbroken. Had it really only been the day before, Creed thought, that he and Gruber had clashed aboard the *Excubitoi Castellum*? He met the man's cold blue stare with defiance, only looking away when Ryse boomed out, 'Creed! Good to see you! Unwounded?'

Creed patted his leg, and pulled a face. A lump of shrapnel was as good as untouched.

Ryse nodded. 'Now are we all here?' He made a signal and the feast hall doors were closed. Ryse's voice lost its jocular note. 'Well. Welcome. I am glad to see you all. For those of you who are unaware, Governor Primus Marus Porelska was killed today in defence of Cadia. Governor Secundus Karwyn is feared lost.'

He listed the dead – the higher ranking ones anyway. Creed bowed his head. Each name brought back the memory of the gory trophy on the *Excubitoi Castellum*'s bridge.

He looked round to see Kell carrying a shot glass and a bottle. He took the glass and knocked it back.

He felt warmth spread through him. 'Thank the Throne,' he said quietly.

'So that is the situation,' Warmaster Ryse concluded. He looked grave. 'As far as we know there have been no other landings. Admiral Elen has locked the planet down.

I have sent an astropathic signal to the High Lords on Terra. We await their response.'

Creed listened in silence to the responses. They all focussed on the Volscani, expressing disbelief that they could have masterminded such an attack. Creed handed his empty glass back to Kell. Kell returned it refilled. Creed knocked it back again.

'This wasn't the work of the Volscani,' he heard a voice say.

Creed's thigh stung. He realised he had stood up, and as everyone was staring at him, he realised that it was he who had spoken. He cleared his throat.

'My men killed General Klief of the Volscani. We killed Luciver Anckor, who was with them as well. Both men died in the first hours of the battle, and it continued without them. They were not the masterminds here. They were pawns. Decoys.'

'What do you mean?' General Gruber demanded.

Creed spoke simply. 'This is war on a scale we have never seen. This, gentlemen...' He paused to look around the room. 'This is a *Black Crusade*.'

There was a murmur of disapproval. 'Hush!' Gruber said.

Creed would not stay silent. 'Yes. Fellow officers, we are not fighting a heretic general or a small warband of traitor Space Marines. We are facing the most ancient of enemies. Abaddon the Despoiler.'

Ryse scowled. 'You should not speak that name,' he said.

'If not naming him would help us, I would not. But let us all be clear. This is the scale of the threat against us. It is the Imperium's most ancient foe.'

'Can it really be him?' A tall, trim equerry in the polished breastplate of the Cadian 101st spoke in an awed whisper. 'After so long. How can he still be alive?'

'I do not care to know the ways of heretics,' Creed said. 'But I am sure we have all seen things that should not be. That reason tells us *cannot* be. All we have are our lasgun, our armour, and our faith in the Emperor.'

Creed felt the mood of the room waver. He stared at the officers. 'I warned you all about this yesterday. None of you listened, despite the evidence. I have no supernatural powers. All I have is the strength of my faith. The power of my troops. The courage of a soldier.'

Warmaster Ryse stepped forward. 'I did not bring you here to argue. I brought you here because we have a great duty upon our shoulders. We have always had two governors on Cadia so that if one was killed the other could rule. Now we are leaderless. Both of them are dead. Until the High Lords appoint another, we need an interim governor.'

'You are suggesting yourself?' Gruber asked.

'No.' Ryse sighed. 'I have been warmaster for seven years. To command Cadia now... It would be too much.'

'Then who?' Gruber turned to face the room. 'General Flowerdew?' The one-eyed commander of the Cadian 910th Airborne regiment shook his head. One by one Gruber went about the room, picking out officers. Each one shook their head. He studiously ignored Creed. At last Gruber turned back to Ryse. 'Then I humbly submit myself.'

'No,' Ryse said. 'I think not.'

'Then who?' snapped Gruber.

Warmaster Ryse sighed. 'I do not know.'

A voice piped up from the shadows. 'May I be permitted to speak?'

Creed knew the voice and turned as the figure stepped out from the shadows. It was Commissar Aldrad.

Even Lord General Gruber straightened up as the commissar stepped forward. Old habits died hard, and commissars were figures of fear, even ones so young.

Aldrad stopped in the middle of the room. His uniform and his very visible injury gave his words gravity. 'I am not a Cadian. I am not even technically a Guardsman. But I alone here represent the Militarum Tempestus.' He lifted the stump of his arm. 'I saw the battle unfold today from the sharp end. I fought all the way from the fens to the very bridge of the *Excubitoi Castellum* where we found the governor dead.' He paused and looked around.

'But for one man in this room, I guarantee that none of us would still be alive. One man commanded Cadia today. It was not Governor Porelska. And it was not you, Lord General Gruber. Nor, with the greatest respect, was it you, warmaster. I have no doubt you defended your Leviathan with great skill and courage, but while you were fighting a private battle here, one man brought the shattered forces of Cadia together. One man combined the Imperium's resources. One man pitted himself against the enemy.

'And he won. Yes, we lost much today. But we were not defeated. We achieved a great victory. We stand.'

'Who are you talking about?' Gruber asked.

'Warmaster, lord generals, I nominate General Ursarkar E. Creed, Castellan of Kasr Rorzann, for the post of interim governor of Cadia.'

There were cheers from scattered officers, but Gruber stepped forward. 'You cannot be serious, Commissar.'

'I am,' Aldrad said.

Warmaster Ryse let out a long breath. He turned to Creed. 'Ursarkar, you have always been a fine and loyal servant. I have learned to trust you more than any of my other commanders. I think this commissar has spoken truly, and I will heed his recommendation. And so I ask you, will you lead us in this, our hour of greatest need?'

'No,' Creed said. 'I do not want to be governor of Cadia.'

'Ursarkar,' Ryse said. His voice teetered between affection and exasperation. 'This is a great honour we are offering you.'

'No, it is not,' Creed said. 'You want to hold me up like a puppet. Cadia needs a commander who has the ability to *lead*.'

Ryse slammed his good hand down onto the table. 'Damn it, Creed. What do you want?'

'What I want is simple, Warmaster Ryse. That I alone rule Cadia until the forces of Chaos are driven from this planet, and from this system.'

'That can't be done!' Gruber roared. 'You want to be a dictator.'

'It can be done,' Creed said. 'It has before. A rank exists. What Cadia needs, gentlemen, is not a governor, but a lord castellan.'

There was stunned silence.

Creed stared them all down. 'It is what Cadia needs. She demands it of us.'

Bodies were piled five deep all along the side of the *Excubitoi Castellum* as Lord Castellan Creed led his commanders to the bridge. It had been sluiced down to get rid of the blood, but it still stank of slaughter. He paused at the threshold of the command deck. He could hear the Cadian troops below. Each crowd had its own note, and this one sounded angry, confused, hurt, leaderless.

Creed had no words ready. He looked around. Warmaster Ryse stood next to him. Kell stood right behind Creed, the banner of the Cadian Eighth in his hand, furled tightly around its pole. He smiled grimly and Creed returned the gesture and stepped over the threshold. He walked alone to the railing, and looked out and down. Arc lumens lit the crowd. The note of the murmuring changed a little as he showed himself. It was expectant now.

Creed felt something being placed in his hand. He looked at it, and saw that it was a voice amplification unit. He swallowed.

'Men and women of Cadia,' he started. He did not know what he was going to say, but he knew he had to say something. 'We lost many today. Friends. Sons. Mothers. Daughters. Comrades. We withstood fire, bombardment, treachery and cowardice. And we did not flinch. We did not turn to ask if another would step up and take our place. We stood, we fought, and we strode forward into battle.'

As he spoke he felt the note of the crowd changing, and for the first time, he had a feeling that Abaddon had not won that day. Yes, he had decapitated Cadia, but Cadia had a new head. And it was stronger, fiercer, more deadly. As the cheers died down, Creed waved a hand.

'Today the High Command have asked me to serve as Lord Castellan of Cadia. I have accepted this weighty honour. Today we have driven the enemy from our home. But the months ahead shall be hard. I offer you nothing but blood and battle. This is our part in a war that has lasted ten thousand years. And today, brothers and sisters, today we – you – have won a great victory that will be remembered for another ten thousand years, or as long as the Imperium of Mankind shall last!'

Creed left the crowd cheering as he walked back inside.

'Lord Castellan.' Castor saluted and fumbled in his breast pocket for a thick silver case, which he opened. Inside were lho-stubs. 'The finest that the Munitorum has to offer,' he said.

Creed took one, and bit it between his teeth as a lucifer was struck and puffed it to life.

'You asked for the maps to be brought here,' Castor continued.

'Yes,' Creed said. 'Thank you.'

Kell handed him a silver tankard. It was full of amasec. Creed barely tasted it as he stood over the table, pulled out the system map and saw it all as he had described it to Porelska just the day before. He saw the terrible brilliance of it all, all the regicide pieces not just of the war on Cadia, but of a Black Crusade like a many-tentacled creature seizing the Imperium in its grip.

'The official records,' he said. 'All reference to traitor Space Marines must be extinguished. This was a treacherous attack by General Klief of the Volscani, aided by the traitor Luciver Anckor. Both were killed in the attack. The Volscani Caraphracts have been destroyed. Governor Marus Porelska died valiantly, fighting on the bridge of the *Excubitoi Castellum*.'

'Yes, sir,' Castor said gravely.

Creed looked up and met the eyes of every man present. 'You shall all keep to this official record. No one will speak of Horus' scions on Cadia's holy soil. Is that clear?'

The men nodded. Creed leafed through the latest reports. He did not know how long he stood there. An hour perhaps. Maybe two. The other men were silent as he went through all the reports that Porelska had been keeping from them. Things were worse than even he had guessed. But as he stood and worked through the data sheets, he felt he was getting a sense of the enemy's strategy.

Strange asteroid activity in the Scarus System. Warp storms off Belial. Contact lost with Chinchare. Sabotage on Belis Corona. Uprisings on St Josmane's Hope.

He stopped at that and took a sip of the amasec. Arcady Pride. He smiled, and felt the eyes of the men in the room on him.

'The Voice' was on Saint Josmane's Hope. He shivered and remembered the figure that had found him in the ruins of Kasr Gallan. 'Get me Admiral Elen.'

Castor nodded. He relayed the command, but paused. 'There's something else. The men want to rename the regiment.'

Creed looked up.

'What do they want to call it?'

'Lord Castellan's Own,' Castor said.

Creed half laughed.

'Do they have your permission?'

'Yes,' Creed said. 'If that is what they wish.'

He took another sip, pulled out another chart and puffed on his lho-stub. He, a mere man, was pitting his skill against the most ancient evil in the galaxy. He drew in a deep breath and thought of all those who had died that day, of the men he had sent to certain deaths. If the Imperium of Mankind stood a chance, then here on Cadia the war would be won or lost. And to win it he had to be harder, crueller and more brutal than his foe.

Creed could feel Cadia as if she was a spirit in the room, standing at his shoulder. Approving. Resolute. Defiant.

'Where is Admiral Elen?' he demanded.

'Sorry sir!' Castor brought a vox-unit. Creed took it.

'Admiral. This is Lord Castellan Creed. There is heresy upon St Josmane's Hope. You will order a fleet there and destroy the planet and all upon it. No. No evacuation.'

The admiral questioned the order, and Creed repeated it. The room was silent, the atmosphere tense. Creed could only imagine what was going through the heads of the assembled officers.

'Yes,' he said, his voice harder. 'Destroy St Josmane's Hope and all on it, admiral.'

Colour sergeant Jarran Kell listened dispassionately. It was chilling hearing his commander – his friend – commit a planet to extinction, but Kell felt hope flare within him too. Creed could win this. Kell now understood why he had always felt so strongly that he had to keep Creed alive. It was for this moment. Because Creed alone could save Cadia, and perhaps the Imperium.

Creed put the tankard down and looked around. His gaze lingered on Kell. Kell nodded, and Creed nodded back.

'Next,' he said, and took another report from Castor's trembling hand.

ABOUT THE AUTHORS

David Annandale is the author of the Horus Heresy novel *The Damnation of Pythos* and the Primarchs novel *Roboute Guilliman: Lord of Ultramar*. He has also written the Yarrick series, several stories involving the Grey Knights, including the novel *Warden of the Blade,* and *The Last Wall, The Hunt for Vulkan* and *Watchers in Death* for The Beast Arises. For Space Marine Battles he has written *The Death of Antagonis* and *Overfiend*. He is a prolific writer of short fiction, including the novella *Mephiston: Lord of Death* and numerous short stories set in The Horus Heresy, Warhammer 40,000 and Age of Sigmar universes. David lectures at a Canadian university, on subjects ranging from English literature to horror films and video games.

Toby Frost is the author of the novel *Straken*, about the eponymous Astra Militarum colonel. His other published work for Black Library includes the short stories 'Lesser Evils', 'A Hero's Death' and 'The Apex', the latter two featuring Colonel 'Iron Hand' Straken.

Braden Campbell is the author of *Shadowsun: The Last of Kiru's Line* for Black Library, as well as the novella *Tempestus*, and several short stories. He is a classical actor and playwright, and a freelance writer, particularly in the field of role playing games. Braden has enjoyed Warhammer 40,000 for nearly a decade, and remains fiercely dedicated to his dark eldar.

Justin D Hill is the author of the Space Marine Battles novel *Storm of Damocles* and the short stories 'Last Step Backwards', 'Lost Hope' and 'The Battle of Tyrok Fields', following the adventures of Lord Castellan Ursarkar E. Creed, as well as 'Truth Is My Weapon', and the Warhammer tales 'Golgfag's Revenge' and 'The Battle of Whitestone' for Black Library.

WARHAMMER
40,000

SHADOWSWORD

GUY HALEY

WARHAMMER 40,000

BANEBLADE

GUY HALEY